STEPHEN BOOTH

Stephen Booth was born in the Lancashire mill town of Burnley, and has remained rooted to the Pennines during his career as a newspaper journalist. He lives with his wife Lesley in a former Georgian dower house in Nottinghamshire and his interests include folklore, the internet and walking in the hills of the Peak District. *Blood on the Tongue* is the third in the series featuring Derbyshire detectives Ben Cooper and Diane Fry. The second, *Dancing with the Virgins*, was nominated for the coveted CWA Gold Dagger Award.

Visit www.AuthorTracker.co.uk for exclusive information on Stephen Booth

www.stephen-booth.com

By the same author

Scared to Live
The Dead Place
One Last Breath
Blind to the Bones
Dancing with the Virgins
Black Dog

STEPHEN BOOTH

Blood on the Tongue

HARPER

This novel is entirely a work of fiction. The names, characters and incidents portrayed in it are the work of the author's imagination. Any resemblance to actual persons, living or dead, events or localities is entirely coincidental.

Harper
An imprint of HarperCollins*Publishers*
77–85 Fulham Palace Road,
Hammersmith, London W6 8JB

www.harpercollins.co.uk

This paperback edition 2007
1

First published in Great Britain by
HarperCollins*Publishers* 2002

A catalogue record for this book is
available from the British Library

ISBN 978–0–00–786633–5

Typeset in Meridien by
Palimpsest Book Production Limited,
Grangemouth, Stirlingshire

Printed and bound in Great Britain by
Clays Ltd, St Ives plc

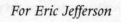

For Eric Jefferson

For their help in the writing of this novel, I am grateful to: Mr F. G. Cejer, Secretary of the Derbyshire branch of the Federation of Poles in Great Britain, for information on Polish language and customs; and the Lincolnshire Aviation Heritage Centre, for a ride on a Lancaster bomber. Any errors are my own.

1

It was an hour before dawn when Detective Constable Ben Cooper first began to get the news. An hour before dawn should be the dead hour. But in the bedrooms of third-floor flats on the council estates, or in stone-built semis in the hillside crescents, there were people blinking in bewilderment at an alien world of deadened sounds and inverted patterns of dark and light. Cooper knew all about the hour before dawn, and it was no time of day to be on the streets. But this was January, and dawn came late in Edendale. And snow had turned the morning into shuddering chaos.

Cooper pulled up the collar of his waxed coat to meet the rim of his cap and brushed away the flecks of snow that had caught in the stubble on his jawline where he had rushed shaving that morning. He had walked down one of the alleyways from the market square, crunching through fresh snow, slithering on the frozen cobbles, passing from light to dark as he moved out of the range

1

of the street lamps. But he had stepped out of the alley into a noisy snarl of traffic that had choked the heart of Edendale and brought its snow-covered streets to a halt.

On Hollowgate, lines of frustrated motorists sat in their cars, boot to bonnet in clouds of exhaust fumes. Many of them had been driving almost blind, their windscreens covered in half-scraped snow or streaks of brown grit that their frozen wipers couldn't clear. The throbbing of engines filled the street, echoing from shop facades and the upper storeys of nineteenth-century buildings. Headlights pinned drivers and their passengers in cruel shadows, like silhouettes on a shooting range.

'We have a serious double assault, believed to be racially motivated. Approximately zero two hundred hours. Underbank area.'

The voice from his radio sounded alien and remote. It was the crackly voice of a tired operator in a control room with no windows, where they would never know if it was still snowing or the sun had risen. Not unless somebody called in and gave them a weather report. We have sporadic outbreaks of violence. Occasional blood on the streets. It's an hour to go before dawn.

Cooper stepped off the edge of the pavement and straight into six inches of wet slush. It went over the top of his shoe and turned his foot into a frozen sponge. Since it was only seven o'clock and still completely dark, it was going to be a long, uncomfortable shift unless he got to his locker at E Division headquarters in West Street pretty soon for a change of socks.

'Two male victims received multiple injuries and are described as being in a serious condition.'

Cooper worked his way between the gridlocked cars to reach the far side of Hollowgate. Around him, fumes rose from the shadows and hung under the lamps, trapped in the street by the freezing temperature and the stillness of the air. They created a grey blanket that absorbed the light and swirled slowly in front of black Georgian windows sparkling with frost.

'Four suspects are currently being sought. All are white males, aged between twenty-five and forty-five. Local accents. One suspect has been identified as Edward Kemp, 6 Beeley Street, Edendale. Thirty-five years of age. Hair short and dark brown, approximately six feet tall.'

The weather changed so quickly in the Peak District that snowfall always seemed to take motorists in the town by surprise. Yet within a few miles of Edendale all the minor roads and passes would still be closed and outlying villages would be cut off until the snowploughs reached them. They might be isolated until tomorrow, or the next day.

Cooper had set off early because of the weather. On his way in from Bridge End Farm, as he steered his Toyota into the tracks left by the first snowplough, the hills around him had been glittering and pristine, like huge wedding cakes covered in sugar icing, lurking in the darkness. But it meant he had missed his breakfast. Now what he needed was a couple of cheese toasties and a black coffee. He was tempted by the lights of the Starlight Café, reflecting off the banks of untouched snow.

'Edward Kemp is described as powerfully built, with a distinctive body odour. Last seen wearing a dark overcoat and a hat. No further description available at this time.'

Cooper peered into the café. Behind the condensation on the plate-glass window there were figures wrapped in coats and anoraks, scarves and gloves, and a variety of hats made of fur, leather and wool. They looked like models posing for an Arctic explorers' clothing catalogue.

'All suspects could be in possession of baseball bats or similar weapons. Approach with caution.'

Now he could almost taste the coffee; he could feel the crunch of the toasted teacake and the clinging softness of the melted cheese. Saliva began to seep on to his tongue. Cooper pulled back his glove to look at his watch. Plenty of time.

While his nose was pressed close to the window, a hand came up and wiped away some of the condensation. A woman's face appeared, her eyes wide with outrage. She mouthed an obscenity and raised two fingers that poked from a blue woollen mitten. Cooper pulled away. There would be no toasties this morning, and no coffee.

'Control, I need a car outside the Starlight Café in Hollowgate.'

'With you in two minutes, DC Cooper . . . Is it still dark out there?'

'It's an hour before dawn,' said Cooper. 'What do *you* think?'

It was the ice and the scouring wind that created the worst of Marie Tennent's delusions. They were like daggers thrust into her brain, plunged in so deeply that their edges scraped together in the middle of her skull, filling her head with noise.

For the last hour before she died, Marie believed she could hear music wailing in the wind, the hissing of wheels on an icy road, and the muttering of voices deep in the snow. Her mind struggled to interpret the sounds, to make sense of what was happening to her. But the music was meaningless and the voices distorted, like the babbling of a badly tuned radio when its batteries were almost dead.

Marie lay amid the smells of bruised snow and damp air, with the taste of her own blood in her mouth and her body a bewildering pattern of cold spots and numbness and pain. Her arms and legs were burning where the snow had melted into her clothes and frozen again. And the ache in her head had flowered into a savage, unbearable agony.

It was because of the pain that Marie knew, in a lucid spell, that the sounds she could hear were caused by the tiny bones of her inner ear shrinking and twisting as they froze. They were grating against each other as they contracted, creating an

5

internal whisper and mumble, a parody of sound that mocked her slow withdrawal from the boundaries of reality. It was a disturbing and inarticulate farewell, a last baffling message from the world. It was the only accompaniment to her dying.

The sun had dropped over the edge of Irontongue Hill, so that the snow-covered moor was in shadow, and the temperature was dropping fast. Marie felt the faint, cold kiss of snowflakes on her face. Yet the top of the hill was still touched by the last of the sun, and the snow on the rocks was turned blue by the light. Irontongue itself was hidden from her, its fissured shaft of dark gritstone poking southwards over the valley. But she caught a glint of water to the north, where Blackbrook Reservoir lay in a hollow of the moors.

The last thing Marie saw before her eyelids closed was a thin, dark shape that sliced the skyline on the hill. It seemed to cut into the grey belly of cloud like the blade of a razor. Her mind clutched at the thought of it as she drew together the dregs of her willpower to fight the pain. In the end, that crumbling memorial in the middle of the snowfield had not been the place she was destined to die. It was for men who had lived and died together. It was quite a different thing to die alone.

A series of out-of-focus slides seemed to flicker across a screen in her mind. They were gone too quickly for her to puzzle out their significance, though she knew they were connected to her life. Each one had vague figures that swung and jerked against a dark background. Each brought with it a momentary burst of smells and tastes and sounds, a kaleidoscope of sensations that dragged all the emotions out of her and ripped them away before she could recognize what they were.

There was a voice, too – the voice of a real, remembered person, not a phantom of the snow. 'We'll be together,' it said. 'Are you happy?' it said.

And then there were just three final words. They came amid an eruption of intolerable pain, the smell of dirty sheets and the sound of scuttling feet above her head. The same voice, but not the same.

'It's too late,' it said.

And Marie Tennent would never see the dawn.

Ben Cooper entered the café. It was full of customers, who sat half-asleep over their mugs of tea, their brains kept barely alert by the tendrils of steam they breathed in through their noses. As Cooper stamped his feet to shake off the snow, a few faces turned away from him, as usual.

One man sat alone near the counter. He was wearing a dark overcoat and a Manchester United hat. Cooper moved up behind him until he was close enough to recognize the smell. The man had an odour about him that identified him against the background of bacon and fried eggs, even among the wet-dog smells from sodden coats and muddy floor tiles.

Cooper moved slightly so that he could see the man's face.

'Morning, Eddie,' he said.

The customer nodded cautiously. It was the best that Cooper could expect, in the circumstances. Eddie Kemp was well known to most of the officers at E Division headquarters. He had visited the custody suite and interview rooms there many times in the past. These days, though, he visited other parts of the West Street station, too, if only from the outside. Eddie Kemp had started a window-cleaning business.

'Bad weather for business, isn't it?' said Cooper.

'Bloody awful. My chamois leathers are frozen solid. Like dried-up cow pats, they are.'

Kemp didn't look too good today. His eyes were red and tired, as if he'd been up all night. The Starlight opened at five o'clock for the postal workers starting their shift at the sorting office, for the bus drivers and railway staff, and even a few police officers. Kemp looked as though he had been here since the doors opened that morning.

'Put your hands on the table, please,' said Cooper.

Kemp stared at him sourly. 'I suppose you're going to spoil my breakfast,' he said.

'I'm afraid you're under arrest.'

The other man sighed and held out his wrists. 'They only got what they deserved,' he said.

Yes, it was the sound of feet. Feet creaking around her in the snow. Marie Tennent's heart lurched

8

painfully against her diaphragm, and a spurt of adrenalin ran through her muscles like acid. She was sure she could hear the footsteps of human rescuers, as well as those of something quicker and lighter that skittered across the surface of the snow. She became convinced that a search dog had sniffed her out, and that arms were about to pull her from the snow and wrap her in a thermal blanket, that friendly hands would bring warmth to her skin with their touch and reassuring voices would ease the agony in her ears.

But the footsteps passed her by. She couldn't cry out for help, because her reflexes failed and her body had no strength left to react. Her lips and tongue refused to obey the screaming in her head.

Then Marie knew she was wrong. The feet she heard were those of wolves or some other wild predators that lived on the moors. She could sense them creeping towards her and scuttling away, dragging their hairy bellies through the wet snow, eager to claim a share of her body. She pictured them drooling in desperation to tear off chunks of her cooling flesh with their teeth, yet afraid of her lingering smell of humanity. The faint tingling on her cheeks and in the folds of her eyes told her the predators were close enough for her to feel their breath on her face. If she had opened her eyes, she knew she would have found herself staring into their jaws, into the drip of their saliva and the whiteness of their teeth. But she could no longer open her eyes; the tears had frozen her eyelids shut.

The fear passed, as Marie's brain lost its grasp on the thought and it went slipping away. The pictures were still in her mind, but the cold had drained all the colours from them. The dyes had melted and run, leaving washed-out greys and dark corners, bleeding the meaning from her memories. She could no longer capture the sounds and scents and tastes, no longer even keep hold of that one overwhelming emotion which had swollen so large that it filled her mind, but which now wriggled away from her grasp. Was it grief, anger, fear, shame? Or was it just the same unnameable longing that had haunted her all her life?

Marie had forgotten how she came to be lying in the snow, with the pain in her head and the blood in her mouth. But she knew there was a reason she ought to get up and go home. And she knew it had something to do with Sugar Uncle Victor. But the fingers of ice were squeezing out her consciousness, so that she would soon know nothing at all.

Marie was unaware of her bladder failing and releasing a warm stream that thawed a ragged patch in the snow. Soon, the physical sensations stopped altogether. As Marie's skin froze and her blood thickened to an ooze, even the illusory sounds retreated beyond the reach of her senses. The footsteps faded and the voices fell silent, because there was no one left to hear them. Her heart slowed until its valves were left fluttering uselessly, pumping no blood through her body.

Finally, Marie Tennent existed only as a speck like a grain of sand floating in an oily residue of memories. Then they, too, swirled away into a hole in the back of her brain, and were gone.

For the fifth time, Ben Cooper turned to peer towards the corner of Hollowgate and High Street. The traffic lights had changed to green, but a queue of traffic was stuck in the middle of the junction.

'Where's the car?' said Cooper, feeling for the radio in his pocket, wondering whether it was worth worsening the mood of the control-room operators at West Street with a complaint about somebody else's slow response. 'It should have been here by now.'

Eddie Kemp was wearing black wellies, with woollen socks rolled over the top of them, and his overcoat was long enough to have come back into fashion two or three times since he first bought it from the army surplus store, probably around 1975. Cooper thought he looked warm and comfortable. And no doubt his feet were dry.

'We could flag down a taxi, I suppose,' said Kemp. 'Or we could catch a bus. Have you got the right fare on you?'

'Shut up,' said Cooper.

Down the road, traffic was still moving on High Street. Cars crawled through white flurries that drifted across their headlights. An old lady in fur-lined boots picked her way over the snow in the gutter. For a moment, Cooper thought of his own mother. He had promised himself he would talk to her tonight, and make sure that she understood he was serious about moving out of Bridge End Farm. He would call in to see her when he finally went off duty.

'I'm not walking all the way up that hill,' said Kemp. 'It's not safe in these conditions. I might slip and injure myself. Then I could sue you. I could take the police for thousands of pounds.'

Cooper wished he could distance himself from Kemp's powerful smell, but he daren't loosen his grip or shift from his eight-o'clock escort position at his prisoner's left elbow.

'Shut up,' he said. 'We're waiting for the car.'

He was aware of customers coming out of the café now and then, the doorbell clanging behind them. No doubt each one stopped for a moment in the doorway, staring at the two men on the kerb. Cooper shifted his weight to maintain his grip. He felt the slush in his left shoe squelch as he put his foot down.

'Maybe the car's broken down,' said Kemp. 'Maybe it wouldn't start. These cold mornings play hell with cheap batteries, you know.'

'They'll be here soon.'

On the far side of Hollowgate, shopkeepers were clearing the snow from the pavement in front of their shops, shovelling it into ugly heaps in the gutter. The beauty of snow vanished as soon as it was touched by the first footstep or the first spray of grit from a highways wagon. By daylight, it would be tarnished beyond recognition.

'I have to tell you I've got a delicate respiratory system,' said Kemp. 'Very susceptible to the cold and damp, it is. I might need medical attention if I'm kept outside in these conditions too long.'

'If you don't keep quiet, I'm going to get annoyed.'

'Bloody hell, what are you going to do? Shove a snowball down my neck?'

A pair of flashing blue lights lit up the front of the town hall in the market square, just past the High Street junction. Cooper and Kemp both looked towards the lights. It was an ambulance. The driver was struggling to make his way through the lines of crawling cars.

'That's clever,' said Kemp. 'Sending for the ambulance first, before you beat me up.'

'Shut up,' said Cooper.

'If you took the cuffs off for a bit, I could use my mobile to phone the missus. She could get the sledge out and hitch up the dogs. They're only corgis, but it'd be quicker than this performance.'

Behind them, somebody laughed. Cooper looked over his shoulder. Three men were standing in front of the window of the café, leaning on the plate glass, with their hands in the pockets of their anoraks and combat jackets. They wore heavy boots, a couple of them with steel toecaps, like the safety boots worn by builders in case they dropped bricks or scaffolding on their feet. Three pairs of eyes met Cooper's, with challenging stares. *Four white males, aged between twenty-five and forty-five. Could be in possession of baseball bats or similar weapons. Approach with caution.*

Finally, Cooper's radio crackled.

'Sorry, DC Cooper,' said the voice of the controller. 'Your response unit has been delayed by a gridlock situation on Hulley Road. They'll be with you as soon as possible, but they say it could be five minutes yet.'

One of the men leaning against the window began to form a snowball between his gloved fists, squeezing it into the shape of a hand grenade with short, hard slaps.

'Damn,' said Cooper.

Kemp turned his head and smiled. 'Do you reckon we could go back inside and have another cup of tea?' he said. 'Only I think it's starting to snow again. We could freeze to death out here.'

By morning, Marie Tennent's body had stiffened into a foetal position and was covered in frost, like a supermarket chicken. Ice crystals had formed in the valves of her heart and in her blood vessels; her fingers and toes and the exposed parts of her face had turned white and brittle from frostbite.

Nothing had disturbed Marie's body during the night – not even the mountain hare that had pattered across her legs and squatted on her shoulder to scratch at patches of its fur. The hare was still brown and ragged, instead of in its winter camouflage white. It defecated on Marie's neck and left a scattering of fur, dead skin cells and dying fleas for the pathologist to find. For a long while afterwards, Marie lay waiting, just as she had waited in life.

Later in the morning, a patrolling Peak Park Ranger almost found Marie, but he stopped short of the summit when he saw more snow coming towards him in the blue-grey clouds rolling across Bleaklow Moor. He turned back to the shelter of the briefing centre in the valley, retracing his own footsteps, failing to notice the smaller tracks that ended suddenly a few yards up the hill.

When the fresh snowfall came, it quickly covered Marie's body, gently smoothing her out and softening her outline. By the end of the afternoon, she was no more than a minor bump in the miles of unending whiteness that lay on the moors above the Eden Valley.

That night, the temperature dropped to minus sixteen on the exposed snowfields. Now there was no hurry for Marie to be found. She would keep.

2

Detective Sergeant Diane Fry knew she was going to die buried under an avalanche one day – an avalanche of pointless paperwork. It would be a tragic accident, resulting from the collapse of a single unstable box file under the weight of witness statements piled on top of it. The landslide would carry away her desk and swivel chair and smash them against the wall of the CID room like matchsticks. It would take days for the rescue teams to locate her body. When they did, she would be crushed beyond recognition, her bones flattened in the same way that the reports on her desk were even now pressing down on her brain.

The piles of paper reminded her of something. She turned her head and looked out of the window, squinting to see past the condensation that had streaked the panes. Oh yes. Snow. Outside, the stuff was piled as high and as white as the paperwork. She couldn't decide which was worse.

Then she felt the touch of warm air. It came

from the noisy fan heater that she had stolen from the scenes of crime department that morning before the SOCOs arrived for work. The paperwork was just about preferable. At least it meant she could stay in the warmth for a while. Only masochists and obsessives chose to wander the streets of Edendale on a morning like this. Ben Cooper, for example. No doubt Cooper was somewhere out there even now, conducting a one-man crusade to clean up crime, despite the icicles hanging off his ears.

Soon, scenes of crime officers would be scouring the building for their missing heater. Eventually, she would have to give it up, unless she could find somewhere to hide it when she heard them coming. You could always tell when the SOCOs were coming by the sound of their grumbling. But the heater was the only source of warmth in the room. Fry put a hand to the radiator on the wall. It was warm, but only faintly. It felt like a body that hadn't quite cooled but had already gone into rigor mortis. No need to call in the pathologist for a verdict on that one. Dead for two hours, at least.

She sniffed. A whiff of sausages and tomato sauce trickled down the room and settled on a burglary file that lay open on her desk. It was the sort of smell that was responsible for turning the walls that strange shade of green and for killing the flies whose bodies had lain grilling for months inside the covers of the fluorescent lights.

'Gavin,' she said.

'Mmm?'

'Where are you?'

'Mmm-mmph-mm.'

'I know you're there somewhere – I can smell you.'

A head appeared above a desk. It had sandy hair, a pink face, and dabs of tomato sauce on its lower lip. DC Gavin Murfin was the current bane of Diane Fry's life – less temperamental than Ben Cooper, but far more prone to dripping curry sauce on the floor of her car. Murfin was overweight, too, and a man in his forties really ought to think about what he was doing to his heart.

'I was having some breakfast, like,' he said.

'Can't you do it in the canteen, Gavin?'

'No.'

Fry sighed. 'Oh, I forgot –'

'We don't have a canteen any more. We have to make our own arrangements. It says so on all the noticeboards. Twenty-two years I've been stationed here, and now they take the canteen away.'

'So where did you get the sausage bap?'

'The baker's on West Street,' said Murfin. 'You should have said if you wanted one.'

'Not likely. Do you realize how much cholesterol there is in that thing? Enough to turn your arteries solid. In another five minutes, you'll be dead.'

'Aye, with a bit of luck.'

The smell of fried meat was doing strange things to Fry's stomach. It was clenching and twitching in revulsion, as if food were something alien and disgusting to it.

'There's garlic in that sausage, too,' she said.

'Yes, it's their special.'

Detective Inspector Paul Hitchens opened the door and seemed to be about to speak to Fry. He paused, came in, and looked around. He sniffed.

'Tomato sauce? Garlic sausage?'

'Mmm,' said Murfin, wiping his mouth with a sheet from a message pad. 'Breakfast, sir.'

'Mind you don't drop any on those files, that's all, Gavin. Last time you did that, the CPS thought we were sending them real bloodstains, just to make a point that we had sweated blood over the case.'

Fry looked at Murfin. He was smiling. He was happy. She had noticed that food did that for some people. Also DI Hitchens was looking a little less smartly dressed these days, a little heavier around the waist. It was four or five months since Hitchens had set up home with his girlfriend, the nurse. It was depressingly predictable how soon a man let himself go once he got a whiff of domestic life.

'I only wanted to tell you Ben Cooper has called in,' said the DI.

'Oh, don't tell me,' said Fry. 'He's joining the sick brigade.' She looked at the empty desks in front of her. With leave, courses, abstractions and sickness, the CID office was starting to look like the home stand at Edendale Football Club. 'What is it with Ben? Foot and mouth? Bubonic plague?'

'No. To be honest, I don't remember Ben ever having a day off sick in his life.'

'He can't get into work because of the snow, then. Well, it's his own fault for living in the back of beyond.'

'That's why he bought that four-wheel drive jeep thing,' said Hitchens. 'It gets him through where other people get stuck, he says.'

'So what's the problem?' said Fry impatiently.

'No problem. He's made an arrest on the way in.'

'What?'

'He collared one of the double assault suspects. Apparently, Cooper came into town early and called in for the morning bulletins on the way. He was intending to stop for a coffee and found Kemp in the Starlight Café, so he made the arrest. Good work, eh? That's the way to start the day.'

'That's Ben, all right,' said Murfin. 'Never off duty, that lad. He can't even forget the job when he's having breakfast. Personally, it'd give me indigestion.'

'It isn't being conscientious that gives *you* indigestion, Gavin,' said Fry.

'Watch it. You'll upset Oliver.'

Oliver was the rubber lobster that sat on Murfin's desk. At a push of a button, it sang extracts from old pop songs with a vaguely nautical theme. 'Sailing', 'Octopus's Garden', 'Sittin' on the Dock of the Bay'. One day, Fry was going to make it into lobster paste and feed it to Murfin in a sandwich.

'Look at that weather,' said Hitchens. 'Just what we need.'

Fry stared out of the window again. The wind was blowing little flurries of snow off the neighbouring roofs. They hit the panes with wet splatters, then slid down the glass, smearing the grime on the outside. She couldn't remember it ever snowing back home in Birmingham, not really. At least, it never seemed to have stuck when it landed; it certainly hadn't built up in knee-high drifts. Maybe it had been something to do with the heat rising from the great sprawl of dual carriageways and high-rise flats she had worked in, the comforting warmth of civilization. Her previous service in the West Midlands was a memory that she almost cherished now, whenever she looked out at the primitive arctic waste she had condemned herself to. She had left Birmingham without a farewell to her colleagues. She might as well have said: 'I'm going out now. I may be some time.'

'Well, there's one thing to be said in its favour,' said DI Hitchens. 'At least the snow will keep the crime rate down.'

And somewhere under the mountains of paper, Diane Fry's telephone rang.

Inside Grace Lukasz's bungalow on the outskirts of Edendale, the central heating was turned up full in every room. Ever since the accident, Grace had been unable to bear the cold. Now, even in summer, she insisted on keeping the windows and doors closed, in case there was a draught. These days, her immobility meant that she felt the chill more than most, and she could not tolerate discomfort. She saw no reason why she should.

This morning Grace had been up and about early, as usual. She had gone immediately to adjust the thermostat in the cupboard in the hallway, and had spent her time gazing with some satisfaction at the outside world beyond her windows, where her neighbours in Woodland Crescent were turning white with cold as they scraped the ice from their cars or slid and stumbled on the slippery pavements. Once, a woman from across the road had fallen flat on her back on her driveway, her handbag and her shopping flying everywhere. It had made Grace laugh, for a while.

But now the stuffy heat in the bungalow caused her husband to frown and turn pink in the face the moment he arrived home from his night duty at the hospital, and it had spoiled Grace's mood. Peter stamped his feet on the mat and threw his overcoat on the stand. Grace wanted to ask him her question straight away, right there by the door, but he wouldn't meet her eye, and he brushed past her chair to get to the lounge door. With sharp tugs of her wrists, she backed and turned in the hallway, her left-hand wheel leaving one more scuff mark on the skirting board. Peter had left the door open for her from habit and she followed right behind him, glaring at his back, angry with him for walking away from her.

He should know, after all this time, how much it infuriated her.

'Did you phone the police?' she said, more sharply now than she had intended to speak to him.

'No, I didn't.'

Grace glowered at her husband. But she said nothing, making the effort to keep her thoughts to herself. She knew him well enough to see that no purpose would be served by pressing him too hard. He would only say she was nagging him, and he would set his face in the opposite direction, just to demonstrate that he was his own man, that he could not be bullied by his wife. Sometimes he could be so stubborn. He was like an obstinate old dog that had to be coaxed with a bone.

'Well, I don't suppose it would make any difference,' she said.

'No.'

Grace watched him wander off towards the sofa, tugging his tie loose. Within a few minutes he would have the TV remote control in his hand and his mind would be distracted by some inane quiz show. Peter always claimed that he needed to turn off his mind when he got home from a night at the hospital, that his brain was exhausted by the stress of his work. But it was never acknowledged that *she* might need to turn off from the things that had plagued her mind all day. No matter what she did, there was far too much time for brooding. She had been used to looking forward to Peter's return home as something to occupy her mind, but these days it never seemed to work.

Peter had brought with him an odour of cold and damp from outside. The smell was on his coat and in his hair, and there had been snow on the shoes that he had left on the wet doormat. For the past few hours, the only thing Grace had been able to smell was the scorching of dust on the radiators, the invisible dust that gathered behind them where she couldn't reach to clean. A few minutes before he came home, she had sprayed the rooms with air freshener. But still he had brought in this unpleasant cold smell, and the world outside had entered the bungalow with him.

'You know it wouldn't make any difference,' he said. 'You're expecting too much, Grace. You're getting things all out of proportion again.'

'Oh, of course.'

She swung the wheelchair towards the centre of the room and lowered her head to rub at her limp legs. She watched him out of the corner of her eye, waiting for a sign that he was weakening. Although he was stubborn, he was susceptible to the right tactics, like any man.

Peter threw himself on the sofa and dug the remote from under a cushion. The set came on with a sizzle of static. There was news on – leading with a report on the effects of the bad weather across the country. Shots of children sledging and making snowmen were interspersed with clips showing lines of stranded cars, airport lounges packed with frustrated holidaymakers, railway travellers staring morosely at information boards, and snowploughs piling up snow twelve feet high by the side of a road in Scotland.

'Where's Dad?' asked Peter.

'He's with his photographs again,' she said.

'It's been a bad night, Grace. We had two young men brought in who'd taken a terrible beating with baseball bats.'

'I'm sorry.'

They sat for a few moments in silence. Grace could tell from the angle of her husband's head that he wasn't taking in the news on the TV any more than she was herself. She waited, aware of the power of silence, calming her breathing until she could hear the ticking of the radiators and the sound of a car engine on the crescent. There was a faint rustling of feathers from the far corner, where their blue and green parrot stirred in its cage, perhaps sensing the atmosphere in the room. It turned a black eye on the couple, then snapped at its bars with a sudden, angry click of its beak.

'If you must know,' said Peter, 'I think he's gone back.'

Grace felt her shoulders go rigid. 'Gone back where?' she said, though she knew perfectly well what he meant.

'Where do you think? To London.'

'To *her*?'

'Yes, to his wife. She has a name.'

'Andrew said she's in America, at a cousin's

25

funeral.' Grace slapped one of her knees as if it had offended her by its inactivity. 'I've tried to phone him again, Peter. He's not answering.'

'We'll just have to wait until we hear from him, Grace. What else can we do?'

Grace manoeuvred alongside one of the armchairs, feeling the wheels slip into well-used grooves in the pile of the carpet. Peter made no move to help her, and he didn't even look to see how she was coping. She was glad he didn't do that any more. Once, she had lost her temper at his clumsiness and had pushed him roughly away. He had said nothing, but she knew he had been shocked and hurt by her violence. Her legs might be useless, but her hands and wrists were strong.

'It doesn't make any sense,' she said. 'Why should he arrive out of the blue like that and then disappear again so suddenly, without a word?'

'There are a lot of things Andrew never got round to telling us about his life.'

'In a day? He didn't have time. A day isn't enough to make up for five missing years.'

'Grace, he has an entirely separate life of his own. You can't dwell on the past for ever.'

She had heard this too often. It had become his mantra, as if it might become true if he repeated it often enough. Grace knew it wasn't true. If you had no present and no future, where was there to live but the past?

'But he's our son,' she said. 'My baby.'

'I know, I know.'

Grace knew she was reaching him. She lowered her voice to a whisper. 'My dear Piotr . . .'

But she heard Peter sigh and watched him finger a button on the remote. A weather forecast was on the other channel. An attractive young woman stood in front of a map scattered with fluffy white clouds that seemed to be dropping white blobs all over northern England. In a moment, Grace would have to go back to the kitchen to make her husband a pot of tea, or his routine would be upset and he would sulk for the rest of the day.

'There's a lot more snow on the way,' he said.

The moment had passed. Grace lifted her hands to her face and sniffed the faint coating of oil on her fingers. The oil and the dark smudges on her hands were the constant signs of her reliance on machinery, of her enforced seclusion from the rest of humanity. She was a great believer in turning your disadvantages into something positive. But sometimes the positive was hard to find.

'Oh, wonderful,' she said. 'That's just what we want. More snow. More excuses for not finding him. Everyone will say they're too busy with other problems. Then they'll say it's too late, that we'll have to accept the fact he's gone.'

Grace stared at the icon of the Madonna in the alcove above the TV set. Tonight, she would pray again for their son. And she would force Peter to pray too.

'It causes a lot of problems, does snow,' said Peter. 'More than people think.'

But on the TV screen, the weather girl smiled out at them cheerfully, as if she thought snow was absolutely the best thing she could imagine in the whole world.

The Derbyshire County Council snowplough was brand new. It was a yellow Seddon Atkinson, with a bright steel blade, and its automatic hoppers could spray grit at passing cars like machine-gun fire. That morning, its crew was working to clear the main Snake Pass route to Glossop and the borders of Greater Manchester, battling through ever deeper drifts of snow as they climbed away from Ladybower Reservoir, with the River Ashop below them and the Roman road above them, skirting the lower slopes of Bleaklow and Irontongue Hill.

Trevor Bradley was the driver's mate this morning. He didn't like snowplough work, and he certainly didn't like getting up in the middle of the night to do it. Even worse, they had been sent to the Snake Pass, which was as desolate a spot as you could find yourself in, when every other bugger was still at home in his bed. They had left the last houses far behind already, and on these long, unlit stretches of road there was nothing to be seen but their own headlights and endless banks of snow in front and on both sides. Bradley was glad when the driver had stopped for a few minutes at the isolated Snake Inn, where the owners had filled their vacuum flasks with coffee and given them hot pork pies from the microwave. The snowplough men were popular at the Snake, because on days like this they made all the difference between customers getting through to the inn and no one getting in or out at all.

A few minutes after re-starting, the snowplough had reached the stretch of road through Lady Clough and the Snake Plantations. Here, the hill became steeper and the headlights fell on even deeper drifts, where the wind had brought the snow down from the moors and blown it round the edge of the woods, sculpting it into strange and unlikely shapes.

Just past the last car park, before the end of the woods, Bradley thought he felt the impact of something solid that dragged along the road surface for a few yards under the blade of the plough. Then he saw a dark shape that was briefly revealed in a shower of snow as the blade lifted it and pushed it into the banking. It was followed by the impression of a man's face hovering near his window for a second, then falling away again. It had been a very white face, quite unreal, and could only have been a trick of the snow and the poor light.

'We hit something, Jack,' he said, sucking the last of the warm jelly from the pork pie off his fingers.

'No kidding?'

Jack stopped the engine, and they both got down. The driver seemed to be more worried about damage to the equipment than anything else. He'd told Trevor that people dumped loads of builder's rubbish in the lay-bys, and stuff like breeze-block and broken bricks could easily chip the blade. The plough was the latest investment by the highways department, and he was conscious of his responsibility for its pristine condition.

Meanwhile, Bradley poked around a bit by the side of the road, scraped some snow away with his gloved hands, and finally lifted a blue overnight bag out of the drift. The bag was empty. He could tell by the weight of it.

'That's careless,' he said.

He pushed a bit more snow aside. It looked as though the clothes had spilled out of the bag on to the roadside, because there was a shoe lying in the snow. It had a smart black leather toe, with a pattern printed on the upper. It wasn't a shoe anybody would have been walking in, of course, so it must have come from the luggage. Probably it had been some of the clothes that he had seen in the headlights – a white shirt, perhaps, crumpled into the illusion of a human face as it was tossed out of the bag by the impact of the plough blade.

Bradley bent down and tried to pick the shoe up, but felt some resistance, as if it were heavier than it ought to be. Maybe it was frozen to the ground. He brushed a bit more snow clear, and then he noticed the sock. It had a green and blue Argyll design, the sort of sock he had seen some of the bosses wearing back at the council offices. He touched it as he wiped away the frozen snow.

It was definitely a sock for an office worker, not for wearing with a work boot. Your feet would be frozen solid out here in the snow, if you wore fancy socks like that.

He realized his mind was wandering a bit. It was a long minute before he finally accepted what his fingers were telling him. There was an ankle in that Argyll sock, and a foot in the shoe. A man lay under the snowdrift.

Bradley straightened up and looked back at his driver, who was still inspecting the plough. The blade was bright and sharp and shiny, and it weighed half a ton. Last winter, with one much like it, they had removed the entire front wing of a Volkswagen Beetle before they had even noticed it abandoned in a snowdrift. Bradley remembered how the blade had ripped the metal of the car clean away, like a carving knife going through a well-cooked chicken. In fact, the Beetle had been a trendy bright yellow, not unlike a supermarket chicken. For a few moments they had both stared at the lump of metal caught on the blade without recognizing what it was, until the wind had caught it and the wing had flapped off down the road, trailing its headlight cables like severed tendons.

Now, Trevor Bradley recalled his impression of the thing that had bumped and dragged along the road under the plough blade a couple of minutes ago. He remembered the glimpse of something that had waved momentarily from the midst of a spray of snow. It was an object which his brain hadn't registered at the time, and which he only now identified as having been a human arm. Then there had been the face. The arm and the face had been all that he had seen of the body as they flailed over the edge of the blade and were jerked back into the darkness.

He gulped suddenly, and decided that he didn't even want to imagine the damage the snowplough could have done to the rest of the body.

Bradley opened his mouth to call to his driver. 'Jack!'

But his voice came out too faintly on the cold air, and it was drowned by the noise of a jet airliner that passed low in the cloud as it manoeuvred for the approach to Manchester Airport. The rumble of the aircraft vibrated the windscreen on the snow-plough and set Trevor Bradley's limbs trembling, too. His stomach decided that, as long as his mouth was open, he might as well be sick.

The noise of the airliner gradually receded as it descended behind the shoulder of Irontongue Hill. It was an Air Canada Boeing 767, and it was at the end of a seven-hour flight from Toronto.

3

A pair of shoes stood outside each door in the bare corridor. There were a set of trainers with thick rubber soles, some brown brogues split down the side, and a pair of high-sided Doc Martens. Right at the end were Eddie Kemp's wellies, with melted snow running off them to form puddles on the floor. In the background, Nigel Kennedy was playing *The Four Seasons*.

'Has he asked for a doctor?' asked Ben Cooper.

'A doctor?' The custody sergeant frowned as he checked over the paperwork carefully. 'No. All he said was that he takes two sugars in his tea, when I'm ready.'

'Give him the chance to ask, just in case, Sarge.'

The sergeant was well over six feet tall. He had the weariness about him that Cooper had seen all custody officers develop after a few months processing prisoners. They saw far too much of the wrong end of life. They saw far too many of the same prisoners coming in and out, over and over again.

'Why, what does he reckon is wrong with him?' said the sergeant. 'Apart from having his sense of smell amputated?'

'He is a bit ripe, isn't he?'

'Ripe? Putrescent is the word that springs to mind.'

There was a strange, rancid odour about Eddie Kemp – not his breath, but the smell of his body, a sourness that oozed directly from his pores. It seemed to eddy in the air around him when he moved, restrained only by his clothes from overpowering anyone within twenty yards. When his old overcoat and body warmer came off, the paint on the walls had almost begun to peel.

They had bagged up Kemp's outer clothes as quickly as they could and sent a PC around the custody suite with disinfectant. There were three prisoners on the women's side, and they'd soon be complaining again. Cooper thought the smell would stay with him all day, like his frozen foot.

'I hope they're not going to be too long coming to interview him,' said the sergeant. 'One of our prostitutes down the corridor there has been reading up on the Human Rights Act. There might be a clause about infringement of a prisoner's right to fresh air, for all I know.'

'I don't know who's going to interview Eddie Kemp, but rather them than me,' said Cooper. 'Besides, I think he might have some popular support out on the streets. I'm sure three of his mates were at the café. But he's the only one we had a witness ID for.'

'Members of the public can't be allowed to take the law into their own hands,' said the sergeant, sounding like a man reading from a script.

Late the previous night, the two seriously injured young men had been found wandering by the road in Edendale's Underbank area, a compact warren of streets that ran up the hillside yards from one of the main tourist areas of the town. Although they had been badly beaten, it had been impossible to get a reason from them for the attack.

This morning, the police had been having difficulty identifying the assailants. Most of the people in the area had seen nothing, they said. But a couple who had looked out of their bedroom window when they heard the noise of the assault had said they recognized Eddie Kemp, who was their window cleaner. Everyone knew Eddie. Cooper had felt the disadvantages of local fame himself, so he sympathized with Kemp a little.

'By the way, I checked the names of the assault victims,' he said. 'They're both regulars of yours, Sarge. Heroin dealers off the Devonshire Estate.'

Along the corridors, it was approaching the end of Spring, according to Nigel Kennedy.

'I can't understand why the radio briefing said the incident was suspected to be racially motivated,' said Cooper. 'One of the victims is Asian, but the other is white.'

'Default position,' said the sergeant. 'We cover

our backs, just in case. Talk about the inmates of the asylum . . .'

Recently, a number of asylum seekers had been dispersed to Derbyshire, and some were housed in Edendale's vacant holiday accommodation. Until now, many residents had rarely seen anyone of a different ethnic origin in their town unless they ran restaurants and cafés, like Sonny Patel, or were tourists and didn't count. The sudden appearance of Iranians, Kurds, Somalis and Albanians queuing at the bus stops that winter had been like someone dropping a drum of herbicide into a pond and watching it seethe and bubble. For the first time, a National Front logo had been scrawled on the window of an empty shop in Fargate, and the British National Party were said to be holding recruitment meetings at a pub near Chesterfield.

'Your prisoner's a bit of a joker,' said the sergeant. 'He gave his name as Homer Simpson.'

'Sorry about that.'

'Oh, think nothing of it. You'd be surprised how many Homer Simpsons we get in here. Some days, I think there must be a convention of them in town. In the old days, it used to be Mickey Mouse, of course. But that name went out of fashion among the custody suite intelligentsia. Anyway, I told him I had to register him in the guest book, otherwise he wouldn't get his breakfast in the morning.'

'I suppose it gets a bit much.'

'Water off a duck's back, my son. You've seen the guidelines, haven't you? "All idle and foolish remarks will be disregarded". It helps no end when some inspector in nappies tries to tell me what to do. You can ignore them and say, "It's in the guidelines, ma'am."'

'What's the point of the music, by the way?' said Cooper.

'It relaxes the customers,' said the sergeant. But Cooper thought he sounded a bit defensive.

'Does it?'

'So they tell me.'

The sergeant paused. They both listened to the Vivaldi for a moment. Kennedy had just reached Summer.

'It's the inspector's idea,' said the sergeant.

'Ah,' said Cooper. 'She's been on a course, has she?'

'Been on a course? I'll say she's been on a bloody course! Show me the week she's *not* on a course. This one was called "Conducting a Resources Audit of Your Public Interface". What the hell does *that* mean? Mark my words, she'll have us putting mirrors and potted palms in here next. Moving the doors and the desk to make the energy flow better or some such rubbish.'

'Feng shui,' said Cooper.

'Sorry?'

'Feng shui.'

'I think you've caught a cold standing out in the snow,' said the sergeant.

'Making the energy flow,' said Cooper. 'It's Japanese.'

The sergeant stared at him. ''Course it is,' he said. 'I must be stupid.'

He was much too tall for the counter he worked at, and he leaned awkwardly to write in the custody record. Unless Health and Safety had conducted a proper workplace assessment in here, there would be more compensation to pay out in a year or two, when the sergeant was walking like Quasimodo. But by then, he'd be haunted by the sound of Nigel Kennedy rather than the bells of Notre Dame.

Cooper felt his pager vibrating in his pocket. It was the fifth call for him in the last half-hour. They had started plaguing him about other enquiries while he was still escorting his prisoner through the snowbound streets of Edendale.

'All these new ideas, what's the point?' said the sergeant. 'I can't get my breath sometimes. A bloody madhouse it is round here. And I don't mean the customers, either.'

A PC came out of the office behind the sergeant and handed Cooper a note. It said: *DC Cooper – report to DS Fry ASAP. Urgent.* Cooper reluctantly gave up the plan he had been nursing for the last few minutes. He had been hoping to call by his locker for some dry socks, then carry out a raid on Gavin Murfin's desk to see if he had any spare food.

'Mind you, you didn't hear me say any of that,'

said the sergeant. 'I'm very happy in my work, I am.'

When passengers reached the arrivals gate at Terminal One of Manchester Airport from Air Canada flight 840, a tall, fair man with a beard was waiting. He greeted the woman by shaking her hand, but they both looked for a moment as though they regretted there were so many people around them on the airport concourse. Alison Morrissey smiled when she heard his strong local accent, as if it made her trip to England seem real.

'So you came,' she said.

'I couldn't think of you arriving on your own and knowing no one.'

'That's kind.'

There was a moment's silence between them. As the crowd of passengers passed her on either side, the woman looked at the unfamiliar names on the airport shops – W. H. Smith, Virgin, Boots the Chemist. For a moment, she looked no older than a schoolgirl as she cocked her head to listen to the announcements.

'We've got a bit of a walk to the car park,' he said, watching her. 'Will you be all right? You look pale.'

'Yes, I'm fine.'

He found a baggage trolley and pushed it for her towards the exit. Alison Morrissey paused to rub her legs, though she had performed her exercises religiously all the way across the Atlantic from Toronto Pearson.

'The weather's not too good outside,' he said. 'But I suppose you're used to snow in Canada.'

'Frank, I live in a suburb of Toronto. No grizzly bears or lumberjacks for miles.'

She looked dizzy and disorientated, but when she shook herself hard, she reverted to a confident woman in her mid-twenties.

'The meeting is set up with the local police, isn't it?' she said.

'Of course. Don't worry about that. It's all organized.'

'I'm sorry, Frank. It just hit me suddenly. This is more than travelling to a foreign country – it's like venturing into the past.'

'I understand that.'

'And it's a dangerous past. I really feel as though I'm on the borders of hostile territory.'

'Don't expect hostility from every quarter,' he said. 'Not necessarily.'

Outside, Alison Morrissey looked at the grey sky and ran a hand across her forehead.

'You're right,' she said. 'Transatlantic flights knock hell out me. I suppose it's past breakfast time here?'

'Nearly lunchtime, in fact. We can find somewhere to eat here at the airport, if you like.'

'May we drive out to Derbyshire first, Frank? How long will that take?'

'It depends whether they've got the A57 clear yet,' he said. 'I had to come here by the motorway. The last I heard on the radio traffic bulletins, the Snake Pass was still blocked. I don't know why – they're usually pretty good at getting the snowploughs out to clear the main roads. Perhaps there's been an accident or something.'

Grace Lukasz peered cautiously round the door into the back room of the bungalow, clinging on to the wheels of her chair to suppress the noise. Zygmunt was in his armchair by the table. He looked as though he might be asleep. His hands lay on the table, the blue veins standing up prominently, as if he really did suffer from the high blood pressure that he had always complained about, but which the doctors said didn't exist. His head was tipped against the back of the chair, and he had taken off his spectacles. Grace could see the red marks on the sides of his nose and the small wings of white hair pushed up over his ears. There were tufts of hair inside his ears, too, and more hair on his neck where he never thought to shave.

The old man's eyes were closed, but Grace wasn't sure that he was really sleeping. Often he sat like this while awake. Zygmunt always said he was thinking, when he took the trouble to explain at all. Grace supposed he was going back over his life in his mind, dwelling on his past. It was all he seemed to do now, to dwell on the past. But maybe she was misjudging him. Perhaps the old man was thinking of his wife, Roberta. She doubted it, though. It was more likely that he was thinking of Klemens Wach. These days, he thought mostly about Klemens.

Next Sunday was the day for the Edendale *oplatek* dinner. Almost the whole of the Polish community would gather for the event in the ex-servicemen's club, the Dom Kombatanta. Grace knew that for Zygmunt this would be the emotional high point of the year, more important even than *Wigilia*, the Christmas Eve celebration. This was the time when everyone began the year anew, but it was also a chance to reflect on their history and their place in the world. Most of the folk who would come to the dinner had not been born in Poland, of course. But since Solidarity and democracy, and the possibility of EU membership, some of those people had begun to talk more and more about their culture, their roots, their place in Europe. Not Zygmunt, though. Zygmunt didn't talk much at all these days. When he did, it was about the past.

But still, there would be the dinner. Though the community celebration had drifted back into January, it was no less of an occasion and everything had to be done just right. Grace could taste already the beetroot soup, the poached pike, the carp with horseradish sauce, the mushroom-stuffed tomatoes. The ladies who organized the dinner clung tenaciously to the traditions, no matter how much trouble they had to go to.

The stops had been pulled out for the family *Wigilia*, too, when all of them had sat down to the traditional twelve meatless dishes, with the extra place set for an unexpected guest. First they had shared the *oplatki* wafers. The symbols of reconciliation and forgiveness meant more this year than ever. Of course, forgiveness wasn't easy. Grace knew Peter was thinking of their eldest son in London, with no family around him to celebrate *Wigilia*, except some skinny bottle-blonde. They had sent an *oplatek* to Andrew as always. But whether Andrew had shared it with his blonde was doubtful. As far as Grace could gather, the apartment they rented in Pimlico contained nothing of relevance to *oplatek*, precious little that spoke of forgiveness.

The younger members of the family would change the traditions, if they had their way. Richard and Alice were embarrassed by the whole business. They would have made a meaningless ritual of *oplatek* just to get it over with quickly, so they could move on to the food and watch some American film on television. But they knew better than to upset Zygmunt, not at this time of year, and particularly not in these last few months. It was the time for reconciliation, when they could forgive each other their faults and their mistakes over the previous year. It was not a time for arguments.

So Zygmunt, as the eldest, had taken the first *oplatek* and offered it to his sister Krystyna, blessing her and wishing her health and a good year ahead. She had then broken off a piece of his wafer and offered her own *oplatek* in turn. And she had gazed into his face as she carefully wished him health and happiness in the year ahead, repeating the words as she was supposed to; but then her voice had broken and the old woman had begun to cry. Grace had edged her wheelchair nearer and put her arm round Krystyna's shoulders. But the old woman had looked as though she would go on weeping for ever, for the whole twelve days of Christmas maybe, right through to the Feast of the Three Kings. The front of her best dress had got stained with her tears.

Zygmunt had simply frowned and waited for her to continue with the ceremony, until everyone had shared their wafers with each other, biting into the nativity scenes moulded into the unleavened bread. And then, and only then, had they sat down to dinner, to the twelve meatless courses, one for each apostle. The family had visibly sighed with relief. Some of them had expected Zygmunt to make a speech, to talk about the mistakes and the sins of the last year, as he said his father and grandfather had always done, listing all the things the young people had done wrong before forgiving them and wiping the slate clean for a new year.

If Zygmunt had done that, it would have made things difficult. It was easier to pretend things hadn't happened when they weren't spoken out loud.

Grace took one last look at Zygmunt, to assure herself that he was still breathing, and backed across the passage. Peter was in the conservatory, among his cacti and the pelargoniums. There remained a thin covering of snow on the glass panels of the roof, and the light beneath it was pale blue.

'Is Dad all right?' he said, without turning from his inspection of a spiky monstrosity on a high shelf. His hearing was attuned to the sound of her chair. Even Zygmunt had acute hearing; Grace wouldn't have been surprised if the old man had known she was there, in the doorway of the room, all the time she had been looking at him. It would have been just like him to pretend he was unaware of her. It was like Peter, too. She could imagine him being exactly the same when he was a decade or two older. They were stubborn and hot-headed in turns, immovable or flying into tempers. His unpredictability had been one of the things that had attracted her to Peter. But recently his temper had been kept firmly in check, corked up inside.

'He's fine,' she said. 'He's been looking at the photo albums.'

It hardly seemed necessary for Grace to say it. The photographs had been in front of Zygmunt on the table where they stayed almost permanently. They were photographs of the family, the bits of the Lukasz history pieced together as best they could be, given the gaps, the sudden ends to so many lives. There was nothing that could be said to explain the page on which a young man of eighteen stood smiling and full of life in one photo, while below it the rest of the page was blank but for an almost indecipherable shot of a metal plaque.

At *Wigilia*, there had been many quiet prayers as

the Lukasz family had tried to connect with their relatives overseas. They had been thinking mostly of Zygmunt and Krystyna's cousins in Poland, but now also of Andrew. Everybody had spoken of him as Andrzej in the presence of the old people.

Krystyna said she always tried to conjure the memory of her dead parents back in Poland to strengthen the connection. Grace wanted to ask her if the prayers actually worked. But a glimpse of Krystyna's face in an unguarded moment told her what she wanted to know.

As always, there had been midnight Mass at the Church of Our Lady of Czestochowa on Harrington Street, under the images of the Black Madonna. Alongside the church was the Polish Saturday School, where a handful of pupils still kept the language alive, studying for their Polish GCSE exams, learning the history of Poland and the Catholic faith. It was the children of the Saturday School who would stage the Nativity play at the *oplatek* dinner next Sunday.

In church they had all joined in the singing. Some of the men smelled of vodka, and even some of the women were flushed too. But they all tried to sing, nevertheless. The Poles never seemed to have good singing voices, but they made up for it with enthusiasm. Even Zygmunt, in his croaky voice, had joined in with his favourite *Koledy*, the Christmas carols that followed Mass.

There had, of course, been the conversation – the catching up on the latest news. All their Polish acquaintances loved a bit of gossip. It was futile to try to keep the intrusion out of their lives. Grace was glad of the snow as an excuse for keeping to the house, because she didn't know what to say when their friends asked after Andrew.

She watched Peter stroke the firm leaves of the cactus and touch the tip of his finger to the points of the three-inch long spikes. He pressed on them until the spikes looked as though they would pierce his skin like nails.

'There was a phone call earlier,' he said.

'Yes?'

'It was that man, Frank Baine.'

Grace froze. Irrationally, she wanted to reach out and grab the pot the cactus was in, to hurl it against the wall and smash it. She wanted to fling it through the glass on to the flags in the back garden. She wanted to crush its ugly, vicious spikes and watch the fluid spurt from its swollen body. But she couldn't even reach that high.

'She's arrived then, has she?' said Grace.

'She flew into Manchester this morning.'

'Are you going to tell him?'

Peter shook his head. 'Let him rest a while longer,' he said. 'He needs his rest.'

Grace recalled the extra place that had been set at the *Wigilia* dinner. For an unexpected guest, Krystyna had said. The old lady never tired of explaining that it was the tradition, that it meant they could provide hospitality for any wanderer who might be travelling along the road that night, for any stranger who might knock at the door, whoever that person might seem to be. For at *Wigilia*, the stranger could be Jesus himself. Grace wanted to laugh out loud at the idea of Jesus wandering along Woodland Crescent, Edendale, on Christmas Eve and deciding to ring the bell at number 37. Surely he had better things to do, just as her parents had told her Santa Claus had at Christmas.

But Grace had said nothing. It had been Zygmunt who had shaken his head and smiled at his sister's words. Then, in his quiet, barely audible voice, speaking in Polish, he had insisted the extra place was set for those who were absent, for members of the family who had died. What he meant, of course, was that this place was for his cousin Klemens. It had been set at *Wigilia* when Zygmunt had first become the head of his own household, and every year since.

But Grace knew this year had been the last time. Next *Wigilia*, the extra place would no longer be for the absent Klemens. It would be for Zygmunt.

It might have been more than the cold that made Alison Morrissey shiver and pull her coat closer around her shoulders. In fact, the sun was already rising over Stanage Edge and Bamford Moor. In another hour it would have eased some of the chill from the air and melted away the mist that clung to the black rampart of Irontongue Hill. Morrissey looked as though the sun would bring her no warmth, as though it would take much more than a dose of winter sunlight to do that.

She was looking across a few yards of rough grass to a snow-covered peat moor and an eruption of bare rock. The wind was scraping across the moor from a more distant mountain to the north.

'The rock there is Irontongue,' said Frank Baine. 'In the distance is Bleaklow.'

'This place certainly looks bleak in the snow.'

'Even without the snow, it's still bleak.'

It was Irontongue Hill that took her attention. Baine had already told her that it got its name from the eruption of black rock on its summit, an uncompromising slab of millstone grit thrown up by ancient volcanic activity.

Morrissey turned away. The valley below them looked vast and mysterious in the darkness. It lay like a rumpled sheet tugged into peaks and valleys by a restless sleeper. But gradually the lights of scattered villages and farms were vanishing into the grey wash of dawn. The shadows of the hills deepened and began to spread dark fingers across a patchwork of fields, groping and fumbling among the yards of stone farmhouses and the gardens of invisible hamlets.

'I didn't anticipate it would be so cold in England,' she said. 'I didn't bring the right clothes.'

'None of your clothes would have been the right ones,' said Baine. 'The weather changes by the minute in these parts. This snow could be gone completely tomorrow.'

'Let's hope so. I've got to see the site. That's very important to me.'

'I understand that,' said Baine.

'The Lukasz family,' she said, 'will they agree to talk to me?'

'No,' said Baine.

'I could persuade them,' she said. 'If only I could get a chance to meet them, face to face, they would see I was human, like them. We all want the same thing.'

'I'm not sure about that.'

'But we do. We all want the truth. Don't we?'

They both stared ahead through the windscreen as they waited for it to clear. The hills in front of them were white and completely smooth, like marble slabs. Morrissey shivered.

'The Poles think they know what the truth is,' said Baine. 'I'm sorry.'

He used his sidelights as he drove on down the A57. Halfway down, Morrissey looked back. Her hand felt in her coat pocket for the little autofocus camera that she had not used. Postcards with photographs taken from this spot always seemed to face the other way, to frame a view of the valley bathed in sunlight. They never pictured Irontongue.

Shortly before the Snake Inn, they had to stop behind a line of cars that were waiting for a policeman in a fluorescent yellow jacket to wave them on. The other side of the road was blocked by two patrol cars with their lights flashing, and a snowplough was standing idle, with more cars pulled in close behind it.

'There, you see,' said Baine. 'I told you there must have been an accident. Somebody's run into the snowplough.'

Morrissey stared at the scene as they went by. She couldn't see any damage, or even figure out what the snowplough had collided with. Maybe they had already towed the other vehicle away. Yet there were people standing by the side of the road, and a woman in a sort of white boiler suit crouching in a snowdrift.

'Downhill all the way now,' said Baine. 'We'll soon be in Edendale.'

He turned on the radio. The sound of the eight o'clock news filled the car, speaking clearly of families going about their ordinary domestic routines, arguing over the use of the bathroom and the last cup of coffee in the pot, rushing to find the right shoes and cursing as they remembered, one by one, all the things they had to do that day. Morrissey closed her eyes.

'Have a doze, if you like,' said Baine.

'Frank,' she said, 'whenever I close my eyes, that's when the pictures come. The pictures of dead men.'

Baine nodded. 'Someone once said that memories are photographs on the wrong side of your eyes.'

'All my life, I've never been quite sure where memory ends and imagination begins. These days,

I can't always say which side of my eyes the dead men are.'

She opened her eyes again. A black, unmarked van with tinted rear windows was passing them slowly, going up the hill. Morrissey twisted in her seat to watch the policeman direct it into the side of the road. A blonde woman wearing a black coat and a red scarf stared at her until she turned away, and they drove on into Edendale.

4

Diane Fry hated these spells of standing around doing nothing. There were plenty of people who were better at that sort of thing than she was. It had been marginally better back at West Street, where at least she might have been able to hang on to the SOCOs' fan heater for a little while longer. But out here there was nothing to keep her warm, apart from the long, red scarf she had bought from Gap at Meadowhall for the winter. There was no shelter, nor even any physical activity to prevent her body from seizing up. She would rather have been the officer directing the traffic – at least he got to wave his arms a bit. But it wasn't the thing for a new detective sergeant to be doing.

Instead, she spent her time going through some discreet exercises, rising up on her toes, stretching her tendons, practising her breathing, feeling for the centres of energy in her body, keeping her circulation moving in her extremities to combat the cold. She became so absorbed in what she was doing that she almost forgot she wasn't alone. Almost.

'No blood,' said DI Paul Hitchens. He folded his arms across his chest as he leaned casually on the wheel arch of the snowplough, whose blade had been hastily covered by a sheet of blue plastic. Hitchens looked relaxed, and he spoke as if he were commenting on the weather. No blood today then, just snow. How boring. But Fry knew the comment wasn't addressed to her. Hitchens had a more appreciative audience.

DC Gavin Murfin had been talking to the county council driver and his mate, who were now sitting in the back of a patrol car. Murfin was wearing a pair of unsuitable fur-covered boots that came up to his knees, like the bottom half of a yeti costume. He stamped his feet on an area of compacted snow as he came round the back of the plough and wheezed faintly in the cold air.

'Blood? Not a drop,' he said cheerfully.

Fry frowned at Murfin as he fumbled among his clothes for a pocket to put his notebook away in. He was wearing so many sweaters that he looked like the original Michelin Man, with layers of rubber wobbling around his middle. Yet his face was flushed with cold. Somewhere in his pockets, she suspected, there might be a secret supply of food – something to keep him going for an hour or two, until he could find the nearest Indian takeaway for a beef biryani to stink her car out again.

'You know, I really hate it when there's no blood,' said Hitchens.

The pathologist, Juliana Van Doon, was suited up and working in the area cleared of snow, while an officer video'd the scene. Mrs Van Doon had the dead man's clothes open across his abdomen to examine a gaping wound. In her white suit, she looked like a badly designed snowman. Fry sighed. A snowman and the Michelin Man. There must be something wrong with her brain today. The cold weather was giving her hallucinations.

'Blood really makes a body, I always think,' said Hitchens. 'It gives it that bit of excitement. A certain *je ne sais quoi*. A subtle edge of implied violence, perhaps. The bitter-sweet taste of mortality. Do you know what I mean, Gavin?'

'Oh, sure,' said Murfin. 'It means you know the bloke's a definite stiff 'un, like.'

Fry thought Murfin's voice sounded slightly muffled, as if he had smuggled something into his mouth without her noticing. She thought she heard the rustle of a chocolate wrapper in his pocket. She looked longingly towards her car. There were things for her to be doing back at West Street. There were *always* things for her to be doing at the moment. Life went on in all its predictable messy ways in Edendale, as it did in every town in Derbyshire, as it no doubt did in every town and city in the country. There were plenty of crimes that went by without being investigated, let alone cleared up. The paperwork was everywhere to

55

prove it – cases that had been allocated crime numbers for insurance claims, and then filed. Everyone was crying out for more police time to be spent on solving crime, as if the world depended on it.

But here, at the foot of the Snake Pass, Fry felt as though she were standing on the edge of the world. On either side of the A57 there was a white wall a couple of feet deep where the snow lay untouched and unnaturally smooth, so that the edges of the road merged seamlessly into the surrounding moorland. The tarmacked surface of the A57 was normally the only sign of civilization this far out of Edendale, and Fry found its disappearance unsettling. It seemed to be telling her she might never get out.

Mrs Van Doon turned for a second to stare at the police officers standing in the road. Their voices carried loud and clear to where she was working. She shook her head and concentrated again on her job.

'You'd think if someone had been cut almost in half by a snowplough, they would bleed a bit,' said Hitchens.

'Yes, you'd think so,' said Murfin. 'A bit.'

'If only out of a desire to be artistically satisfying in their final moments.'

Hitchens caught Fry's eye and nodded at her, as if she had said something intelligent. She knew he sensed her antipathy to Murfin and her irritation at the way the DI was encouraging him. But Hitchens smiled, like a man who had all the time in the world at his disposal and had chosen to spend part of it right here, in this isolated, snow-covered spot, with a handful of fellow police officers, two distraught council workmen, and a body with no blood.

'Mind you, it's probably a clue,' he said.

Fry watched the pathologist taking a temperature and examining the corpse's skin for lividity. The dead man was dressed in a dark suit that bore the marks of the snowplough blade where it had gouged into him and tossed him on to the roadside verge like a sack of rubbish. The blue overnight bag that had been found with him stood a few feet away. He could almost have been a passenger stranded at a snowbound airport, sleeping uncomfortably on the floor of the terminal as he waited for a flight that would never leave.

Murfin surreptitiously chewed something and swallowed. When he opened his mouth, Fry imagined she could see tiny particles of chocolate hanging in the cloud of his breath, perhaps a sweet-flavoured mist that drifted and dissipated in the sharp air. 'I think I've got it, sir,' he said.

'Yes, Gavin?'

'The snowplough driver is a vampire. He sucked all the blood out of the body, and he never left a drop.'

Fry turned away so that they wouldn't see her expression. She felt the irritation turning to exasperation, and she had to take a few deep breaths of the ice-cold air to control it. She wanted to slap DC Murfin round the head a few times, but she couldn't do it with the DI present. Worst of all, she knew that Murfin would be hers for the duration of the enquiry.

'Well, well,' said Hitchens. 'Our first vampire killer in E Division. That's going to be a tricky one to do the paperwork on, Gavin. I don't think we've even got a form for it.'

Murfin grinned. His lips began to move, and he patted his pockets, seeking something else to eat – a Snickers bar, a packet of sweets, there would be something there. Fry could see that he was thinking. His brain was occupied with a difficult challenge, and it wasn't the detection of a crime.

'Everybody has their *cross* to bear, sir,' he said.

Mrs Van Doon turned, distracted by the chatter. 'If you really want to know, this man's heart had long since stopped,' she said. 'No heart pumping means no blood. Your corpse was already quite dead when the snowplough hit him.'

The pathologist began packing her bag. Fry wanted to help her. In fact, she wanted to go with her, to get out of the atmosphere here and into a nice warm mortuary, among peaceful company that didn't crack stupid jokes or leave prawn crackers trampled into the carpet of her car. Mrs Van Doon looked tired. Like all of them, she was overworked at the moment.

Fry did one more stretch, inhaled and exhaled

deeply, and felt her body tingle with the extra oxygen.

'I dunno about that,' said Murfin. 'I still like the vampire theory myself.'

'Excuse me,' said the pathologist. 'I think I'm finished here for now.'

Fry had to stand back out of the way to allow her past. She wanted to exchange a look, to share a little sympathy. But the woman's head was down, and she didn't look up. There were tired lines around her eyes and blue patches under them. Fry recalled that, according to the gossip at divisional headquarters, their old DCI, Stewart Tailby, had once had a personal interest in Juliana Van Doon, but nothing had come of it. Tailby was soon to make the move to an admin job in Ripley. Now Mrs Van Doon looked as though she had seen too many dead bodies.

'You see, I reckon I know that bloke who was driving the snowplough,' said Murfin. 'And I've never seen him out in the sunlight.'

The pathologist walked back to her car and began stripping off her suit. Fry picked up Mrs Van Doon's case and held on to it for a moment as the woman reached out to take it from her. Their eyes met, but neither of them spoke.

'What do you think, Doc? Should we take a blood sample from him?' called Murfin. 'I don't mean the dead man, I mean the undead one, so to speak. We might get a *cross*-match.'

Murfin barked with laughter. It was a very realistic bark, like the 'arf-arf' of a fat King Charles

59

spaniel. It echoed off the banks of snow on either side and caused little avalanches on to the roadway. Mrs Van Doon took off her overshoes, piled her gear into the back of her car and drove off without another word, spraying a gallon of slush on to Murfin's fur boots as she accelerated away.

'Was it something I said?' asked Murfin.

'Oh no,' said Hitchens. 'You've been eating garlic for breakfast again.'

Ben Cooper found the CID room icy cold and deserted. Obviously, the central heating radiators on this floor weren't working again. He could smell food. Tomato sauce and garlic. So Gavin Murfin hadn't been gone all that long. At any other time, Cooper would have opened a window to let in some fresh air, but his fingers were already starting to go so numb that he could barely hold a pen.

There were files piled on his desk, with yellow notes stuck all over them. It looked like a crop of daffodils had suddenly bloomed, despite the chilly air. He saw that one of the notes was much bigger than the others and was written in black marker pen of the kind used for exhibit labels. He didn't know what to do with it, or whether he should even touch it. For all he knew, it might be vital evidence in a forthcoming prosecution. All it said was: 'We've got our heater back, you bastards!'

Cooper rang down to the control room.

'DC Cooper here. Can you tell me what's going on?'

'DC Cooper? We've been trying to contact you since seven forty-two.'

'Well, I'm here now. What's going on?'

'You were supposed to be on duty at seven.'

'Yes, I know. You must have a record of the way I was left stranded with a prisoner on Hollowgate for half an hour waiting for a pick-up that never came? I had to walk up Spital Hill and meet a PC who couldn't even stay on his feet for thirty seconds. He looked like a reject from the Northern Ballet Company. Since I got here, I've been processing the prisoner through custody.'

There was a pause as the operator consulted somebody in the control room. 'We're a bit stretched at the moment,' she said.

'Tell me about it.'

'There are several messages from DS Fry,' said the operator accusingly. 'Three of them are marked urgent.'

Cooper sighed. 'So where am I supposed to be, apart from three places at once?'

'The body of an unidentified white male was found on the A57 Snake Pass, two hundred yards west of the Snake Inn,' said the operator.

'Is the road clear?'

'According to our latest information, it's passable with care.'

'OK, I'm on my way.'

'Er, we do have some later messages,' said the operator.

'Yeah?'

'I could probably just skip to the last one. It says: "Don't bother."'

'What does that mean?'

'I suppose it means they've managed without you, dear.'

Cooper blinked. Suddenly, the control-room operator sounded like his mother. Or at least, like his mother used to before she became ill.

'Thanks a lot,' he said, and put the phone down. He looked again at the files on his desk. It seemed he was muggins again, the sucker landed with the work that nobody else wanted, not when there was something more interesting to do. And it was all because he had set off for work early and found Eddie Kemp in that café. Next time, he would know better. Next time, he would pretend he hadn't recognized the suspect, as ninety per cent of his colleagues would have done when they weren't officially on duty. That's exactly what he would do next time. Maybe.

Cooper slouched across the room to see if he could dredge any warmth out of the radiator. As he moved, his left foot squelched.

Frank Baine banged the bell for a third time. There was no response.

'Well, if you're sure you'll be all right,' he said.

'I'll be fine,' said Alison Morrissey.

She stood in front of the deserted reception desk with her bags. The lobby was like no other hotel she had ever seen. It was dark, and it seemed to be full of ancient potted plants and stuffed fish in glass cases. It was also deserted. Baine had already put his head round all the visible doors to try to find a member of staff.

'Someone will appear in a second,' said Morrissey.

'We've got the meeting with the police at nine o'clock tomorrow morning,' said Baine. 'I'll pick you up here about eight-thirty, shall I? It isn't far.'

'That will be great. And thank you, Frank.'

Finally, he left. Morrissey gazed at a trout the size of a small dog. It stared back at her glassily, its mouth hanging open as if it might say something to her in a minute.

'Can I help you?'

A receptionist.

'A room,' said Alison. 'I have a room reserved. And I'm about ready to die unless I get to it soon.'

After she had showered and rested, she got out the files again. There were files on every member of the crew of Sugar Uncle Victor. Some, of course, were slimmer than others. The thickest was that on her grandfather, Pilot Officer Danny McTeague. But at the top of the pile, the one Alison Morrissey would look at first and read again tonight, was the file marked 'Zygmunt Lukasz'.

Later in the morning, Ben Cooper discovered who was going to have to interview Eddie Kemp in connection with the double assault.

'There isn't anybody else,' he was told. 'They're all out.'

Kemp looked almost pleased to see him. He seemed to feel they had struck up a close friendship waiting at the side of Hollowgate, as if a bond had been forged between them by performing a bit of early-morning street theatre for the customers of the Starlight Café. Cooper wasn't sure how long the theatre would have lasted, without turning into a tragedy, if it hadn't been for the appearance of Sonny Patel and his two oldest sons, brandishing brushes and shovels. They had made a great ceremony of sweeping the pavement clear of snow, until the three men leaning against their plate-glass window had shuffled their feet and moved on.

'The tea's not bad here,' said Kemp. 'But they're going to have to turn the bleedin' music off. It's doing my head in.'

Cooper and the PC accompanying him tried to keep their distance from the table, so they could breathe more easily. With the triple tape deck running and the duty solicitor sitting alongside Kemp, they took him through the events that had led to the injuries to the two young men at Underbank in the early hours of that morning. Kemp made no attempt to deny that he had been involved, but insisted that he had been assaulted first and had acted in self-defence.

'That old one,' said Cooper.

'They're known villains,' said Kemp. 'They're dealers off the estates.'

'And you say they attacked you first?'

'Yes.'

'When you arrived here, you were given the opportunity to see a doctor. You didn't report any injuries.'

'Well, I know how to handle myself,' said Kemp.

Now that Eddie Kemp wasn't wearing his Manchester United hat, Cooper could see that his hair was dark and wiry. He had the beginnings of a moustache, something more than a case of not having shaved this morning.

'Who were the other men who took part in this incident?' asked Cooper.

'No idea.'

'Complete strangers?'

'I reckon they were just passing and came to help,' said Kemp. 'Good Samaritans, if you like.'

'Who had the baseball bat?'

'Baseball bat? I didn't see that.'

'A snooker cue, maybe.'

'Dunno. Perhaps those lads that came to help me had been playing snooker at the club.'

Eddie Kemp looked at the solicitor and smiled happily. Kemp was experienced enough to know that witness identification was rarely sufficient in itself for a prosecution to go forward. Among a group of six men, it would have been impossible to say who had done what. And it had been at night, too. He was quite safe, for now.

'The victims were seriously injured, you know.'

'They deserved it,' said Kemp. 'They're scum. We don't want them coming around Underbank.

We don't want them getting our kids involved in hard drugs. If a beating keeps them away, that's a good thing. Your lot can't seem to do anything about them, anyway.'

'Assault is still a crime, Eddie, no matter who the victims are.'

'There's a crime, and then there's justice.'

'Which one is this, in your view?'

'I reckon it could be both at once.'

'Well, aren't you the philosopher then?' said Cooper impatiently. 'Two contradictory ideas in your head at the same time.'

Kemp nodded. 'You're right. Only I don't think they're contradictory. Not always.'

Diane Fry and Gavin Murfin finally blew in through the door of the CID room like Santa Claus and one of his elves. Their clothes were plastered with patches of snow and their faces were bright pink.

'Ah, Ben, at last,' said Fry, beating her hands together.

'I've been here all morning.'

'Got much done?'

'I've worked my way through most of the daffodils.'

'Sorry?'

'Yes, I've done quite a bit of work.'

'Oh well, whatever. I've got some jobs for you.'

'Fine.'

But Ben Cooper got that sinking feeling again. No job that Diane Fry had for him would ever be something he could get excited about. He suspected he would be spending the rest of the afternoon chasing phone calls and shifting yet more paperwork.

'We need to put a name to the Snowman,' said Fry.

'The Snowman?'

'One white male, unidentified.'

'Right.'

'And dead,' said Murfin.

Cooper listened as Fry explained the details they knew, which weren't many. There had been no obvious identification on the man, though they would have his clothes to work on when the body was dealt with in the mortuary. There was also the overnight bag that had been lying nearby. Like the body itself, the bag had been scraped along the ground by the blade of the snowplough. It was scuffed and ripped, and it was soaking wet from the time it had spent underneath the snow. Worst of all, it was empty. Even a toothbrush and a can of anti-perspirant could have helped them to build up a picture that would identify the Snowman.

'What we need are some mispers,' said Fry.

Cooper had only that afternoon been dealing with some reports relating to a missing person. It was easy to refer to them as 'mispers' when they were merely a set of details in a computer database. But when you started to look into an individual case, they suddenly turned into people. They sprang out of the screen and became unhappy teenagers or abused wives, confused old women or businessmen who had hit fifty and decided to recover their youth with the girl from the marketing department.

'What age are we talking?' he said.

'Early thirties. Good physical condition. Well dressed.'

'Mmm. Right profile anyway.'

'For what?'

'Well, for going missing.'

'You need to be a particular type of person?'

'Apart from youngsters, the people most likely to go missing are men aged between twenty-seven and thirty-four.'

'That puts you right in the frame, then, Ben.'

'Are we talking death by misadventure? Or suicide, or what?'

Fry hesitated. 'Don't know,' she said.

'If it's murder,' said Cooper, 'you don't need a profile for that. Anybody will do for a victim these days. Have we got any evidence? I thought he was hit by the snowplough?'

'He was already dead before then.'

The Snowman's priority rating depended on the pathologist. If he had merely suffered a heart attack by the roadside, then he would be likely to stay on ice for some time before he was claimed. But Fry wasn't taking that line.

'An instinct, Diane?' he said.

But Fry ignored the question. 'So you and Gavin have got work to do. Let's have a list of possibles, soon as you can. Neighbouring forces, obviously. Don't forget he was found on the A57. Greater Manchester must have a whole book full of missing persons.'

'No doubt.'

'Get on to the Missing Persons Helpline. And don't forget the national forces – Transport Police, Ministry of Defence. Oh, and the Northern Ireland Police Service.'

'Oh, great. Terrorist execution by snowplough.'

'You never know.'

E Division's commander, Chief Superintendent Colin Jepson, had agreed to see Alison Morrissey himself. But of course he demanded support from his junior officers. There was strength in numbers, he said – as if the visitor were the advance party for an enemy horde about to invade E Division. But numbers were something they didn't have at the moment. The duty inspector had said she was too busy, and nobody from the community safety department was available, either. Ben Cooper's name had been mentioned.

'Here are the files the Local Intelligence Offi-cer has put together for the Chief,' said DI Paul Hitchens after telling Cooper the news, just before he went off duty that night.

'If the LIO produced the files, why can't he go to the meeting?' asked Cooper.

'He's got flu. So it'll have to be you, Ben.'

'Why?'

'The Chief is afraid he'll be asked questions that need a bit of local knowledge. You know he's never quite managed to work out which county he's in since he transferred from Lancashire. He has you marked down as the local lad who can answer all the difficult questions the rest of us can't – you know, like how to spell "Derbyshire".'

'No, I meant – why?' said Cooper. 'It sounds as though this Alison Morrissey is on some kind of holy mission to clear her grandfather's name. All ancient history, isn't it?'

'That's about right,' said Hitchens.

'So why are we doing this at all?'

'Ah. Political reasons.'

'Political? What's political about it?'

'We owe favours,' said Hitchens.

'We do?'

'When I say "we", I mean the Chief, of course. Maybe you don't remember the big fraud case a few years back, Ben. The main suspect got out of the country and ended up in Canada, masquerading as a lumberjack or whatever. The Mounties weren't too co-operative at first, but the Chief talked to the consul in Sheffield. They'd played golf together once or twice, and the consul pulled some strings. Anyway, the net result was that our Chief Superintendent made some new bosom buddies over there in Ottawa. They discovered they had similar handshakes, if you know what I mean. And one of them turns out to be this Morrissey woman's uncle. That's what I mean by politics.'

'So we're putting on a show.'

'Up to a point. We're not actually going to *do* anything.'

'How do you know that, sir, if we haven't even talked to her yet?'

'Oh, you'll see,' said Hitchens. 'Even political influence can't produce resources out of nowhere.'

Finally, Cooper went off duty and made his way directly across town to the Old School Nursing Home. In one of the lounges, he found his mother waiting. She was sitting up in an armchair, tense, staring at the wall, her thoughts far away in some world of her own making.

'Do you remember what I said, Mum?' he asked. 'About moving out of the farm?' He tried to say it casually, to make it sound as though he were only planning to pop out to the shop to buy some tea bags.

Isabel Cooper didn't say anything, though her eyes shifted from the wall to his face. Cooper took her hand. It felt limp and lifeless.

'I've decided I've got to live in my own place for a bit,' he said. 'It'll only be in Edendale. I'll still come and see you every day, don't worry.'

Her eyes remained distant, not focused on him at all. But a momentary shadow seemed to pass across her face, a faint echo of the expression she had always used when she thought she had caught him out in a lie.

'You'll never know any difference, Mum,' he

said. 'You'll see as much of me as you always have. Too much, as usual. That's what you always used to say, whenever I got under your feet.'

He wished that she would smile at him, just once. But her face didn't move. Part of that was the drugs. The drugs were doing their job, controlling the involuntary spasms, suppressing the facial twitches that had so often turned her into someone else, nothing like the mother he had known.

He patted the back of her hand, leaned forward and kissed her. Her cheek was cold, like the face of a statue. He heard her release her breath in a long sigh, and felt her relax a little. It was the only response he was likely to get.

For a moment, Cooper thought of going back on his decision. But it didn't matter to his mother now, did it? It didn't make any difference to her where he lived, now that she was in the nursing home and not likely to return to Bridge End Farm. It was his own reluctance that he was having to deal with, his own sense of leaving a large part of himself behind.

He had promised to call at the nursing home to see his mother every day, and so far he had done it. It meant he could keep telling her every day about his decision to move out, until they both believed it.

Cooper had left the farm too early that morning to collect his mail when the postman came. It was usually approaching nine o'clock by the time the post van made it out as far as Bridge End. So the estate agent's details were waiting for him when he arrived home that evening. Everyone could tell what the envelope contained. He had told his family that he planned to move out, but he could see that they hadn't really believed it until now. One of his nieces, Josie, handed him the envelope without saying a word, but with a reproachful look. She almost seemed to be about to burst into tears.

'Anything interesting?' said Matt, watching his brother open the envelope from the estate agent.

Cooper could see straight away that there was nothing suitable. All the agents had available were a couple of three-bedroom semis in Buxton and a furnished first-floor apartment in Chapel-en-le-Frith. Apart from the fact that they were too far away, the rent for each of them was well outside the limit of his resources. But it seemed like an admission of failure to tell his family there was nothing. Worse, it might raise expectations that he would never find anything and that he would be forced to stay on at the farm. Once that idea became accepted, it would be all too easy to fall in with it himself. And that would be that. He would be here until he retired, or until Matt decided to sell the farm, which would be a disaster in itself.

He looked at Matt. He wasn't altogether sure how his brother felt about the prospect of him moving out. It was a big step, to be sure. But wouldn't it leave more room for Matt and Kate and the girls to live their own life? Even inside the estate agent's, though, he had felt embarrassed to explain what he was doing. He was nearly thirty years old, and it wasn't an age where you could comfortably announce that you were thinking of leaving home for the first time. He imagined the sideways glances at him, the speculation about his relationship with his mother.

'I might have a look at one or two of these places tomorrow,' he said.

He could only hope. Things might look completely different tomorrow.

Diane Fry stayed behind in the office for a while after everyone else had gone. The night shift was practically non-existent, and the station became like a morgue. It was the time she liked most, when there were no distractions and she could think out problems without being interrupted by singing lobsters or, even worse, her colleagues. People always had their own demands to make on her.

From a locked drawer in her desk, she took out a manila folder, which had Ben Cooper's name on it. It contained copies of his personnel files. She knew when he had been recruited into Derbyshire Constabulary, what grades he had got in his training and where his first posting had been. She had the date of his transfer from uniform to CID, a couple of commendations from senior officers, and a special note from the Divisional Commander referring to the death in service of his father, Sergeant Joe Cooper. Ben had been given compassionate leave and counselling. A note said 'no long-term problems'.

There were also the results of his examinations for the rank of sergeant, all good. Then the outcome of his interview board, when he had withdrawn his application. That had been when Fry got the sergeant's job herself. Did the change in Cooper stem from that time? It would be understandable. But she didn't think it was quite that – although the disappointment of missing out on the promotion he had banked on could have been the cause of what she suspected he had done later. She was almost sure he had concealed evidence, or at least not reported his suspicions, all out of misguided loyalty.

Fry touched the scar on her face, which had healed but not yet faded. She had no evidence against him – that was the problem. There was no proof. Unfounded allegations against a colleague would blight her own career as surely as anything else she could do. Especially when they were against Mr Popular, the man who had lived in the Eden Valley all his life and knew everyone. She would get no benefit from stirring up trouble against fellow officers, unless she was absolutely sure of her ground. And that was particularly true when one of them had died in the course of his duty.

Fry knew nothing could do more damage to her relationship with her colleagues. She could imagine even now the officers drawing away from her in the corridor, the cooling of attitudes from senior staff, gradually freezing her out. Finally she would get the message and either transfer back to where she had come from, the West Midlands, or leave the police service altogether, knowing no one would care which she chose.

She frowned at the memory of the way Ben Cooper had looked today as he went off duty. He had been wearing that ridiculous waxed coat with the long skirts and the vast inside pocket he called his poacher's pocket. The coat was dark green, as if he were trying for a camouflage effect. It wasn't much use in the snow – he would be a sitting duck for an angry gamekeeper with a twelve-bore shotgun. But somehow it made him look as if he belonged where he was, like a man who was at ease with himself and his own place in the world. And then there was the tweed cap. In the shadow of its peak, you could barely see his eyes.

Fry shook herself. There was no one she could ask about Ben Cooper. Perhaps her view of him was somehow distorted. Maybe her antennae were deadened by her preoccupations with her own problems. One thing was certain, Cooper was a man orbiting somewhere beyond the reach of her detection systems. But he wouldn't need to put a foot too far wrong before his orbit brought him right back into her sights. Maybe tomorrow.

5

By the next day, the skies had cleared. Overnight frost had sprayed glitter on the snow that lay on the moors, and the air crackled like static electricity.

Ben Cooper sighed as he stumbled around his room, determined not to miss breakfast today. First thing this morning he had to attend the Chief Superintendent's meeting with the Canadian woman. He hoped it was something that could be got out of the way as soon as possible. It was an irrelevance, and a waste of time. From what he had read of the files produced by the Local Intelligence Officer, it was more than a cold case she was asking Derbyshire Constabulary to take up – it was no case at all.

Cooper was sure it was just another fuss being kicked up by somebody with an obsession about the past and the history of their family. The Canadian would be sent packing by Chief Superintendent Jepson pretty quickly.

She was unimportant, anyway. At the moment,

until he was fully awake, Cooper couldn't even remember the woman's name.

Alison Morrissey had brought Frank Baine with her to West Street for support. Baine described himself as a freelance journalist who had researched local RAF history and the background to the aircraft wrecks that littered the Peak District. He hinted at a book yet to appear. He was also the man who had liaised for weeks now on behalf of the Canadian, pestering for information and a confirmed date and time for the meeting. Though the Chief Superintendent had at no stage spoken to Baine himself, he had already managed to become irritated by his persistence, communicated to him by his staff. That Canadian Consul must really be a valuable contact.

The four of them met in the Chief Superintendent's office amid a flurry of cappuccino served by the Chief's secretary, and an offer of the Bakewell tarts that Jepson kept for the purpose of demonstrating his Derbyshire street cred to visitors. Cooper couldn't remember when he had tasted real coffee at West Street before. He had heard they actually served it to customers in reception at the new B Division headquarters, but he wouldn't believe it until he saw it for himself.

The meeting opened with some half-hearted pleasantries about the health and welfare of Miss Morrissey's uncle, his family, his dog and his golf handicap. The Chief Superintendent eventually ran out of small talk and sat looking at his visitors in silence. It was an interrogation technique that he fell back on from force of habit, from his long-past days in the CID. It worked, though. Alison Morrissey began talking almost immediately.

'As you know, gentlemen, I asked for this meeting because I am attempting to clear the dishonour on the name of my grandfather, Daniel McTeague, who was an officer serving in the Royal Canadian Air Force. He was reported missing while on attachment to the RAF in January 1945.'

'All of fifty-seven years ago,' said Chief Superintendent Jepson. He was smiling amicably, but he was putting down his marker from the start.

'I happen to know that your neighbours the Greater Manchester Police re-opened a case last year that was exactly fifty-seven years old,' said Morrissey, looking him straight in the eye. 'The length of time that has passed seems to me to be irrelevant, if there's been a miscarriage of justice.'

Cooper sneaked a look at her over the files he was pretending to study. He hadn't expected her to be so young. If he had bothered to think about it, he would have been able to work out her possible age range, of course, since he knew it was her grandfather that she was here to talk about. It was mentioned in the files that Pilot Officer McTeague had been twenty-three when he went missing. His daughter, Alison Morrissey's mother, had been born only days before he disappeared, which would make her fifty-seven now.

79

She must have been one of those women who waited until her thirties before having children, because Morrissey could barely have been more than twenty-five or twenty-six. Cooper liked the way she had answered the Chief Superintendent. She had plenty of determination. And she knew her stuff, too.

'There was never a court case,' pointed out Jepson. 'Justice was not involved.'

'Natural justice,' said Morrissey.

The Chief Superintendent sighed a little. 'Go on.'

'My grandfather was the pilot of a Lancaster bomber based at RAF Leadenhall in Nottinghamshire, part of 223 Squadron of Bomber Command. He had been flying with the RAF for two years, and he had an excellent service record. He was awarded a Distinguished Flying Cross after bringing home a damaged Wellington from a successful raid on German U-boat bases near Rotterdam. He ordered his crew to bail out once they were over England and landed the aircraft single-handedly. And that was despite the fact that he had himself been wounded by shrapnel from enemy anti-aircraft fire. As soon as he recovered from his injuries, he retrained on Lancasters and was posted to RAF Leadenhall.'

'Very interesting,' said Jepson. 'But can we move forward to January 1945?'

'You need to know what sort of a man my grandfather was,' said Morrissey.

Cooper watched her eyes harden with a momentary anger as she spoke. Her age might have taken him by surprise, but he certainly hadn't expected her to be so attractive. She had that style and confidence that made a woman stand out from the crowd. He was enjoying her display of assurance and pride. He was surprised that Jepson hadn't softened to her more by now – he usually had a weakness for an attractive young woman himself. But the Chief must have hardened his heart, and once he did that, there was no way he would back down. This meeting could have only one possible outcome. Cooper was already beginning to feel sympathy for the Canadian woman. Jepson would let her go through her paces, but in the end, she was going to be disappointed.

'This is a photograph of my grandfather,' said Morrissey. She slid a picture across the table to the Chief Superintendent, then one to Ben Cooper. She had hardly looked at him so far, except for a quick glance of appraisal when they had been introduced. He had the impression that she was a woman who knew exactly what she aimed to achieve, and who was most likely to be able to help her. Now, she fixed her gaze on Chief Superintendent Jepson again.

'That photograph was taken when he was pro-moted to the rank of Pilot Officer on joining 223 Squadron,' she said. 'Because of his service, he was a year or two older than most of his crew. That's why they called him "Granddad".'

The photo was something that the LIO hadn't been able to produce for the files. Yet surely it must have been readily available, if it was an official RAF shot. Morrissey had been better organized, or had better help. Cooper glanced at Frank Baine. He had heard of Baine vaguely. He recollected having seen a television programme the journalist had featured in, which had been commemorating the sixtieth anniversary of the Battle of Britain. The only thing Cooper remembered clearly from the programme was the fact that some of the Lancaster bombers used by the RAF during the Second World War had been built at a factory in Bamford, only a few miles from Edendale. Of course, the factory was long since gone, as were all the Lancasters it had produced. A woman who appeared on the programme had spoken of working on the aircraft as a girl, and of being told by an officious foreman in a bowler hat that if she made any mistakes she would be responsible for allowing the Germans to win the war.

'I want you to look at the photograph,' said Morrissey, 'because you will be able to see how proud my grandfather was of his uniform.'

Pilot Officer McTeague was immaculate in his RAF uniform, with his peaked cap, brand new hoops on his sleeve, and a medal on a ribbon pinned to his breast pocket. He stood almost to attention, with his arms at his sides. His tie was perfectly straight, and there were sharp creases in his trouser legs. The uniform would have been blue, of course, though the photo was black and white. Probably the original print had been sepia

– this looked like a computer-enhanced copy. It had brought out the features of McTeague's face – a small, dark moustache, a proud smile, and a direct gaze at the camera from a pair of clear eyes. He was a good-looking man, who must have turned the heads of a few girls in uniform. And, yes, there was a definite resemblance in his eyes to the granddaughter who sat across the table from Cooper now.

'He's wearing his Distinguished Flying Cross, as you can see,' said Morrissey.

Jepson put his copy of the photograph down on his file. 'January 1945,' he said.

Morrissey nodded. 'On 7th January 1945, my grandfather was at the controls of Lancaster bomber SU-V,' she said. 'The crew called their aircraft Sugar Uncle Victor.'

It was Frank Baine who took up the story. This was his expertise, his specialist field of knowledge. Baine had shaved his head, a fashion that had ousted the comb-over as a means of hiding the beginnings of baldness. As soon as he began to talk, Cooper saw why Alison Morrissey had brought Baine along. He hardly needed to refer to any notes to deliver the facts of what had happened on 7th January 1945. The facts as far as they were known, anyway.

'Lancaster SU-V had suffered damage to the outer starboard engine from an attack by a German night-fighter during a bombing raid on Berlin,' he said. 'The engine had been replaced with a new one, and the crew were on a flight to test the new engine. It was routine – they were due to fly from their base at RAF Leadenhall in Nottinghamshire to RAF Benson in Lancashire. It was a distance of no more than a hundred miles. This crew had flown several operations over Germany and had returned safely. But something went wrong over Derbyshire. SU-V crashed on Irontongue Hill, ten miles from here. There were seven people on board. Five of them died in the impact.'

Cooper found the crew list in front of him. Seven names. Only one of them was familiar so far – that of the pilot, Daniel McTeague. 'Hang on a moment,' he said. 'Which crew members were killed?'

'First of all, the wireless operator, Sergeant Harry Gregory,' said Baine.

'Yes.' Cooper put a small cross next to his name on the list.

'The bomb aimer, Bill Mee, the mid-upper gunner, Alec Hamilton, and the rear gunner, Dick Abbott, who were all British RAF sergeants.'

'And one more?'

'One of the Poles,' said Baine. 'The navigator. Pilot Officer Klemens Wach.'

'Apart from McTeague, that leaves just one who survived,' said Cooper.

'Correct.'

'The last one then is the flight engineer. I'm not quite sure how to pronounce it . . .'

'It's Lukasz,' said Baine. 'Like *goulash*. The other survivor was Pilot Officer Zygmunt Lukasz.'

*   *   *

84

Grace Lukasz noticed that Zygmunt showed no interest now in attending Dom Kombatanta, the Polish ex-servicemen's club. She was glad about that. These days, the old soldiers and airmen seemed to talk of nothing else but war and death, as if the lives they had lived over nearly six decades since 1945 had been telescoped into a fortnight's leave from operational duties. She had heard one former paratrooper who had drunk too much vodka in the club one night say that he had never been so alive as when he was facing death. And that's what they were doing now, too – the old servicemen were standing by to climb on board for their last journey, their final venture into the unknown. This time, their transport would be a hearse.

At one time, Zygmunt and his friends had taken an interest in British politics. They had discussed endlessly what they thought was an amazing apathy on the part of the British themselves, who hardly seemed to want to bother voting, let alone listening to what the politicians had to say.

'They haven't been the same since Winston Churchill,' Zygmunt had said one day.

'Dad, that was nearly sixty years ago,' said Peter.

'That's what I mean!' said Zygmunt. 'It's been downhill ever since.'

But that had been in the days when he would still speak English.

The old man had a knack of making Grace feel

foreign. It was an uncomfortable feeling, which she had never quite got used to since marrying Peter. Before, her name had been Woodward, and she had never even considered her national identity. She had been British, and that meant you didn't have to think about it. But suddenly one day, her name was Lukasz, and people treated her differently, as if she had been re-born as a foreigner. Even people she had known all her life and had been to school with seemed to imagine that she might have forgotten how to speak English.

And then, after the accident six years ago, Grace had found herself being glad to feel foreign. Now, when she went into a shop and people fell suddenly silent, she was able to believe that it was because they had heard only her name and mentally labelled her as some kind of East European asylum seeker. There were plenty of asylum seekers now, in the guest houses in Buxton Road.

Grace had read stories in the newspapers recently about groups of East European women and children visiting shops in local villages supposedly asking for directions and distracting the shopkeepers while their children stole from the shelves. She had no doubt it was true. Most of these people were gypsies anyway, and Edendale had suffered its share of gypsy problems for many years. One year, a tribe of them had parked their lorries and caravans in a field next to Queen's Park. From the corner of the Crescent, she had been able to see their washing lines and their children playing in the hedge bottoms; she had watched their dogs running wild and their rubbish piling up day by day in the corner of the field. It had been like watching the coming of winter and the dying of the landscape, like waiting and waiting for the first day of spring, when the sun eventually came out and it seemed possible to make things look neat and respectable again. She had experienced the same sense of impotence, the same impatience, as she waited for an irritation to be gone from her life.

But finally, one morning, the gypsies had departed before dawn, leaving a sea of mud in the field and litter of all kinds strewn down the banking towards the road. What did it matter to her where the gypsies went when they moved on? What did it matter to her where the snow went? The snow was absorbed back into the earth somehow, that was all that mattered. There was a cleansing rhythm to nature that she found comforting.

Grace turned back to the room. Her eye immediately fell on the Lukasz family photograph in the alcove near the door. Herself and Peter, Zygmunt and Krystyna, with the grandchildren at their knees. She had once, before they were married, tried to persuade Peter to change their surname. She thought it would be best for their future children. A good alternative would have been Lucas, she had said. It would only have been a change in spelling really; the pronunciation was almost the same. Peter had said no. He had said it in a tone of voice she had not heard from him until then, a tone that made her hesitate, then decide not to argue. He had never given her a reason, and she had not asked, in the end.

She looked at the face of the old man, Zygmunt, at the proud tilt of his head and the direct stare. Peter was becoming more and more like his father with age. Sometimes, if she watched him carefully, she saw a different look in her husband's eyes when the old man called him 'Piotr'. It was a look that she had never been able to bring to his eyes, even in their most intimate moments. No matter how many times she whispered his name, she could never bring the same look of pride. The meaning wasn't there for him in 'Peter' in the way it was when he heard his Polish name. For a moment, she wished she could do it by calling him 'Piotr' herself. But she knew it was too late to change a habit now.

Grace went quickly to the window when she heard the sound of a car. A Ford had pulled up at her kerb beyond their hedge. She could see a man with fair hair in the driver's seat. It wasn't Andrew. A woman got out on the passenger side. She met Grace's eyes for a moment. Then she turned away and walked to a house two doors down, while the driver waved and drove off. Grace let go of the breath she had been holding. It wasn't her either. Not yet.

Frank Baine waited to be sure he still had their attention. Alison Morrissey had her gaze fixed on Chief Superintendent Jepson. She seemed to be trying to will the Chief to listen, though Ben Cooper knew Jepson well enough to see that his brain had switched off already. Probably he had decided in advance the amount of time he was prepared to give. Cooper wondered how fast the clock was ticking down.

'Former Pilot Officer Zygmunt Lukasz is the sole surviving crew member of Sugar Uncle Victor,' said Baine. 'Lukasz was one of the youngest of the crew, but even he is seventy-eight now. As it happens, he lives here, in Edendale.'

'No doubt you'll be visiting him,' said Jepson, as if suggesting there was no time like the present.

'We have been in contact with the Lukasz family,' said Baine. 'It would be fair to say that they're not keen to co-operate.'

'Pity,' said Jepson.

'On the day of the crash, the skipper had filed a visual flight record with flight control, as was normal practice,' said Baine. 'He'd been briefed on broken clouds at two thousand feet and poor visibility. But somehow he went off course and found himself over the Peak District. He discovered the fact too late, when he nosed the aircraft down through the overcast to establish his position. Directly in front of him was Irontongue Hill. He never stood a chance of avoiding it.'

'Five men died in the crash. There were two who survived.'

'Yes, the seventh was the pilot, my grandfather,'

said Alison Morrissey. 'After the crash, he was never found.'

Cooper was ready for this. It was the whole point of the meeting, after all. The rest was just preamble. 'He was listed as having deserted,' he said. 'In the air accident enquiry, he was also blamed for the crash.'

Morrissey turned on him suddenly. 'He was the pilot. He was in command of the aircraft. Since there was no evidence given of enemy action or mechanical fault, he was bound to take the blame. He was branded guilty by default. And there's absolutely no evidence that my grandfather deserted. Absolutely none.'

'But he was seen leaving the area,' said Cooper.

'No – he was not.'

Chief Superintendent Jepson stirred slightly, his interest piqued by the suddenly raised voices. He studied the report that had been prepared for him by the Local Intelligence Officer. 'According to my information, two young boys were spoken to, who said they had seen an airman walking down the Blackbrook Reservoir road, from Irontongue Hill towards Glossop. That seems fairly conclusive.'

'Their statement was crucial. I'd like to find them now to talk to them, but the boys aren't named in the reports I have.'

'That might be unfortunate from your point of view, Miss Morrissey, but they were only children, after all. Twelve years old, and eight. Why should they lie about something like that?'

'I have no idea.'

'Also, it appears that a man in uniform was reported to have been seen heading away from the area later that day. In fact, he was picked up by a lorry driver on the A6 near Chinley. That was a perfectly normal thing for a driver to do back then.'

'The man was never positively identified as Pilot Officer McTeague,' said Morrissey.

'We used to do it until quite recently, in fact. But not for a few years.'

'Do what?'

'Give lifts to servicemen. They would stand at the roadside with their kitbags and a sign saying where they were going, and motorists would stop for them. You could see what they were by their haircuts, because all the other young men of their age had long hair then. I can remember picking a few soldiers up myself on the M6 roundabout near Preston, in the days when I was serving with the Lancashire force. These days, though, you can't trust anybody. You never know who might have got hold of an army uniform or a bit of equipment. Let them into your car and you could be mugged in a minute, or worse. I would advise members of the public against it, for their own safety.'

Alison Morrissey stared at the Chief Superintendent, and Cooper saw her redden slightly. The extra colour made her look even more attractive, but Jepson didn't seem to have noticed. He had gone into public-meeting mode, as if he were addressing members of the Chamber of Commerce or a police liaison committee.

'That man was never positively identified as my grandfather,' repeated Morrissey.

'Yes, I see that,' said Jepson, looking at his report.

'And how did he get to the A6? Let's consider that for a moment. I've studied the maps of the area, and the place this man was picked up was over ten miles from the scene of the crash. Is my grandfather supposed to have walked all that way? And why didn't anybody else see him earlier?'

'It was dark,' pointed out Cooper.

The Canadian woman caught his eye. He had the feeling that, in different circumstances, she might have smiled.

Jepson nodded at Cooper gratefully. 'Of course it was. It was seven o'clock in the morning when the lorry driver picked him up. It's still dark at that time in January round these parts. Ben knows, you see. He's a local lad. There's nothing like a bit of local knowledge. It's better than any number of bits of paper you can produce, Miss Morrissey.'

The Chief Superintendent pushed the report aside, as if he didn't need it any more, and beamed at Morrissey. Cooper recognized it as his politician's smile, the one he normally only used for visiting members of the Police Authority when he was hoping they would go away and leave him in peace.

'The lorry driver couldn't even say that it was

an airman's uniform this person was wearing,' said Morrissey, starting to sound a little desperate.

Jepson pulled the report back towards him. He glanced at the first page, then at Cooper, who mouthed three words at him silently.

'It was dark,' said Jepson hesitantly. 'Yes, of course it was – it was dark, as we've already established. Miss Morrissey, we can't expect a lorry driver to have noticed details of a serviceman's uniform in the dark. There were no street lights at that time, you know. There was –'

'– a war on,' said Morrissey. 'Yes, I know.'

Jepson steepled his fingers and looked round the meeting with some satisfaction, as if the point were proved. 'Did you have any more information you wished to produce, Miss Morrissey? Any *new* information?'

'My grandfather didn't desert,' said Morrissey quietly.

'With respect,' said Jepson, getting into his stride as he saw the home stretch appear, 'I don't think there's anything you've told us that could be considered new. There is no reason to believe that anything happened to your grandfather other than that he left the scene of the crash before the rescue teams arrived, he hitched a lift from a lorry driver on the A6 and . . .'

'And what?' said Morrissey.

Jepson flicked the report over uncertainly. 'Well, presumably he somehow managed to get out of the country and back to his home in Canada.'

'And how easy would that be for a deserter?' said Morrissey. 'Especially as there was a war on?'

The Chief Superintendent looked to be about to shrug his shoulders, then changed his mind at the last minute. He had been told in senior management training sessions that it was a gesture that gave out the wrong message.

'Please. My problem is that, without being able to trace the two boys who saw my grandfather, my only possible sources of information in the area are Zygmunt Lukasz and a man called Walter Rowland, who was a member of the RAF mountain rescue team called out to the crash. Frank has contacted them, but both are refusing to speak to me.'

'Miss Morrissey, I'm sorry, but I really can't do anything for you,' he said.

'It's not that you can't – you won't,' said Morrissey.

'If you wish. But the fact is, I don't have resources to spare even to advise you on your mission.'

Ben Cooper could see that Alison Morrissey didn't like the word 'mission'. Her jaw tensed, and her expression became obstinate. But she began to fiddle with the catch of her briefcase, as if she were about to put her papers away.

Cooper took the opportunity to ask a question. 'Miss Morrissey, what exactly do *you* think happened to your grandfather?'

Morrissey met his eye, surprised for a moment, and pushed her hair behind her ear with a quick flick of the hand. 'I think he was injured,' she said. 'Probably dazed or concussed, so that he didn't know what he was doing or where he was. Possibly he couldn't even remember the crash. I think he took off his flying gear and left it by the side of the road because it was too heavy for him to carry. I think he reached a house somewhere nearby, perhaps a farmhouse, and the people took him in.'

'Took him in?'

'Looked after him and gave him somewhere to stay.'

'Knowing who he was? They must have heard later that there had been an air crash. Why would they keep him? Why not hand him over to the authorities? If he was injured, they would at least get medical treatment for him.'

'I don't know why,' said Morrissey stubbornly. 'I do know that the man who hitched a lift on the A6 was not my grandfather. I believe that man was an army deserter who had gone absent without leave from the transport depot at Stockport. He was a man named Fuller. The police arrested him later at his parents' house in Stoke-on-Trent.'

'But your grandfather?' asked Cooper. 'What makes you think he stayed in this area? It seems very unlikely.'

'*This* is what makes me think so,' said Morrissey. She pulled a plastic wallet from her briefcase. Cooper could see that it contained a medal on a red-and-gold ribbon. The medal was perfectly polished, and it gleamed in the fluorescent lights, flashing in their eyes as if sending a message across the decades.

'What is it?'

'It's a Royal Canadian Air Force Distinguished Flying Cross,' said Morrissey. She turned the medal over in her hands. 'It arrived at my grandmother's old home in Ottawa one day during the summer. There was a note with it, too. It was addressed to my mother, and it just said: "Remember your father, Pilot Officer Danny McTeague."'

Cooper leaned closer to look at the medal. 'This is your grandfather's medal? But where did it come from?'

'All we know,' said Morrissey, 'is that it was posted here, in Edendale.'

6

The body from the Snake Pass had arrived in the mortuary at Edendale General Hospital, where it would be kept on ice, at least until it could be identified and somebody claimed it. When Diane Fry had driven up to the mortuary, she had left DC Murfin in the car, where he was no doubt adding to the pile of toffee wrappers on her floor.

Inside the mortuary, it was warmer than out on the street. The air smelled better, too – it was full of disinfectants and scented aerosols to suppress the odours of body fluids and abdominal organs.

'We don't get many of these now,' said Mrs Van Doon. 'People carry all sorts of identification with them these days, don't they? But if not, we can usually match up their fingerprints or dentition, or their DNA. No luck your end so far, I take it? Nothing we can match him to?'

'Nothing,' said Fry. 'We're putting appeals out, of course. But at present his description doesn't match the details of any missing person we know of.'

'So maybe no one's noticed he's missing yet.'

'There seem to be a lot of people who go around not noticing things,' said Fry.

The pathologist gave her a brief, quizzical look. 'He doesn't look like the average missing person to me,' she said. 'He's too clean and well dressed, for a start. Those shoes he was wearing are expensive.'

'I know. His shoes and the rest of his belongings are our best hope. They're distinctive.'

'He wasn't a hiker, not wearing those on his feet. The snow has ruined them.'

'No, he wasn't a hiker.'

'A stranded motorist, perhaps? Trying to walk back to civilization from an abandoned car?'

'That's possible. All the cars found so far have been matched up with living owners, but there are a few side roads the snowploughs haven't reached yet.'

'You don't sound convinced of that, either.'

'No, I'm not.'

'Any particular reason?'

'Look at him. Look at his clothes. You pointed out yourself how expensive they are. Would he really set off walking in the snow dressed like that? With no coat? Why didn't he stay where he was until he was found? It's not exactly the Antarctic – somebody would have come across him within twenty-four hours at the most. And why didn't he phone for help? For God's sake, every schoolkid has a mobile phone these days. I can't believe a man like this didn't have one.'

'You're right, I suppose. I should restrict myself to the physical evidence and let you deal with the psychology.'

'I didn't mean that,' said Fry, noting the pathologist's defeated air.

'It's all right.'

'And another thing. Are we supposing that he set off walking down the road and that the first people who came along were some opportunist muggers who just happened to be driving over the Snake Pass in a blizzard?'

'I couldn't possibly say.'

'I'll take that as a no.'

Fry glanced at the body. It had been cleaned and covered up. But the face of the man was still visible. He was aged about thirty, she supposed, a little thick about the neck but otherwise in reasonable shape. His hair was dark, cut short and tidy, with a few flecks of grey at the temples. The stubble growing on his cheeks looked wrong; he was a man who would normally have been close-shaven. She looked at his hands. They were strong, but free of calluses, and the nails were trimmed.

'What about the injuries?' she said.

'There is one major ventral wound to the abdomen, which opened up the abdominal cavity and the lateral muscles and almost severed his left arm above the elbow.'

'That was the blade of the snowplough, presumably?'

'All I know is that it was a sharp metal object about ten feet wide and weighing approximately half a ton,' said Mrs Van Doon.

'Right.'

'There are a number of abrasions on the head, face, back and legs, probably caused by the body being dragged along the road surface for a short distance. There's plenty of bruising, and he also has two cracked ribs on the right side of his chest from a fall.'

'A fall?'

'All right, look. From the position in which he was found, I'd say that particular damage might have been caused by him being dropped by the snowplough on to some small rocks by the side of the road. He was found lying half on the rocks, and half off. A few inches to either side and he would have had a much easier landing – on snow or soft ground.'

'I don't suppose it made much difference to him by then.'

'Not a bit. All the injuries I have mentioned were suffered post-mortem.'

'After he was dead.'

'That's usually what post-mortem means. Otherwise, it would come as a bit of a shock to my customers when I remove their internal organs.'

'The one million pound question, then . . .' said Fry.

'What *did* kill him, you mean?'

'Of course.'

'I'll need to do some more tests,' said the pathologist. 'Contrary to your inspector's impression, I do
actually have the services of a modern laboratory
to call on.'

'But . . . ?'

'I need to study the configuration of the major
wound more closely before I can be certain of
anything.'

'I'm not sure what you mean by that.'

'Circumstantial evidence,' said Mrs Van Doon.
She pointed at one of the plastic bags containing
the victim's clothes. 'Your inspector was also wrong
when he said there was no blood. There *was* blood.
Not much, but some. It wasn't noticeable at the
scene because it had been absorbed by his clothing.
He was wearing a thermal vest, a shirt and cotton
sweater. A small amount of blood had penetrated
the layers of clothing to stain the inner lining of
his suit jacket, which is why it wasn't visible. It was
lucky that he had been dead for some time when
the snowplough hit him. If there had been a lot of
bleeding from the major wound, I might not have
noticed anything.'

Fry was listening carefully, trying to work out
the direction of the pathologist's thinking. 'Do you
mean you think there is an earlier wound which
has been masked by the later one?'

'Exactly. At least, that is one theory I'll be
exploring. The edge of the snowplough blade is
regular in shape. I'm told it's a new one, which
is useful. But there's an irregularity in the shape

101

of the wound which matches the position of the bloodstain on the clothing. We need to do some matching. And I need to go deeper into the tissues to tell you more.'

'Deeper? A knife?'

'Possibly. My conclusions will be in my report.'

'So he was stabbed, then dumped from a vehicle.'

'If that's the case, then it helps your time frame, too, doesn't it?'

'But he was already dead some time before he was found . . .'

'Yes, but if he was dumped from a vehicle, *when* was he dumped? My impression from the scene was that the body would have been in full view of passing traffic, if it hadn't been for the snow. But then, I suppose there *was* no traffic on that road after the snow had fallen.'

Fry thought carefully about what she was saying. 'If somebody dumped him, it has to have been when it was already snowing heavily enough to have discouraged drivers from attempting the Snake Pass, so that there was no one passing to be a witness. Probably the snow-warning lights at the bottom of the road were already on, so drivers were turning back. We can check what time they were switched on. But it also has to have been before the road became completely impassable. In a heavy fall of snow, that can't have been more than a half-hour window of opportunity. And we have to be looking for a four-wheel drive vehicle of some kind. No one in his right mind would have risked it otherwise. They could have found themselves stranded up there with a dead body in the boot. That narrows it down a lot. Thank you.'

Mrs Van Doon brushed a stray lock of hair from her forehead and smiled tiredly. 'You can deduce so much from a small amount of blood,' she said. 'I agree with your inspector on that, at least. Blood *does* make a body rather more satisfactory.'

Ben Cooper escorted the visitors back down the stairs and along the corridor towards reception. Alison Morrissey walked quickly, looking straight ahead, but Frank Baine tended to linger, glancing curiously into the offices they passed. Cooper was eyeing the slim black briefcase that Morrissey carried. He would have loved to get hold of all the files that he had glimpsed in there, and to immerse himself in the details of the story whose surface they had barely scratched during the meeting. The LIO's briefing had been good, but it didn't tell him anything about the human dimensions of the tragedy, which he could see were what drove Alison Morrissey.

As soon as the thought crossed his mind that Morrissey might let him read the files if he asked her, Cooper dismissed the notion as mere escapism. There was more than enough for him to do right now. Just because something interested him, it didn't mean it was his job to look into it.

As Cooper held open the security door for the

visitors to leave, Morrissey turned to look at him. Her gaze was direct and disconcerting. He felt as though she were seeing him fully, reading everything about him from his face and his manner, in a way that people rarely did. Cooper self-consciously straightened his shoulders and felt the beginnings of a flush rising in his neck.

'And what did *you* think?' she said. 'Wouldn't *you* want to know what happened?'

'It's not my job to take a view on the subject,' said Cooper. 'I just do what I'm told.'

She stared at him, with a small, sceptical smile. He hadn't been sure before, but now he could see that her eyes were pale grey. Cooper felt uncomfortable, unable to move from his position until Morrissey and Baine had passed through the door. But Baine was hanging back, watching them patiently. Morrissey held her gaze for a moment longer.

'That's a shame,' she said.

Cooper felt as though he had been summed up and found wanting. He watched Morrissey walk briskly across the reception area, looking like a smart business executive with her black suit and briefcase. Frank Baine stopped in the doorway.

'Take my business card,' he said. 'In case I can help.'

Cooper took the card almost absent-mindedly. 'Thanks.'

Then Baine leaned towards him, nodding slyly towards the disappearing figure.

'And remember – there's no stopping a woman when her passion is roused,' he said.

Eden Valley Books was in Nick i' th' Tor, one of the cobbled passages running between Edendale market square and the Eyre Street area. The bookshop was a high, narrow building that looked as though it had been jammed between two much wider ones as an afterthought, or a mere space-filler – something to use up all the leftover oddments of stone when the builders had finished work on the Yorkshire Bank next door. But it was three storeys high, with books on the first two floors, and from the tiny windows set into the gabled roof, it looked as though there were attic rooms, too. Ben Cooper recalled there was even a cellar that ran under the street, full of more books.

There were bookshops in Edendale that were more modern, but Cooper had browsed in Eden Valley Books many times, and he was hopeful he would find what he wanted here, even during the half-hour he could spare during his lunch break. The owner, Lawrence Daley, seemed to specialize in gathering together obscure books on esoteric subjects.

The concept of a window display hadn't reached Eden Valley Books yet. All Cooper could see through the streaked glass were the ends of some wooden bookshelves plastered with fliers advertising local events which had taken place several months ago. A concert by a folk group, a psychic evening at the community centre, an autumn fair in aid of the Cats Protection League.

The snow in Nick i' th' Tor was rapidly turning to slush, and water ran down the cobbles into the square. The front door of the bookshop was narrow, and it stuck in the frame when he tried to open it, so that he had to lean his weight against it before it gave way. It reminded him more of a defensive bastion than of an entrance – especially when a warning bell jangled above his head, causing a nervous stirring somewhere inside the shop.

Immediately, Cooper was surrounded by books. They were crammed on to shelves right in the doorway, so that he couldn't get past without brushing against them. Further in, the tiny rooms had been stuffed with books from floor to ceiling. They were piled on the floor and on the bare wooden stairs, and no doubt they filled the upper rooms as well. On a table, Cooper saw a set of Enid Blyton's Famous Five stories and a 1935 almanac with board covers mottled with mould. There was an overwhelmingly musty smell of old paper – paper that had soaked up the damp from many decades spent in unheated stone houses on wet hillsides.

'Hello?' called Cooper.

Lawrence Daley wore a silk waistcoat with a fancy pattern that was none too clean, and his brown corduroy trousers had become baggy at the knees from hours of crouching to reach the lower shelves. On occasions, Cooper had seen Lawrence wearing a bow tie. But today he had an open-necked check shirt, with his sleeves rolled back over pale forearms. His hair was uncombed, and he looked dusty and sweaty, as if it were the height of summer outside with the temperature in the eighties, rather than creeping up from zero towards another snowfall.

'I've been trying to sort out the Natural History section,' said Lawrence when he saw Cooper appear round the stacks. 'Some of these books have been here since Granny's day. They're still priced in shillings, look. A customer brought one to me yesterday and insisted on paying fifteen pence for it. I couldn't argue, because that was what the price on the label converted at in new money.'

'Are you throwing them out?' asked Cooper, wrinkling his nose at the musty smell and the cloud of dust that hung in the air.

'Throwing them out? Are you kidding? I can't throw them out. They just need re-pricing.'

'But if they've been here since your grandmother ran the shop . . .'

'I know, I know. They're not exactly fast sellers. But if that were all I was interested in, I'd stack the place to the ceiling with Harry Potters, like everyone else does. It's Detective Constable Cooper, isn't it?'

'Ben Cooper, yes. I wondered if you had any books on aircraft wrecks. There are so many wrecks around this area – there must be something published about them.'

'If you go right to the back and through the curtain on the left, then down a few steps, you might find something halfway up the shelves,' said Lawrence.

'Thanks.'

Cooper made his way through the aisles of books. He passed Poetry and Literature, Biography and Philosophy, until he reached a dead end at Geography. He turned left at Art and found Music lurking in a curtained-off alcove at the head of a flight of stairs leading down into a cellar. The sides of the stairwell had been filled with more bookshelves. A few creaky steps down, Cooper came across Air Transport. It seemed a curiously modern subject for Eden Valley Books, and he wasn't surprised that it was hidden away. He looked down into the darkness at the bottom of the stairs and wondered what Lawrence had chosen to confine to the cellar. Probably something like Computers and Information Technology.

But there, sure enough, were two slim volumes on Peak District aircraft relics, exactly what he wanted. He wondered if this place was really some kind of Aladdin's Cave where you could find anything you truly wanted, if you wished hard enough. Lawrence Daley made a strange genie, though.

'Just the thing, Lawrence,' he said, when he had made his way back to the counter. 'I found two.'

'Amazing,' said Lawrence. 'And is there a price on them?'

'Well, no actually.'

Lawrence sighed. 'Then I can't charge you anything at all, can I?'

'Of course you can.'

'Not if there's no label. It's against the Trade Descriptions Act.'

'I'm not sure that's how it works,' said Cooper. 'Anyway, I can't take them without paying you for them.'

'Well, fifty pence then.'

'If you say so.'

Cooper began to go through his pockets. He found the estate agent's leaflets and pulled them out of the way while he felt at the bottom for some change. His pager was vibrating again, but it could wait.

'Hello,' said Lawrence, 'have you fallen into the company of conmen and thieves?'

'Sorry?'

'Estate agents,' he said, pointing at the leaflets. 'Are you buying a house?'

'I can't afford that,' said Cooper. 'I'm just looking for a place to rent for a while.'

'Ah. Striking out on your own? Or is there a live-in partner involved somewhere?'

'On my own.'

'Oh. And have you not found anywhere yet?'

'No.'

Cooper handed over his fifty pence, and Lawrence rattled it into the drawer of his till, then found a striped paper bag from somewhere under the counter. Cooper stood looking at some postcards and fliers stuck to a board near the counter. Most of them were advertising the services of typing

agencies, clairvoyants and aromatherapy special-
ists, but there was one that caught his eye.

'There's a furnished flat advertised here,' he said.
'It's in Welbeck Street, by the river.'

'Oh yes,' said Lawrence.

'That's handy for town. I could walk to work
from there. And it sounds quite a reasonable
rent, too. Do you know who this person is? Mrs
Shelley?'

'I'm afraid so. It's my aunt.'

'Really?'

'She lives in Welbeck Street herself, but she
owns the house next door as well,' said Lawrence.
'My uncle had dreams of knocking the two places
together and creating some kind of palatial town
house to swan around in. God knows why – there
were only ever the two of them, with no children.'

'I have an uncle like that, too – he loves unfin-
ished projects. It seems to give him a sense of
immortality. He doesn't think he can possibly die
until all the jobs are finished.'

'It didn't work with Uncle Gerald – he died before
he could even get round to knocking any walls
down.'

'I'm sorry.'

'Aunt Dorothy wasn't. She was over the moon to
be rid of him. She had the house next door split into
two flats. She had a proper job done of it. I think
she wanted the workmen to pound the memories
of Uncle Gerald into dust with their sledgehammers

and cover him over with a nice layer of plaster and some magnolia wallpaper.'

'And one of the flats is empty, is it?'

'It was, when she asked me to put the card up,' said Lawrence. 'It might have gone by now, she hasn't said. I've told her to make sure she lets it to the right sort of person. Reliable and trustworthy professional people only, you know. I do worry sometimes about who she might take in, if she's left entirely to her own devices.'

'I think I'd be interested, if it's still vacant,' said Cooper.

'It might not be up to your standards, you know. Aunt Dorothy is getting a bit vague in her old age. Not quite barmy or anything, you understand. But vague about life's little details.'

Cooper looked at the card again. 'Reliable and trustworthy? Do you think I would qualify, Lawrence?'

'No, but you could lie.' The bookseller laughed. He reached out a hand and patted the corduroy collar of Cooper's waxed coat. 'I love the cold-weather gear, by the way,' he said. 'Policemen usually dress so boringly, don't they? But the cap really suits you. It shows off your eyes.'

Cooper edged away a few inches. 'I might give the flat a try,' he said. 'Mrs Shelley, 6 Welbeck Street? I'll mention that you recommended me, shall I?'

Lawrence chuckled. 'Believe me,' he said, 'you'd be better off lying.'

On the way out, Cooper noticed a morocco-bound volume of *A Tale of Two Cities*, which lay in the dust on the top of a set of shelves. It looked almost as if Mr Dickens himself had wandered into the shop one day and put the book down on the shelf, where it had stayed ever since.

Outside, in High Street, Cooper watched a Hulley's bus splash slowly by like a dark blue ship. It threw a bow wave of slush to either side, which threatened to sweep away the pedestrians walking on the pavement.

As he walked back past the Clappergate shopping precinct towards West Street, Cooper patted his pockets thoughtfully. In the huge poacher's pocket inside his coat were the books on Peak District aircraft wrecks, including the crash of Lancaster SU-V, which had brought Alison Morrissey to Edendale. In another pocket he had the estate agent's leaflets for unsuitable properties. Cooper knew he didn't really want to live on his own. He was moving out of Bridge End Farm because he felt so strongly it was time for a change in his life – and that was all.

He wondered whether Alison Morrissey lived on her own. Probably not. And she was nothing to do with him, anyway. She was in Edendale only as a passing visitor. Soon, she would be flying back to Canada, to an entirely different world, and he would never see her again after today. But perhaps he could hope that there was a person a bit like Alison Morrissey, waiting for him somewhere.

7

Diane Fry was waiting for Ben Cooper when he arrived back at divisional headquarters in West Street. She glared at him as he came into the CID room.

'You didn't answer your phone,' she said.

'I was in the middle of something,' protested Cooper. 'I was going to call you back. How's the double assault case shaping up?'

'Oh, you can forget about that for now.'

'Forget it? There were a couple of serious assaults, wounding with intent, possession of offensive weapons Not to mention being potentially racially motivated'

'Yeah, yeah, and somebody probably dropped some litter on the pavement as well when you weren't looking. Forget it.'

'But, Diane –'

'Add it to your pending file, Ben. We've got more important things to do.'

'What's so important? Have we got another body or something?'

'What's so important,' said Fry, 'is that we've got a meeting on the Snowman case. It just became a murder enquiry.'

Without really thinking about it, Ben Cooper had expected E Division's new Detective Chief Inspector to be female. If not, then a member of an ethnic minority. Or at least gay. It was almost inconceivable that a senior appointment had been made without an attempt to address the balance of gender, ethnicity or sexual persuasion.

But no matter how carefully Cooper studied DCI Oliver Kessen, he still seemed to be a middle-aged white man with receding hair and bad teeth, an ill-fitting suit and a paunch. Seated next to their old DCI, Stewart Tailby, Kessen was the centre of attention for the entire room. It was the first time anybody there had set eyes on him, though he had only come from D Division, which wasn't exactly Australia.

'Good afternoon, everybody,' said Kessen. 'Glad to meet you all. Is everything under control?'

Several people opened their mouths to reply, but didn't manage to get a word out when they saw the expression on DCI Tailby's face. He looked like a headmaster who had warned his pupils not to talk to strangers.

'Yes, I'm sure it is,' said Tailby.

'Well, I've just arrived and I've got to settle in here, so I rely on you people to bring me up to date.

But I dare say everything is going smoothly. I can see Mr Tailby has been running a good team.'

The new man nodded round the room, trying to make eye contact with as many officers as possible. Cooper saw several of his colleagues freeze like rabbits caught in car headlights, their social skills failing them disastrously when faced with suddenly conflicting demands from two equal-ranking senior officers. Kessen must have thought he had walked into a waxworks from the amount of response he got. With the right lighting, it would have made a tableau for the chamber of horrors.

It was always a bit awkward when new bosses came. But it had been Stewart Tailby's own decision to move on, to take up a desk job at headquarters. So he could hardly object to the new man's arrival, and he could hardly resist having his successor sitting next to him and addressing his staff. Kessen was too inexperienced to be Senior Investigating Officer on a major enquiry. So until E Division got a Detective Superintendent to be its new CID chief, Tailby was trapped. There were others here who had expected to get Tailby's job when he moved, but that was a different matter. It was no use telling *them* not to be resentful.

'As some of you know, we have the preliminary results from the postmortem examination of the unidentified body of an adult male found on the A57 Snake Pass,' said Tailby. 'As a consequence of those results, we have opened a murder enquiry. I appreciate that all of you here have other enquiries on which you're engaged, and I don't need telling that we're short of manpower. We're hoping to get some help from other divisions, and the Chief is on the phone right now. But I have to tell you that everybody seems to be in the same boat as regards resources.'

It was true that the room seemed more sparsely occupied than for any major enquiry Cooper could remember. It was ironic that the crisis in manpower should coincide with an unidentified murder victim and a serious assault with multiple suspects. There was a lot of routine slog involved in those cases, and not many people to do it.

'DI Hitchens and DS Fry will fill you in with what information we have so far,' said Tailby.

The Snowman's blue bag was on the table at the front of the conference room, wrapped in latex to preserve it as evidence. Everyone kept glancing at the bag, as if somehow it might tell them everything they needed to know. Paul Hitchens stood up and prodded it with a finger.

'The bag was found with the body by the snowplough crew,' said Hitchens. 'It's a common make, though not cheap. One of the first jobs will be to trace shops in the area that sell this type of luggage. Unfortunately, there are no labels on it, and no contents to help us identify the owner.'

'The bag was completely empty?' asked Cooper.

'There was so much empty space inside this bag,

you'd think it was a Derbyshire CID room,' said Hitchens. 'Except it smelled better.'

Cooper saw DCI Kessen's eyes open a little bit wider. He stared at Hitchens, then turned to Tailby, who ignored him. For the first time that morning, a small smile had crept on to Tailby's face.

'Somebody went to great lengths to remove evidence of his identity, then,' said Cooper.

'Yes and no,' said Hitchens. 'They removed the clothes from the bag, but left him with what he was wearing. They took his wallet and maybe his mobile phone, if he had one, but left the contents of his pockets. In fact, why did they leave the bag itself? If the perpetrators handled it, they were taking a risk. Why not dispose of it with the clothes? It doesn't really make sense.'

'What about missing persons?' suggested DCI Kessen.

'I'm sure that's under control, too,' said Tailby.

'Of course. Who's dealing with it, I wonder?'

Gavin Murfin tentatively raised a hand. His mouth was full of chocolate, and he began to chew a little bit faster as both chief inspectors turned their attention on him.

'This is Detective Constable Murfin,' said Tailby.

'Good afternoon, Murfin,' said Kessen. 'DC i/c mispers, eh?'

Murfin's mouth opened. But all that came out was the sound of masticated food and a faint choking at the back of his throat.

'Anything worthwhile, Murfin?' said Tailby.

'No, sir. There's a list on file, but nothing that jumps out at you, like.'

'National forces?'

'They've all been circulated,' said Murfin. 'There's some we haven't had a response from yet.'

'Keep on to it, Murfin.'

'Yes, sir.' Murfin seemed to realize that his hand was still in the air. He lowered it, looking round at his colleagues in embarrassment.

'And who's the lady?' said DCI Kessen suddenly. Everyone looked round at the door, wondering who had walked into the room. But there was no one there. Cooper kept his eyes straight ahead and saw DCI Tailby's jaw tense. There was only one woman in the room this afternoon, and she was no lady – she was Diane Fry. Eventually, a few officers managed to follow Kessen's gaze and realized who he was looking at. He was smiling, and he had raised one eyebrow at a jaunty angle, a mannerism he must have practised while watching Sean Connery videos.

It was Fry herself who answered him. She got out of her chair and stood up to speak. Nobody else ever bothered doing that during a meeting.

'Detective Sergeant Diane Fry, sir.'

'Good afternoon, Diane. And what are you working on?'

'DS Fry is one of my best officers,' said Tailby, his expression tightening ominously.

'I'm sure she is. She looks it. But I rather think she's one of *my* officers now, Stewart.'

118

'We've circulated a description of the man to all the media and have appealed for information,' said Fry coolly. 'We've also had officers out at checkpoints on the A57, stopping motorists in the vicinity who might have seen something. We are also seeking sightings of a four-wheel drive vehicle in the area around the time that the body was dumped. And, naturally, we're following up leads from the man's physical appearance, his clothing and his possessions. His clothing seems to offer us the best chance at the moment.'

DCI Kessen nodded and smiled approvingly.

'We also have a small tattoo on the left forearm of the body,' said Fry. 'A dagger and a snake. It's a common motif, but it might help identification.'

'I'm sure you'll do an excellent job, Detective Sergeant Fry,' said Kessen. 'An excellent job.'

'Shall we move on?' said Tailby. 'There's a lot to do today.'

Fry turned round so that she could see Cooper and Murfin. They were careful not to smile.

'Explain the timing for us again,' said Tailby.

Fry set out the time line – the narrow window in which the killer or killers had the opportunity to dump the body on the Snake Pass without being seen.

'So we're looking for a four-wheel drive vehicle, almost certainly,' she said.

'There are lots of those around.'

'Eddie Kemp has one, for a start,' said Murfin.

'Who?' said Tailby.

'The bloke that we had in on suspicion for the double assault.'

'Really?'

'Do we have a suspect in custody?' asked Kessen. 'I didn't know this. Whose arrest was it?'

'Mine,' said Cooper. 'But it was a completely different incident.'

'Are we sure of that?'

'It happened the same night,' said Murfin.

Cooper hesitated. 'There's no obvious link. Except for the timing.'

'He has an Isuzu Trooper. I've seen it parked outside when he's been doing the windows.'

'Doing what?'

'He's a window cleaner,' said Murfin. 'But anyway, he isn't in custody any more – he's been sent home. He's had his twenty-four hours.'

Tailby pulled a face. Too often it had been known for the police to have a suspect in their custody, only to release him before the crucial evidence turned up to justify a charge. 'We'd better be absolutely sure there's no link,' he said. 'Someone check that out.'

Cooper realized he was the one the DCI was looking at. 'Yes, sir,' he said.

DI Hitchens interrupted. 'We're currently tracking down some CCTV footage. In view of the location of the assault, we're hoping either the suspects or the victims might have been caught by one of the town centre cameras.'

'That's good,' said Tailby. 'Now let's have some

attention on identifying the Snowman. It's going to be a long haul. Without an ID, we're in difficulties. We need to get assistance from the public, of course. But since he's probably not from this area, that's going to take some time. That means there are plenty of jobs to do. Mr Kessen thinks everything is under control, so let's not disappoint him.'

Diane Fry looked distracted. Ben Cooper leaned over towards her as the meeting broke up.

'Whoever killed the Snowman, it sounds as though we're looking for amateurs anyway,' he said. 'They weren't thinking things through properly. There's no logic to what they did. No system, no planning. That's good, isn't it? It means they'll be worrying now about what traces they left behind.'

Fry shrugged. 'That's not quite true. The timing of it looks planned. Somebody thought that through, all right.'

'Unless they were just lucky.'

'There's not much we can do about luck, Ben.'

'Yes, there is,' said Cooper.

'What?'

'We can get lucky ourselves.'

'Yeah, right.'

But Ben Cooper believed in luck. He believed that, if you worked hard enough and long enough at something, then eventually luck would start to operate in your favour.

What Cooper failed to realize was that he had already been given the most important piece of luck he would get that week.

After the enquiry teams had been hastily assembled, Cooper walked back from the incident room with Diane Fry and Gavin Murfin. The only sound between them was Murfin humming to himself. Cooper listened, trying to identify the tune. It sounded like an old Eagles song, 'New Kid in Town'.

'Well, a new broom sweeps clean,' said Murfin as he reached his desk and began to hunt through his drawers. 'So my old mum used to say, like.'

Cooper saw that Fry couldn't bring herself to say anything. She was pale and held herself rigidly, as if she were freezing cold. And it *was* cold in the incident room, too. You could have broken up the air with an ice axe.

'Always the optimist, aren't you, Ben?' she said. 'You talked about getting lucky. Well, take a look around you. We're at rock bottom for resources and we have an unidentified body on top of all our other enquiries. We have a new DCI, the Chief Super is cracking up, and Gavin here is our number one asset. Even the weather is against us. Does it *look* as though we're likely to get lucky?'

'Well, you never know.'

'Do you think we could persuade Mr Tailby to stay on?' said Murfin.

'I don't think it would take much to persuade

him,' said Cooper. 'He's not really all that keen on the HQ job.'

'He's even less keen on the new DCI.'

'Mr Kessen will settle down, Gavin.'

'It could take time, I reckon. I don't know, Ben – they call some of us old coppers dinosaurs. But it's like a proper Jurassic Park on the top corridor sometimes.'

'So why did you bring up Eddie Kemp? Trying to score some points with the new DCI? Kemp has nothing to do with it, has he? What have you got against him?'

'Maybe he didn't clean my windows properly,' said Murfin. 'Well, I don't know. Kemp and his mates might have been cruising for victims. Got the taste for it with the other two, then picked some poor bugger up at the roadside out of town.'

'I talked to Kemp's wife,' said Cooper. 'According to her, he didn't come home at all that night. He went to the pub at eight o'clock and she knew nothing until she got a call next morning to tell her he was in custody. She also says the Isuzu was gone all night. According to her story, somebody brought it back early next morning and put the keys through the door.'

'One of Kemp's associates, presumably, since he was in custody at the time,' said Fry.

'Presumably. But we ought to check.'

'Does Mrs Kemp know her husband's friends?'

'Knows them, but doesn't want to, I'd say.'

'No names supplied?'

'No. She's not happy, but she's not giving evidence against her husband. The two victims might be more help when we can get full statements from them, but I doubt it. They're part of the Devonshire Estate gang – they think talking to the police is like committing suicide. So all we have against Eddie Kemp is the identification of the old couple who looked out of the window and say they recognized him as part of the group. You know how reliable witness identifications are in those circumstances. Eddie himself says if he hit anybody, he was acting in self-defence.'

'I don't suppose he's identified the other three?'

'Are you kidding? Somebody is going to have to enquire into his associates.'

'God knows who,' said Fry. 'And God knows when.'

'I bet it'll be me,' said Cooper. 'I seem to have got Kemp's car on my list.'

'Hey,' said Murfin, 'did you realize that the new DCI's name is Oliver?' He held up the rubber lobster of the same name.

'Are you telling us it's a coincidence, Gavin?'

Diane Fry had been tapping her fingers on her desk. Now she seemed to make a decision, shake her head and was suddenly her proper self.

'You'd better go and take a look at his car, then, Ben,' she said. 'And take Gavin with you.'

'I'm on missing persons,' said Murfin.

'Let the allocator know where you're up to, then you'll have to leave it for an hour or two. Ben can't

124

go to see Kemp on his own. He's doing enough solos as it is.'

Murfin left, grumbling all the way. With a spasm of concern, Cooper watched Fry as she stared out of the window for a while, the muscles at the side of her mouth tight with tension. She fiddled at a strand of her fair hair in an uncharacteristically uncertain gesture. Her hand was pale and slender, with tendons that he could have traced with his finger.

'A new broom sweeps clean?' she said. 'I'll stick a broom up his *arse*.'

Cooper nodded. He didn't think she was talking about Gavin Murfin.

8

The Buttercross area of Old Edendale had its own personality, its own picturesque gloss, which had been carefully polished and maintained over the years for the benefit of visitors. It was here that the town's antique shops clustered, some of them stuffed with gleaming mahogany furniture and brassware, but others dim and dusty, with nothing in their windows but a few coloured bottles and a Queen Victoria diamond jubilee biscuit tin.

There were shops here that Ben Cooper had never seen open, not in all his life spent in and around Edendale. Today, as usual, the 'closed' signs hung on their doors, with no indication of when their owners would be available to do business. Maybe they only appeared on special occasions, such as bank holiday weekends, when tourists thronged the Buttercross with money to spend. Maybe the dealers sold enough bottles and biscuit tins on those days to see them through the rest of the year. On the other hand, maybe they all had proper jobs to do.

The Buttercross certainly lived up to the tourist brochure image this afternoon. The lying snow and the weathered stone and mullioned windows of the buildings hit just the right Dickensian note to set off the antique furniture. Sadly, there were no tourists in January to appreciate it.

Between two of the shops, a narrow street lurched suddenly uphill. There were steel handrails set into high limestone walls on either side for pedestrians, but no pavements to separate them from any cars that might scrape their way round the corner. The walls had been the traditional dry stone when they were first built. But now they were held together by mortar, and they had periwinkles growing out of their cracks – forlorn green strands encased in frozen snow.

Gavin Murfin swayed against the side of Cooper's Toyota as they bumped over the cobbles, took a sharp turn and then made another steep climb to emerge into the Underbank area. The streets here were even narrower, and the doors of the houses had tiny knockers shaped like owls or foxes, with their numbers picked out in coloured tiles set into the stonework. Further up the hill, a set of three-storey Regency houses stood near a youth hostel. Several of the houses had been converted into flats, but one at the far end looked empty and uncared for. A broken window on the first floor had been left unrepaired.

Beeley Street was hardly more than an alley, with an unmade surface just wide enough for one vehicle to pass. Cooper and Murfin walked up the street and crossed a patch of snow-covered grass.

'Well, that's Eddie Kemp's car,' said Murfin. 'I've seen it many a time at West Street.'

It was a silver Isuzu Trooper with a set of ladders clipped to its roof rack, and it was parked on a raised concrete platform in front of Kemp's house, with its headlights looking down the street towards the Buttercross. The council binmen had left a new plastic refuse sack wedged behind a downspout near the front door. They wouldn't be coming up here again with their wagon soon, though, unless the snow cleared.

Eddie Kemp himself emerged from the house when they knocked.

'Oh, it's you,' he said. 'I've answered all the questions I'm going to.'

'Is this your car, sir?' said Cooper.

'Are you deaf? I just said I've answered all the questions I'm going to.'

'It won't take a minute to check with the DVLC if you're the registered owner.'

'Why, what's wrong with it?' said Kemp.

'I don't know, sir. Is there something wrong with it? Would you like us to have a look while we're here?'

'No.'

'It's a nice motor,' said Murfin cheerfully. 'It looks really useful, like.'

'Well, you know damn well it's mine anyway,' said Kemp. 'All you coppers know. I park it up at your place regularly when I'm doing the windows.'

'Four-wheel drive, isn't it?' said Cooper.

'Of course it is.'

'Good in snow?'

'It has to be.'

'Were you driving this car on Monday night, sir?'

'It was parked here.'

'From what time?'

'Has somebody said they saw me in it?'

'That isn't an answer.'

Murfin leaned against the concrete platform. 'You ought to answer DC Cooper,' he said. 'If he gets annoyed, he stops calling you "sir". That can be very nasty.'

Cooper stepped up on to the platform and looked at the tyres of the Isuzu. They wouldn't tell him anything at all, but Kemp didn't know that.

'What time do you finish work, sir?' he said.

'When it starts going dark.'

'About quarter past four, then, at the moment. Did you come straight home from work on Monday night?'

'I've got a wife and a kid,' said Kemp. 'They expect to see me occasionally.'

'I'll take that as a "yes", shall I?'

'You can take it as what the hell you like. What are you looking for?'

Murfin pointed down the street towards the Buttercross. 'I had a girlfriend who lived around here once. I seem to recall there was a little Indian takeaway on the corner, near the hairdresser's. Is it still there?'

'Yes, it is,' said Kemp.

'What time does it open?'

'How the hell should I know?'

There was mud on the tyres of the Isuzu and small stones embedded in the tread. Streaks of brown grit ran along the sides of the vehicle. Cooper worked round the back and looked in through the tailgate.

'What time did you go out again on Monday, sir?' said Cooper.

'I went to the pub for a bit,' said Kemp. 'What are you looking for?'

'Which pub?'

'The Vine. I told them all this yesterday.'

'Is that where you met your mates?'

'I've got a lot of mates,' said Kemp.

'Really?'

'And some of them drink at the Vine.'

'Do they serve food at this pub?' said Murfin.

Kemp came up on to the platform and stood next to Cooper, though it was more in an effort to get away from Murfin than a desire for companionship. Kemp was an inch or two shorter than Cooper, but he was powerfully built. They both looked through the tailgate at the contents of the Isuzu. There were buckets, sponges, plastic trays of cloths and wash leathers. There were also two rolls of stiff blue plastic sheeting, each about four feet long, with mud stains on their outer surfaces.

'What do you use the plastic sheets for?' said Cooper.

'Standing the ladders on, so they don't make marks on anybody's fancy paving, and such.'

'What time did you get home from the pub on Monday?'

'When it shut. I said all this.'

'Did you go out in the car again?'

Kemp said nothing. Cooper could see fresh grazes on his knuckles when he leaned on the car. He was also standing quite close now, and the freezing cold air did wonders for clearing the sinuses and sharpening the sense of smell. Cooper thought of the people who claimed to be able to see auras. Was it possible to *smell* auras, as well as to see them? If he could see Eddie Kemp's aura, it would be a sort of bilious green, shot through with yellow streaks, like pea soup flavoured with cinnamon.

'Did you decide to drive up the A57 with your mates?' said Cooper.

Kemp still said nothing.

'Which of your mates were with you? The same ones you met in the Vine? Did you find more than two victims that night? Did something go wrong?'

Kemp began to walk back to his house.

'Can you recommend a good chippie then?' said Murfin as he passed.

'We're going to have to take your car away to have a look at it, sir,' Cooper called after him.

Kemp put a hand in his pocket, turned and threw a set of keys on to the concrete platform.

'Give it a wash, then, while you're at it,' he said, and slammed the front door.

Ben Cooper and Gavin Murfin sat in Cooper's Toyota to wait for the vehicle recovery team to arrive. It was cold, and it was starting to get dark already. Cooper kept the engine running so that they could have the heater on, and wondered what he could do with his time while he waited. He looked at Murfin, but as soon as he'd felt the warmth from the heater, Murfin had put his head back on his seat and closed his eyes. His mouth hung open slightly. Not much hope of conversation, then.

Cooper tried the radio. There was a sociological discussion programme on Radio Four, a phone-in on Radio Sheffield, and pop hits of the 1980s on Peak 107. He poked around among his cassettes and found nothing he hadn't listened to already in the last few days. Then he remembered the books he had bought from Lawrence Daley, which were still somewhere deep in his poacher's pocket.

He switched on the courtesy light and flicked through the contents pages of the two books. He quickly found the chapter about the crash of Lancaster SU-V, Sugar Uncle Victor. It was one of many aircraft that had fallen victim to primitive navigation equipment and treacherous weather conditions over the Peak District. Some of them were aircraft the Germans hadn't been able to shoot down, but which the hills of the Dark Peak had claimed.

Ironically, Mk III Avro Lancaster W5013 had been built locally, by Metropolitan Vickers at their factory in Bamford. So it had started life only a few miles from where it had finished its days. From a recent photograph of the wreckage, he could see there were still several of the larger pieces left – part of the tail, a wing section, and engine casings minus their propellers.

Like Frank Baine, the author of these books had done plenty of research, and the details of SU-V's crew were comprehensive. As Baine had said, there had been seven men on board the Lancaster – four British RAF men, two Poles and the Canadian pilot, Danny McTeague.

Of the British crew, the bomb aimer and rear gunner, Sergeants Bill Mee and Dick Abbott, had been found dead some distance from the aircraft. The text described them as 'severely mutilated', but Cooper recognized the euphemism. The phrase was still used today, in official statements to the press on the victims of serious road accidents or suicides on the railway line. It meant their bodies had been dismembered. The wireless operator, Sergeant Harry Gregory, and the mid-upper gunner, Sergeant Alec Hamilton, had been trapped inside the wreckage and had died in the fire that consumed the central section of the fuse-lage. Burned beyond recognition, they had been identified by the uniforms under their flying suits, and by the contents of their pockets, after their bodies had been taken to the RAF mortuary at Buxton.

Cooper put the book down for a moment. He wondered whether Alison Morrissey had considered the possibility that one of the bodies had been wrongly identified. Perhaps, after all, her grandfather had died in the crash. All this time, it might have been some other member of the crew they should have been looking for. And he wondered about Pilot Officer Zygmunt Lukasz, the flight engineer, who had survived and was now seventy-eight years old.

Gavin Murfin stirred and grunted in his seat. His eyes opened.

'Where are we?' he said.

'Underbank,' said Cooper. 'We're waiting for the recovery crew.'

'There's a good Indian takeaway around here somewhere,' said Murfin. Then he snorted, and his head fell back again.

Weather conditions and primitive equipment – Cooper supposed that was the standard explanation for many of these incidents. Otherwise, the crash of Sugar Uncle Victor seemed inexplicable – the aircraft was flying much too low, and it was off course. But it was hinted in the book that the reason it was off course was that the skipper had apparently ignored the navigator's instructions. So was it another example of a pilot caught in the trap between high ground and low cloud, finding mountains suddenly in front of him when he thought he was approaching his home airfield in Nottinghamshire? Or had something else gone wrong?

One of the eye witnesses quoted in the account of the fate of Sugar Uncle Victor was the former RAF mountain rescue man, Walter Rowland, who had also been mentioned by Alison Morrissey. Like Zygmunt Lukasz, he had been unwilling to talk to her. Unwilling, or unable? Rowland was described as being eighteen years old at the time of the crash. After all that time, memories faded. But sometimes there were memories which were too clear for anyone to want them reviving.

'No sign yet?' mumbled Murfin.

'Not yet.'

'It's no good, Ben. I'm having curry-flavoured dreams. I'm going to have to go and see if that Indian is open.'

'Fair enough. I'll still be here when you get back.'

'Do you want anything?'

'Some naan bread.'

'Is that all? You can't live on that.'

'I wasn't intending to,' said Cooper.

Murfin slipped out of the car, and Cooper watched him stumble down the street, clinging precariously to the steel handrail to stay on his feet. If he made it back up with a set of foil trays and a bag of naan bread intact, it would be a miracle.

Cooper looked at his mobile phone. He was trying to remember whether Frank Baine had said where Alison Morrissey was staying, but he couldn't recall. There weren't all that many hotels in Edendale, and he could easily give Baine a call in the morning to find out. He might also ask the journalist for Walter Rowland's address.

Then Cooper laughed to himself. He was thinking all these things as if he were intending to investigate the fifty-seven-year-old mystery, which was ridiculous. The Chief had already sent the Canadian woman packing, and quite rightly. There was certainly no time to be spared on pointless sidelines, by himself or anyone else. He had more than enough to do. So what use would it be for him to know where Morrissey was staying? Why should he need to visit Walter Rowland? No reason at all.

Thinking he had finished the chapter on Sugar Uncle Victor, Cooper turned the page. He found himself looking at photographs of the wreckage taken shortly after the crash. Sections of broken fuselage lay in the snow, being examined by policemen and servicemen in long overcoats. The letters SU-V were clearly visible on the airframe in one shot. There was no sign of Irontongue Hill in the background, but the photographer had provided a distant glimpse over the moors to a glitter of water on Blackbrook

Reservoir, which established the location beyond doubt.

Then, with the next series of photos, the story suddenly took on a human dimension. The first picture was a 'team line-up' of the Lancaster crew – seven young men dressed in Irving suits and flying boots, with their fur collars turned up and the wires from their headsets dangling round their shoulders. They were standing in front of the fuselage of an aircraft, which was probably Uncle Victor himself. The sun was low and falling directly on the men, making their eyes narrow and their faces pale, like miners who had just emerged from underground into the light. They were managing smiles for the camera, though they looked exhausted.

Cooper thought the comparison to miners wasn't a bad one, because working in dangerous conditions forged a bond between men that was hard to break. These young airmen had flown thousands of miles in cramped and difficult conditions night after night, heading into hostile territory, with no idea whether they would make it back to base. And not one of them looked older than his early twenties.

There was a picture of the ground crew and armourers getting the aircraft ready for its mission. This was definitely Uncle Victor, judging from the pawnbroker's sign painted on the nose of the Lancaster – 'Uncle' being the common euphemism in those days for a pawnbroker. He noticed that the ground crew barely seemed to have a standard uniform – they wore leather jerkins, sea-boot socks, gumboots, battledress, oilskins, tunics, scarves, mittens, gloves, balaclavas.

On the facing page was the most atmospheric picture of all. It had been taken inside the aircraft, and it was grainy and spattered with white specks where there had been dust on the negative. The curved interior structure of the aircraft could be seen, and the lettering on an Elsan chemical toilet. In the foreground, a young airman was half-turned towards the camera. His sergeant's stripes were clearly visible on his arm, and he wore a leather flying helmet and the straps of a parachute harness over his uniform, so he must have been preparing for take-off.

But the airman was surely no more than a boy. There was no caption to say who he was, and it was difficult to identify him as one of the men on the facing page. The photographs must have been taken at a different time, because this young man had a faint moustache, while the only airman in the group photograph with a moustache was identified as the pilot, Danny McTeague. This wasn't McTeague. This young man had a prominent nose and a narrow face, and a small lock of dark hair that had escaped from under his flying helmet on to his forehead. Cooper decided he must be Sergeant Dick Abbott, the rear gunner. He had been eighteen years old, and the crew had called him Lofty because he was only five foot six inches tall.

Cooper stared at the photo for a long time, forgetting to read about the many other aircraft that had come to grief in the Dark Peak. He felt as if the young airman were somehow communicating with him across the distance of more than five decades. It didn't seem all that long ago that he too had been the same age as this airman. Cooper could sense himself slipping into the young man's place in the aircraft. He could feel the straps of the parachute over his shoulders and the rough uniform against his skin, hear the roaring of the four Merlin engines and feel the vibration of the primitive machine that would hurtle him into the air. He was eighteen years old, and he was frightened.

Ben Cooper was hardly aware of the vehicle recovery crew negotiating their truck into Beeley Street with lights flashing and diesel engine throbbing. His attention was taken up by trying to analyse his feelings about the photograph, so that he was hardly aware, even, of Gavin Murfin tapping on the window, unable to open the door because of the leaking trays he was balancing.

When Murfin was back in the car, it immediately began to fill with smells of curry and boiled rice. The steam from the trays fogged the windows, so that Beeley Street and Eddie Kemp's Isuzu gradually vanished in a fog.

'Here's your naan bread,' said Murfin. 'Dip in, if you want.'

But the naan bread sat in his lap unopened, the

grease gradually soaking through the paper on to his coat.

Cooper finally realized that it was the look in the young man's eyes that was completely different from the group picture; it was a look which made him unrecognizable from the line-up of smiling heroes. It was the blank, empty stare of a man who had no idea whether he would be coming back to his home base that night. The young man's stare spoke of resignation at the prospect of sudden death as a German night-fighter raked Uncle Victor with machine-gun fire, or the Lancaster's engines failed and they were forced to ditch in the icy North Sea. According to the text, Lancasters were notoriously difficult to escape from when they were in the water.

In fact, that haunted look and the grey, grainy quality of the photograph made the airman appear almost as though he wasn't there at all. He might have been no more than a faded image superimposed on the interior of the aircraft, the result of an accidental double exposure on the film.

To Ben Cooper, it seemed that the photographer had captured a moment of presentiment and foreboding, a glimpse into the darkness of the near future. Sergeant Dick Abbott, only eighteen years old, looked as if he were already a ghost.

9

Back at West Street, Ben Cooper dug through the
paper that had been collecting on his desk until he
found the file produced by the Local Intelligence
Officer for the meeting with Alison Morrissey. It
didn't have anything like the amount of detail
about the crash and the Lancaster's crew that
was in the book from Lawrence's shop. But the
LIO's file did have one advantage – it had the
names of the two boys who had reported seeing
the missing airman walking down the Blackbrook
Reservoir road that night.

Cooper had remembered that point, because
Morrissey had complained during the meeting
that she was unable to track them down since
their names weren't given in the reports. It hadn't
seemed wise to admit that he had the information
in front of him; the Chief Superintendent would
certainly not have approved of too apparent a
willingness to assist. But it meant the LIO had
done a good job collecting the information. Either

that, or Alison Morrissey's research was badly flawed.

'Do you know Harrop, Gavin?' he said.

Murfin sniffed. 'Godawful place. Back of the moon that is, Ben. That's not where you're thinking of moving to, is it?'

'No. I don't think I've ever been there.'

'It's up the top of the Snake Pass somewhere, on the way to Glossop.'

'It must be over the other side of Irontongue Hill.'

'That's it. I bet they were cut off up there today all right. There's no bus service in Harrop. No bus route, so no priority for the snowplough. Somebody will dig them out tomorrow, maybe.'

The names of the boys were Edward and George Malkin, aged twelve and eight, of Hollow Shaw Farm, Harrop. From what Gavin said, Harrop sounded the sort of village where families might stay in one place, generation after generation of them sometimes. Cooper found a telephone directory. Sure enough, there was a G. Malkin still listed at Hollow Shaw Farm. There seemed a good chance that this was the same George Malkin, then aged eight, now sixty-five.

'Knocking off, Ben?' said Murfin. 'Fancy a pint?'

'I'd love to, Gavin,' said Cooper. 'But I've got things to do. Places to look at.'

'Ah, the pleasures of house-hunting. It kind of ruins your social life, like.'

*   *   *

Cooper drove eastwards out of Edendale. He climbed the Snake Pass and descended again almost into Glossop before he turned north and skirted the outlying expanses of peat moor around Irontongue Hill. The buttress of rock on top of the hill was a familiar sight to him, as it was prominently visible on a good day from the A57. The rock was certainly tongue-shaped when you looked at it from this direction, with ridges and crevices furrowing its dark surface. It wasn't a human tongue, though. There was something reptilian about its length and the suggestion of a curl at the tip. And it was colder and harder than iron, too – it was the dark rock that millstones had been made out of, the sort of rock that the weather barely seemed to touch, even over centuries. The wind and rain had merely smoothed its edges, where the tongue lay on the broken teeth of volcanic debris.

Tonight, Irontongue was visible even in the dark. It uncoiled from the snow-covered slopes to poke at the sky, with dribbles of white lying in its cracks.

Cooper found that Harrop was barely big enough to be called a village, yet the roads were clear enough of snow for the Toyota to have no problems. Above Harrop there was a scatter of farms and homesteads with those austere Dark Peak names – Slack House, Whiterakes, Red Mires, Mount Famine and Stubbins. They clung to the edges of the mountain like burrs on the fur of a sleeping dog.

The lane up to Hollow Shaw Farm passed a single modern bungalow and an isolated row of stone cottages. Past the bungalow, the lane was no longer tarmacked. After the cottages, it ceased to have any surface at all. Cooper hadn't seen any street lights for the last few miles. He had to slow the Toyota to a crawl and swing the steering wheel from side to side to avoid the worst of the potholes, but in the total darkness he couldn't see some of the holes until he was almost in them. It was sudden death for suspension systems up here. This was the sort of lane that delivery drivers and salesmen would avoid like the plague, the kind of track that people needed a good reason to live at the end of. As he climbed to Hollow Shaw, Cooper wondered what George Malkin's reason might be.

He parked in front of the old farmhouse and got out. A few yards away, a man was leaning on a wall. It was so quiet here that Cooper could hear rustling from the field on the other side of the wall, and the faint snorting of a flock of sheep. Somewhere in that direction must be Blackbrook Reservoir. He knew it wasn't a large reservoir like those in the flooded valleys, where the vast stretches of Ladybower and Derwent attracted the tourists. Blackbrook was small and self-contained, just enough at one time to supply drinking water for the eastern fringes of Manchester.

'Mr Malkin?' said Cooper.

'Aye. That'll be me.'

Cooper made his way across the garden to where the man stood. Malkin was wearing a pair of blue overalls and a black anorak, and a cap like a lumberjack's, with woollen ear-flaps. Cooper thought at first that he was bundled up with sweaters round his waist, but when Malkin moved he saw that the man was actually pear-shaped, with wide hips like someone who hadn't ever got enough exercise. Cooper introduced himself and explained the reason for his visit.

'I wonder if you could spare a few minutes, Mr Malkin? Nothing to worry about.'

'You'd better come in the house.'

This was one farmhouse that had never been converted to the standards of modern living. There was no double glazing and no central heating – a spiral of smoke from the chimney testified that there was still at least one coal fire inside. The last modernization had been in the 1960s by the look of the front door panelled with frosted glass and the blue linoleum visible in the hallway.

Malkin took off his anorak and cap. His skin was weathered and he looked like someone old before his time. George Malkin had been eight years old when the Lancaster crashed, so he could only recently have started drawing his pension.

'Excuse the mess,' said Malkin. 'I don't get a lot of visitors.'

Cooper shivered. There was an unrelenting coldness in the house. Partly, it was the sort of chill that came from years of inadequate heating and a

145

Pennine dampness that had soaked into the stone walls. And now the winds that spiralled down off Kinder and moaned through the empty fields had found their way into Malkin's house for the winter. The draught had crept under the back door and slithered through gaps in the frames of the sash windows, wrapping itself round the furniture and draping the walls in invisible folds. The chill seemed to Cooper like a solid thing; it moved of its own accord, butting against his neck as he walked across the room, and hanging in front of him in every doorway, like a wet curtain.

'It's none too warm today,' said Malkin, watching Cooper turning himself slowly in front of the fire in an effort to absorb some warmth from the flames.

'No, it isn't.'

'This old house takes a bit of heating in the winter. But I suppose I've got used to it. I grew up here, you see, and lived here all my life. I've never known any different. They reckon your blood gets thinner – to compensate, like.'

There was no escape from the chill anywhere. Even when Cooper stood directly in front of the coal fire, there was only warmth on one side; the cold still fastened to his back like a parasite, draining his body heat and sucking at his kidneys. Its presence was part of the house, an icy phantom that would need exorcizing with central heating, double glazing and a good damp-proof course.

'You certainly get a bit of weather up here. Do you get snowed in much?'

'Oh, aye. It's the first place that gets filled in when it snows. It comes down the valley there, you see, and the hills funnel it right into Harrop. When there's a bit of wind behind it, there are some grand drifts to be seen down here. You should have been here in the winter of 78. That was a winter and a half, if you like. We lost our car for days on end. A Ford Escort it was, as I recall. When we finally dug it out, the engine compartment was solid with frozen snow. Aye, there were people walking along the toppings of the stone walls out the front here, because the lane was so deep in snow the walls were the only solid surface you could see for miles.'

'Actually, I do remember it,' said Cooper. He had, after all, been six years old at the time, and he had missed school for a few days. Probably he hadn't been let out in the snow at all, but had watched it from his bedroom window with his nose pressed to the cold glass, drawing patterns on the frost on the inside. Perhaps his parents had finally allowed him to go out when most of the snow had gone. He remembered being pelted by his brother Matt with snowballs that felt as hard as mahogany when they hit him, but which melted into cold, wet slush inside the hood of his anorak and ran down the back of his neck. There hadn't been snow like that since then, as far as he could remember. Not real snow.

'Come on through to the room,' said Malkin. 'Get yourself warm.'

What Malkin called 'the room' was a kind of sitting room, dominated by a large oak table. Its legs only stood on a carpet at one end. At the other, the carpet had been rolled back to expose the bare floorboards, which looked as though they were still drying out from recent damp. Because the boards were old, there were large gaps between them. Where Cooper stood, he could feel icy draughts rising around him as if he were standing on top of an open chest freezer. A bottle of milk and an unsliced loaf of bread stood on the window ledge alongside some steel cutlery, and several weeks' worth of old newspapers were stacked near an old armchair under a standard lamp. An oil painting on the wall showed a herd of brown cattle against a sombre winter landscape. The mountains behind the cows looked more Switzerland than Derbyshire. Real peaks.

'Fancy anybody remembering the Lancaster crash,' said Malkin. 'A long time ago, that was.'

'Fifty-seven years,' said Cooper, trying to find a patch of carpet to stand on.

'I was only eight years old then.'

'You haven't forgotten, though, have you?'

'No, of course I haven't forgotten. It made a big impression on me. Those things do, when you're that age. I'm getting so as I can't remember what I did five minutes ago, but I remember that plane crash as clearly as if I was there now.'

'You're not all that old,' said Cooper. 'Sixty-five? It's nothing these days. Retirement age, that's all.'

'Retirement? They retired me a few years back. These days, you're useless long before you get to sixty-five.'

A mantelpiece supported ornaments, knick-knacks and assorted junk, and there was a television set standing on what might have been a Victorian aspidistra stand. In an alcove, an electric socket had been pulled out of the skirting board and the wires had been left hanging.

'You were a farmer, weren't you?' said Cooper.

Malkin laughed. He had a rattling laugh, with phlegm shifting noisily in his throat. 'Farmworker. Hired labour, that's all. Shepherd I was, and a good 'un, too. But it doesn't matter how good you are at your trade when it comes down to cutting costs. It's the hired labour that goes first. Sixty-five? Maybe. But it's not a matter of how many years you've lived. It's carrying on doing something useful that stops you being old. The minute you stop being useful, you might as well be dead.'

Malkin's middle-aged spread and the roundness of his belly were emphasized by the tightness of a hand-knitted green sweater that must have been a size too small even when it was made. Of course, farmers weren't as physically active as they used to be. They could spend days sitting in the heated cab of a tractor or combine harvester, hours punching buttons on feed mixers or filling in endless paperwork. Just like coppers, in fact. A modern farmer

149

didn't toss bales of hay or carry stranded sheep on his back any more than a bobby was expected to pound the beat or pursue a suspect on foot. Modern methods made for a different shape of man – a man with a body moulded to the shape of padded seats and computer workstations.

'I wondered if you had kept any souvenirs from the crash,' said Cooper.

'Souvenirs?' said Malkin.

'From the aircraft itself?'

'We picked up a few bits and pieces, me and Ted. There's not much left now, though.'

'Ted's your brother, is that right?'

'Aye. He was four years older than me. I followed him round like a dog, the way kids do. I must have been a right nuisance to him sometimes.'

'Where is he now?'

'Long gone,' said Malkin.

Near the fire, a wooden rack was draped with washing left to dry. There was presumably no spin drier in the house, and if left outside on the line, any garment would soon freeze to the consistency of cardboard. Malkin disappeared and returned a few moments later with a mug of tea, which he handed to Cooper. A thin scum floated on the surface, but it was hot.

'Let me get the box,' said Malkin. 'Stay by the fire and keep yourself warm.'

'Thanks.'

While Cooper waited, he worried about the

drying clothes. They seemed to be a little too near to the fire. Wisps of steam and a warm, foetid smell rose from the lines of damp socks and white Y-fronts. Cooper thought that in another few minutes there would be singe marks on the cotton. Across the room, he could see a short passage into what might have been a kitchen or an old-fashioned scullery. There was an earthenware sink with an enamel drainer and a cold tap, a geyser on the wall for hot water, a cupboard with a flap that let down to create a work surface. He tasted the tea and put the mug down. It had been made with sour milk.

When George Malkin came back with a little wooden box, the first item he produced from it was a photograph. They were always the most treasured items among anyone's collections of mementoes, those little snapshots taken on box Brownies.

This photo – a tiny black-and-white snap with a wide border – dated from 1945. One corner was turned over, and when Cooper straightened it out he discovered a cobweb of lines formed by dust ingrained into the creases in the paper. The photo showed a section of the crashed Lancaster shortly after the accident, when it had become a focus of attention for sightseers. The wreckage was almost unrecognizable: bits of ripped and crumpled metal, trailing strands of wire, scattered with dark soil thrown up from the peat moor by the impact.

In the background, two men in trilbys could be seen peering into a section of fuselage through holes torn in its side. But in the foreground was another figure – a small boy. He was only about eight years old, but with that curious look about his face of far greater age and knowingness, a look that seemed a peculiarity of old photographs, as if children in those days had grown up long before they should have done. People often said that modern youngsters grew up too soon. But their knowledge these days was mostly about sex and drugs, a streetwise awareness that set them apart from their parents and the older generations. Children growing up in the war years were wise about other things. For a start, they knew all about death.

The boy was dressed in knee-length shorts and a pullover with a white V-neck collar and elasticated cuffs. His socks had crumpled around his ankles, and his heavy boots were laced up tight. A lock of hair fell over his forehead, but at the sides it was cut short and his ears stood out from his head. He was staring directly at the camera with an intense look, striking a self-conscious pose, his left hand raised to rest on one of the huge engines that protruded from the debris. The engine was still intact, and each of the curved propeller blades was taller than the boy. It seemed incredible that souvenir hunters would later cut away those propellers from the engine and remove all trace of them from the moor. It must have taken at least two men to carry one blade, and they would have struggled over the rough ground and the steep slopes to get it back to the road. What motivated them to go to such trouble? And where were the propeller blades and the other aircraft parts now?

'Who is this boy?' asked Cooper.

'Who do you think?' said Malkin.

Cooper looked from the photograph to the man across the table. Though the hair was grey now, and no longer fell over his forehead, the style was much the same as it had been in 1945, and so were the protruding ears. And the direct stare was the same, too – then, as now, it was the stare of someone who had grown too old too soon.

'So you walked up to Irontongue to look at the crash?'

'It was a great bit of excitement in those days. There was no telly, of course. These days they wouldn't shift themselves away from the goggle box or their computers, would they? My dad was too busy to bother with us, but we went up with our Uncle Norman, who lived just outside Glossop. I talked about it at school for months afterwards. I was a real centre of attention for a while.'

'Did you come away with any souvenirs yourself?'

'Well, of course. Everybody did. Only a few mementoes, you know. We used to swap them with other lads; the American stuff was what we wanted most, unless we could get hold of something from a German plane. There were plenty of bits and pieces lying around then. But I got rid of nearly everything.'

'Did you happen to find any medals?'

'Medals?' Malkin looked surprised. 'Medals would have been worth something, I reckon. But they would have been on the bodies, probably, wouldn't they?'

'Probably. What did you take, then?'

Malkin pulled the box towards him and poked through its contents. 'There are some newspaper cuttings here, if you want to see them.'

'I've seen most of them already, I think.'

'Fair enough.' He continued to fumble. 'I think it's here somewhere. Ah yes. This is the only thing I've kept.' He produced a round metal object with a blackened casing. Cooper had expected some unidentifiable part of the aircraft superstructure, but this seemed more familiar.

'It looks like a watch,' he said.

'Yes, it is.' Malkin slid the cover away. The blackened face wasn't metal after all, but glass fused by intense heat. Underneath, the face of the timepiece was pretty well intact, though the metal frame had buckled slightly and there was a scorch mark below the figure twelve. The hands had stopped a fraction short of ten to eleven.

'Ten forty-nine,' he said. 'That was the exact time the Lancaster crashed.'

'You mean one of the crew was wearing this watch when the aircraft crashed?'

'I expect so. I found it lying in the peat, half-buried. I didn't show it to my uncle or anyone, just shoved it in my pocket and took it away with me. I only ever showed it to Ted and to my pals at school. Do you think it would be worth much?'

'It was from the body of a dead man,' said Cooper.

'That was what gave it a bit of excitement,' he said. 'Don't you see? The most exciting things are the ones you know are wrong.'

Cooper looked back at the photograph of the eight-year-old boy, while Malkin continued to finger the broken watch. The knowing expression on the boy's face as he leaned against the wrecked propeller gave him an uncomfortable feeling.

Malkin noticed his expression as he stared at the photo. 'Oh, yes,' he said. 'I already had it in my pocket when my uncle took that snap.'

Cooper put the picture back carefully in the box. 'It *was* you and your brother who saw the airman?' he said. 'The one who disappeared?'

'Yes, you're right. Who told you that?'

'It's in the reports. Did the police interview you?'

'Aye, a bobby came here the day after the crash. We'd told our dad about seeing the airman, and he reported it to the local police station. Everybody round here was talking about it by then.'

'Tell me where you saw the airman, Mr Malkin. What did he look like?'

'Nay, I can't tell you that – it was dark. He was in a flying suit, that's all I know, with his leather helmet and all. He had a torch, and we saw him going along the road that runs round the reservoir and off down the hill. It comes out near the old toll cottage on the Crowden road.'

'Can you show me?'

'I'll point you to it,' said Malkin.

They went back outside and walked back along the wall towards Cooper's car. The sheep munched and snorted quietly in the field.

'Look at that,' said Malkin, waving a hand at the field as if it had been bright daylight rather than the true darkness of the countryside. 'Good, rich land, that is. The best grazing for miles. It used to be a quarry years ago, but they filled it in. Now these Swaledales are prized for miles around for their meat. They produce the tastiest lamb chops in Derbyshire, my mate Rod says. If you like, I'll get you a couple.'

'Thanks. This reservoir road . . .'

Malkin pointed into the darkness. 'Over yonder. Can you see the line of the wall, with a bit of a gate and a hawthorn bush?'

'Just about,' said Cooper, though all he could distinguish was the general direction the other man was pointing in.

'That's where the water board road runs. It has a locked gate on it now, but it was only a bit of a dirt track in those days, just made for the maintenance men to get up to the reservoir. I bet that airman was glad to find it, though. He would have had to hike across the snow from Irontongue, and it must have taken him an hour in the dark, I bet. Ted and me, we went along the reservoir wall to get up near the crash – we could see the fire burning from the house. I suppose we wouldn't ever have seen the airman if he hadn't been waving a torch around all over the place. Aye, but we heard him.'

'Heard him? Was he shouting?'

'Singing,' said Malkin.

Cooper stared at him. He couldn't see anything of Malkin's face at all under the cap and the ear-flaps, but from his voice he didn't sound as though he were joking.

'*Singing*? Singing what, Mr Malkin?'

'As I recall, it was "Show Me the Way to Go Home".'

10

Next morning, Ben Cooper was on duty early again. As soon as he arrived, he went to check out the morning's action forms for the Snowman enquiry. With no one in yet to allocate the jobs, he might get away with picking out something interesting. He could say he thought he ought to get on with it, since he was in early. That was something the snow could be thanked for – everybody was arriving at work after him these days. The only people in the station were those on the late shift, who would be going home soon, and the deskbound personnel didn't start until nine.

'Keen, Ben?'

Diane Fry was unwinding her red scarf from her neck, pulling her hair out from under a high collar and shaking it like a dog emerging from water. When she took her coat off, she looked half the size. Cooper's mother would have said she was too thin, that she needed a layer of fat to keep out the winter cold.

'I thought I might as well make a start,' he said. 'There's no time to lose, is there? Considering the shortage of manpower we keep hearing about.'

'Take a gold star. But actually, you're not alone. Even the Chief Super is in. And I just saw DI Hitchens on his way up to the top floor.'

There wasn't really much among the actions to be done. Not surprising, really, since the Snowman had still not been identified. But one form stood out. It related to a woman who had phoned in last night when she had heard about the body on the news. Most of the phone calls had been discounted, or the details filed for later reference. But this one had sounded to the operator as if it might be worth following up and it had been passed on to the incident room. The woman claimed to have seen a man who answered the description of the Snowman, right down to the smart clothes and polished shoes, though minus the blue overnight bag.

Cooper also thought the woman sounded worth talking to. Her name was Lukasz.

Cooper showed the form to Diane Fry.

'Look at this,' he said. 'This call came from a woman called Mrs Grace Lukasz, Woodland Crescent, Edendale.'

'So?'

'Lukasz . . .' he said. Then he remembered that Fry knew nothing about Alison Morrissey, Pilot Officer Danny McTeague, or the crew of Sugar

Uncle Victor. 'Well, it was a name mentioned in the meeting with the Chief yesterday.'

'What? Oh, the Canadian woman. What on earth was all that about, then? Some old wartime story, people have been saying. Why does she think she has the right to waste our time?'

'Somebody in Edendale sent her a medal belonging to her grandfather, who went missing in 1945. He was a bomber pilot, and he was supposed to have deserted after his aircraft was wrecked near here.'

'Yeah?'

He could tell Fry had lost interest already. And why *should* she be interested? There was nothing in the story to concern the police. Not unless Morrissey produced some evidence of a crime. A lost medal that turned up after fifty-seven years was far from that.

'It's a bit of a coincidence, that's all. It's an unusual name.'

'You know what it's like,' said Fry. 'You notice an unfamiliar word or name for the first time, then you seem to keep hearing it again for days afterwards. It's just that you never noticed it before.'

'If it was a common name in Edendale, I think I would have noticed it before now.'

'Oh, I forgot – you're Mr Local Knowledge. You probably have the phone book memorized.'

She took the action form from him and studied it. The name of Lukasz meant nothing to her – she was assessing the action purely on its merits.

160

Cooper found himself silently willing her to hand it back. But then she began to look through the rest of the forms.

'OK, but take these others as well,' she said. 'Kill several birds with one stone. Then I can justify you missing the morning meeting. I dare say we'll cope without you, for once.'

'All right, then. You know I still have several enquiries outstanding?'

'Haven't we all?'

Before he went out, Cooper checked the electoral register for the address given by Grace Lukasz. The entry for 37 Woodland Crescent showed three registered voters living in that household – Piotr Janusz Lukasz, Grace Anne Lukasz and Zygmunt Henryk Lukasz. So he had tracked down the survivor of the Lancaster crash without even trying. Maybe Diane was wrong about their luck – it looked as though it might be changing.

Not that he had any reason for wanting to find Zygmunt Lukasz. Not that there was anything he could ask the old man. Not officially. But on a personal level, he would be interested to hear Lukasz's version of the crash of Sugar Uncle Victor and of what happened to Pilot Officer Danny McTeague. It might put his mind at rest, settle down the uneasiness that had been aroused by seeing the photographs of the crew, particularly the young airman who seemed to have had death written on his face.

Besides, he personally thought that Alison Morrissey was justified in searching for answers about the fate of her grandfather. He could see she was hoping beyond reason that the medal sent to Canada had come from Danny McTeague himself and therefore meant he was still alive somewhere in the area. It almost certainly meant someone knew more about McTeague than had ever been told. Cooper knew he would have wanted to do the same in her position. It was a little hard that he wasn't able to help her when he was ideally placed to do so. If only he didn't have so much else to do.

Cooper wrote the names of the Lukasz family in his notebook. He would leave them until after he had visited the other addresses. He liked to save the best until last.

Chief Superintendent Jepson was standing at the window of his office on the top floor of divisional headquarters, looking down on to the car park at the back of the building. Some of the snow had been swept to the sides to clear a bit of space, but cars and vans were parked at all sorts of angles, making the place look untidy. He watched a figure cross the car park. It was dressed in a long waxed coat and a peaked cap.

'Ben Cooper is a good lad,' said Jepson. 'I don't want him left out in the cold for long.'

DI Paul Hitchens was in early because he had been told to be. He was standing in the middle of the room waiting for the Chief Super to get round to saying whatever it was that he had on his mind. So far, they had touched only on the weather.

'I must admit, there's been some muttering in the ranks,' said Hitchens.

'Muttering? What do you mean?'

'Cooper is popular here. A lot of people think he's been badly treated, promotion-wise. Another one passed over for a newcomer from outside, they're saying.'

'Yes. Well, perhaps they're right,' said Jepson. 'I'd like to be sure that now DCI Kessen has arrived he's made fully aware of Cooper's strengths and potential. It doesn't do to start off with the wrong impression. And, Paul . . .'

'Yes, Chief?'

'That applies more generally.'

'I'm not sure what you mean.'

'I mean starting off with the right impression. The first impression someone has of you can last a long time.'

'I understand.'

'So let's have a bit more of a positive attitude, shall we? Less of the cheap humour.'

'Certainly, sir,' said Hitchens. 'I'll make sure my humour is more expensive in future.'

Of course, Diane Fry was right. It was the wrong time to expect a bit of luck. Two of the people on his list had been far too vague about the man they had seen to be any help at all in identifying

163

the Snowman. Predictably, their descriptions had fallen apart and become useless when they were questioned closely. And, even if they *had* seen the Snowman, they could not say who he was, where he had been going, or where he had come from.

The first witness had been an old lady with bifocals and thinning hair, who had seen a strange man walking down her street, stopping to look at the numbers on houses. She hadn't seen him call at any particular address. And, unfortunately, she hadn't noticed a car that might have belonged to him, which would have helped a lot.

The second woman was younger, a divorcée with two young children at primary school. This witness had a more detailed eye, and her encounter had been at closer quarters. She had observed a person very like the Snowman doing his shopping in Boots the Chemists on Clappergate, where he had bought razor blades and a bottle of Grecian 2000 in a dark brown shade. She had noticed that he was well dressed, with nicely polished shoes, and that he had paid for his purchases with a brand new £20 note. She had been standing right behind him in the queue at the till, and she thought his aftershave was Obsession. Afterwards, she had watched him walk off towards the market square, but had lost him when he crossed the road near the High Street junction. That was the way she had put it – she had 'lost him'. Cooper had been impressed. With a bit more training, she might have made a useful surveillance operative.

As it happened, the third woman had been out. Cooper had put his card through her door with a note asking her to contact him. This witness lived in one of the crescents that clustered on the hillside above Edendale. Most of the addresses here were bungalows dating from the 1960s or 1970s, some of them quite large, with well-established gardens or dormer windows built into their roofs.

That left the address he had saved until last. Cooper consulted the street map in the glove compartment of his car. Woodland Crescent was only two blocks down the hill from the street he was in, a few hundred yards away. He left the Toyota by the kerb and walked downhill towards Edendale, carefully sticking to the middle of the pavement to avoid sinking his shoes into more snow.

He came across a little grocer's shop and a corner post office that had billboards outside advertising the *Derbyshire Times* and *Daily Mail*. A small flatbed lorry with the name of a local builder on its cab door stood in a driveway next to an outdoor aviary full of fluttering zebra finches. Two hundred yards away, on the main road, was a Case tractor dealership, directly opposite Queen's Park, the town's largest open space.

Woodland Crescent was much like the other streets: more bungalows, and a few newer homes at the top, with open-plan lawns separating their drives. A man of about sixty, dressed in yellow waterproofs like a fisherman, was slowing pushing snow off the pavement with a brush. He stopped

165

as Cooper passed and gave him a nod. He was flushed and breathing hard. The clouds of his breath reminded Cooper of the early-morning cars standing in exhaust fumes pumped from cold engines.

There was a woman sitting in the window of number 37, the Lukasz home. It was a large bungalow with a built-in garage and a sizeable conservatory, which he could see down the passageway separating it from the bungalow next door. Cooper guessed the woman must be Grace Lukasz. Was she the wife of Piotr?

Cooper walked up the driveway past a blue BMW to the bungalow, conscious of the woman's eyes on him. She was watching him suspiciously, as if he might be somebody undesirable – a Jehovah's Witness or an insurance salesman. Near the front door, he stopped and looked at her. The woman was still staring at him. And her expression was more than suspicion – it was fear.

By the time he rang the bell, the face of the woman had disappeared from the window, though he hadn't seen her stand up. He saw movement through the glass panels of the door, and then realized why the woman hadn't stood up. She was in a wheelchair.

Cooper introduced himself, and showed his identification, interested by the woman's nervous manner. She relaxed, though, when she discovered who he was and why he had come. She almost pulled him into the hallway of the bungalow and closed the door behind him. Then she leaned forward in her chair to fiddle with a draught excluder shaped like an elongated sausage dog.

'If you wouldn't mind taking your shoes off,' she said. 'There are some spare slippers in the cupboard.'

The heat in the bungalow was already bringing Cooper out in prickles of sweat under his coat. The difference between this and Hollow Shaw Farm was like getting on a plane in Iceland and stepping off in tropical Africa. Grace Lukasz was wearing a cream sweater and slacks, managing to look both comfortable and smart. While he put on the slippers, Cooper looked at the passages going off the hallway in two directions. It was certainly a large bungalow. Four bedrooms, at least. He wondered what Piotr Lukasz did for a living.

'I'm not at all sure,' said Mrs Lukasz. 'It's just that the description sounded similar. And since the police were appealing for help . . .'

'Quite right. We always welcome the public's help.'

She tilted her head slightly to one side to look at him, an amused smile on her face. She wasn't one to be easily fooled. Cooper could see that she had been an attractive woman, too. Still was, for anybody who saw past the wheelchair. She had no trace of an accent. That didn't necessarily mean she wasn't of Polish origin herself, but he was working on the assumption that she was English and that she was Zygmunt Lukasz's daughter-in-law.

'Have you found out who he is yet?' she said.

Cooper was taken aback to find that Mrs Lukasz had seized the initiative in asking the questions. He was forgetting what he was here for, speculating too much about the old airman who had flown on Sugar Uncle Victor. He knew himself well enough to understand that a thing like this could become an obsession, if he wasn't careful. But he very much wanted to see Zygmunt Lukasz, to compare him to the photographs in the book, to see whether he was the young man who had seemed to communicate with him across those fifty-seven years.

'No, we haven't, Mrs Lukasz. That's what I was hoping you might be able to help us with.'

'I see.'

She seemed irrationally disappointed. 'But he didn't tell me his name, I'm afraid. He came to the house, but I sent him away.'

'When was this again?'

'Monday morning. I rang yesterday, after I heard it on the news. You've taken a long time coming, haven't you?'

'We have a lot of people to speak to,' said Cooper.

He suddenly got the feeling he was being watched from another part of the room. He looked round and met the sceptical eye of a blue and green parrot. It had its head cocked at him in almost the same way as its owner.

'I thought he was selling insurance or replacement windows,' said Mrs Lukasz. 'We get so many of them here. I knew he wasn't a Jehovah, of course.'

'Oh?'

'They stopped coming when they found out we were Catholics. It's a shame. I always hoped I might have been able to convert one of them.'

'The man who came to the house on Monday,' said Cooper, 'he didn't say what he wanted?'

'I didn't give him a chance,' said Mrs Lukasz. 'I don't want to be sitting on the doorstep in the cold, arguing with salesmen. I nearly sent you packing, too, but I could see you weren't selling anything. Not in that coat.'

Cooper fumbled with his pen, embarrassed by the double stare from the woman and the parrot. 'Could you give me a description of him, please? As much detail as you can remember.'

Grace Lukasz gave him the description succinctly. It fitted the Snowman exactly, down to the shoes. She was an observant woman, for somebody who hadn't even given the man a chance to speak.

'Did he have a car?'

'Not that I saw.'

'Did you notice which way he came from, or which way he went when he left?'

'Not particularly.'

'Is there anybody else in the household I might ask, Mrs Lukasz?'

She hesitated and began to look suspicious again. Cooper almost brought out his ID for a second time, just for its reassurance value.

'His car might have been parked somewhere else in the Crescent,' she said. 'Try our neighbours. I expect he went down the whole street if he was selling something.'

'I'll certainly do that.'

'Will you let me know who he was when you find out?'

Again, Grace Lukasz had taken him by surprise. But she was waiting expectantly for his answer, as if the information should be part of their deal. It was understandable, he supposed, that she should want to know who the man was who had been on her doorstep and had died shortly afterwards.

'I'll see what I can do,' he said. 'In the meantime, we like to get as much corroboration as possible. So while I'm here . . .'

'Well, my husband is home at the moment,' she said. 'And there's my father-in-law. But neither of them saw him.'

'Perhaps we could check with them, to be sure. It would be very helpful.'

Mrs Lukasz seemed almost to be laughing. 'Come this way.'

She led him down a passage to the back of the bungalow, where she knocked on a door and called a name. Cooper noticed that she called 'Peter', not Piotr, as her husband was listed in the electoral register. A man came out, and Cooper caught a glimpse of a bright conservatory full of plants. Lukasz had dark hair and long, slim fingers, which he wiped on a cloth. His eyes looked rather tired.

'No, I didn't see him,' said Lukasz stiffly when he was asked. But Cooper was getting the same feeling that he'd had from the man's wife. With each of them, there was that brief moment when they might have answered differently, but held something back.

'Are you quite sure, sir?'

'Yes, I'm certain,' said Lukasz. 'I wasn't even at home by then. I'm a consultant in the Accident and Emergency Department at the hospital, and I'd stayed late that morning because we had a crisis.'

'I believe your father lives here also.'

'I don't think he would be able to help you.'

Cooper was considering how hard he could risk pushing his luck, when the doorbell rang. He heard Grace Lukasz go back into the hall to answer it. Automatically, Cooper turned towards the front door. So he was standing in plain view next to Peter Lukasz when Grace opened it.

And then he wished he had been standing somewhere else at that moment, anywhere else at all. Waiting on the doorstep of the Lukasz bungalow were Frank Baine and Alison Morrissey.

'We need some clothes,' said DI Paul Hitchens. 'Otherwise, all we have are the bare facts.'

There were photos of the Snowman pinned to a board behind the two DCIs. There was no hope of an identification yet. One idea being considered was the production of an artist's impression of the dead man, to be reproduced in the papers and on the local television news, and for officers to show to drivers at checkpoints on the A57. Motorists had already been stopped, but nobody could recall seeing a man walking along the roadside with a blue bag, or a vehicle parked in the lay-by where the Snowman's body had been found. A picture might make all the difference to their memories.

Diane Fry thought DCI Kessen looked as though he hadn't yet adjusted to the sense of humour in E Division. According to the grapevine, he had not been popular in D Division. The theory was that when the new Detective Superintendent arrived, it would be someone who could keep him from causing too much trouble.

'So our task for today is to find some clothes,' said Hitchens. 'And I'm in charge of the shopping expedition.'

DI Hitchens looked in his element when he was the centre of attention. He stepped up to a map pinned to the wall and tapped it with a ruler. He was pointing to an area to the west of the lay-by on the A57 where the Snowman had been found. A search of the lay-by itself had recovered plenty of assorted debris from under the snow, but nothing that might have been the contents of the blue bag – unless the Snowman had been in the habit of wearing hub caps and cushion covers.

'Here's the place to start,' said Hitchens. 'Right below the road here is an abandoned quarry. It's well within reach of the lay-by and a favourite spot for fly-tippers. This is what you might call the Knightsbridge boutique of our shopping trip. It could have exactly what we want – but it's difficult to get into.'

Fry didn't see many officers laughing at the joke. Even DCI Tailby frowned. Since Hitchens had moved in with his new girlfriend to a modern house in Dronfield, he had definitely gone upmarket. It sounded as though he had been dragged off to London at some point to learn what shopping was all about. An inspector's salary was a nice step up from a mere sergeant's.

'If the bag was emptied in situ, chances are the contents will be somewhere down here, in the quarry,' said Hitchens. 'Unfortunately, when the quarry was abandoned, the owners spared no effort in blocking it off to stop people getting in. They piled rocks up in the entrance like they were building the pyramids of Giza, and the sides are sheer. I suppose they must have been worried about somebody stealing their leftover millstones.'

Hitchens twirled his ruler happily, as though he were conducting a tune. The two DCIs sat stony-faced at their table, refusing to sing.

'The net result is that there's no way we can get into that quarry without the use of heavy machinery,' said Hitchens. 'And that would take time – not to mention money. Since we have neither, we're falling back on a bit of good old-fashioned improvisation. To put it bluntly, we've decided to use a man with a long rope and a careless disregard

173

for his personal safety.' Hitchens smiled. 'Now all we need is a volunteer. Don't all shout at once.'

Nobody moved. Nobody so much as let his chair creak.

'I have some photographs to encourage you,' said Hitchens.

He picked up a large print of a photo taken from the fence at the edge of the lay-by, looking down into the quarry. The sides were almost smooth, except for patches where the stone was crumbling away. There was snow at the bottom, but it looked a long way off. It covered large, uneven shapes, like a white dust sheet thrown over a room full of modern furniture. They all knew there were rocks littering the floor of the quarry under that snow, guaranteed to break a few ankles.

'No one?' said Hitchens. 'Then I suppose I'll have to nominate a volunteer.'

Peter Lukasz had reacted so angrily to the presence of the two people on his doorstep that Ben Cooper had begun to think he would have to intervene to prevent a breach of the peace, or an outright assault. Until that moment, Lukasz had seemed an ordinary, reasonable man – but he had changed into a snarling guard dog. He had pursued Alison Morrissey and Frank Baine from his property, seen them right down the driveway, then had come back in and slammed the door after them.

Breathing hard, Lukasz had answered Cooper's questions with a distracted air, and terse replies.

He knew nothing, and he hadn't seen the man that his wife was talking about, he said.

Cooper got ready to move on. He would have to call on the neighbours, to see if they, too, had been visited by the Snowman but had not noticed a resemblance to the description given out on the local news. Maybe one of the neighbours had bought some double glazing from him, which would be a stroke of luck indeed. There was also the third witness, who hadn't been home when he called. And no doubt there would be other jobs waiting for him back at West Street.

But Cooper was reluctant to leave too quickly. He tried to stretch out the process of changing back into his shoes, while squinting through the glass door to see if anyone was hanging around outside.

Then he noticed that Lukasz hadn't disappeared back into the conservatory but had turned towards another room next to it. As he opened the door, Cooper caught sight of a third person, seated at a table. It was an old man, with thin, white hair receding from his forehead and brushed back over his ears. He had wire-rimmed glasses worn on the bridge of a Roman nose, and he was wearing a heavy brown sweater that made his shoulders look out of proportion to his body. The old man looked up as Peter entered, and Cooper saw his eyes. They were pale blue and distant, like glimpses of the sky through broken cloud.

It was only a second or two before the door

closed again. But Ben Cooper had been given his first glimpse of Zygmunt Lukasz.

DI Hitchens folded his arms and looked around the room, which had gone horribly quiet. No volunteers came forward for the privilege of being lowered into the quarry. There were officers here who were likely to have a panic attack if they thought the stairs were too steep. There were others whose technical capabilities fell short of inadequate. There was Gavin Murfin, for a start. Give him a rope, and he would try to eat it.

DI Hitchens gazed at Murfin briefly, and passed on. Then he stopped, and looked round the room again with a frown.

'Hold on,' he said. 'There's somebody missing.'

11

Ben Cooper had never quite got used to the sensation of stepping backwards into space. That second before his boot connected with the rock face was like no other experience. It went through his mind every time that he might never touch ground again – or rather, that he would hit it only once more, down at the bottom.

But the soles of his boots landed gently on the gritstone surface. The rope in his hands vibrated, and the harness tightened round his body. He let out more rope until he was leaning well back, gaining stability by pressing his weight into the rock. Then he adjusted his grip and bent his torso forward. The angle had to be just right. Too narrow an angle and his feet would slide off the smooth surface and he would smack into the wall face-first.

Cooper looked up at the edge of the quarry, and saw two members of the Buxton Mountain Rescue Team peering down at him, their faces already too small and out of proportion against the sky.

'OK, Ben?'

'Fine.'

To his right, one of the scenes of crime officers, Liz Petty, back-pedalled to the edge and took her first step backwards. She was bundled up in her blue overalls and a yellow waterproof jacket, with a red helmet pulled low over her eyes.

Cooper had been initiated in the pleasures of abseiling by his friends in the MRT, and he knew it was a lot easier than it seemed to a spectator up top. For one thing, you didn't have to look all the way down as they did. Your eyes were on your rope, on where your feet were going, and on the rock face in front of you. Once you had turned your back on that dizzying drop and braced yourself for the first step into nothing, it was easy.

He paused to manoeuvre around a gritstone outcrop. Liz came alongside him, and she turned to smile. It was the conspiratorial smile shared by rock climbers. Liz's face was flushed with cold and excitement, and her eyes shone with pleasure from under her helmet.

'Going down?' she said.

Cooper felt his foot slip off the rock. He put out his left hand to steady himself and stop his weight making the rope swing. He twisted his torso slightly to look down at his brake hand as he fed the rope through the figure eight of the descender. The gristone was hard and bruising to the fingers;

yet in some places it was crumbly and unsafe, its stability undermined by decades of quarrying.

They moved on a bit further. The officers at the top kept calling down to ask if they were OK, as if somehow they might get lost on the way down. Cooper promised he would be sure to let them know if the rope broke. They laughed, but not much.

A few yards from the bottom, Liz paused. Cooper watched her wrap the rope round her thigh with three loops. This freed her brake hand, and she reached into the pocket of her jacket for her digital camera to take an establishing shot of the quarry floor. They didn't know what to expect down there. Probably it was a futile effort. But there had been too many instances when small items of forensic evidence had been overlooked until it was too late.

Liz was lighter than Cooper, and had perfected that effortless rhythm that allowed her to float down in easy steps. She had already unclipped her belay and removed her harness by the time he touched bottom. She shouted up to a colleague at the top, and her case was lowered down to her.

'Right,' said Liz, as Cooper unclipped his straps. 'Let's see what we've got.'

The floor of the quarry was littered with lumps of gritstone blasted away from the walls. To the east, a vast stack had been heaped up to block access to the site. Liz Petty took some shots of the quarry floor. Then she crouched by a large rock, opening her case and unfolding a tight stack of evidence bags.

'We're looking for clothes, right? Well dressed? Casual, or what?'

'Yes, well dressed.'

'We can discount the donkey jacket, then.'

Cooper leaned over her shoulder. She was pointing to a dark, sodden mass on the ground. It reeked of mould, and patches of the fabric were turning green with mildew. There were rips in the leather patches on the shoulders.

'It's been there too long, anyway.'

'Pity. It could probably have told you a lot about the owner. What he had for breakfast, for a start. Those encrusted stains have survived well.'

Much of the debris and rubble from the quarrying operations had simply been left in place, and there were still lethal shards of buried metal and invisible holes to fall into. Cautiously, they picked their way among the stones, glad of the boots that protected their feet from the sharp edges and the sudden shifting of the ground that could turn an ankle.

Cooper pointed up to the edge of the quarry. 'If the clothes were thrown over the side of the quarry, it would have been from up there somewhere.'

Liz tried to push her helmet back from her eyes, but it soon slipped forward again as she bent to clamber over a boulder that must have weighed a couple of tons. Now and then, she stopped to examine something more closely. Cooper waited patiently each time, holding out little hope that the grubby-coloured scraps of material lying among the debris had belonged to the Snowman.

'This is more like it.'

She was taking photographs again, manoeuvring for different angles to identify the exact spot, then going for a close-up.

'What have you got?'

Liz held up a blue garment, her tweezers gripping a corner of fabric. 'Knickers. They're quite recent. A bit damp, but no more than lying in the snow would cause.'

Cooper considered the scrap of material. 'If those are out of the Snowman's bag, it casts a new light on the enquiry.'

'It tells you something about his sexual inclinations, perhaps.'

'I was thinking more of a woman accompanying him. We had assumed we were looking for male clothing.'

Liz chose a paper bag as a temporary container for her find. The blue pants would have to be allowed to dry out naturally in the air, rather than sealed in airtight plastic that would encourage the proliferation of micro-organisms.

There were shouts from on top of the cliff again. Cooper turned, gave them a thumbs-up and pointed at the bag.

'DI Hitchens says this quarry is a Knightsbridge boutique,' he said.

Liz held up the bag and studied the underwear critically. 'If you ask me,' she said, 'we're in an Age Concern charity shop.'

Diane Fry found herself feeling a little guilty about Ben Cooper's allocation in his absence to the quarry job. But she reassured herself by reflecting that, if he had actually been at the meeting, he would certainly have volunteered anyway. He was that sort of man. No sense at all.

But to help him out she went to have a look at what he had on his desk, in case there was anything urgent that needed to be dealt with. The first file she noticed was the one on Eddie Kemp, the window cleaner. Since Kemp had been arrested, there had been a positive snowstorm of calls, accusing him of every offence in the book. According to the callers, he had been getting up to everything from flashing to stalking, from social security fraud to child abuse. And there were at least three calls naming him as the killer of the man found on the Snake Pass.

The information had been copied to the incident room, but the reports were lacking in convincing details like names, places and times. An absence of detail was usually the giveaway for malicious calls. Eddie Kemp wasn't top of the popularity stakes among his neighbours, by the look of it. So it might come as a shock to some of them to find out that he had already been bailed and was back at home. What the police really needed was reliable intelligence on his associates, and witnesses to the assault or the events just before it.

But there was one useful piece of information that had come through. One of the rolls of blue plastic sheeting from Kemp's car had revealed the impression of two objects shaped like baseball bats, and traces of both human blood and sweat had been obtained from the plastic. DNA analysis could provide a match if the division was willing to pay for samples to be sent to the Forensic Science Service laboratory. So progress on that had become a budgetary decision.

Fry wrote a note for Ben Cooper to read when he eventually returned to his desk. There were other enquiries piling up for him, too, and most of the files had messages attached to them – phone calls from the Crown Prosecution Service, officers in other departments or other sections, and even the victims of crimes themselves, wondering what was happening to their case, desperate to contact the person they naively thought was busy investigating it. But they would all have to wait. She just hoped that Cooper was wearing a safety harness. The last thing they needed was another casualty.

Fry's phone rang again. It had that tone which usually meant a call she didn't want to answer. This time it was the control room informing her that the search of the quarry had been abandoned. The mountain rescue team had pulled out to respond to an emergency call, and had since located a body on nearby Irontongue Hill. Police officers at the quarry had been diverted to attend. Control were letting her know as a courtesy, because DC Cooper was one of the officers at the scene.

Fry rested her head in her hands and stared across the room at her remaining staff.

'*Ooh-wee, baby . . . ooh-we! Won't you let me take you on a sea cruise.*'

'Gavin,' she said. 'Shut that bloody lobster up, or I'll throw it out of the window.'

Marie Tennent was barely recognizable as human at first. By the time Ben Cooper arrived at the scene, someone had scraped some of the ice from her, so that now she at least looked like a pile of wet clothes abandoned on the hillside. The frozen snow clung to her in small lumps. Cooper had tried to brush a patch clear near her pocket, but the crystals were attached firmly to the fibres of her coat.

He stood around with the other police officers and members of the mountain rescue team, who were stamping their feet as they waited for the doctor to come and certify that the woman was indeed dead, rather than cryogenically frozen and in a state of suspended animation. One of the rescue team was a middle-aged Peak Park Ranger, who had seen his fair share of bodies. He made a joke about the doctor needing to borrow an ice pick before he could use his rectal thermometer, and everyone laughed uneasily.

Liz Petty had walked to the site with him, though she wouldn't be of any use just yet. She was still wearing her helmet, and her eyes were bright with speculation as she looked up at Cooper.

'Mrs Snowman, by any chance?'

'Who knows?'

'Give me a shout if I can help, when you're sure she's dead.'

That morning, the pilot of a small plane had finally seen Marie Tennent's outline against the peat as the snow had begun to slip from her shoulders. It was none too soon – the snow had come again since then, and Marie might have stayed undiscovered for another few days by the look of the sky in the north.

Cooper found Liz was still standing next to him, watching him deep in thought.

'It could be suicide, I suppose,' she said.

'The assumption will be death by misadventure.'

'Tried to climb a mountain in bad weather, then fell, and died of exposure before she could be found? It sounds reasonable.'

'It's the sort of thing people do all the time around here. It's as if they think bad weather isn't real, just a bit of gloss added by the National Park Authority to make the scenery more picturesque.'

Cooper turned and looked over the surrounding moorland. Today the Peak District really did look like a scene from one of those old-fashioned winters that people always talked about. The snow that had fallen earlier in the week had smoothed out the familiar features of the landscape, until the hills and valleys had become unrecognizable.

Everyone who had lived in the area before the mid-1980s had their own tales of deep snows that brought everything to a halt, of chest-high snow-drifts and people skating on iced-over rivers. It was said that Burbage Edge had once been covered in drifts thirty feet deep, that it had taken years for its birch trees to recover from the damage after the weight of snow had snapped their boughs like matchsticks and ripped them limb from limb where they stood. On days like that, it was foolhardy to venture on to the moors.

Cooper turned over the plastic bag contain-ing the woman's purse, which he had found in the left-hand pocket of her coat, the first part of her to emerge from the snow. A cash card and bank statement revealed her name to be Marie Tennent, of 10 Dam Street, Edendale. Why had no one reported Marie Tennent missing? He knew without checking that she wasn't on the missing persons list – he had been through it only yesterday with Gavin Murfin, and she had been lying here longer than that. So where were Marie's family? What about her friends and neighbours?

The postmortem would tell them whether Marie Tennent had been injured or had collapsed through the cold, or had simply lain down and frozen to death. The physical circumstances could be established in the mortuary; but no amount of examination of the brain would prove her state of mind.

'I can see some animal traces,' said Liz. 'They might help with time of death.'

'Yes. Thanks.'

But Cooper was looking at the dead woman's face. She lay curled on her side, and her head was towards him, with her hands at her temples, as if she had been covering her ears to shut out the sound of approaching death. Her eyes were closed, and the skin of her face was white and rimed with a thin layer of frost. Her nose and lips were already starting to turn black.

Cooper knew his colleagues sometimes accused him of being over-imaginative. And he wasn't supposing that he could read the expression of a corpse. But he did know one thing, which a quick glance over his shoulder confirmed. When she died, Marie Tennent had been facing towards Irontongue Hill, not away from it. The remains of the tail fin of the wrecked Lancaster bomber SU-V were plainly visible from here. The last thing Marie would have seen in life was a rusty fragment of Sugar Uncle Victor.

Cooper recalled what Diane Fry had said about a name you heard for the first time, which then seemed to crop up again and again. He had been vaguely aware since his childhood of the wreckage of the Lancaster bomber on Irontongue Hill. It was a story that would have appealed to him as a boy, when war had seemed exciting and glamorous, probably because it was something so distant that it was never likely to touch him personally. He had missed the height of the Cold War, when people had believed they were in daily danger of being wiped out in a nuclear holocaust; he had been too young to remember Vietnam. It was all history, as remote as World War Two, not affecting real people that he knew. Yet the wreck had always been there, at the back of his mind.

Cooper didn't think he had heard the name of the aircraft before yesterday. Lancaster SU-V. Sugar Uncle Victor. He was sure it would have stuck in his mind. It sounded so innocuous for a machine designed to kill and destroy. He didn't think he could have missed the irony. Now the flight engineer of Sugar Uncle Victor had been drawn to his attention twice in two days. And here was a woman who might have been heading either towards or away from the wreck when she died.

There were too many assumptions that could be made in a case like this. The first assumption would be that Marie Tennent had been responsible for her own death, in one way or another. Suicide or misadventure. Did it matter? Perhaps only to the High Peak coroner, who liked his records to be neat.

'Ben?' called Liz. 'I think you're wanted over here.'

'Coming.'

The doctor had been lowered on to the hill by the RAF rescue helicopter, which still hovered overhead, waiting to take the body up on the winch.

Cooper took a last look at the tattered tail fin barely visible above the rocks on Irontongue Hill. He would have to get up there one day soon and take a closer look at what was left of the aircraft that Pilot Officer Danny McTeague had walked away from. He couldn't imagine what connection there might be between the wreck and two sudden deaths. But he had a strong feeling that they were rapidly going to become intertwined.

It was as if the phantom shape of Sugar Uncle Victor was circling the Eden Valley again, its Merlin engines rumbling beneath the cloud cover, its slaughtered crew returning for a final mission. It was as if the ancient Lancaster had flown in under the slipstream of Alison Morrissey's Air Canada Boeing 767 from Toronto.

12

Frank Baine leaned against the wall of the post office next to the Buttercross. He lit a cigarette and tossed the match into the snow, where it fizzled briefly. He drew hard on the smoke and held the cigarette cupped in his hand as he watched two teenage boys lean their bikes against the window of the post office and run inside.

A DAF articulated lorry came down Buxton Road towards the roundabout. Instead of turning on to the relief road, it came straight on towards the Buttercross. Baine let out a lungful of smoke, noting the lorry's registration number automatically as its driver applied the air brakes and pulled up a few yards short of the traffic lights. A line of cars immediately began to build up behind the lorry as it blocked the carriageway.

A man climbed down from the passenger side of the cab. Baine couldn't see him until the lorry indicated and pulled away again towards the lights. Then he watched George Malkin cross the road.

Malkin didn't look at him until he was within a few feet.

'Frank Baine?'

'That's me. I love the transport.'

Malkin didn't answer.

Baine smiled and drew on his cigarette. 'OK,' he said. 'Let's talk about money.'

The lower eastern slopes of Irontongue Hill were a favourite area for motorcycle scramblers, bikers who liked to get off-road with their machines and spray a bit of dirt.

Only last Sunday, before the snow came, there had been a confrontation here between a party of hikers and a group of scramblers. For some time, there had been complaints that the motorcyclists had been churning up the pathways, turning the surface into mud impossible for walkers to cross without sinking up to their knees.

This morning, someone had stolen a scramble bike from a trailer parked in a farmyard outside Edendale. A patrol car driving up the A57 saw a rider in a lay-by next to the woods above the inn and stopped to question him. But he rode off as soon as he saw them, and they gave chase. The police crew were in a Range Rover, but they knew they wouldn't have much hope of catching the biker if he went off-road. A hundred yards away was an open gateway leading on to one of the paths favoured by scramblers.

The motorbike slid across the gateway and

ploughed through a snowdrift, scattering a white spray against the stone wall. The Range Rover skidded as the driver braked, but he kept control and turned into the gateway to follow the bike up the track.

The track rose steeply and started to get narrower.

'We'd better call it off,' said the passenger.

'Just round this next bend, we'll be able to see where he goes,' said the driver. 'Anyway, he'll be struggling if the snow gets any deeper.'

'Watch out!' shouted the passenger.

The bend had been too sharp and too sudden for the Range Rover. The driver skidded again, but this time failed to control the vehicle. It went off the track and slid a couple of yards into a streambed, ending up with its bumper and front wheels in the water.

The driver turned off the engine. 'Damn and blast,' he said.

'The garage won't be pleased,' said his passenger. 'It had a new radiator only last week.'

'Call in,' said the driver.

He opened his door and stepped into a couple of inches of freezing cold water. The streambed was full of uneven stones, and he had difficulty keeping his balance as he tried to get to the side against the force of the water. He reached out a hand to grasp the branch of a birch sapling growing out of the bank and found himself clutching something else – an item of clothing. It was a shirt – a blue shirt, with a thin white stripe and white cuffs. He could see the label inside the collar and recognized that it was from a well-known manufacturer, not one of the cheap Portuguese things that he bought himself from the bargain shops in Edendale.

The driver looked up, and saw that the streambed was full of clothes. There were shirts and trousers draped across the stones, and socks and jockey shorts with water bubbling over them as if somebody had decided to do their washing the primitive way. A blue and red striped tie hung from a clump of dead heather. A shoe had filled with water and sunk to the bottom, where its laces waved in the current like strands of seaweed.

Then the driver remembered the unidentified body found near here, the man who had been hit by the snowplough. There had been an overnight bag with the body, but it had been empty of clothes.

'Have you called in yet?' he shouted to his partner.

'Yes.'

'Do it again, then.'

Ben Cooper had decided to walk to Dam Street. The house where Marie Tennent had lived was no more than half a mile from divisional headquarters, just across town in the tangle of backstreets near one of the old silk mills. It hardly seemed worth getting a car out, not when the streets were still clogged with crawling vehicles and pedestrians slithering around in the roadway because the pavements hadn't been cleared yet. Besides, there were few enough places to park in the Dam Street area, even without the snow. The millworkers' houses had been built long before anybody needed either garages or streets wide enough to park cars on.

The silk mill itself had recently been converted into a heritage centre. The old three-storey stone building had become derelict and for years had been in danger of demolition, but now a new café and shop had been built. Cooper wondered what on earth had possessed the designers to build the extension out of red brick when the old mill and all the other buildings around it were stone. The Peak District was stone country. Brick felt like an alien substance.

On the corner of Dam Street, a man in a hooded parka was walking a Doberman tightly held on a chain. He eyed Cooper suspiciously, hauling back on the dog's lead as if trying to give the impression it would attack at the slightest provocation.

Cooper let him pass and walked on until he located Marie Tennent's house. It was at the end of a terrace, with a tiny front garden and a view to the side over the millpond at the back of the heritage centre. Between the house and the one next door was a high stone wall that effectively prevented any communication with the neighbours. It seemed peculiarly quiet at this end of the street. Part of the effect was perhaps caused by the stretch of water, which was covered by a thin skin of ice. Cooper looked at the houses on the opposite side of the street. Their windows and doors were boarded up. They were either awaiting renovation or demolition.

First he knocked on the neighbour's door, but got no reply. He had decided to try again after he checked out number 10 when there was a voice behind him.

'Yeah?'

It was the man with the Doberman, and he was fiddling with the chain as if he were about to let the dog loose. The dog didn't look particularly interested, but Cooper didn't feel like taking a chance. He showed his ID.

'Do you live here, sir?'

'I suppose so. What do you want?'

'I'm making some enquiries about your next-door neighbour, Marie Tennent.'

'Scottish lass?'

'I don't know.'

'I think she's Scottish.'

'Her name's Tennent.'

'That's it. Like the lager. What's she done, then? Sit!'

The Doberman sat with a sigh of relief. On closer inspection, the dog looked worn out, as if it had been pounding the streets for too long. In fact, it looked like some of the Edendale coppers used to when they had done a quick shift change-over and had been on duty eighteen hours out of twenty-four.

'I'm afraid she's had an accident,' said Cooper.

'That's copper's talk, isn't it? You don't know how to say what you mean, you lot. Dead, is she?'

'Yes. Did you know her well?'

'Hardly at all. Kept herself to herself, she did.'

'Perhaps she was frightened of dogs.'

The man watched Cooper walk to the door of number 10 and open it with the key he had been given by the agents. Cooper glanced back for a second. Two strings of saliva had run out of the Doberman's mouth and were dripping on to the pavement. The muscles in its shoulders and haunches had tensed. He was glad when the door opened at the first attempt, letting him into the cold interior of Marie Tennent's home.

The first thing he saw in the hallway was the green message light flashing on an answering machine. He pressed the button and got a Scots voice. Not Highland, more urban Scots – maybe Glasgow or Edinburgh, he was never sure of the difference. It was a woman, middle-aged, who didn't bother to identify herself. There was no phone number given either for the return call.

'Marie, give me a ring when you can. Let me know how you're going on, so I don't worry about you.'

There were bills piled up on a table and yellow Post-it notes stuck to the bottom of the mirror. There was a red coat hanging on a hook behind the door, a pair of shoes under the table, and a box of books on the floor that had been delivered by the postman but not opened.

Cooper paused, trying to assimilate the immediate impressions of the house. There was something in the atmosphere that didn't seem quite right. In an apparently empty house, an unexplained noise was immediately noticeable. But it wasn't a noise that he had heard. He moved his head from side to side, sniffing carefully for gas or the smell of burning, or for the odour of something dead and decomposing. But there were none of the smells that would normally have set his alarm bells ringing. There was a faint, elusive scent in the hallway, but it evaded his senses after the first whiff, before he could identify it. He wasn't sure which direction it was coming from. It could simply be a lingering squirt of air freshener or a suggestion of recently used disinfectant.

The hallway was cold, but no colder than any other house that had been standing empty for a couple of days. He supposed there was no central heating in these cottages. Or, if there was, it would be on a timer, to save gas. If that was the case, then this was a time of day when Marie would not have expected to be at home, and that might have meant she had a job to go to.

Cooper stood completely still and listened. Somewhere, a clock was ticking. It was one of the worst sounds you could ever hear – the ticking of a clock in an empty house after its owner had died. It was a reminder that the world would carry on just the same after you had gone, that the second hand wouldn't even hesitate in its movement as you passed from living to dying. Tick, you were there. Tick, you were gone. As if you had never mattered. It was a sound that struck straight to some primal fear in the guts – the knowledge that time was steadily counting you down to your own death.

Your clock ought to stop when you died. Cooper knew it was one of those irrational things, something that welled up from a deep superstition. But he wanted to climb up on a kitchen chair and take the battery out of the clock or remove its counterweight, to bring its hands to a halt. He wanted to demand silent respect in the presence of death. But he didn't do it. Instead, he allowed the ticking to follow him around the house as he moved from room to room; he permitted it to mock him with its sound, like the chuckle of a malevolent mechanical toy.

The first door off the hallway opened on to a sitting room. Cooper walked straight to the fireplace and checked the items on the mantelpiece. A recent gas bill had been shoved behind a cracked Chinese willow-pattern bowl, and there was a Somerfield's checkout receipt with it. He turned to the fold-out mahogany dining table in the corner. There was a glass vase containing a dried-flower arrangement standing on a raffia mat. But there was no suicide note.

The room also contained a desk, which was

packed with bank and credit-card statements, letters and old photographs. Cooper carefully separated some of the more recent letters to study them for the names of Marie Tennent's closest contacts. He took a few moments to make a note of some names and addresses. None of them was local, and none sounded like a boyfriend. One was called John and seemed to be a relative of some kind who was at university in Glasgow.

Then he saw that some paper had been burnt in an otherwise unused grate behind the gas fire. He crouched to look at it, already beginning to speculate why Marie would have written a suicide note, then burned it – or whether somebody else might have burned it for her. But when he got a closer look, he could see that it wasn't a suicide note at all. It was a letter which said Marie Tennent, of 10 Dam Street, Edendale, was a confirmed finalist for a £250,000 cash prize. She was invited to state how she would like to receive the money, and the letter gave suggestions as to how she might spend it – a brand new car, a Caribbean holiday, a dream home in the country. Cooper poked the letter, and the blackened parts crumbled into dust. If you were already feeling desperate enough, the cynical irony of that bit of junk mail might be the thing to push you over the edge.

Cooper lifted all the cushions on the sofa and the two armchairs. He found three ballpoint pens, a handful of small coins and a dog's squeaky toy in the shape of a bone. Did Marie have a dog somewhere? But she had been living in the cottage for only eighteen months, according to the agent. The dog could have belonged to a previous tenant. There were no dog hairs on the furniture or the carpet that he could see. There was a small damp patch on the wallpaper on the outside wall, but that looked more like poor maintenance. The windows hadn't been cleaned for some time, either. The view of the boarded-up houses across the street was grey and smeared, spattered with small gobbets of dirty snow and dry streaks of bird droppings.

Cooper worked his way back through the hallway and checked the cupboard under the stairs, where he found the controls for the central heating system. The heating was set to go off at 9 a.m. and come back on at 3 p.m. The more meticulous suicides would have turned the central heating off to save unnecessary gas, knowing that nobody would be home that afternoon to need it. For others, the more impulsive or self-absorbed, it would never have crossed their minds. He didn't know enough about Marie Tennent yet to be able to say which type she was.

When he reached the kitchen, he finally recognized the smell. It was so distinctive that he couldn't believe that it hadn't registered with him immediately. It was composed of wet nappies and plastic bottles, warm milk and sterilizing fluid, washing powder and soiled liners. It was the smell of a baby in the house.

13

Ben Cooper banged on the door of number 8, then tried the next house, and the one beyond that. He got no answer at any of them. Even the man with the Doberman seemed to have disappeared, or was refusing to answer his door.

After he had called in for assistance, Cooper went back into Marie Tennent's home and walked quickly through all the rooms again. He was sweating now from a surge of panic at the thought that there might be a baby lying somewhere in the house. How long could a baby survive if it was left on its own? He had no idea. He had a vague feeling that a baby's demands for food and attention were pretty constant, but it was only an impression gained at a safe distance from watching his sister-in-law Kate when his two nieces had been very young. Josie and Amy had cried when they were hungry, or when their nappies needed changing. If there had been a baby left alone in this house, it would surely be crying by now. Long before now. The neighbours would have heard it, wouldn't they? Of course they would. And they would have reported *that*, even if they hadn't bothered to report the fact that they hadn't seen the baby's mother for a while.

The thought made Cooper feel a little better as he opened cupboards and wardrobes. But then he looked at the walls of the house and realized how thick they were. These were stone cottages, a hundred and fifty years old, built for millworkers at a time when houses were intended to last several lifetimes. They had solid walls, not those timber and plasterboard things you could put your fist through. Without the door or a window open, he could hear nothing from outside the house. He knew it was possible that a baby could have cried and cried in here, and not have been heard. It was possible that it could have cried itself to death.

He pulled aside some clutter at the back of the cupboard under the stairs – a vacuum cleaner, a roll of carpet, cardboard boxes, an abandoned glass-topped coffee table. Each time he moved something out of the way, he expected to see a small bundle in a corner. But there was nothing.

'Ben?'

For once, he was glad to hear Diane Fry's voice. 'Through here,' he said. 'I'm glad you came.'

Fry paused in the doorway, gazing round the room, but without seeming to look at Cooper at all. She walked round the sofa, stopped at the window and rubbed her finger through the grime on one of the panes. 'Do people *never* clean their own windows round here?'

'It depends whether you want to see out,' said Cooper.

'You're being enigmatic again, Ben. It doesn't suit you. Where have you looked?'

'Everywhere, but not properly.'

'You take down here then, and I'll do upstairs. Take it steady, be thorough. There's no need to panic.'

'Yes, OK.'

Fry headed for the stairs. Cooper felt some of the weight lift from him.

'Diane?' he said.

'What?'

'Thanks for coming.'

'I had to – I'm paid to look after you now.'

Back in Marie Tennent's kitchen, Cooper decided to look in the automatic washer. Like everybody, he had read newspaper stories of children getting trapped in washing machines. But this one was half-full of underwear. Nearby, several nappies were drying on a rack near a radiator.

Then there was the refrigerator. It contained fruit juice and yoghurt, grated carrot and frozen oven chips, some of them well past their best-before dates. A mouldy piece of cheese and a half-used tin of marrowfat peas occupied the top shelf. In the cupboards, there were lots of pans and cooking utensils, but little food. What there was seemed to consist mostly of pasta and lentils, baked beans and cheap white wine. There was no sign of any dog food, or of feeding bowls, so it looked as though the odds were against a dog. There were more notes stuck to a cork board – phone numbers and shopping reminders. No suicide note.

He opened the back door and found himself looking into a small garden, with a washing line draped across a paved area. The line was encased in frozen snow, like insulation round an electric cable. Cooper couldn't see what else there was in the garden, because of the unswept snow, but he imagined a few bare flower borders around a patch of grass. Birds had been scratching at the snow, and in one corner there was a little brown heap where a neighbourhood cat had thought it was burying its faeces, only to find the heat melting the snow around them. Similar gardens ran off to the left, separated by low walls and fences. None of the houses overlooked Marie's garden. The view straight ahead was of the rear wall of the mill, where the windows were few and tiny, dark squares in the snow plastered to the stone. There was a coal bunker against the wall of Marie's house. As Cooper lifted the lid, a layer of snow slid back and piled against the wall. Nothing inside.

That left only one place to hide something – the green wheelie bin pushed against the wall near a gate that must lead on to a tiny back alley under the shadow of the mill. To reach it, he had to cross the garden, unsure where the path might be under the snow. There was a padlock on the gate, and it was secure. From here, the mill wall seemed to tower above him like a fortress, blank and forbidding. Of course, this was the northern side. All the windows were on the southern wall, to provide light for the millworkers who had overseen the looms. It was interesting to note that they would have had light for their work, but none on their homes – the shadow of the mill saw to that.

As soon as he touched the wheelie bin, Cooper could tell there was something inside. An empty bin was so light on its wheels and so tall that it could be tilted with one finger when it came time for it to be retrieved from wherever the binmen had left it. This one had weight in the bottom. It bumped against the sides a little as he pulled the bin away from the wall to allow room to open the lid. He pushed the snow aside from the lid, staring for a moment at the High Peak Borough Council label that had been stuck to the green plastic. It gave dates for refuse collection arrangements over the Christmas and New Year holidays.

When the lid came open, Cooper winced at the smell that rose towards him. Something wrapped in a Somerfield's supermarket carrier bag rolled around in the bottom as he tipped the bin. Half an inch of dark liquid moved with it, gathering into a corner and revealing all sorts of dried debris stuck to the bottom. Cooper looked back at the house, wondering whether to call Fry down from upstairs. But instead he removed his woollen gloves and put them in his right pocket. From the left, he took a packet which contained a different pair of gloves. Latex and sterile. With a stretch, he managed to reach down into the wheelie bin and hooked a couple of fingers through the handles of the carrier bag. The handles had been tied together to seal the bag, tightly enough for it to take him more than a few seconds to get them open.

Despite the smell, he was smiling by the time he could see what was inside the bag.

Cooper re-entered the house and went upstairs to find Diane Fry. There was only one bedroom and a bathroom on the first floor. Although Marie had a double bed, there were pillows on only one side.

'Anything?' said Fry.

'A few days ago, Marie Tennent roasted a leg of lamb, but never ate any of it,' he said. 'I'd say she left it in the fridge until it started going off, then chucked it in the bin. It could mean something.'

'Like what?' said Fry.

'You don't normally cook an entire leg of lamb for yourself when you live on your own. Or so I imagine.'

'Right. You think she might have been expecting a visitor who never came?'

'It seems the bins are emptied here on a Monday normally. The collections were out of routine at the New Year, but they should have been back to normal this week. The lamb was the only thing in the bin. That means she threw it out after the binmen came on Monday at the earliest.'

'How on earth have you found out when the binmen come?'

'They left a note.'

Cooper stood on the tiny landing, watching Fry move around the bedroom. He felt a slight draught, and looked up.

'There's a trap door over the landing,' he said. 'There must be a loft.'

'Can you reach it with this chair?'

Cooper managed to get the trap door open by standing on the chair. Fry handed him a small torch, and he was able to heave himself up on his elbows enough to see that the loft was tiny – barely more than a crawl space beneath the rafters, with a layer of ancient insulation nibbled into holes by burrowing mice. He shone the torch into all the corners. Nothing.

He climbed down and took the chair back into the bedroom. Fry had just pulled out a picture that had been stored under the bed. It was wrapped in an old sheet and covered in dust.

'There's no baby in this house anyway,' she said.

'Thank God for that. Now all we need to do is find out who she left it with.'

'Yeah.'

Cooper watched her unwrap the picture she had found.

'It's a print of Chatsworth House,' he said, recognizing the distant view over parkland to a vast, white Palladian facade. It was the home of the

Duke of Devonshire and one of the area's biggest tourist attractions.

'Very picturesque. But she obviously didn't like it.'

Cooper took it and turned it over. 'It was bought at the souvenir shop at Chatsworth itself,' he said.

'Not recently, though, by the looks of it.'

'No, but I wonder if she bought it herself, or whether it was a gift. Chatsworth is only a few miles away. She might have been there for a day out.'

'Ah. With the anonymous boyfriend, you mean.'

'It's the sort of thing you might buy someone as a gift, as a memento of a day together.'

'Is it?'

'If you were that way inclined.'

'How much would it cost, do you think?'

'A print this size? It could have been thirty or forty pounds, I suppose.'

'We can soon check.'

'Interesting,' said Cooper. 'Apart from the usual household items, that print must be one of her most valuable possessions.'

The wardrobe had mostly trousers and jeans, sweaters and long skirts. A pair of child's sandals was in the bottom, but they surely wouldn't have fitted Marie's baby for a couple of years yet. A black evening dress was still on a hanger from the dry cleaners.

'Bathroom?' said Cooper.

The bathroom cabinet contained toothbrush and

toothpaste, floss, mouthwash, a bottle of migraine tablets and a foil sheet of contraceptive pills, with half the blisters still full.

'The pills are an old prescription,' said Fry. 'Well past their use-by date.'

'More than nine months past?'

'Yes, but that doesn't necessarily mean it's her own baby she was looking after.'

'Might she have wanted to keep it secret?'

'Why? She was an adult – and it's not a sin any more. You don't get put away in a lunatic asylum for being an unmarried mother these days. Not even in Edendale. They tell me you even stopped burning witches last week.'

'Maybe there was one particular person she didn't want to know about the baby.'

'One particular person? Who?'

'The boyfriend,' said Cooper.

'Him again. Mr Nobody. We know nothing about him at all.'

Cooper placed a secondhand pair of baby shoes on the table. 'On the contrary,' he said. 'I think I'm starting to get a feeling for him.'

'You were always one for empathy. You can check with her GP, when we leave here. And the hospital and Social Services. We need any clues they can give us about where to look for the baby.'

Fry was staring at the bookshelves. She touched the spines of the books gingerly, as if they were some inexplicable religious icons. Cooper joined her and examined the mixture of modern novels, celebrity biographies, cookery books, diet books and self-improvement programmes.

'She was a great reader, by the looks of it,' he said.

'Too much imagination, I suppose. It never does anybody any good.'

Cooper picked up a copy of a Danielle Steel novel that was lying face-up on the shelf. It had a well-worn cover, and it looked as though it had been through more than one pair of hands. 'Why not?' he said.

'Well, look at this stuff. Half of it is about other people's miserable lives. Let's face it, life turns out shitty for everybody in the end, no matter who you are. What's the point of reading about how bad it is for somebody else?'

Cooper turned the book over in his hands and read the blurb on the back. 'Maybe it helped her to feel she could connect to other human beings in some way.'

Fry curled a glance at him from the corner of her eye. 'Oh, my God. Let's have less connecting and more detecting, please, Ben.'

Cooper smiled. 'Eden Valley Books,' he said.

'What?'

He held up an imitation leather bookmark that had been nestling between chapters 26 and 27 of Danielle Steel. 'I've detected where Marie bought her books from.'

'Is it here in town?'

'Just off the market square. Never noticed it?'

'If I had, I wouldn't have to ask.'

'The bloke who owns it is called Lawrence Daley. I've been in there a few times.'

'Oh? Get your Barbara Cartland fix there, do you?'

'He found me some old song books once. For the male voice choir, you know.'

'Lovely.'

'Also he had a couple of burglaries at the shop, not long after I transferred to CID. God knows why – there's nothing in the place worth nicking. We thought it was probably some heroin-fuelled dork who'd been watching *Antiques Roadshow* or heard about antiquarian books being sold for big money at Sotheby's, and thought he could lay his hands on some of the same stuff. I don't suppose a set of old Agatha Christie paperbacks fetched him much to feed his habit with.'

'And your point is?'

'I know Lawrence Daley slightly. He's a bit of a character, but he's OK.'

'Ben, I'm well aware that you know everybody round here.'

'I was thinking – if Marie Tennent bought so many books, Lawrence might know something about her. He's the sort who'd want to chat to his customers and find out a bit about them.'

Fry nodded. 'Yeah, it's worth a try. I can't see that we're going to turn up much else in here.'

'When I've finished with Social Services and the

hospital, I'll call at the bookshop and have a word with Lawrence.'

'I've got a meeting this afternoon. Let me know how you get on.'

They cleared up the books and put Marie's junk mail back on the hall table.

'What about this box?' said Fry, pushing at the carton near the door with her foot.

'More books.'

'Have you had a look at it?'

'Not yet.' Cooper pulled out a penknife and cut the tape. 'I think they call this Chick Lit, don't they?' he said, opening the box to reveal books with bright pink and yellow covers, the sort of book no man would ever willingly be seen reading. 'Looks like they're from a book club.'

'Is there a delivery date on the box?' said Fry.

Cooper inspected the delivery company's label. 'Monday.'

'The day she went walkabout.'

'She signed for the delivery herself. But she never opened the box.'

'No.'

'If it were me,' said Cooper, 'I would have opened it straight away, to see what I'd got.'

'But if she wasn't intending to read them, why should she bother?' said Fry.

'Good point. But she must have been intending to read them when she ordered them.'

'Right. So something happened between her placing the order for the books and getting the

212

delivery. Something changed her view of things. Her books had suddenly become an irrelevance.'

Cooper flicked through the pages of one of the books and turned to the back cover. According to the blurb, it was a hilarious, sexy account of a thirty-something woman's search for Mr Right and her disastrous encounters with a series of Mr Wrongs. The cover showed discarded underwear among a scatter of wedding confetti and a bride's bouquet.

'There's always the possibility,' said Cooper, 'that they were all too relevant.'

When they had finished, they locked Marie's front door on the way out.

'If only she'd made it a bit easier for us,' said Fry. 'If the binmen left a note, why couldn't she?'

Cooper looked at the boarded-up windows of the other houses, at the high wall to the side of Marie's garden, and finally at the dark expanse of stagnant water that shut off the end of the street like an icy wall.

'A note?' he said. 'Who to?'

After they had spoken to the staff at the estate agent's, Diane Fry called in and reported their failure to locate the missing baby. While she was using the radio, Cooper irritated her by standing outside the estate agent's office to look in their display windows. It was on the corner, with one window looking on to Fargate that was full of photographs of houses, with their prices and details alongside.

Fry could never understand what it was about these windows that seemed to distract so many people. Maybe it was the fascination of seeing the price of properties that other people lived in, of weighing up the unattainable and working out the mortgage that would be involved if they were ever to achieve their dream. It was another form of living out a fantasy, much like reading Danielle Steel novels.

She watched Cooper become absorbed in something towards the bottom corner of the display.

'What are you looking at?' she said, when she finished her call.

'Mm? Oh, they've got some properties to rent, look.'

'So? Why are you interested?'

'I told you a while ago, didn't I? I'm going to move out of Bridge End Farm. It's just a matter of finding somewhere to live that I can afford.'

'You're really going to do it, then?'

'Of course.'

'I never thought you would, Ben.'

'Why not?'

Fry shrugged. 'You're too much of the home boy. Too much of a man for having his family round him, all cosy and smug at night.'

'You mean "snug".'

'Do I?'

Cooper bent to peer at the properties lower down, at the cheaper end of the display. It was funny how estate agents' windows were designed so that rich people didn't have to bother bending to look at suitable houses.

'No, I didn't think you would ever move out,' said Fry. 'Not until you had a wife of your own to settle down with and have kids. Then you'd be looking for one of those little executive semis over there. Something like that one –' She pointed to the other side of the window. The houses displayed there were made of stone, but were newly built. The one she was indicating was a rectangular box with a garage door that seemed to dominate its frontage. It had a bare patch of soil at the front, and no doubt a barbecue patio at the back. The house to the left of it looked identical. And the one to the right did, too. And so, she was sure, would the one behind it, and the one across the road, and all the others that spread across the hillsides in the new residential developments south of the town. She had seen those developments, and they had a comforting anonymity; they were a bit of the city dropped into the uneasy quirkiness of Edendale, like the advance paratroopers of an urban invasion.

'It's conveniently close to schools, shops and other amenities,' she said. 'And only a few minutes' drive from the A6 for those wishing to commute to the cities of Manchester or Derby.'

'And nobody knows the name of their next-door neighbour, I expect,' said Cooper.

'Maybe. Is that necessary in your world?'

'I suppose it is.'

'All right. So what's special about this flat, then?'

'Nothing special really. But it's right here in town. It isn't too big. And the rent's reasonable.'

'You haven't got any money put aside to buy something, then?'

'No way. It's what I can afford on a police salary or nothing.'

Fry thought of her own flat in Grosvenor Avenue, in the land of student bedsits and laundrettes, Asian greengrocers and Irish theme pubs. 'A cheap rent just means something really grotty that nobody else wants,' she said.

Cooper sighed. 'I suppose so,' he said. 'The perfect place to live seems very hard to find.'

'Impossible. Most people have the sense to give up trying.'

'Yes, you're right.'

Fry walked to the car. She had wasted enough time humouring Ben Cooper. Her efforts to understand the members of her team were over for the day, as far as Cooper was concerned. But when she opened the driver's door, he still hadn't moved away from the estate agent's window.

'For heaven's sake, are you coming?'

'Diane?' he said.

'What now?'

'If it's so hard to find the perfect place to live – how difficult do you think it is to find the perfect place to die?'

14

High above Irontongue Hill, another Boeing 767 left its white track across the lightening sky as it approached Manchester. It was a few minutes late, and it was waiting for clearance behind a shuttle from Paris. Much lower in the sky, a small plane banked and turned and came in slowly, as if someone in the cabin might be taking photographs.

On the hillside below, four people turned to watch the smaller aircraft as they heard its engine. They lifted their heads into the wind, squinting their eyes against the brightness of the sky and the hard flecks of snow driven into their faces from the higher ground.

'It's a Piper Warrior. A Type 18,' said Corporal Sharon Thompson. Her plump cheeks were bright pink from the cold, and her hair was pulled back tight under her beret and the hood of her cagoule. 'It's probably from Netherthorpe Airfield.'

Flight Sergeant Josh Mason glanced at the underside of the aircraft as it drew away from them.

'Don't talk crap,' he said. 'Any idiot can see it isn't a Type 18. Haven't you done your aircraft recognition?'

Thompson went a shade pinker, but her expression became stubborn. 'Come on, Flight. We've got a long way to go yet. We don't want to be out here all day. It'll be dark before we get back.'

'Well, as matter of fact, we're nearly there.'

The cadets scrambled through a snow-filled gully and up the slope on the other side. They slipped and slid until they were near the top and were able to clutch at bits of dead grass to pull themselves the last few inches.

'There you go,' said Mason proudly. 'The trig point. The Lancaster should be a hundred yards north north-west, just over that next rise.'

The cadets groaned. 'Why do we have to do this, Flight?' said Cadet Derron Peace. He brushed snow off the knees of his fatigue trousers where he had slipped into a snowdrift.

'We're supposed to be on a navigation exercise,' said Thompson. 'If the skipper finds out . . .'

'Well, he won't find out, will he?' said Mason.

'It's foolhardy to take people out on the moors in this weather. We're not properly equipped.'

'All right, stay here then.' Mason began to walk away through the snow towards the next rise.

'But you're the one with the map and compass,' said Thompson.

The cadets looked at each other and began to follow him. The cabin windows of the Piper caught a flash of sunlight as the aircraft banked and turned over the hill ahead of them, the note of its engine dropping to an ominous grumble as the sound bounced off the rocky outcrop called Irontongue.

Chief Superintendent Jepson closed his eyes in pain. For a moment, he thought he might be having a heart attack. It was a fear that crossed his mind often these days, ever since his doctor had told him he had high blood pressure and needed to lose weight. Every time he felt a spasm of discomfort or a touch of cramp, he thought he was having a heart attack. He would sit back in his chair and breathe slowly, and reach for the aspirin to thin his blood, before it was too late. But it had never been a proper heart attack, not yet. Usually it was just the effects of one more bit of stress piled on to him by one of his junior officers, eager to tell the Chief Superintendent about the latest disaster in E Division, careless of the damage they might be doing to his cardiovascular system.

And the news this morning was so typical. For fifty-one weeks of the year his resources were stretched, but not so stretched that they couldn't cope. In fact, they coped so well that Constabulary HQ in Ripley used it as a reason to fend off his demands for more officers. They always pointed out that E Division saw less major crime than any of the other letters of the alphabet from A to D. But they also said that he was managing the division brilliantly, that he was an example to the other commanders of the way intelligence-led policing should work, that his intelligence and information were so good that the question of how many officers he had on duty at any one time had become academic. It was supposed to make him feel better.

And then came the one week in the year when the whole system collapsed. The one week when traffic ground to a halt in snowdrifts on every road out of town and his officers were tied up trying to move abandoned vehicles. It was the week when half his available manpower seemed to have fallen over on the ice and broken their collarbones, or sprained their backs shovelling snow from their driveways, while the other half had phoned in sick with the 'flu. The same week when some idiot rammed a patrol car into a stone wall on Harpur Hill, and an even bigger idiot got his dog van nicked and burned out by two teenage burglars he was supposed to be arresting. Her Majesty's Inspector of Constabulary was asking questions about how the administration budget was being spent. And the Police Complaints Authority had received yet another allegation of racial abuse from one of those thieving gypsy bastards camped on the council golf course.

And now the division had not just one body, not even two bodies – but maybe three, if the missing baby didn't turn up soon. One body was bad, and two was unlucky. Three would be a catastrophe. In fact, three was a whole mad rush of bodies.

Chief Superintendent Jepson felt he could see them toppling towards him like a set of skittles, or like mummies tumbling out of their coffins and landing at his feet, grinning up at him from their wrappings. It seemed as though there were bodies littering the landscape everywhere. They were worse than the abandoned cars; worse than the police officers with sprained backs laid out flat on their settees at home, who ought to have been dead but weren't.

Intelligence-led policing methods ought to enable him to direct a solitary officer to the right addresses with a sheaf of arrest warrants in his hand. But intelligence had grown tired of doing all the leading and had trotted off in the opposite direction, where it would no doubt get lost on the moors in the dark and fall over a cliff.

'So who *have* we got available?' he said, opening his eyes just enough to examine the expression on DI Hitchens' face. The Chief was seeking enough evidence of insolence from the DI to justify losing his temper. But, as usual, Hitchens knew how to tread the line.

'The underwater section is at full strength,' said the DI. 'Otherwise, we have three traffic wardens. After all, there's not much else for them to do – the snow is covering up all the yellow lines.'

Jepson let out a sound more like a whimper than a sigh. 'That isn't funny,' he said.

'Well, you know yourself, Chief, that we've been

talking about putting the division on emergency-only response.'

'I never thought it would seriously come to this. But a double assault, two bodies and a missing baby, on top of everything else . . .'

'And there's the ambulance, of course,' said Hitchens.

'What ambulance?'

'I'm surprised the press boys haven't been on to this one yet. It's the sort of story they love. They're bound to see it as another opportunity to bash the police – I can see the headlines now in the *Eden Valley Times*.'

'What ambulance?' said Jepson.

'Maybe it's a bit too early for the reporters, though. I expect we'll be inundated with them later on. Oh, and uniformed section say a couple of photographers turned up at the scene, so I suppose we can look forward to some pictures on the front pages, too.'

'*What ambulance?*'

'Sorry, Chief. I mean the ambulance that ran into one of our traffic cars on Buxton Road. There wasn't a lot of damage to the vehicles, mind you. It was just a shunt, really. A buckled boot on the Vauxhall and a cracked radiator on the ambulance.'

Jepson closed his eyes again. 'Tell me there wasn't a patient in the back of the ambulance.'

'There wasn't a patient in the back of the ambulance, Chief.'

The Chief Superintendent's eyes popped open in amazement. 'There wasn't?'

'Actually, there was. I was lying.'

'Oh Jesus. But hold on – a buckled boot? The ambulance went into the back of our vehicle? So it wasn't our driver's fault. That's some consolation. He had to brake a bit suddenly, perhaps?'

'You might say that,' said Hitchens. 'I suppose.'

Jepson ran a hand across his chest, feeling for movement under his shirt. He held it over the spot where he thought his heart ought to be. His fingers flickered, as if tapping out a beat. It was an irregular beat, more syncopation than rhythm. There was a faint answering flutter. He was still alive.

'What are you saying?'

'Well, it's just that the driver of the damaged milk tanker might tell a different story when it comes to court.'

'I think you can tell me the rest later.' The Chief Superintendent looked at Diane Fry, who was standing by impatiently. 'This woman they found, the suicide case –'

But Hitchens hadn't finished. 'They haven't managed to get the tanker out of the ditch yet,' he said. 'There's milk all over the road. Frozen solid it is, too, like a giant slab of vanilla ice cream. I'm told it looks delicious.'

Fry stirred restlessly at the DI's interruption. 'You mean Marie Tennent, the woman on Irontongue Hill, sir.'

'Yes,' said Jepson. 'What can you tell us about that, Fry?'

'It's an unusual way to choose to commit suicide,' she said. 'But perfectly effective, if that's what she did. There was no way she would have survived the night. She wasn't dressed for it, for a start. And she seems to have made no attempt to save herself. As far as we can tell, she simply lay down and froze to death.'

'It wouldn't be my choice of a way to die,' said Jepson, as if he had already spent some time weighing up his personal options.

'Marie Tennent was aged twenty-eight. She had been working as a shop assistant until the baby was near. Her GP confirms she was in a nervous state about the baby, even before it was born. Who knows what goes through the mind of a woman in that state? Maybe she found the responsibility too much and couldn't face it.'

'She didn't leave a note?'

'No.'

'That's a problem. The coroner won't bring in a suicide verdict without a note, or at least some conclusive evidence from her family or close friends about her state of mind. And this Marie Tennent has no husband, I suppose?'

Fry didn't even bother to answer that question. 'The main problem is the baby,' she said. 'I'm afraid we're going to find it dead somewhere. The question then will be whether it died before the mother or after.'

224

Jepson sighed. 'Oh, that's terrible.'

'No neighbours came forward to report Marie missing. She has no family locally, but we've traced her mother in Scotland. She says the baby's name is Chloe, and she's only six weeks old.'

The baby's fate would be causing concern everywhere. In the morning the newspapers would be asking: '*Have you seen Baby Chloe?*' The publicity would be their best hope of an early result.

'And there's no husband?' said Jepson. 'No fiancé? A boyfriend maybe?'

'Not that we can find so far.'

'There must be someone, Fry. I mean, nine months ago, there must have been *someone*.'

Fry shrugged. 'It was probably another case of a Saturday night out in Sheffield.'

'I beg your pardon?'

'That's what some women tell the Child Support Agency when they ask who the father was. They say they don't know, that it was just a night out in Sheffield.'

'Jesus. A Saturday night out in Sheffield? In my day, all that meant was that you woke up next morning with a hangover. Or a bit of vomit on your shoes, at worst.'

'With respect, sir, you were a man.'

Jepson smiled tiredly. 'So I was, Fry, so I was. You must have been looking at my medical records. But don't they have a "morning-after" pill these days?'

Fry laughed. 'Yes. And they've had condoms

for decades, and lots of other methods of contraception too. I suppose I don't have to mention that the man could have exercised some responsibility . . .'

'All right, all right. Did Social Services have no reports of any potential problems with this woman?'

'None.'

'And we weren't involved anywhere along the line? There was no information received from neighbours worried about her welfare? No anonymous tip-offs about babies that had suddenly gone missing? Please tell me there weren't any reports that we never got round to following up.'

'I haven't checked yet, sir.'

'Better do it sooner rather than later, Fry, before someone goes to the press with that as well. Two dead bodies are enough. That's all we need right now.'

'The patient in the ambulance died, by the way,' said Hitchens.

The Chief Superintendent was so still and pale for a few moments that Diane Fry began to wonder whether she ought to start cardiac massage. Then Jepson stirred. When he spoke, it was clear he had decided to ignore the ambulance.

'Thank God we got rid of the Canadian woman. The last thing we need is that sort of distraction.'

'But Marie Tennent,' said Fry, 'we need to find out who she left the baby with. And how do we know for certain she left it with anyone?'

'We don't,' said Hitchens.

'And where's the damn father?' said Jepson.

'Marie's mother might give us some clues,' said Fry. 'She's arriving tomorrow morning.'

'Diane, you've got another case here,' said Hitchens.

'Thank you. I was so hoping you'd say that.'

'Use available resources where they're needed most,' said Jepson, like a man repeating a mantra.

'What does that mean exactly?' asked Fry. She looked at the DI.

'It means you get half a traffic warden,' said Hitchens.

Jepson tried breathing deeply through his nose, filling his lungs with oxygen until his head became pleasantly light.

'You can tell me about the ambulance now,' he said.

On the television monitor, a street scene appeared. Ben Cooper recognized it as Fargate, with the antique shops in the Buttercross area in the background. Two figures were visible, waiting to cross the road. There was no snow on the ground. The display gave the date as 8th January, and the time was 01:48.

One of the figures in the CCTV footage was a tall, slim, white youth of about eighteen with a prominent nose and an aggressive haircut. He was followed across Fargate by an Asian of the same age, less tall and wearing a heavily padded jacket that made it impossible to judge his build. They walked with a kind of overly casual swagger that suggested they had been fuelled by alcohol to an artificially heightened bravado.

When they reached the antique shops in the Buttercross, one of the youths tapped the other on the arm as they came up behind a third figure, someone heavier and slower. The two youths broke into a run over the last few yards and pounced on their victim, fists flying. What they intended wasn't clear – whether it was an attempted mugging, or merely a moment of casual violence. But their attack didn't last long. They were near the corner of one of the shops, where Cooper knew there was an alleyway leading up towards the Underbank area. And suddenly there were more figures appearing from the alley, and the two youths were in the middle of a melee.

Cooper cursed the lighting that threw too many shadows on faces and washed out the colours of clothes. It was impossible to be sure how many newcomers were involved in the attack, but there were at least three. The white youth pulled something from his coat that looked like a knife, and a weapon that might have been a baseball bat was swung at him. Cooper saw one youth go down, then the other, and a boot connected with someone's ribs so hard you could almost hear the thud on the videotape.

The fracas was over quickly. It was going to be very difficult to sort out who did what, even if

anybody could be identified. Cooper knew Eddie
Kemp, but he could not have been sure that he
was among the group that had been lurking in the
shadows.

He had almost stopped the tape when he saw a
group appear further up the road, walking away
from the camera. There were four of them, probably all male, and it was possible they had cut
through one of the alleyways to avoid passing in
the direct line of the CCTV surveillance. There
were cars parked by the roadside, but the group
had disappeared from view before they could be
seen approaching a particular vehicle.

Cooper re-wound the tape. At accelerated speed,
the group backed down the street, and the two
youths stood up and drew back. When he ran
the tape forward again, he confirmed what he
had glimpsed the first time. There was a second
when one of the men walking away turned to
look back over his shoulder at the youths, and
his face was partially exposed to the light from
a street lamp. The picture would be grainy, but
the frame was good enough to be usable in court.
Eddie Kemp would have a lot of talking to do to
get out of this one.

The air cadets found the wreckage easily. There
was no mistaking it once it appeared out of the
snow. For a while they poked around the scattered
pieces. There was probably more under the snow,
but the smaller fragments would not re-appear

until the thaw. The cadets were growing colder and more unhappy as they watched Flight Sergeant Josh Mason clamber over the undercarriage and sit astride an engine casing. He waved his arms like a rodeo cowboy.

'Watch me ride this bugger!'

'Can't we go back now?' said Sharon Thompson.

'Don't you want to look at it, now we're here? It's a Lancaster bomber. You won't see one of these very often. Do you know how many pounds of bombs these babies carried?'

Mason tugged at the wing section, lifting it an inch or two from the ground, revealing a dark cavity between mounds of peat, and a trickle of gritty sand. Then he stopped and braced himself against the weight, his cagoule flapping suddenly in a spiral of wind.

'Hey,' he shouted, 'I think they missed one of the crew!'

'What?'

'There are bones under here. It's a skeleton! A dead body.'

'Don't talk daft.'

'It's a missing airman from 1945.'

The cadets laughed uneasily. They knew Mason had found nothing more than the remains of a sick sheep or abandoned lamb that had crawled under the wing section to die.

With a grunt, Mason heaved up the wing. Peat dribbled from the underside of the metal in dark, wet gobbets. Reluctantly, the others moved closer, prepared to humour him for a minute or two longer as he play-acted over a dead sheep.

The bones lay in a hollow where the wing section had protected them from the weather and the attention of scavengers. They appeared to be almost intact – the skull still attached to a fragile neck, the thin bones of the limbs still jointed in the proper places, and tatters of skin still hanging from the ribcage and the lower legs. But the cadets could see that the body was too small to be a sheep. And it wasn't curly grey wool they could see clinging to the decomposed skin of the skull but something man-made and far more shocking. It was something that cried out to them from the dark peat.

With a jerk, Mason let go of the wing. There was a thud and a scatter of wet snow across their boots as it slammed back into place, plunging the tiny skeleton again into darkness. The cadets gasped in horror, shuffled backwards, and shook their heads to clear the image. Then they stared up at Josh Mason, as if he alone were responsible for putting the picture in their minds.

But they had all looked at the bones under the wing. And they had all seen the white knitted jacket and the ridiculous pink bonnet. They had seen quite enough to know that the flaps of the bonnet were designed to cover the tiny ears of a human baby.

15

Today there seemed to Ben Cooper to be even more books in Lawrence Daley's shop, if that were possible. Could they have been secretly breeding overnight? Or was it only a different arrangement that made the stacks look dangerously unstable?

'It seems to me these books are just taking up space,' said Cooper when Lawrence emerged from the back of the shop. 'You said yourself you don't have enough room to get new stock in.'

'That's not the point at all.' Lawrence sighed and wiped his forehead with a sleeve. He sat down on a wobbly pile of ageing volumes. Near the top were *Observations in the Field from the Lower Derwent Valley* and *A Comprehensive Record of Bird Migration in Western Derbyshire 1925–1930*. Lawrence had a coating of brown dust on the lenses of his glasses, which must have made the books all around him look mustier than ever.

'So what *is* the point, then?' said Cooper.

'The point is that the old books are the ones my customers expect to see in the shop. They come for the character of the place, don't you see? The ambience. They like to touch the books and soak up the feel and the spirit of them. Do you think that customer the other day would have come in here at all if I were selling Harry Potters instead of this stuff?'

'No, but . . .'

'It's all about targeting. Finding your niche. You've got to identify the needs of your own unique marketplace and cater for its specific requirements.'

'You've been reading magazine articles,' said Cooper.

'Yes, there was a feature in last week's issue of *The Bookseller* about the survival of independents,' said Lawrence. 'Basically, it said I had to identify my niche market or die. Unfortunately, it seems the people who constitute *my* niche market don't actually want to buy books. They just want to browse among dusty old tomes, with handwritten prices that say "three shillings and sixpence". It's part of the visitor experience.'

Cooper picked up one of the booklets published by the Edendale Historical Society. It was called 'Folk Customs of the Eden Valley'. 'Marketing strategies, eh? We get those sort of articles in the *Police Gazette*, too,' he said.

'Oh? And what are customers in *your* niche market looking for, pray?'

'Pretty much the same, I suppose – image and no substance.'

Lawrence laughed. 'Do you want a coffee? That's something else I provide free, along with the ambience.'

'Yes, as long as it comes with a bit of information on the side.'

The bookseller rolled his eyes. 'Well, fancy that – a policeman wanting information. You're sure a chocolate digestive wouldn't do instead?'

'No.'

'I could stretch to a jammy dodger, if you smile at me nicely, young man.'

'White with no sugar, thanks,' said Cooper.

Lawrence passed him a roll of adhesive labels and a ballpoint pen. 'Make yourself useful then, while I put the kettle on.'

'What do you mean?'

'You can price up some of these books.'

'Wait a minute, Lawrence . . . I don't know the first thing about the price of antiquarian books.'

'For heaven's sake, put what you like. It's bound to be more accurate than three shillings and six-pence, isn't it?'

Lawrence trotted through into the back of the shop in a sudden waft of body spray. Cooper caught a glimpse of a tiny kitchen area. He looked at the labels and the nearest pile of books. He shrugged. Then he began to stick labels on the covers of the books, adding handwritten prices. He varied the amount between £1 and £5, according to the size and thickness of the volume. Cooper had a vague idea that the age and rarity of the book ought to count towards the price, too, but it was too complicated for him. He hoped that some poverty-stricken book-lover might benefit one day by discovering a terrific bargain in the Natural History section of Eden Valley Books. Perhaps he could suggest to Lawrence that it would be a selling point. He could put a sign in the window – *Books priced by Ben Cooper. Don't miss this sensational opportunity while stocks last!* On the other hand, putting anything at all in the bare windows of Eden Valley Books might spoil the ambience.

He priced a tattered copy of *The Natural History of Selborne* at £2.50 and added 'Or Near Offer' for a bit of variety. His attention began to wander, and he looked around the shop. On the floor, between two sets of shelves, he noticed a telltale scattering of black mouse droppings. In a pigeonhole behind the counter there was a half-drunk tumbler of whisky. So that was how Lawrence kept himself from dying of boredom during the day.

'How are we doing?' called Lawrence.

'We're doing fine,' said Cooper. 'With a bit more practice, I could get a job filling shelves in Somerfield's supermarket.'

'I like a man with ambition.'

The bookseller manoeuvred a tray carefully along the passage, swaying his hips to dodge some of the unsteady stacks of books. He looked approvingly at the newly priced labels.

'There – wasn't that worth coming in for? You've learned a new skill.'

'I want to ask you about a woman called Marie Tennent,' said Cooper, when he had his coffee in his hand.

'Do I know her?'

'That's the question, Lawrence.'

Lawrence had brought a plate of biscuits, too, but he didn't seem to mind eating them all himself. In fact, he was stuffing them into his mouth absent-mindedly, the automatic movement of somebody used to snacking all day long.

'Oh, I see,' he said. 'Marie . . . what was it?'

'Tennent. She'd be aged about twenty-eight, medium height, dark hair, a little on the plump side maybe. She could have been buying books by Danielle Steel.'

'Oh, a customer? That would be a novelty.'

In between biscuits, Lawrence began to fiddle with his glasses, leaving crumbs on the frames and a large thumbprint on one of the lenses.

'Do you remember her coming in here, Lawrence?'

'Would this have been recently?'

'I'm not sure. It could have been any time. She bought a few modern novels, fitness books, autobiography.'

Cooper's phone rang. He found it in his pocket, looked at the display, and sighed as he pushed the button to end the call. There was always another job waiting for him.

'Danielle Steel, did you say? I don't have many customers who buy Danielle Steel novels. They're a bit too popular, if you know what I mean.'

Cooper was starting to get irritated by Lawrence's constant fiddling with his glasses. He found it distracting not to be able to see someone's eyes when he was talking to them.

'You don't stock them, then?'

'I didn't say that, quite,' said Lawrence. 'Down at the end there, I do have a few boxes of books that I've bought at auctions and never bothered sorting out. People can have a rummage in there, if they want to. Anything they find, they can have for 10p. There might have been some Danielle Steels. There was a Jeffrey Archer found in there once.'

'You would remember Marie Tennent, if she'd been a frequent customer, I suppose?'

Lawrence picked up the last biscuit and broke it in half, then into quarters, scattering crumbs on the desk and on to the floor. More food for the mice tonight.

'Yes, of course. I know my regular customers pretty well – I can usually guess what they're looking for.'

'But you don't remember her?'

Lawrence shook his head, then clapped his hand over one side of his glasses as if he were testing the eyesight in the other eye. 'Sorry. Local, is she? Not a tourist?'

'Local. She had a baby recently. You might

have noticed her if she came in when she was pregnant?'

Finally, Lawrence took his hand away from his face. Cooper noticed that one of the bookseller's eyes was looking rather strange behind the lens of his glasses. It was slightly drooping and lop-sided. He wondered if Lawrence had suffered a minor stroke recently, which had left the muscles weak on that side of his face. But then the lens of Lawrence's glasses dropped out and landed on one of the books in front of him on the desk, and his eye looked normal again. Cooper realized it had been working loose for the past few minutes.

'Damn and blast,' said Lawrence. 'They're a real bugger to get back in once they come out. Especially when you can't see what you're doing properly because your lens has fallen out.'

'Haven't you got a spare pair?'

'Somewhere,' said Lawrence vaguely. He peered around the shop with his other eye, and Cooper began to worry that the bookseller was going to ask him to look for his spare glasses among the mountains of books. But Lawrence was prepared – he carried a tiny screwdriver on a little chain round his neck.

'What's the problem with this Tennent woman?' he said. 'What has she done?'

'She's dead,' said Cooper.

Lawrence laid his glasses on the counter and bent over them short-sightedly as he tried to tighten the screws holding them together. Watching him,

Cooper thought the job might take him a long time. His hands were too unsteady either to keep the screw in position or to fit the screwdriver on to it.

'Ah, well,' said Lawrence. 'So that's another customer gone, then.'

Cooper hadn't held out much hope of Lawrence. Even with so few people visiting his shop, it was asking a lot to expect him to remember a particular one. It was painful to watch him struggling with the screw, and it meant talking to the top of his head. But Cooper wasn't going to volunteer to help.

'I forgot to go and see your aunt about the flat,' he said.

'Not to worry,' said Lawrence. 'It probably isn't your sort of place.'

'No, I'm sure it's fine. I meant to give her a call last night, but I was busy.'

'There will be somewhere a lot better waiting for you. Have you tried the estate agent on Fargate? They've got some nice properties.'

'I can't afford them.'

'Aunt Dorothy is getting a bit eccentric anyway.'

'No, I'll go.' Cooper looked at the board. 'I see you've taken the postcard down.'

'Oh, yes. The flat has probably been let by now.'

'Has it?'

'I don't know.' Lawrence was mumbling over his counter, so that Cooper could hardly hear what he was saying.

'Sorry?'

'I just thought the card was getting a bit faded.'

'It's worth a try then. I'll call round at Welbeck Street tonight.'

It was in that moment of saying it that Cooper knew he had committed himself. If the flat was even half habitable, he wouldn't be able to find a reason to get out of taking it – not without long and impossible explanations to make.

He left the bookseller still trying to fit the lens of his glasses back in. Near the counter, he saw a set of illustrated Thomas Hardy novels: *Far from the Madding Crowd*, *Under the Greenwood Tree*, *Jude the Obscure*. Cooper had loved Thomas Hardy as a teenager. *Jude* had been one of his A-level set books, and he had read all the rest one after another, drawn into the evocation of a remote yet familiar world. These editions were in gold covers with coloured panels, protected in a cardboard slipcase, and they were priced at £45. Cooper wondered what the profit on that was for Lawrence Daley. Assuming that he ever sold them, of course.

It had already been dark for over an hour by the time Ben Cooper got to the house in Welbeck Street. It was across the river from the Dam Street area where Marie Tennent lived. If it hadn't been for the houses behind, he might have been able to see the roof of the heritage centre in the old silk mill.

Dorothy Shelley stood in the hallway of the

ground-floor flat at number 8 and looked him over. She was a slender woman wearing a cashmere cardigan, with another slung over her shoulders. The cardigans looked a bit frayed round the edges, and they gave her an air of decayed gentility, which might have been natural, but could just as easily have been the image she was aiming to present. Cooper was initially pleased with the look of the flat, which comprised the ground floor of a stone-built semi-detached house, solid and sympathetically converted, with the occasional incongruity of stud wall and plastic coving.

'If you could perhaps tell me what's included in the rent,' he said. 'What about Council Tax and water rates?'

'Do you have any objections to cats?' said Mrs Shelley.

'None at all. We have several back home. Well, they're farm cats really. They're supposed to be outside, but they spend as much time in the house as they do in the outbuildings.'

'That's good,' said Mrs Shelley 'Only, there's a sort of a lodger, you see.'

'Oh?'

'She stays in the conservatory, except to go out in the garden to do her duty. She's no trouble at all.'

'You mean there's a cat? That's all right, as long as the central heating works and there isn't too much damp. Who's responsible for the maintenance work?'

'I call her Miranda,' said Mrs Shelley. 'She's a stray, but she seems to have moved in for a while. I'm glad you don't mind, because I couldn't throw her out. Not now.'

'Well, I'm sure it won't be a problem. Is the electricity supply on a coin meter? Or would I get a separate bill? I could do with an estimate of the running costs, so I can tell whether I can afford it.'

'Actually, I'm worried about Miranda,' she said.

'Oh?'

'I know she's only a stray moggie, but I took her in because I could see she was pregnant. I couldn't bear the thought of her having her babies out in the cold and the snow.'

Cooper opened a cupboard door, hoping to find the electricity meter. But the cupboard was full of cleaning equipment and empty boxes.

'So I brought her into the conservatory and made her a little bed in there,' said Mrs Shelley.

Cooper sighed. 'And has she had the kittens?'

'No. That's what I'm worried about.'

'You wouldn't mind if I bought a few small pieces of furniture, would you? The odd chair, a writing desk. And I need somewhere to set up a personal computer. Perhaps over here, near the power points. I'd have to move the sideboard a bit.'

'She seems to be getting bigger and bigger, but nothing's happening.'

'The sideboard would go nicely in that corner,

Mrs Shelley. If I moved the table over a foot or two . . .'

She wrung her hands. 'In fact, since you're here, would you mind having a look at her? At Miranda, I mean.'

'Mrs Shelley, if there's a problem with your cat, I really think it would be a better idea to let a vet have a look at her.'

'I know, but vets are so expensive, aren't they? Won't you please have a quick look? You said you live on a farm, so you must know about animals. I'm sure you'll be able to tell whether I'm panicking for no reason.'

'I'm not sure I've got time. I only popped in from work. I really should be getting back. If you could just let me know a few things. I was wondering about a parking space for my car.'

'If you tell me the poor thing needs a vet – well, I suppose I'll find the money somehow.'

Cooper sighed again. 'All right. I'll take a quick look.'

Mrs Shelley led the way through the kitchen into the little conservatory. Cooper followed, pausing to examine the electric cooker and the fridge. They looked reasonably new and in good condition, but there were hardly any work surfaces, and the cupboards were old and starting to look chipped around the edges.

'Is there a freezer, or enough space to put one in?' he said.

'She's in here,' said Mrs Shelley, 'the poor love.'

243

Miranda was jet black, with thick fur that looked as though it had recently been groomed. The cat lay curled in a wicker basket padded with cushions and part of an old blanket. The basket was pulled up close to where the flue from the stove passed through the wall, and it looked the warmest and most comfortable spot in the entire house.

'What do you think, dear?'

'I think a freezer would go better in the kitchen,' said Cooper.

Mrs Shelley looked at him in complete bafflement. 'You haven't even looked at her,' she said.

Obediently, Cooper bent down, and the black cat opened a wary eye at him. It was a sharp, yellow eye set in a broad face that was almost Persian. He could see that the cat's stomach was pretty large. In fact, the animal had to lie sideways in the basket to accommodate its bulk.

Cooper put a hand out cautiously, fighting memories of cats that had taken exception to being touched by a stranger and had left their claw marks on the back of his hand to reinforce the message. But Miranda didn't move as he stroked her side and felt the rounded swelling under the black fur. A faint, rumbling purr started up, like the revving of a tiny motorbike, and Cooper gently eased his hand underneath to where the cat's belly rested on the blanket.

'How long has she been this big?' he asked.

'Well, she was quite large when I took her in,' said Mrs Shelley. 'And she seems to have got bigger and bigger since then. It must be six weeks now.'

'Six weeks? Are you sure?'

'Oh, yes.'

Cooper moved his hand over the cat's belly, feeling carefully for signs of engorged teats, then moved it backwards. Miranda didn't protest as he raised one back leg and took a quick peek at the rear end hidden under the fur. He lowered the leg and looked at the floor to the side of the basket, where there were several saucers, one containing fresh milk and the other three with various tasty-looking delicacies – one seemed to be tuna, and there were some scraps of chicken, too.

'I hope you haven't been spoiling Miranda too much,' he said.

'She has to eat properly,' said Mrs Shelley, following his gaze. 'It's very important in the later stages of pregnancy. I make sure there is always plenty to tempt her appetite. I give her a few little tidbits. Nothing wrong with that, is there?'

'Not within reason.'

Cooper let the cat settle back into its position. It eased itself over to allow space for its rounded belly and looked up at him. The cat's stare was faintly challenging, but full of conspiratorial know-ingness. A message seemed to pass between them, an acknowledgement by the cat that it had met someone who understood these things. A warm basket, as much food as you could want, a bit of affection and no demands made on you at all. It sounded idyllic to Cooper, too.

'I don't think Miranda will be having kittens any time soon,' he said.

'Oh dear, what's wrong?'

'There's nothing wrong really. Nothing that a little less rich food and a bit more exercise wouldn't help.'

'Oh, but poor Miranda –'

'And you might think about changing his name as well,' said Cooper.

The cat gave him that look again. It was a steady gaze, resigned but with no hint of shame. 'Man to man,' it said, 'you'd have done exactly the same.'

'Well, if you've *quite* finished,' said Mrs Shelley. 'Are you going to tell me what you think of the flat?'

Cooper hesitated. He looked at the side wall of the house next door, at the cat hairs tangled on the floor of the conservatory, and at a raffia chair with black specks of mould, which sat under the boarded window. He still had no idea as to the whereabouts of the electricity meter, the size of the Council Tax bills, or who paid for the maintenance. In the pause before he answered, Cooper could hear nothing in the house but the purring of the cat and the ticking of the radiators, like a faint background heartbeat, the sound of somebody sleeping.

'It'll do fine,' he said.

*   *   *

That night, at home at Bridge End Farm, Ben Cooper discovered that the Canadian woman, Alison Morrissey, had taken her story to the media. In fact, she must have contacted them in advance of her arrival with information on the purpose of her visit. It had been a clever move, and he wondered if someone had been advising her on a public relations strategy.

The regional television stations had picked up her story and there were items about her that night. Morrissey was a gift to the screen – her face played well for the cameras, being striking as well as full of both passion and intelligence. There was a particular scene in a *Calendar* piece on YTV that showed her against the backdrop of a snow-covered Irontongue Hill, where the wreckage of her grandfather's Lancaster bomber still lay. Morrissey's face was flushed with the cold, and her dark hair was in constant movement in the wind as she spoke to the interviewer. Her voice came across calmly and with absolute clarity against the bluster of the wind on the microphone. She was an articulate woman, too. There were no signs of the usual stumblings and 'ers' and 'ums' that were so irritating in people unused to being interviewed.

Cooper watched as the camera finally pulled away and lingered on a shot of Alison Morrissey gazing at the hill, her face in profile, her expression a picture of common sense and determination, but with a hint of strong emotion held in check. It wasn't quite clear how she achieved that effect – it was something about the way she tilted her head, or the angle of her neck. He didn't think it was entirely an act for the camera.

This woman wasn't some nutcase whose life had been taken over by an irrational obsession. Determined and clever Morrissey certainly was, but she seemed to be sincere too. Sincere people could be the most trouble.

The sight of Morrissey on the screen had made him forget for a while all the noise around him. The noises were the sounds of his brother Matt's family going about their usual evening activities, which seemed to consist mostly of shouting and arguing, laughing and singing. But even these seemed to retreat into the background as Cooper watched the piece shot on the hillside. He could see it had been filmed early that afternoon, with clouds already starting to build up in the east, but shafts of sunlight lit up the outcrops of rock on top of Irontongue Hill. The producer must have been delighted with the effect, as well as with the performance in front of the camera by Alison Morrissey herself.

She had certainly been a contrast to DCI Kessen, who had made an appearance in the main news bulletin, appealing to the public for information about the whereabouts of Marie Tennent's baby. 'We're very concerned for the safety of this child,' he said. In fact, he said it three times, and still failed to get any sincerity into his voice.

When the next item came on the TV – a funny piece about a quaint rural tradition in North Yorkshire – Cooper continued staring at the screen for a while without seeing it.

There was so much happening in his life at the moment that it seemed inconceivable he should be developing an interest in something fifty-seven years old. But the signs were there of the beginnings of a fascination. They always included a desire to find out everything there was to know about a subject, and a tendency to be thinking about it even when he was supposed to be on duty.

He was lucky that he had survived this long in the job when his mind was so prone to flights of imagination. Imagination was a trait that didn't always fit with routine police work. Up to now, his supervisors had given him plenty of leeway on the strength of his reputation. And, of course, because of who he was. He was Sergeant Joe Cooper's son. Who wouldn't find it understandable if he seemed to be a little distracted occasionally? But now, more than ever, Cooper was aware that he ought to watch his step.

He turned off the TV and looked at his watch. The man he most wanted to talk to at this moment was Walter Rowland, the former member of the RAF rescue team who had been on the scene of the Lancaster crash. Aside from Zygmunt Lukasz, Rowland was the only surviving witness he knew of. But it had been a long day and he was exhausted.

Maybe tomorrow he would find a chance to contact Rowland. Probably it would be a waste of time. It all happened a long time ago, after all, and Rowland was an old man by now – no doubt he would have forgotten the whole thing.

Because he had turned off the TV, Cooper missed the news bulletin later that night, when it was announced that human remains had been found at the site of an old aircraft wreck on Irontongue Hill.

Ever since he had retired, Walter Rowland liked to listen to the radio in his workshop. The sound of the voices soothed him as he worked, helped him to forget the increasing pain that would knot his hands into claws for days. The news readers' talk of events going on in and around Derbyshire was somehow reassuring; it made him feel that he was well off where he was, lucky to be out of the constant mad whirl of car crashes and house fires and endless incomprehensible arguments about subjects he would never have to understand. But tonight, what he heard on the radio made him pause on his lathe. He stared at a curl of wood as it hung from the chair leg, ready to fall. He had forgotten what he was supposed to be doing.

Rowland had been just eighteen years old when the RAF Lancaster crashed on Irontongue Hill. He had enlisted twelve months before the war ended, and had never seen any action. Instead, he had been recruited into the RAF mountain rescue unit based at Harpur Hill. Then he had seen a bit of action all right, and plenty of dead and injured men, too. But the bodies had all been from his own side – British and American airmen, or Canadians, Australians and Poles. They had not been killed by enemy action, but had died on the hills of the Peak District. A lot of them had flown unwarily into the deadly embrace of the Dark Peak, into that old trap that lay between low cloud and high ground.

They didn't say much on the radio news late that evening. But he heard the newsreader mention human remains and an aircraft wreck on Irontongue Hill. The words were enough to take Rowland back over half a century, to a scene of carnage and a burning aircraft on a snow-covered hill. There had been human remains then, all right. There had been pieces everywhere, and men charred like burnt steaks in the wreckage.

He thought about the possibility that there might, after all, have been another body the rescue team hadn't found, a fatally injured crew member who had been overlooked. But then Rowland remembered how thorough the search of the wreckage had been, not only by the rescue teams and the local police, but also later by the RAF recovery squad. And he recalled how many of the fragments of the aircraft had disappeared over the years, scavenged by souvenir collectors or tugged loose by curious walkers and left to be scattered by the ferocious gales that blasted those moors in winter.

Rowland brushed the wood shavings off his overalls with the backs of his hands.

'No way,' he said to the chair leg sitting on his workbench. 'No way on this earth.'

He had lost interest in the chair. The smooth surface and delicate turns seemed irrelevant now, an old man's preoccupation, no more than a means of keeping himself occupied and away from his memories. His hands weren't as good as they used to be now, anyway. The arthritis had progressed too far, and the pain was so great that it was impossible to keep his grip on the wood. He knew he would suffer for the rest of the week now, as a result of the short time he had spent working on the chair. Some folk would tell him to stop, to give in and accept that he was wasting his effort. Aye, and the day that he gave in would be the day that he died.

Rowland opened the back door of the workshop and coughed out a mouthful of sawdust on to the side of the path, staining a patch of snow. Then he lifted his head slowly and spoke to the night sky, as if the cold air might somehow carry his voice to the place on Irontongue Hill where the wreckage of Lancaster SU-V lay.

'All of them that died in that crash, we got out,' he said. 'And the one that should have died – that bastard walked away.'

16

The tiny bones looked pathetic on the slab. Dark peat had dried and crumbled away from the skeleton, to be carefully swept into an evidence bag. Some of the bones were crushed or were freshly broken where Flight Sergeant Josh Mason had dropped the wing of Sugar Uncle Victor on them.

'If it weren't for the skull, you could be forgiven for thinking you had found a dead lamb,' said the pathologist, Juliana Van Doon. 'At this age, they're barely formed.'

'What age?' said Diane Fry.

'Mmm. Two weeks, perhaps. We'll ask a forensic anthropologist to take a closer look. The only injuries I can see are definitely post-mortem.'

'Blasted air cadets.'

'It's hardly their fault.' The pathologist used a small steel instrument to remove a live insect that had been hibernating in the corner of the jaw. It went into another bag. 'I see from the newspapers you've been searching for a small child. "Have you seen Baby Chloe?"'

'That's right,' said Fry.

'Well, I don't know the sex of this child. But there's one thing for sure – it isn't Baby Chloe. This baby has been dead for years.'

Fry nodded. She looked at the evidence bags containing the pink bonnet and the knitted white jacket found with the bones.

'On the other hand,' she said, 'the clothes it was wearing are brand new.'

By Friday morning, DC Gavin Murfin had still not come up with a match for the Snowman on the missing persons databases and was showing signs of giving up. There were the usual missing husbands and sons on the list. There were the middle-aged men who had succumbed to their midlife crises and walked out on the boring wife, and the teenagers who had suffered their midlife crisis early and walked out on the real world. And plenty more besides.

The trouble was that none of them sounded like the owner of the expensive suit and the brogues. Strangest of all, a house to house in Woodland Crescent had established that the man Grace Lukasz described had called at no other addresses except hers.

'We're going to get Mrs Lukasz in to make a formal statement,' said Diane Fry when she came back from talking to their senior officers.

'There must be a clue there somewhere to who this man was, and what he wanted in Woodland Crescent.'

The Snowman enquiry and the hunt for Eddie Kemp's associates in the double assault were taking up most of the resources that E Division had available. And they still had a missing baby to find, and nothing was more important than that. Meanwhile, undetected crimes and unresolved enquiries were piling up. The Crown Prosecution Service was kicking up a fuss about the delay in producing files for court cases, which they had to postpone.

Ben Cooper had more actions on the Snowman enquiry that morning. There were several more visits in Edendale, and a drive out to the Snake Inn to talk to the staff once more.

'By the way, I think Eddie Kemp is going to find himself called in for questioning again,' said Fry.

'Did Forensics get something from his car?' asked Cooper.

'Nothing definite yet. But we badly need to be questioning somebody. Who's going to make the decision, I'm not sure. It might be Mr Tailby, or it might be Mr Kessen. Talk about too many chiefs and not enough Indians.'

'Are we going to get any help, or what?'

'God, I hope so. But as for who's going to organize that . . .'

'I get the picture.'

Fry watched him sifting through the files on

his desk. 'Have you found anywhere to live yet, then, Ben?'

'As a matter of fact, yes. I went to see a place last night. A flat on Welbeck Street, close to town. It belongs to Lawrence Daley's aunt.'

'Whose aunt?'

'Lawrence Daley. He owns Eden Valley Books. You remember, where Marie Tennent bought her books?'

'Oh, yes. So you did some private business while you were there, did you, Ben?'

'Well, not really.'

'And you bought some books as well, if I remember rightly.'

'It didn't take me two minutes.'

'Better make up for it with some interviews. There are plenty to be done.'

'You know there's still the Marie Tennent file outstanding?' he said.

'Mrs Van Doon won't be getting round to her yet, so the inquest won't open for a few days. It's a matter of priorities. We have to move on with the Snowman. We have to get an identification. The woman can wait.'

'That was a false alarm about the remains, then. It wasn't Baby Chloe?'

'No, this one was long dead.'

'Poor beggar. What do you think? An unwanted child? Teenage mum?'

'Never mind teenage – they have them by the time they're ten.'

'The clothes, though . . .'

'Forensics will tell us more,' said Fry. 'But they were new. It got out on the news bulletins last night, and we've been coping with phone calls about missing babies ever since.'

'Nothing from the person who actually has Baby Chloe, I suppose?'

'No.'

'If the clothes turn out to belong to Marie's baby . . .'

'OK, we're still very concerned about Chloe. Officers visited all the neighbours last night, when they got home. No one knows anything about the baby. They're going to take another look round the Tennent house today, just in case, and Marie's mother is coming in this morning. She lives in Falkirk and says she hasn't seen her daughter since not long after Chloe was born. Marie was due to go up to Scotland to visit her in the spring, but in the meantime they only communicated by phone, says Mum. We might get some more out of her when she arrives.'

'Marie *did* have a baby then?'

'Why, what did you think, Ben?'

'She might have been looking after somebody else's baby. She might have been babysitting for a friend. She might have been working as an unregistered childminder. She might have been one of those women who are so desperate for a baby they take somebody else's. There are lots of possibilities.'

257

'Not according to Grandma. Anyway, if you spent less time in bookshops and more time reading the files, Ben, you'd know that Marie's GP has removed any doubts on that score.'

But Cooper hadn't really been in any doubt. The impression from Marie Tennent's house had been quite clear. Marie had been a mother, and her baby was somewhere they hadn't looked yet.

'What about the garden?' he said.

Fry sighed. Despite what she had said, Cooper knew she was thinking the same as he was.

'The uniforms are being issued with spades,' she said.

Mrs Lorna Tennent was brought back to West Street after identifying her daughter in the mortuary at the hospital. She was made tea and settled in an interview room. She cried for a while until her eyes were red and swollen, and then she talked about her daughter and about the baby, little Chloe.

'Of course, I came down to be with her when the baby was born,' she said. 'I stayed with her for a week, but I had my job to go back to in Falkirk.'

'Did she seem all right?' asked Fry. 'Able to cope with the baby?'

'She was taken up with Chloe completely. But Marie wasn't very practical. I wanted her to come back with me to Scotland, so I could help her to look after the little thing. But she wouldn't do it. She wanted to be on her own with her baby, and she didn't want Granny being in the way. She hardly even seemed to want the little jacket I knitted for her.'

'A jacket? What colour?'

'White.'

'Would you be able to identify it?'

'Of course. Have you found it?'

'We might have.'

Mrs Tennent nodded sadly. 'Marie didn't want Chloe wearing it. She thought I was interfering. You're right, she wasn't really up to coping properly, but she wouldn't take any help. Of course, it's always a bit difficult with a first baby?'

Fry paused. 'Mrs Tennent, are you sure this was Marie's first baby?'

The woman stared at her, then her tears began again as she understood what Fry was saying. 'I always wondered,' she said. 'There was a time when I thought she might have been pregnant.'

'When was this?'

'Over two years ago. She'd come to live down here because she fell in love with the area. We used to visit Edendale every year when she was younger.' Mrs Tennent paused. 'I suppose she had an abortion, did she? She wouldn't want to tell me, because we're Catholics, you see. Marie was brought up a Catholic.'

'No, I don't think Marie had an abortion,' said Fry. 'I think she'd given birth before.'

'But . . .'

Fry showed her a cutting from that morning's

newspaper. 'We think this could have been Marie's first baby. This was also where the jacket was found which I'll ask you to identify.'

Mrs Tennent read the article twice. 'Do you know how the baby died?'

'Not yet. In fact, we may never know. But from the baby's age, it seems most likely that it died, and Marie hid the body.'

'Marie told me she had a new job in a clothes shop and was too busy to come to see me, or to let me come and see her.' Mrs Tennent sighed unsteadily. 'I should have followed my instincts, and I might have been able to do something. I suppose nobody knew she'd had that baby at all?'

'It seems possible, I'm afraid.'

But, like Fry, Mrs Tennent was following a line of logic. 'Poor little Chloe,' she said. 'It's terrible to think of all the things that might have happened to her. Marie wouldn't have done anything deliberately to hurt her, though. I'm sure of that.'

'Her doctor says she was suffering from some anxiety about the baby, even before it was born.'

'I know, I know. But that's not the same as wanting to hurt her, is it? I thought she would get on better once she'd got rid of the old boyfriend – if you could call him a boyfriend. He was married, of course. He went back to his wife after a few months, but not until after he'd knocked our Marie about a bit. She always had poor taste in men.'

Fry sat forward with more interest. 'Who was this boyfriend?'

Mrs Tennent had looked ready to start crying again, but she scowled at the question.

'I told and told her she could do a lot better for herself. Marie said he ran his own business. But after all, he was only a window cleaner.'

The number of potential interviewees had been mounting steadily, without a matching increase in the number of staff for the enquiry teams, although a trickle of officers had been seconded from other divisions. Ben Cooper had been knocking on doors fruitlessly with a file full of interview forms in his hand, when he had found himself within half a mile of Underbank. It occurred to him to wonder whether Eddie Kemp's car had been returned. Kemp would find it impossible to do his work without it.

Rather than attempt the steep, cobbled street from the Buttercross itself, which hadn't been cleared of snow, Cooper chose to approach the Underbank area from the opposite direction. He worked his way to Eddie Kemp's street, and noted that the Isuzu wasn't on its concrete apron.

Now he was nearly half an hour ahead of schedule. Next on his list of tasks was a visit to the Snake Inn, where he was supposed to take statements from the staff and try to jog their memories about vehicles that might have passed the inn after the Pass had been closed because of the heavy snow on Monday night. Half an hour in a cosy pub with a blazing fire and a pint of beer sounded attractive. Then his mobile phone rang. It was Diane Fry.

'Ben – I know you're busy, but I need you to meet me at Eddie Kemp's house in Beeley Street in half an hour.'

'Half an hour?'

'Can you make that?'

'Of course, but –'

'We've just had Marie Tennent's mother in,' said Fry. 'Guess who used to be Marie's boyfriend until he went back to his wife?'

'Not Eddie?'

'Yes. That sounds like a desperate woman to me.'

'Maybe he's got hidden qualities.'

'Yeah, she probably liked him for the size of his squeegee.'

'Do you think he might have the baby? I hope so.'

'Do you? He wouldn't be my idea of the perfect father.'

'No,' said Cooper. 'But it's better than some of the alternatives.' He looked at the street where he had parked. Eddie Kemp's house was just round the corner. 'Half an hour you said, Diane?'

'I've got to show my face at a meeting first, so I can't make it any sooner. Is that OK?'

'No problem at all.'

When Cooper finished the call, he checked an address in his notebook and turned the car round. The former RAF mountain rescue man, Walter

262

Rowland, lived only a couple of streets down from Eddie Kemp, in a terrace of houses that hung over the antique shops in the Buttercross like a line of birds perched among the trees.

Rowland's front door was one of two narrow entrances which shared a wooden portico carved with stylized flower designs. A stone mounting block found at one of the former coaching inns in town now stood outside the cottages among the remains of some frost-blackened petunias. On the end of the row stood a modern Gospel Hall, and further up, on the corner of Harrington Street, was another church that Cooper didn't recognize.

He looked up at Rowland's cottage. The first-floor windows had tiny glass panes, so grubby and dark that it was obvious neither Eddie Kemp nor any of his window-cleaner colleagues had called this way recently with their ladders and chamois leathers. The putty was crumbling away from the window frames, and the lintels were badly worn where the weather had eaten deep chunks out of the soft golden sandstone. From outside, it looked as though only the ground floor was occupied. The lower windows were stuffed with cheaper versions of the brass in the nearby antique shops, along with pot plants and porcelain figurines in front of the net curtains. These objects were the traditional barricades against the prying eyes of the tourists who passed by in the street during the summer, only inches from the private lives of those who lived here all year round.

*   *   *

Walter Rowland was in his mid-seventies and looked like a man who had been accustomed to doing things with his hands, but no longer could. He had deformed fingers, in which the tendons twitched occasionally, their movement clearly visible under the skin, like the strings of a puppet. Ben Cooper found the movement distracted his eye from Rowland's face and the sound of his voice.

'Yes, you can come in,' said Rowland. 'I don't know what you want, but I don't get much company.'

The cottage was a traditional two up and two down, clean and neat. On the ground floor there was a combined sitting- and dining-room looking on to the street, and a kitchen at the back. Rowland led Cooper through the front room, which was dominated by a pine table and black iron fireplace with an incongruous gas fire that pumped out enough heat to wipe out memories of the cold outside.

In the kitchen, Cooper saw an open back door, which didn't lead directly to the outside but into a small workshop that had been built on to the house. He saw a wooden workbench, with a gleaming lathe and tools hanging neatly in racks. There were old wood shavings on the floor and several half-finished objects on a table.

Rowland closed the door to the workshop. He did it awkwardly, not using his hands, but leaning into it with his elbow and shoulder. Then, without

264

even bothering to ask whether his visitor wanted a cup of tea, he switched on an electric kettle that stood next to the sink under the back window. Cooper noticed that the skin of the old man's face was translucent, like his hands. You could see the veins in his temples and the light from the window shining through his ears.

'Of course I remember the crashed Lancaster,' said Rowland. 'I remember all the crashes I went to, every body or injured airman I helped to carry off the mountains. That's not the sort of thing you forget. And the Lancaster was the worst of them all.'

'Do you remember the fuss about the Canadian pilot who went missing?'

'That one walked away,' said Rowland. 'The pilot. McTeague. Murder, that was, pure and simple. That man left four of his crew dead, and another one dying, and he walked away. He didn't care about them, did he?'

'Maybe it was shock. People behave in strange ways in those circumstances. He might not even have known where he was, or what had happened.'

Rowland sniffed. 'I'll give you that. Sometimes we had men that would wake up in hospital and not know why they were there, let alone remember anything about a crash. Yes, it happens. But I reckon this one was different.'

'But why?'

Rowland walked back into the front room and

sat at the table. Cooper followed, wincing at how slowly and painfully the old man walked.

'He'll be dead by now, I expect,' said Rowland.

'I don't know.'

'There's no good comes of talking ill of the dead. I wouldn't want people to talk ill of me, when I'm dead. It won't be long now, so it's something I think of, I suppose.'

'Apart from McTeague, there was only one survivor from that crash,' said Cooper.

'And has *he* said anything?'

'No.'

'Loyalty, that is. The skipper could do no wrong. That was the way they were.'

'Yes,' said Cooper. 'You're right, they were like that.'

'I always thought they would find him pretty quick afterwards,' said Rowland. 'But they reckon he made it down to the road and hitched a lift. Dumped his flying gear somewhere and legged it.'

'There was a lorry driver who said he picked a serviceman up on the A6 a couple of hours later and took him to Derby,' said Cooper. 'He never spoke much on the journey, he said. If it was McTeague, they never established how he got from Harrop to the A6.'

'Folk round here picked servicemen up all the time,' said Rowland. 'That was how the lads got home when they were on leave, and back to their bases again. Everybody did it. Nobody would think of asking any questions.'

'I realize that. And it was only because the lorry driver was local that he heard about the missing airman when he got back home from his trip. But McTeague was a deserter. They would have looked for him.'

'A deserter? Aye, maybe. But he was one among hundreds,' said Rowland. 'Blokes went AWOL all the time, but they kept that sort of thing as quiet as they could. It was bad for morale, you know. They couldn't have the public thinking their brave boys were too scared to fight.'

'It was a different time altogether, wasn't it?' said Cooper. 'A foreign country.'

Rowland nodded, recognizing the reference. 'The past is always like that, even if you lived through it.'

Cooper stayed silent for a moment, letting the old man's memories drift slowly into his head. He knew what distant memories were like – a vast sea that seemed to approach with the tide, but then merely touched the shore and withdrew again, leaving just a trace of its passing, a damp boundary along the shoreline.

'McTeague,' said Rowland thoughtfully. 'He told his crew he was going for help, but saved his own skin. Now, if he had been the one that died and the others had survived, then it would have been justice. There was no excuse for what he did. None. I just hope those four dead men were on his conscience for the rest of his life.'

'Perhaps they were.'

Cooper controlled a smile. It hadn't taken much for the old man to break his own rule about not speaking ill of the dead.

'Two of the crew were Poles, weren't they?' said Rowland.

'Yes, that's right.'

'Brave lads, those. A bit clannish, maybe, but they fought well. They hated the Germans with a venom. They hated the Russians too, mind. Good haters all round, the Polish blokes. They had their beliefs, and they stuck to them – you couldn't have convinced them to do anything else. You never heard of any of *them* deserting.'

'They were fighting for something more immediate – they wanted to get back to their homes and families in Poland. That must concentrate the mind.'

'But they didn't go back to their homes, a lot of them,' said Rowland. 'They stayed on here. That was because of the Russians. They didn't fancy Communist Poland.'

'And because they married English girls and settled down.'

'Aye, that's right. Can't blame them, I suppose. I recall the local girls seemed to like them. They were a bit glamorous, mysterious – romantic, too. Well, the lasses like that sort of thing, don't they?'

'I suppose the British servicemen must have resented it sometimes?'

'Maybe so. But the Poles were better than the bloody Yanks, anyway. If I had to choose, give me the Polish lads any time. I was glad they were on our side, though. I wouldn't like to have them against me.'

'No,' said Cooper. 'I doubt they'd soon forget a grudge.'

Rowland stared silently past his shoulder. The old man's hands moved slowly towards each other on the table, as if they could bring comfort to each other by touching. Cooper heard the electric kettle steaming in the kitchen, then a click as it switched off. Rowland didn't move.

'You know nothing about it, do you?' he said. 'You weren't there, like I was. You didn't have to pick up the bits. And there were lots of bits, you know. The Polish chap – Zygmunt, they called him. We managed to save him, but there was his cousin that died.'

'Klemens Wach,' said Cooper.

'Aye. Have you talked to old Zygmunt?'

'Not yet.'

'He won't tell you much. No, not him. He wouldn't tell you that, when we found him, he was holding on to his cousin like a mother holding a baby. He won't tell you that his cousin's arm had been cut off at the shoulder, and that Zygmunt was trying to hold it on, with the blood spurting everywhere in the snow. His flying suit was covered in it. When we found them, we thought for sure that we had two dead ones together, but he was alive, just. It was his cousin's blood that he was soaked in. You might get the impression that I think badly

269

of McTeague. But imagine how old Zygmunt feels. And they say he's never talked about it all these years. A thing like that eats at a man. He won't have forgotten, or forgiven. Take my word for it – the one wish of his life would have been to find McTeague. It stands to reason. I would have done the same, too.'

Cooper nodded. 'Mr Rowland, has anybody else been to talk to you about this?'

'Like who?'

'I was thinking of a Canadian woman called Alison Morrissey.'

'Ah,' said Rowland.

'Has she been?'

'No, but there was a bloke called Baine. A journalist. He's been here, and he mentioned the Canadian. He said she's related to Pilot Officer McTeague.'

'She's his granddaughter.'

'I don't know what he thinks I might tell her,' said Rowland. 'I couldn't tell her any more than I've told you. And I don't suppose that's what she wants to hear, is it?'

'No, I don't think it is.'

'Well, then. I'm not going to lie to the woman. So what's the point of her coming here? She won't like what I have to tell her. I told that to Baine. And do you know what he said?'

'I can't imagine.'

'He said that perhaps my memory was faulty anyway. Can you credit that? Perhaps my memory was faulty. I didn't reckon much to that. Did he mean he wanted me to lie?'

'You can only remember what you saw and heard,' said Cooper.

Rowland watched him, his mouth moving silently in the automatic grimace of habitual pain.

'Do you think I should talk to her?' he said. 'Is that what you're here for?'

'It's entirely up to you,' said Cooper. 'It has nothing to do with me at all.'

'Aye?'

Rowland tried to rest his hands in his lap, but didn't seem to find the position any more comfortable. He moved restlessly in his chair. He appeared to be saying it was almost time for Cooper to go.

'There must have been a lot of people up there after the crash,' said Cooper. 'Members of the mountain rescue team, local police, RAF investigators . . .'

'All of those. And the Home Guard,' said Rowland. 'You remember the Home Guard?'

'Mr Rowland, I don't remember any of it.'

'Aye – too young, aren't you? Everybody's too young these days. The Home Guard were blokes who were too old or not fit enough to join up. And there were some that were in the reserved occupations – farmers and miners and such. It was Home Guard men who were set to watch over the wreck, but they were none too keen on their task.'

'Would any of them still be around?' said Cooper.

'Nay, long gone. We're going back fifty-seven years, you know. There's only a few of us left, the ones like me, that were only lads at the time. The rest are pushing up daisies. There's only me that remembers the crash, and the Pole, Zygmunt. And George Malkin.'

'Do you know Malkin?'

'Oh yes, I remember both the Malkin boys. They were kids back then – lived on a farm the other side of Blackbrook Reservoir, just across the moor. I remember seeing them hanging about on Irontongue Hill – we had to chase them away from the wreck a time or two. Their dad came and took them home eventually. But they were both that sort of lad – inquisitive, adventurous.'

'An aircraft crash must have been quite an adventure if you were a child.'

'Yes, the Malkin boys,' said Rowland, 'they used to get everywhere. Their dad had taught them to be independent, and it would never have occurred to them that they couldn't look after themselves. It's something the kids don't learn these days, independence.' Rowland shook his head. 'If you ask me, they're ruining a whole generation.'

Cooper's questions seemed to have sparked Rowland's memories. His eyes had developed a familiar distant stare, the look of a man recalling a time when he had been needed by his country, instead of being discarded.

'Those Poles,' he said. 'Do you know what they called Britain when they came here? I mean the ones that came over from France to carry on fighting when the Germans invaded?'

Cooper shook his head. 'No idea.'

'They knew there was nowhere else for them to move on to after Britain,' said Rowland. 'There was nowhere left for them to go to carry on fighting against Hitler. So they called us "Last Hope Island".'

17

Some officers were starting to call Edendale's two Detective Chief Inspectors 'Tweedledum and Tweedledee', because they were rarely seen except when they were sitting alongside each other at the head of a briefing. Everyone knew that a Senior Investigating Officer was unlikely to get involved directly in the day-to-day enquiries on a major case. Sometimes, as now, the SIO seemed to be completely out of step with what was happening on the ground.

'Which car is this?' DCI Kessen was saying as Fry slid into the meeting and sat at the back. Being at the back gave her very little protection, because most of the seats in front of her were empty. Both Cooper and Murfin were among the missing this morning.

'Edward Kemp's car,' explained DI Hitchens. 'The suspect for the double assault. The Isuzu Trooper with the window-cleaning gear in it.'

Fry noticed that the officers present had split

into two groups, one on either side of the room, like opposing teams, with the two DCIs as the captains. She thought at first there was some kind of team-building exercise going on. Then she realized that they were all sitting up against the radiators on the walls. There was no warmth in the centre of the room – only an icy draught that ran from the door straight down the middle to Tweedledum and Tweedledee, who were prevented by their status from moving nearer to the warmth.

Fry took out her notebook and tapped her pen on it. With so few officers doing interviews, the regular briefings were starting to look like a waste of time, especially when there were two bosses to be kept up to speed. She ought to be out on the streets herself, keeping an eye on what was happening. She ought to be conducting interviews of potential thugs. She ought to be finding a missing baby. She had written two words at the top of her pad for the meeting. It said: 'More staff?' and was underlined.

'We're looking for a four-wheel drive because of the time line,' said Hitchens. 'We think the body was dumped in the lay-by after the Pass had already been closed because of the snow.'

'Ah, yes.'

'Forensics are still going over the Isuzu. According to Kemp's wife, he was missing all night, as was the car. And DC Cooper spotted some rolls of blue plastic, which are the sort of thing we think might have been used to wrap the body in when it was transported.'

'Right.'

'Cooper apprehended Edward Kemp on suspicion of the double assault next morning. Kemp was identified by witnesses as one of four men committing the assault. But he was released on bail.'

'Released?'

'We can soon locate him again,' said Hitchens confidently.

'But we're still looking for the three other suspects in the assault case, aren't we?' said Tailby.

'If you can call it looking,' said Hitchens. 'We've got a couple of people sitting by telephones, hoping members of the public will do the looking for us. I know DS Fry feels the same, but we were hoping there might be news of some extra staff being allocated.'

The comment seemed to go right over the heads of the two DCIs, like a passing breeze that barely ruffled Tailby's hair. Tweedledee and Tweedledum seemed to move a little closer together.

'I'll take some convincing about this,' said DCI Tailby. 'It's rather optimistic to imagine that Kemp is going to help us clear up both enquiries. Not that I wouldn't be grateful to him, but I don't believe in luck like this.'

Fry raised her hand.

'Ah, DS Fry,' said Kessen. 'What good news have you brought us?'

She filled the meeting in quickly on her interview with Mrs Tennent.

'I'll have to leave shortly,' she said. 'I'm going

to visit Kemp's house. Of course, there's no one else free to do it.'

'The missing baby?' said Tailby. 'That would be very convenient, wouldn't it? Three enquiries at once. I think I'm more interested in the clothes. They might constitute hard evidence.'

The clothes found by the traffic officers in the streambed were laid out in latex bags. There were several shirts, two pairs of trousers, underwear, a dark blue sweater and three or four odd socks. They had been air-dried and closely examined for traces of blood, sweat or other substances that might help an identification.

'We thought at first there was a good chance they belonged to the Snowman,' said Hitchens. 'The shirts are a similar quality to the one he was wearing.'

'But . . . ?'

'They're the wrong size.'

'Damn.' Tailby's face creased in annoyance. 'Do you mean some idiot's been spreading clothes around the landscape just for a bit of a joke? Do these people do it on purpose to waste our time?'

'They may actually have come from the blue bag, for all we know,' said Hitchens.

'But if they're the wrong size –'

'It's only an assumption that the bag was the Snowman's. There was other rubbish dumped in that lay-by.'

'Good point.'

'However, we do have this,' said Hitchens. 'We

found it in the pocket of the coat he was wearing.'

He held up a smaller evidence bag. Whatever was in it was so small that officers a few feet away had to lean forward to be sure there was anything there at all.

'It got a bit wet from the snow, but fortunately the printing is good and hasn't washed away. Aside from the Snowman's apparent visit to Woodland Crescent on Monday, this is the best lead we've had to date, folks.'

'What is it?' said Fry.

'An admission ticket. It's for entry to an air museum at a place called Leadenhall.'

When Ben Cooper left Walter Rowland's house, he walked into an awkward *déjà vu*. Alison Morrissey was standing in the road, with her hands shoved in the pockets of her coat. A few yards away, Frank Baine stood by a black Ford estate.

Morrissey watched Cooper as he began to walk back towards his car. For a futile moment, he thought he was going to get away without speaking to her.

'Detective Cooper, isn't it?' she said. 'Can I have a word, please?'

Cooper pulled his coat up round his ears. 'Is this a coincidence?' he said.

'No,' said Morrissey. 'Frank lives near here and he saw you arrive, so he phoned to tell me. I've been waiting for you to come out of there.'

Cooper couldn't read her expression, but he didn't think she was happy. It might have been the cold making her face flushed, but on the other hand, it could have been anger.

'I accepted that the local police aren't going to help me,' she said. 'But I didn't realize they would set about interfering and trying to stop me.'

'That's not what I'm trying to do,' said Cooper.

'No? It looks very much like it from where I'm standing. You appear at the home of the Lukasz family, and you pop up here, checking on people I want to talk to.'

'I have no intention of interfering.'

'I presume your superiors have given you instructions to keep an eye on me, in case I cause trouble.'

'Nothing like that.'

'But you visited the Lukasz family. I suppose you talked to the old man, Zygmunt. And I suppose it was you who warned them not to speak to me.'

'Why should I do that?'

'You've had your instructions, I expect. I was disappointed that the police wouldn't give me any help. But I never expected that they would set out to actively hinder me.'

Embarrassed, Cooper tried to edge towards his car, which was parked on the steepest part of the street. But Morrissey moved with him.

'Well, let me tell you something, Detective Cooper,' she said. 'Your attempts to obstruct me will only make me more determined to find out the truth. I guess I'm just that sort of person. I've always been pretty awkward – I tend to go the opposite direction to the one I'm being pushed in.'

'I wasn't able to speak to Zygmunt Lukasz,' said Cooper.

'Oh, no?'

'No.'

She hesitated, as if not sure whether to believe him. 'You had a long chat with his family, though, I bet.'

'I had to see them about a few other things.'

But even as Cooper said it, he knew it sounded weak and unconvincing. Morrissey gazed at him with something like contempt.

'I don't know why you bother to lie to me about it. Not when you were at Mr Rowland's house as well. Are you going to tell me that you had to go and see him about a few other things too? That really would be a coincidence, wouldn't it?'

'There doesn't seem to be much point in me telling you anything, Miss Morrissey. I can see you're not going to believe me.'

Cooper had almost reached his car, but Morrissey moved too quickly. She was light on her feet, and she managed to get in front of him. She stood close to him – too close for Cooper's comfort.

'I have no reason to believe you,' she said. 'But I want you to know that, whatever you do, you won't make me give up. I'm in no hurry to go back to Toronto. No hurry at all. I'll stay right here in

Derbyshire for as long as it takes. I'll keep trying until I wear down Zygmunt Lukasz and Walter Rowland. And I *will* wear them down in the end. I'll certainly wear *you* down.'

Cooper began to button up his coat. This wasn't what he wanted to hear, not from Alison Morrissey. He had enough to cope with from Diane Fry. Fry was good at wearing him down, too.

'I've spent enough time here. I've got other things to be doing,' he said.

'Of course you have,' said Morrissey. 'You're short of resources, aren't you?'

'Yes, we are. That's why the boss told you we couldn't help. To be honest, I think he'll already have forgotten about you by now. He has other things to worry about. You're not important to him.'

'Well, thanks.' She looked at him searchingly. Then the dismissive comment finally seemed to make her accept that he might be telling the truth. 'So what then?'

'Sorry?'

'So why do you keep popping up asking questions wherever I go?'

Cooper didn't know how to answer her. He wasn't sure of the reason himself. Maybe it was something to do with his fascination for family ties, the sense of loyalty that drove people's lives. He sensed in himself a need to understand it when he saw it in others. He saw it in the Lukasz family, certainly. And he saw it in Alison Morrissey, too.

281

Morrissey was still watching him. 'You're a strange cop, aren't you? I can't make you out.'

Cooper inclined his head, accepting the judgment. 'You've nothing to worry about from me,' he said.

'Walter Rowland has talked to you, hasn't he?' she said.

'Yes.'

'These people will talk to you when they won't give me the time of day. They see me as a threat. But not you. There's something strange about that. Why isn't a cop a threat?'

Cooper only shrugged.

'What did he tell you?'

'Who?'

'Rowland, of course. What did he say to you?'

'You don't know what I was asking him about.'

'No, but it's a pretty safe bet it was something to do with the crash.'

'Not directly.'

Morrissey fixed him with her grey eyes. 'You could help me,' she said.

'Could I?'

'I mean, if you're not here to hinder me, like you say, then there's no reason why you shouldn't help me. These people won't talk to me, but they'll talk to you. You could get them to tell the truth.'

'My Chief Superintendent has already told you, Miss Morrissey –'

'Yeah, yeah. No resources to spare. His officers don't have the time, blah, blah. But you're already putting in the time here. For what reason, I don't know. But if you're already putting in the time with Lukasz, and with Rowland, then I'm not using up your Superintendent's precious resources, am I?'

'I'm sorry, I can't help you.'

'Your boss said he *would* help me, if he could,' said Morrissey.

'No. I'm sorry. You'll get me into trouble.'

'And I wouldn't want that, would I?' she said.

Cooper felt he ought to get in the car and drive away, but something kept him. He knew she hadn't quite finished what she wanted to say. After a second, she took a small step closer and put her hand on his arm.

'At least give me a chance to tell you why it's so important to me,' she said.

Cooper hesitated. He wanted to say 'yes'. He wanted to hear her explain it, to know what was driving her, to share her passion for finding the truth. Instead, he finished pulling on his gloves.

'I don't have the time,' he said.

Diane Fry and Gavin Murfin drove into the Buttercross area and parked in front of one of the antique shops. A vanload of uniforms was due to meet them at Eddie Kemp's house, which they would be going over hoping for some sign of Baby Chloe.

Fry had chosen to stop by Decker and Miller – Purveyors of Antiques and Collectibles. From here, she could see Ben Cooper's red Toyota halfway up a steep, cobbled street, which was still covered in a sheet of compacted snow. Her Peugeot would never make it up there. It had never occurred to her when she bought it that she might have need of a four-wheel drive.

And there was Ben Cooper himself, standing at the top of the street in his thick-soled boots and ridiculous poacher's coat. He was talking to a woman Fry didn't recognize. She was wearing a red jacket and black jeans, and her dark hair was pushed behind her ears. Fry could tell by Cooper's posture and manner that the woman was nothing to do with the enquiry he was supposed to be on. She could see his ears glowing pink even from here. The woman was probably some old flame he had bumped into – at least, that was the most charitable assumption. If he had arranged to meet her when he was supposed to be on duty, she'd crucify him. He was wasting enough time as it was.

Fry slammed her door and set off up the street. But the shoes she was wearing weren't made for walking on frozen snow. She felt herself slithering as soon as she set foot on the slope, and she had to hang on to the iron rail fixed to the wall to pull herself up. She was concentrating so hard on keeping her feet that, when she looked up again, the woman had gone. Cooper was standing in front of his car, waiting for her to reach him.

'Who was that you were talking to?' she said.

'Nobody in particular.'

'Well, you've no right to be talking to nobody in particular, Ben. Damn it, you're supposed to be interviewing potential witnesses.'

'Yes, I've done that.'

'And? What did they say?'

'"We don't know nothing, and if we did, we wouldn't tell you." If you want the expletives, they'll be in my report.'

Fry took her hand away from the rail to make a gesture at him, but she didn't quite complete it. The movement shifted her balance and she felt herself beginning to slip backwards. She grabbed at the nearest object, which happened to be the wing mirror of Cooper's Toyota. It folded in towards the car, but was enough to save her from plummeting headlong down the slope into the road. Cooper stepped forward as if to help her, but she glowered at him, and he dropped his hand.

'You need to get yourself some shoes with a bit of grip in the soles,' he said. 'If you're not careful, you'll be joining the bad back and twisted ankle brigade. We can't have that. How would we cope?'

Fry bit her lip. 'Ben, if by any chance you've finished chatting up every passing female, perhaps you could shift your snow shoes and your four-wheel drive and get yourself up to Kemp's house. Then I've got another job.'

Fry tried to turn, slipped, and had to cling on to Cooper's car even harder. She stared at the uneven slope ahead of her, which ran down towards the antiques shop and her own car parked on the road below. She felt as though she were facing a two-thousand foot ski slope without any skis.

'Maybe you should just hang on to the car,' said Cooper, 'and I'll tow you down.'

Vicky Kemp looked like a woman who was never surprised to see the police on her doorstep. She greeted the sight of the detectives' IDs and the uniforms behind them with a weary gesture of her hand across her face, followed by an invitation to stand in her hallway so that she could shut the door and keep out the cold.

'He's not here, of course,' she said.

'Your husband?' said Diane Fry.

'I haven't seen Eddie since yesterday morning.'

'Where has he gone?'

'All he said was that he was getting out of the way for a bit. He said you lot would be coming back to make trouble for him again. He was right, wasn't he?'

'We're not the ones causing trouble, Mrs Kemp,' said Fry.

'What? You've taken his car away. How is he supposed to keep his business going? How is he supposed to earn a living for us? It's bad enough as it is. He has me stuffing envelopes all day for one of those home-working things. I hate it. But there wouldn't be much housekeeping if I didn't do it.'

'Do you have a family?'

'One boy, Lee. He's twelve years old.'

'He'll be at school, then.'

'Probably.'

Fry raised an eyebrow. 'You might have heard that we're looking for a missing baby,' she said.

'It was on the local news last night,' said Mrs Kemp. 'Baby Chloe. Only a few weeks old, isn't she? Poor thing. You never know what's going to happen to your kids these days.'

'Do you have any idea of the whereabouts of that baby?' said Cooper.

'Me? Why should I?'

'The name of Chloe's mother is Marie Tennent. We understand that your husband lived with her for a while.'

'Oh.' Mrs Kemp's eyes flickered from side to side uncertainly, as if she weren't quite sure how she was supposed to react. 'It's her, is it? I thought it might be. It's a bit of an unusual name for round here.'

'You know about your husband's affair with Miss Tennent?'

'We went through a bad patch about eighteen months ago and Eddie left me for a bit. I know it was her he lived with. People aren't slow to tell you things like that in this town. But he came back to me, and we've been back together for nearly six months. He knew it was best for Lee if he came back. Eddie is very fond of his lad. So it's all sorted out now.'

'Nearly six months?'

'Last July.'

Fry and Cooper both watched Mrs Kemp. She stared at them curiously, until a slow realization came over her face. 'You reckon that Eddie is the baby's father? Is that what you mean?'

'It seems a possibility,' said Cooper.

'The bastard,' she said. 'He never told me anything like that.'

'Has he never mentioned a baby? Have you seen no signs of a baby?'

'Not here,' said Mrs Kemp. 'He never brought it here. Eddie? Why would he?'

'If the child was his . . .'

'Not here,' said Mrs Kemp firmly. 'I'd soon have shown him the door again. Believe me on that.'

'We're going to have to take a look in the house.'

'I suppose so.'

'And are you sure you've no idea where your husband has gone?'

'No, I haven't.'

'Is there anywhere you might expect him to go? To a friend's? A relative's?'

'I don't know,' she said.

'And who did he go with?'

'It would be one of his friends,' she said. 'He went down to the pub to meet them. The Vine, that's where they all go. I'm not telling you any more.'

'He's in breach of bail, Mrs Kemp. Are you sure you can't give us the names of any of his friends?'

Mrs Kemp paused, maybe picturing Marie Tennent and the missing Baby Chloe. 'I'll think about it,' she said.

Within a few minutes, Diane Fry began to get restless as she watched the uniformed officers examining the Kemps' house and garden. Vicky Kemp showed no interest in the proceedings, except to follow round straightening cushions and rubbing invisible fingerprints off cupboard doors. Fry gestured Ben Cooper outside the house, while she phoned in and reported Eddie Kemp's breach of bail conditions. He was supposed to reside at his home address so that they could find him easily when they wanted him. Now, he would be arrested again when he was found.

'Ben,' she said. 'Do you know of an aircraft museum at a place called Leadenhall?'

Cooper was startled. 'Where did you say?'

'Leadenhall.'

'Leadenhall?' he said.

'Are you going deaf or something? Has the snow got in your ears? Apparently, there was an old RAF station in Nottinghamshire called Leadenhall, but now it's an aircraft museum.'

'I only heard of it for the first time recently,' said Cooper. 'Not the museum, but the airfield.'

'Oh? Heard of it in connection with what?'

'It was where Sugar Uncle Victor was based. The aircraft flown by Pilot Officer Danny McTeague and his crew.'

'Ah. You're talking about Miss Alison Morrissey again,' said Fry.

'Yes.'

'I can't believe this. Why does everything seem to come back to that in your mind?'

'I can't help it. You asked me about Leadenhall, and that's where I heard of it, from Alison Morrissey and her journalist friend, Frank Baine. McTeague's Lancaster bomber was flying from Leadenhall to an airfield in Lancashire when it crashed on Irontongue Hill.'

'Ben, I'm working on a line of enquiry which relates to an aircraft museum. I'm talking about here and now, not something that happened half a century ago. You're obsessed with the past.'

'Surely that's what a museum is all about – the past? Anyway, don't forget the baby. The fact it was found at the crash site makes a connection worth considering, doesn't it?'

She sighed. 'All right. Where is this Leadenhall place? I expect you've located it precisely, with your usual attention to detail when something interests you. You can probably give me the exact map co-ordinates *and* the course directions your World War Two pilot was supposed to be following.'

'It's near Newark, in the Trent Valley area of Nottinghamshire.'

'Think you can find it?'

'Of course. Why?'

'That's where we're going this afternoon.'

'What about Eddie Kemp and the baby?'

'Gavin and the search team can cope here. It's obvious they're not going to find Baby Chloe being cared for by Vicky Kemp. Her darling husband will be picked up somewhere in due course. You know there's no point in us chasing our backsides over that.'

'I suppose not. But Leadenhall . . .'

Fry waved his protests aside. She wasn't going to be put off her chance to go somewhere and do something at last.

'We're going to follow the footsteps of the Snowman,' she said.

18

The Leadenhall Aircraft Museum opened on some days during the winter months, but it was obvious that hardly any visitors came. Diane Fry and Ben Cooper found the gates open and a few volunteers taking the opportunity of the lull to carry out restoration and maintenance work on their aircraft.

The main hangar was gloomy and cavernous. Inside, a Spitfire had been roped off and the armour plating round its nose had been dismantled. A man in blue overalls was doing something with a wrench deep inside the engine. The clink of metal against metal echoed in the hangar like a pebble rattling at the bottom of a deep well.

A twin-engined Vickers Wellington seemed to be the central exhibit. Cooper edged towards the information board under its nose. This wartime bomber had been recovered from a remote Norwegian fjord where it had crashed in 1941 after being damaged by a German fighter. Its canvas fuselage had been torn away in large sections, exposing a metal grid-like structure underneath and offering glimpses of the flight cabin and the navigator's table. The aircraft's upper surfaces were painted a camouflage green, but underneath it was black, where it would be seen only against the sky.

The Wellington had a powerful presence, even in this setting, and it reminded Cooper of something. He learned from the information board that Wellington bombers had been referred to affectionately by their crews as 'Wimpeys' after a fat, hamburger-eating character in the Popeye cartoons. But the impression it made on him was far from cartoon-like. There was nothing harmless and bumbling about this machine. The comparison he was trying to grasp was more animal-like.

After they had crossed the concrete floor, Cooper turned for another view of the Wellington. The Perspex panels of the cockpit were like a pair of dark eyes staring down the long nose and over the front gun turret towards the sky beyond the hangar walls. For Cooper, there was nothing cosy or nostalgic in the impression at all. The aircraft had a snout like a muzzled hunting dog.

'How recent was the Snowman's visit here, Diane?' he said.

Fry paused by the sliding doors of the hangar, near a set of display boards filled with newspaper reports of Second World War air battles. *Fighter Command Spitfires destroy eight Messerschmitts over English Channel.*

'Sunday 6th January.'

'The day before he was killed, probably.'

'Somebody might remember him – it was only a week ago. And look at this place – it isn't exactly heaving with crowds, is it?'

'No, you're right. But, Diane . . .'

'What?'

'I'm supposed to be interviewing the staff at the Snake Inn this afternoon, trying to jog their memories about four-wheel drive vehicles. You could have brought Gavin here with you. They didn't need *him* at the Kemps either.'

'Yes, I could have brought Gavin.'

'So why am I here?'

'Perhaps I wanted to keep an eye on you.'

Outside, an elderly man in an ill-fitting flying suit with wing insignia was washing the fuselage of an Avro Shackleton. He had a stepladder, a bucket of water and a cloth, and he went about his job lovingly, with complete absorption and wonder, like a grandfather who had been asked to change the nappy of a brand new grandchild.

'Perhaps we could ask him to do the windows at West Street,' said Fry, 'now that Eddie Kemp has gone on strike. He looks as though he'd make a nice job of it.'

'I think it's a labour of love,' said Cooper.

Fry snorted. 'Cleaning?'

'It's a question of *what* he's cleaning.'

'It's a plane,' said Fry.

'Yes, it is.'

She shook her head, exasperated. 'Well, he's obviously only the hired hand. Let's find someone who knows what's what around here.'

They asked at the shop about possible sightings of the Snowman, but the woman behind the counter said that she didn't normally work on Sundays and directed them back to the Shackleton and the man with the stepladder.

'Mr Illingworth?' said Fry.

'That's me.'

They introduced themselves. 'We're enquiring about this man,' said Fry. 'We believe he visited last weekend. Sunday 6th January.'

Illingworth looked at the photograph. 'Is he dead, then?'

'I'm afraid so, sir.'

'Funny,' he said. 'I don't think the other lot knew that.'

'Other lot? What other lot?'

'The last lot of police that came.'

'Sorry?'

'It was only two days ago. I suppose you've found him since then, have you?'

'Mr Illingworth, are you saying some police officers have been here already asking about this man?'

'Yes, but they had a photograph of him when he was alive.'

'Where were these officers from?'

'Sorry, I can't remember. Weren't they your lot?'

'I don't think so,' said Fry. 'We're from Derby-shire.'

'Ah, out of your area, then. I assume they were Nottinghamshire Police.'

'And they were trying to identify this man?'

'No, no, they seemed to know who he was. They had a name, even.'

'Which was?'

'Sorry . . .'

'You can't remember. That's OK.'

Cooper looked at her. He knew what she was thinking: a lack of communication somewhere had not only led to duplication of effort, but a waste of several days of their time in trying to identify the Snowman. Surely Gavin Murfin had contacted Nottinghamshire for their missing persons – they were one of Derbyshire's neighbouring forces. Fry's jaw clenched. Somebody was going to be in trouble. And for once, it wasn't Ben Cooper.

'Wait here,' she said, 'while I make some calls.'

As she walked off, Illingworth shrugged. 'Sorry I can't remember any more,' he said. 'Sounds like a bit of a cock-up, doesn't it?'

'You've got a Lancaster here, haven't you?' said Cooper.

'Ah, you're interested in the Lanc, are you? Yes, one of the few left, she is. Do you know we had to buy this one from Canada? All but a couple of the RAF's Lancs were scrapped. Or left to rot.'

'Where is it?'

'She's in a separate hangar of her own. We're still working on her. There's a bit of restoration to do yet. In fact, I think they're bringing her out now to turn over the engines.'

The doors of the next hangar stood wide open. Although the displays were protected by wooden barriers, Cooper was able to reach across and touch the side of the Lancaster. To his surprise, it felt light and fragile. It was nothing more than a series of sheets of thin alloy, held together by thousands of tiny rivets. That it had ever travelled to Germany and back was a miracle.

A shaft of winter sun came through the Perspex panels in the hangar roof. The weak light lit up tiny details here and there on the Lancaster – a patch of worn red paint on the fuselage markings, a stencilled number on an escape hatch cover, and the rust caked on the barrel of a Vickers machine gun that poked from a shattered turret.

A small tractor attached to the undercarriage of the Lancaster was slowly towing the big aircraft out on to the tarmac. It was a very tight fit – the wing tips cleared the side of the hangar entrance by only a foot or two on either side.

'Most of the people who work here are volunteers, I suppose – enthusiasts,' said Cooper.

'That's right. We couldn't do without them. They put their own time and effort in, and their own money, too. It's an expensive hobby.'

There was a metal ladder leaning against the fuselage of the Lancaster. Cooper couldn't resist a peep inside the open door. He was amazed by the confined space inside the aircraft, which looked so large from outside. Forward from the door, the main spar half-blocked the passage, narrowing it to two tiny compartments behind the cockpit.

Cooper glanced back at Illingworth. 'Which crew members sat in these compartments?'

'The wireless operator and the navigator. Then there's the flight engineer's position, right in the passage between the navigator and the pilot. And down there, under the pilot's feet, is the bubble where the bomb aimer lay. The best view in the aircraft, he had.'

Some of the Perspex looked very new and clear to Cooper. But inside the aircraft, the instruments and equipment were all obviously original. To his left, towards the tail, the fuselage narrowed even more. Down at the end of a dark tunnel was a glimpse of curved sliding doors, left partly open.

'That must be the rear gunner's turret.'

'Correct,' said Illingworth. 'That's Tail-End Charlie's place. The coldest, loneliest spot on a Lancaster, without doubt. It was so cold back there that the rear gunner had to wrap himself up in an electrically heated suit, so that his arms and legs didn't seize up completely and leave him useless.'

Cooper could see that the rear turret was also the most vulnerable position. And in fact, it was the one where you would be unable to see anything of your own aircraft, as you were flying backwards.

The space in there was tiny, barely big enough for a man to sit. The breech blocks of four machine guns jutted through the Perspex, and it would be impossible to move your feet more than a couple of inches either way because of the ammunition feeds, rising like conveyor belts from the base of the turret.

Illingworth was warming to Cooper's interest in the aircraft. 'You'll notice that the only crewmen with a proper view out of the aircraft were the pilot, the bomb aimer, and the flight engineer, all up front. The navigator had to work in a curtained-off area – he wouldn't have any idea what was going on outside, except for what he heard on his headphones. That glass bubble above his position is the astrolabe, for making sightings of the stars – all very well, as long as there were no clouds.'

'Of course.'

But on the night Uncle Victor had crashed, there had been plenty of cloud over the Peak District. Cooper's eyes were drawn back to the rear gunner's turret. Because of the cramped space, the rear gunner couldn't have been a big man, or he wouldn't have fitted. Of course, Sergeant Dick Abbott had been only five foot six inches tall. The doors would have slid shut behind Abbott quite easily as he sealed himself up for his last journey.

Cooper shuddered. Noticing his expression, Illingworth smiled grimly. 'The Lancaster was known to be the worst aircraft to get out of in an emergency. And the quickest to sink, if it was ditched into the sea. Makes you think, doesn't it?'

Surely this Lancaster would be haunted. Cooper could imagine the aircraft standing at night in its darkened hangar, full of spectral sounds – the quiet throwing of switches and levers, the muttering of conversations on the intercom.

'We're going to have to ask you to stand clear now,' said Illingworth. 'They're going to start her up in a minute. You don't want to be turned into mincemeat by the propellers.'

Cooper climbed down reluctantly. 'How much would this aircraft be worth?' he asked.

'Worth?' The man looked astonished at the question, as if someone had suggested selling the Queen Mother. 'How can anyone say what she's worth? She's priceless.'

'Where on earth do you get the parts to restore it?'

'Wherever we can. Aviation scrapyards, dealers, other museums. Some bits have to be made new, of course. We need a new main spar for the Lanc if we're ever going to get her airworthy again. You don't find many of those lying about, so we'll have to get somebody to make one. That's a long way in the future, though, for this aircraft.'

'Have you got a collection here, too? I mean memorabilia, that sort of thing?'

'Yes, lots of stuff. There's a display over in the old control tower building.'

'And I suppose some of your volunteers have their own collections.'

'Of course they do. They're enthusiasts. Some of them get into it in a big way. They spend all their money filling their homes with stuff. You wouldn't believe it. But I suppose it's like anything else. If you get keen on it, you'll go to any lengths to collect whatever you can get your hands on.'

'They're men usually, I imagine,' said Cooper.

'Well, as it happens, yes.'

'Who have you got here who's like that? Can you give me a few names, sir?'

Illingworth began to reel off names until Cooper stopped him.

'Who was that last one?'

'Graham Kemp. Now, he's a complete nutcase for collecting. Graham travels all over the country if he hears of something that might be interesting. He even takes his holidays in places where he can look at aircraft wrecks or scrapyards. His wife gets totally naffed off about it.' There was a burst of noise, and the propellers of the four Merlin engines began to turn. Illingworth had to raise his voice against the noise. 'We haven't seen him around here for a bit, but he's one of the keenest collectors I know. He's from your area, too – Edendale. Is it Kemp you're interested in?'

'Graham Kemp,' said Cooper thoughtfully. 'Perhaps it is.'

Fry appeared at the corner of the hangar. She didn't look any happier. 'Nottinghamshire don't know what the hell I'm talking about,' she said.

301

'But they're going to ask around.'

'Great.'

'Great? Oh, it's absolutely bloody marvellous.'

Then the engines of the Lancaster caught with a roar. Cooper could see the frame of the aircraft shaking so hard that it was a surprise the rows of rivets didn't pop out. No wonder the crew had come back deafened and wobbly when they set foot on the ground again.

The noise of the engines was deafening, but exciting too. It reminded Cooper of the sound of an orchestra tuning up before a concert. There was nothing except roar and discord, but it held out the promise of something entirely different to come.

Diane Fry listened sceptically while Ben Cooper told her about Graham Kemp.

'Some relation of your friend Eddie's?' she said.

'Quite possibly. I've an idea that he has a brother.'

'Maybe he knows where Eddie is, then.'

'I can soon track him down.'

'No, Ben. It'll have to wait.'

Then Fry was silent for a while. For half an hour, Cooper was left to his own thoughts as he drove towards a yellow sunset, which dripped over the Dark Peak hills like honey running away into the east. Everything he could see ahead of him was distorted by long shadows lying flat on the landscape. In this light, snow could be black, while the bleak gritstone tors could shine like polished gold.

By the time they were approaching Edendale

itself, though, the sunset had gone. They were left with the street lamps and the wet roads, and the stained heaps of snow lying in the gutters. In every house they passed, curtains glowed and flickered in the windows as people hugged their own little lives to themselves. But the hills were lost in the darkness somewhere above the town.

'You've still got a job left to do, haven't you, Ben?' said Fry as they approached West Street.

'Have I?'

'Interviews with the staff at that place near where the Snowman was found.'

'The Snake Inn,' said Cooper.

'You've got it.'

'It's quite a long drive from here.'

'You'd better get going, then.'

They saw Gavin Murfin in the car park chatting to members of the task force. He shrugged when he saw Diane Fry.

'I take it there was no Baby Chloe at Eddie Kemp's house, Gavin?' she said.

'Not a sign. Not a single used nappy.'

'Why doesn't that surprise me? If anything goes right this week, I'll buy you another singing lobster.'

The licensees of the Snake Inn ought to have been the best people to remember vehicles passing along the road after the heavy snowfall had started early on Tuesday morning. There were hardly any buildings for miles in either direction on the A57, and the inn relied on tourists or passing trade between

Derbyshire and Manchester. They would notice when no vehicles were passing; and they were the first place to be cut off when the snow came.

Yet when Ben Cooper went through their statements with them carefully, they could remember nothing except the snowploughs battling their way over the Pass from either direction. The plough from the east they remembered particularly, because its crew had stopped at the inn to fill up their flasks, shortly before they found the body. That was the sort of incident that focused the memory wonderfully. But no matter how many times Cooper went over their statements, the Snake Inn licensees recalled no four-wheel drive cars struggling through the snow that morning.

So had somebody been very lucky indeed? Or had the Snowman's body been in the lay-by during the night, in full view of passing traffic? Cooper sighed. He was going to have to tell Diane Fry to re-draw her time line.

On the way back from the Snake Inn, it wasn't a long diversion from Manchester Road into Woodland Crescent, Edendale. In fact, it could even be called a short-cut. Cooper drove down the Crescent first, then reversed and came back again, checking for signs of Alison Morrissey or Frank Baine hanging around the Lukasz bungalow. The blue BMW was parked in the drive again, and its windscreen was clear of snow and frost, which suggested it had been out and had returned quite recently. If Peter Lukasz had just finished a shift at the hospital, it might be a good time to catch him.

'We're rather popular, aren't we?' said Lukasz when he answered the door. 'Some people can't keep away.'

'I wondered if this was a better time to speak to your father,' said Cooper.

'It's never a better time.'

'Could we try? Just for a minute?'

'Very well. If that's what it takes to convince you.'

Zygmunt Lukasz was sitting at a small table in the back room, with a pad of lined A4 paper open in front of him. He was writing with a thick rollerball pen, which produced a convoluted black script. There was line after line of it building up, creating a dense scrawl on the page. Cooper noticed that the old man's left hand had the two middle fingers missing. There were two stumps where the fingers had been cut off below the bottom knuckle.

'Can I talk to you, Mr Lukasz? I'd like to ask you a few questions.'

The old man didn't look up from the table. He spoke a few words in a language Cooper took to be Polish. He looked at the younger Lukasz, who seemed a little embarrassed.

'My father says he has nothing to say to you.'

'Have you explained to him why I'm here?' asked Cooper.

'Yes, of course.'

Then the old man spoke again, more urgently.

'And that was?'

'He says the Canadian woman can go to hell,' said Peter. 'I'm sorry.'

'Did he say "sorry"?'

'No – I did.'

The old man continued to write. The pen moved slowly but steadily, filling in the lines of the page with solid, black letters that flowed and overlapped until they had created an intricate spider's web, each word entwined with the ones above and below it. Cooper watched as Zygmunt reached the bottom of the page, turned to a new sheet and continued writing in an almost unbroken movement.

'Why does your father refuse to speak English to me?' said Cooper.

Peter shifted from one foot to the other uneasily. There was a silence for a moment, except for the faint scratching of the pen. Then the old man placed a firm full stop and looked up for the first time. The blue of his eyes was so pale that it was almost ash grey. Even the sky was only ever that shade of blue in the winter, seen on a bright, cold day from the top of the moors.

'You don't understand,' said Peter.

'I understand that Mr Lukasz speaks English perfectly well. He knows what I'm saying to him. But he hasn't the courtesy to answer me in a language I can comprehend.'

'It isn't a matter of courtesy. My father finds he isn't able any longer to think in two languages

306

at once. He's working in Polish, therefore he's thinking in Polish. Of course, he understands what we're saying, but his brain isn't able to translate his own thoughts in reply.'

'It's a pity he's forgotten how to communicate as well as he did with his English-speaking comrades in Sugar Uncle Victor,' said Cooper, holding the old man's stare. He was pleased to see an expression of pain drift across the blue eyes, like the gap in the clouds closing for a moment.

'Please,' said Peter. 'I don't think this is helping.'

'The police can call on the services of an official interpreter,' said Cooper. 'We have an entire list of them. But then it would have to become a formal interview, at the police station.'

Cooper hoped they didn't realize how far he was flying a kite. There was no way he could get approval to pay for an interpreter. He shouldn't even be spending time here himself. There was no official police enquiry that would justify the use of resources.

Zygmunt spoke for the final time. The last couple of words were said with a jerk of the head and an explosive sound made on the lips, which sent a spray of saliva over the pages he was writing on.

'What was *that*?' said Cooper.

'My father says let the Canadian woman pay for an interpreter herself,' said Peter.

'And the last part of it?'

'And good luck to her.'

'Oh, yes?'

The old man lowered his head and went back to his writing. Cooper saw the black ink blur where his saliva had wet the page. But the pen skated over it and continued to flow until it was approaching the foot of another page. Staring at it made his eyes cross. There didn't seem to be a single paragraph break in the whole lot.

Cooper turned and walked out of the room. Peter Lukasz followed him, closing the door carefully so that they were out of earshot of the old man.

'I'm sorry,' he said.

'So you said.'

'It isn't you,' said Peter. 'He won't talk to us in English either. Can't, I suppose I mean. His brain just doesn't seem to be able to cope with it at the moment.'

'What is it he's writing?' asked Cooper when they were back in the hallway.

'I thought you would have guessed that,' said Lukasz.

'No.'

'For some reason, he can only write it in Polish. I think it's all been there in his mind for years and years, waiting to come out, waiting for him to pick up that pen. Finally, he's decided to do it, before it's too late.'

'To do what?' said Cooper.

'To put the record straight. You see, my father is writing his account of the crash of Sugar Uncle Victor.'

308

19

DCI Kessen buttonholed Diane Fry in the corridor on her way back from the interview room. He put a hand on her shoulder to delay her as Gavin Murfin walked ahead.

'Detective Sergeant Fry – everything under control?'

Fry felt the muscles in her shoulder knotting where his hand was touching her. She drew in her breath steadily to control the reaction, which she knew was unreasonable. She wondered whether DCI Kessen had been made aware of her background, her reason for transferring to Derbyshire from the West Midlands. Some men had no idea how to behave towards a woman who had been a rape victim. On the other hand, maybe he had too little interest in her even to have read her file. She was afraid he was measuring up to be her worst nightmare – a large stumbling block in her progress up the promotional ladder. A transfer from E Division was starting to look even more attractive.

'Yes, sir,' she said.

'Good team that you have, I expect?' he said.

'Excellent.'

Kessen took his hand off her shoulder, but he was still standing too close, several inches inside her personal space. Fry could see that he was the sort of man who wasn't aware of the effect he had on people. Probably he had been walking a fine line for a while, waiting for someone to put their hand up and complain.

'DC Cooper now – a very conscientious officer, isn't he? An example to some of the others.'

'Sure,' said Fry. Well, compared to the ones who rang in sick with bad backs, she thought. But where the hell was this paragon of virtue right now? Just like yesterday, he had managed to make a few simple enquiries last for hours.

Fry looked at her watch. If only she could get away from meetings for a while, she would get out there and find that example to the others, and kick his arse.

'Gavin, has Ben Cooper called in yet?' she said as she caught up with him in the CID room.

'No. He's interviewing the staff at the Snake Inn, isn't he?'

'Let's hope so. He should have called by now.'

'He'll be having a pie and a couple of pints while he's there,' said Murfin. 'I would.'

'Back to the phones, Gavin.'

'Yes, ma'am.'

'And leave the lobster alone.'

*　　*　　*

Ben Cooper perched on the sofa in the sitting room of the Lukasz bungalow. It was much too warm for him. Even with his heavy waxed coat hanging in the hallway, he still felt stifled by the central heating.

'You don't sound as though you're interested in the past,' he said. 'Doesn't your father's history interest you?'

'Oh, it used to,' said Peter Lukasz. 'But time passes, and people change. There comes a point when we have to move on.'

'Perhaps your father doesn't feel able to move on yet.'

'Oh, I think that's exactly right,' said Lukasz.

Grace Lukasz had disappeared somewhere to the back of the house to leave them alone. Her departure had left Peter looking uncertain. He was reluctant to sit down, but instead stood on the rug in front of the fireplace, swaying gently on the balls of his feet, his gaze tending to drift past Cooper's shoulder to the window that looked out on Woodland Crescent.

'We all treasure our Polish heritage, of course,' said Lukasz. 'But most of us have become as much British now as Polish. My father is going the other way; he's going backwards, regressing into his past, almost into a time when he knew no English. Being two nationalities is a delicate enough balance as it is. I don't need my father trying to push me the wrong way.'

'But you were born here, weren't you? Is it such a difficult balance?'

311

'You'd be surprised,' said Lukasz. 'Of course, I'm half English. But every time I'm asked to spell my name, I feel a bit foreign. Some Poles came up with anglicized versions when they settled here. My name, for example, could so easily have been changed to Lucas. Nobody would have questioned it then. Peter Lucas. It sounds fine, doesn't it? You couldn't get much more English than that. But there are other people who believe it would be a betrayal of some kind, a denial of our nationality, a sacrifice of a vital part of ourselves.'

'Your father being one of those people?'

'Yes, my father. And his sister, my aunt Krystyna.'

'But what do *you* think?'

'It has to be what seems right for the individual, doesn't it? It has to be a question of how we see ourselves, whether we think of ourselves as English or Polish, or whatever. All that matters is what each person thinks his own identity is, and whether he's willing to sacrifice any part of it to be able to fit in. That's the question we have to ask ourselves.'

'Not as easy a question as it sounds.'

'Did you notice my father's hand?' asked Lukasz.

'You mean the fingers he has missing?'

'Yes. He lost them as a result of frostbite and his injuries in the crash. It was caused by the delay in rescuing them from the moor afterwards. My father took his gloves off to try to staunch blood from the wounds that Klemens had suffered.'

Cooper nodded. But that hadn't been in the books he'd read.

'My father and Klemens were more than just cousins,' said Lukasz. 'They were very close, like brothers – and that's not an exaggeration. Not for Poles. They had been brought up together in their village in Polskie province. They escaped together when the Germans came, and they went to France. They had to leave when France was invaded too. Hitler called the Polish servicemen "Sikorski's Tourists" after their commanding officer, and because they moved from one country to another. He shouldn't have been so contemptuous, because they were some of the best fighters there were. They had passion, you see. They had an enemy to fight. Eventually, Zygmunt and Klemens arrived in England to fight with the RAF. The British airmen used to called them "The Terrible Twins" because they were always together and they thought they looked alike.'

'Were they really very much alike?'

'Not all that much.'

'Do you have a photograph?'

'My father has some. They're very precious to him, but I suppose he won't mind you seeing them.'

Lukasz was gone only a moment. But when he re-appeared he looked almost furtive, as if he were carrying something shameful.

'This one was taken when my father and Klemens Wach were first based in Britain. They were billeted

313

in a hotel in Brighton. I think they probably had a good time there for a while.'

'Who were the girls?'

'I've no idea. There were always plenty of girls, according to my father. Plenty of girls for a good-looking young man in a pilot's uniform. And the Polish airmen were a bit exotic too, I suppose. Why do you ask?'

'I was thinking one of them might be your mother. A wartime romance, was it?'

'Oh no, they didn't meet until after the war.'

'I see.'

As far as Cooper could tell, almost the only thing that made Lukasz and Wach look like twins was the uniform. Almost the only thing. But there was also something about the jaunty angle of their caps, the way they held their shoulders, and a certain Slavic set of the eyes. Zygmunt Lukasz was taller and more heavily built and had a greater air of maturity. In the picture, he had one arm round a girl with dark permed hair, and the other across the shoulders of his slighter cousin, Klemens. He looked not so much like a twin, more like an uncle, or at least an older brother.

'According to the inquest report, Klemens Wach died of serious multiple injuries. They weren't specific about what caused them.'

Peter Lukasz shrugged. 'My father has never talked about the details of the crash. It was pretty horrific, by all accounts. Some of the British crew members were actually dismembered, I gather.

They were thrown through the framework of the aircraft. Two others burned to death, trapped in the wreckage. McTeague had a lot to answer for. He was lucky they never tracked him down.'

'Do you think McTeague is dead, Mr Lukasz?'

'I don't know. My guess would be that he got back to Canada as soon as he could. McTeague had a wife and a newborn child over there, remember. Apparently, he talked about them all the time, and said he was desperate to get back home and see them. You know, at one time, my father even talked about going to Canada to look for him. But I think, in the end, he preferred to carry the pain and the memories with him intact. His hatred of Danny McTeague has been like a talisman to be cherished; it's kept his memory of Klemens fresh and alive, if that makes sense. If he knew McTeague had died peacefully in his sleep somewhere, it would be like losing that talisman. Then there would be nobody left to hate. And then, worst of all, there would be nothing more that he could do for Klemens. His memories would begin to fade. Do you understand what I'm trying to say?'

'Yes, I think so.'

Lukasz nodded. 'I've thought about it a lot over the years. My father and I are alike, I think. That's the way I would feel, too, in the same circumstances. Hatred and a desire for vengeance are things you can hold on to. They are solid things. They give you a focus.'

'A purpose in life?'

'If you like. But, as I say, it would have undermined all that if my father had ever met McTeague again and discovered he was only another human being. Of course, McTeague was just a man who made a mistake, a man who was afraid and let down his comrades. But it was better for my father to preserve his picture of a monster. It was the only thing that made the death of Klemens more understandable. It was the only way to make sense of something that was ultimately senseless.'

Cooper listened for a moment to the claws of the parrot rattling on the bars of its cage in the corner of the room.

'It's ironic that it should come up now,' said Lukasz. 'It's against the spirit of *oplatek*.'

'Sorry?'

'*Oplatek* is our tradition of forgiveness and reconciliation. It's symbolized by eating the *oplatki* wafers. And this Sunday is the *oplatek* dinner for the Edendale Polish community, down at the ex-servicemen's club, the Dom Kombatanta. It's one of the high points of our calendar. It certainly means a lot to my father.'

Cooper had never heard of such a thing, and he couldn't quite picture how to spell the word that Lukasz was pronouncing. Forgiveness and reconciliation? Well, there was certainly plenty of scope for that.

'Do you know somebody called George Malkin?' asked Cooper.

Lukasz frowned. 'Malkin? Should I? What's the connection? Was he in the RAF?'

'No. He's a local man. He lives near the place where the Lancaster crashed.'

'I'm sorry, it doesn't mean anything.'

Cooper handed the photograph back reluctantly. 'They were all brave men,' he said.

Lukasz laughed. 'That's what everybody says. Everybody who wasn't involved, anyway. But it isn't what my father says. He says that none of them was brave; he says it wasn't about bravery at all. In his view, they did what they could because they were part of a crew, a team, and it was impossible to consider letting your comrades down. They were very close, you know, and the circumstances brought them even closer. It's impossible for us to understand now how close they were.'

'Like a family, in fact. It's always worse when things go wrong within a family. It feels like a betrayal.'

'Yes. But these days, even families aren't as close as that. Ask my son.'

'Your son?'

'Andrew. He lives in London now, but he's been visiting us recently.'

'Is he still here?'

'No. He was only visiting.'

'When did you see him off?'

Lukasz seemed to hesitate about answering. 'He hasn't been here since Sunday,' he said.

'Was he going straight back to London?' said Cooper. 'Was he travelling by train or did he have a car? It might have been difficult in the snow.'

It was Grace Lukasz who answered. She had approached quietly behind her husband's back to listen to the conversation, as if drawn by the merest mention of her son's name.

'He arrived in a taxi. And we didn't see him off,' she said.

'Oh? Why?'

'I was on duty at the hospital on Sunday night,' said Lukasz. 'As I told you, I work in the A&E department. By the time I arrived home, Andrew was gone.'

'Was there a family row of some kind?' asked Cooper. The Lukaszes both looked embarrassed at the question. 'It happens in every family, I know.'

'Andrew went off without saying goodbye at all,' said Grace Lukasz.

Cooper looked at the heaps of snow piled up outside on Woodland Crescent. The snow was becoming stained with car exhaust fumes and soot from central-heating flues. It didn't say much for the air quality in the Crescent.

'Mrs Lukasz, do you mean that your son just disappeared?'

'Well, in a way.'

'Did he have any luggage with him?'

'Yes, of course.'

'Have you reported him missing?'

'He isn't missing,' said Peter Lukasz. 'He left a little suddenly, that's all. I presume somebody came for him. A taxi, whatever.'

'He promised he would phone me,' said Grace. 'I've called his home in London several times, but there's only an answering machine. He said his wife is away in America, and we don't have his mobile number.'

'He probably has some urgent business to deal with,' said Peter. 'Andrew is regional sales manager for a medical supplies company.'

Cooper began to get exasperated. People could sometimes be so slow to accept that tragedy could intrude directly into their own comfortable lives.

'Could you describe your son, please? How old is he? How tall? Is he dark or fair? What was he wearing?'

'Well, Andrew is dark, like me,' said Peter Lukasz. 'He's thirty-two. I don't know what he was wearing. What's this all about?'

But his wife's face was already growing pale. 'The man found dead on the Snake Pass,' she said. 'But that's the man who called here at the bungalow on Monday, isn't it?'

'*Is it?*' said Cooper.

They both stared at him wordlessly. A faint sheen of sweat glistened on Peter Lukasz's forehead. He seemed to find it too warm in his own bungalow.

'I'm afraid I'll have to ask you to come in and

have a look,' said Cooper. 'In case you're able to help us identify him.'

Grace Lukasz shook her head. 'But that wasn't Andrew,' she said. 'Surely that's not what you're saying?' She gave a short laugh. 'I know my own son.'

Peter Lukasz seemed to understand better. 'It's ridiculous,' he said. 'Quite ridiculous. But I'll do it, if it helps to get the idea out of your head.'

'Thank you, sir. However, I think we'll need both of you. Your wife was the only one who saw the man who came to your door.'

Cooper got ready to leave the bungalow. Peter Lukasz saw him out, but paused on the doorstep in his slippers. Lukasz seemed as though he might have something else he wanted to say, but Cooper didn't know what question he should be asking him.

'How long has your father been working on his story?' said Cooper.

'About a week.'

'Is that all? What made him decide to start it now?'

'Oh, I think that's because he knows he's dying,' said Lukasz. 'He has advanced liver cancer, and all that can be done for him now is to control the pain. We've been told that he'll be dead within a few months.'

Ben Cooper stood in the CID room as he stripped off his coat and stared at his shoes, which were

320

turning a strange grey where they had once been black. He flicked through the messages and memos on his desk, allocating them to three piles in order of priority. He had learned the technique on a time-management course. Important and urgent, important but not urgent, urgent but not important. In this case, only the first would get dealt with. Towards the bottom, he stopped and read a telephone message more carefully. There was no pile this one would fit into. It didn't fit into his duties at all.

He put the message aside carefully on his desk while he dealt with the important and urgent tasks. A CPS lawyer needed a report for an assault case that was due before the magistrates first thing on Monday morning; a family in Edendale whose burglary he was supposed to be investigating had been burgled again and needed calming down; a superintendent had invited him to volunteer for a farm security working group and wanted an answer yesterday.

Diane Fry watched Cooper going through the ritual. She wasn't sure why it was that she found him every bit as irritating as Gavin Murfin. Murfin was stupid and lazy, but she could understand that. Ben Cooper was neither of those things.

'Ben, you took a long time at the Snake Inn,' she said.

'Sorry.'

'Do you realize how stretched we are here?'

'Of course,' he said.

'I'm not asking you to cut corners,' she said, 'but I need you to be making the best use of your time. So let me know where you are in future, if you're going to be delayed.'

'Listen, Diane, I've asked Peter and Grace Lukasz to try an identification on the Snowman.'

She stared at him. 'Have you now? Ben, are you working this enquiry on your own?'

'No, but –'

'So how come you talked to the Lukasz family again? Was that on your list of actions?'

'No. I used a bit of initiative.'

'Well, don't.'

'They don't know the whereabouts of their son. They haven't seen him since Sunday.'

Fry stopped and stared at him. 'Have they reported it?'

'No.'

'Description?'

'It's a rough match with the Snowman. Besides, Grace Lukasz is the only one who saw this man who's supposed to have visited Woodland Crescent on Monday.'

'*Supposed* to have?'

'I don't think she's telling the entire truth,' said Cooper. 'Her husband wasn't home, and her father-in-law is in some world of his own. As for the neighbours, it seems the man who called at the Lukasz bungalow didn't visit anybody else in the street. That doesn't sound like any salesman I ever heard of. It will be interesting to see what she makes of the Snowman, anyway.'

'All right,' said Fry. 'But for God's sake let me know what you're doing in future, Ben.'

'There's another thing,' said Cooper.

She sighed. 'Go on.'

'The staff at the Snake Inn remember no four-wheel drives. Is it possible the Snowman's body was left in that lay-by overnight, before the snow started?'

'Not possible. There was snow underneath the body. And take another look at the video of the scene. It's perfectly obvious that the body would have been visible to traffic coming up the hill. Even in the dark, you would see it in your head-lights.'

'It wouldn't be the first time people had just driven on by.'

Fry tapped her fingers. 'That would mean we'd have to do roadside checks on motorists. That's more time and more staff.'

'Sorry.'

'I'll let the DI know. Anything else?'

'Not for now.'

'Clear up your messages, then.'

Fry watched him for a few minutes longer as he began to make phone calls. She listened to him placating people who were becoming more and more anxious that nothing had been done on their enquiries. He was good at that – people on the other end of the line started off angry or upset and went away feeling that they had his full attention and sympathy. Fry wondered how she could get Cooper's full attention. Maybe she ought to get angrier herself, or more upset. Nothing else seemed to work.

Cooper picked up the message form he had put aside. Urgent or important? Neither, of course. Yet, of all of them, this was the call he most wanted to make. He put it into his pocket, pulled on his coat and carried his cap as he followed Fry to the car park.

He found the cold air outside refreshing. To get to his car, he had to cross a treacherous rink of compacted ice where dozens of police vehicles had spun their wheels on their way in and out of the compound. Someone would have to clear the ice soon, or there would be members of the public falling and breaking their legs, and the county court would be full of negligence cases against the police. That would play hell with the budgets, all right.

Cooper supposed he ought to make an effort not to get himself into trouble with Diane Fry. Not only was she his supervisor, but she already had a hold over him, a suspicion that had never been mentioned between them, only ever hinted at, so that it might only have been his own delusion that she knew his secret. But one thing was sure. One more wrong move could blight his career. He could end up one of those embittered old warhorses who had given up hopes of promotion or recognition. He could end up like Gavin Murfin, who no longer cared whether everyone thought he was a joke.

But there was something about the way Fry approached it that rankled. Every time she gave him the benefit of her advice, it made him want to do entirely the opposite. It was exactly what he heard married men say about their nagging wives.

Cooper looked again at the message form he had put in his pocket. Miss Alison Morrissey had called to speak to him and would like him to phone her back. It was an Edendale number, so he guessed she was still staying at the Cavendish Hotel. He hadn't yet decided whether he was going to talk to her; he wanted to be sure of his ground before he had the confidence to face her.

But Alison Morrissey needed his help. Fry didn't need him at all – in fact, she would be better off without him, because she could get on and organize everybody the way she wanted them. The contrast between the two women couldn't be clearer.

The Snowman looked as though his eyes might open at any moment. The colour of his skin reminded Ben Cooper of the real snowman that someone had built in the churchyard at All Saints. It was close to the road, and over the last few days the fumes from passing traffic had turned it grey and unhealthy.

He looked at Peter and Grace Lukasz. They had

already looked upset when they had arrived at the hospital mortuary.

'Are you sure you're all right?' he said. 'We can do this tomorrow morning, if you prefer.'

'No, it's all right,' said Lukasz.

The mortuary assistant drew back the plastic sheet fully from the face of the corpse. Cooper watched the couple carefully. Lukasz actually seemed to become calmer when he saw the face. But his wife was riveted by the sight. She edged her wheelchair a little nearer to study the details of the Snowman's hair and skin.

'Well, it certainly isn't our son,' said Lukasz. 'I've never seen this man before in my life.'

'Mrs Lukasz?' said Cooper.

'Of course it isn't Andrew.'

'But have you seen him before? Do you think this is the man who called at your home on Monday?'

'It's difficult to tell,' she said. 'Seeing him like this . . . and, well, I met him for only a moment or two. But I think it could be him.'

'Have you thought of anything else that might help to identify him? Any little detail at all?'

'I don't think so.'

'Thank you.' Cooper nodded at the attendant and watched him cover the Snowman's face. The Snowman had been travelling, and he seemed to be unknown locally or in neighbouring areas. He wondered whether Gavin Murfin had contacted Europol yet.

'Mrs Lukasz, did you happen to notice whether this man had an accent at all?'

Grace Lukasz rubbed her hands on the wheels of her chair and looked up at her husband. 'He didn't say much, so I couldn't tell.'

'What did he say exactly?'

'He asked if Mr Lukasz was at home. That was all.' She turned away, and they began to head for the exit.

'But which Mr Lukasz did he want?' said Cooper.

Grace stopped. Her back was towards him, her shoulders tense. Her husband stepped behind her to push the wheelchair. 'I don't know,' she said. 'But Peter wasn't home, and I couldn't let him bother Zygmunt.'

Cooper frowned at their backs, irritated by their apparent lack of imagination, their readiness to ignore the possibilities.

'It didn't occur to you that he might be looking for *Andrew* Lukasz?' he said.

'But Andrew had already gone,' said Peter.

'Exactly.'

On her way home to her flat in Grosvenor Avenue, Diane Fry called at the shop on the corner of Castleton Road. It was run by a Pakistani family, who were unfailingly polite to her, whatever mood she was in. Some days, she left the shop feeling guilty that she had failed to respond to their kindness. But those were the days when Edendale was the last place she wanted to be, anyway.

Fry had bought a bottle of milk and a frozen pepperoni pizza. Near the counter, she picked up some newspapers, in case there was nothing on TV tonight that she could bear to watch. She had lived alone for a long time, but she was hardened to it. She was able to hold back the tide of loneliness quite easily now, as long as there were no people around. The difficult times were when she heard the students who lived in the other flats laughing and calling to each other, coming back from the pub with their friends and playing music as they sat around putting the world right. That was when she needed all her strength. It was clear to her that Ben Cooper would not be able to cope with living alone. He had no idea what it was like.

When she reached the flat, Fry glanced at the local papers while she heated up the pizza and boiled the kettle. The first thing she realized was that the Canadian woman, Alison Morrissey, had been to the newspapers.

The *Eden Valley Times* had done a full-page feature on her; so had the *Buxton Advertiser*. There had been items in the city papers, too, the *Sheffield Star* and the *Manchester Evening News*. Each of them carried pictures of the woman herself. Fry recognized her immediately as the woman she had seen talking to Ben Cooper at Underbank.

20

Ben Cooper awoke on Saturday morning thinking of Marie Tennent. He had been dreaming that his limbs had frozen together, that frostbite had eaten through the membranes of his ears and nose, and that his eyes would never open again. But finally they did open, and he saw his bedroom. It was the same bedroom he had slept in nearly all his life.

He pulled back a corner of the curtain at his window. The room looked out on to the yard at the back of the farmhouse, and above it a steep hill that was covered in dark conifers until the top hundred feet, where the moors burst through. In his childhood, he had peopled those wooded slopes with all sorts of imaginary beasts and adventures. He had followed his brother Matt into many scrapes that had been terrifying and exciting in equal measures. The memory gave him only a small pang of regret at the thought of leaving it behind.

Though the yard was pitch-dark, Cooper could see there would be no more snow this morning.

The black sky was full of stars that were piercingly bright. There would be ice lying on the moors, just as there was on the night Marie Tennent died. For a moment, he tried to put himself inside Marie's mind, struggling to grasp the compulsion that had driven her up to the top of Irontongue Hill in the worst possible weather. Had it really been a need to cover the bones of a long-dead baby, wrapping it against the cold that it would never feel?

Cooper shook his head. He knew it was one of those things he would never be able to understand, even if Marie had been here now to explain it to him in her own words. There was too much emotion in it, and too little logic.

On Monday, Marie Tennent would not be his first priority, though a copy of her file still sat on his desk. How much time was he likely to get to spend on her? Maybe he would have to shelve her altogether, until there was more time, or her baby was found, or the pathologist got round to a postmortem examination. He added Marie to a long list of frustrations, cases where he was powerless to help. On Monday morning, the Snowman would again be the main priority, because postmortem results had identified him as a murder victim. He was urgent and important.

Today, though, it was Saturday, and Cooper was off duty. Today it was time for him to leave Bridge End Farm. It didn't take him long to pack his possessions.

'I've got the pick-up ready,' said his brother

Matt over breakfast. 'I'll give you a hand to load up.'

'There isn't all that much to take,' said Cooper. 'The flat's furnished, so I don't need much furniture. And it's surprising how little stuff I've collected over the years, when I look.'

'What about your guns?'

'I'll have to leave them behind. They'll have to stay in the cabinet here. I've got nowhere to keep them.'

'It'll be the competition again soon, Ben. You should be practising.'

'I know.'

Matt sat and looked at him helplessly. Neither of them knew what to say. Matt got up from the table so that he wouldn't have to struggle to find the words.

'Give me a shout then, when you're ready.'

All Cooper needed were his clothes, his computer and stereo, a few books, CDs and pictures. He felt like a student setting off for his first term at university, his anxious parents insisting on ferrying him to his halls of residence to settle him in. There were some things he could leave behind at Bridge End Farm. So it would still, in a way, be his home.

The first picture he took down was the one that hung on the wall opposite the foot of his bed. He realized he hadn't looked at the picture for a while. But then, he didn't need to – he knew every detail of it. He was familiar with every face on each of the rows, even with the patterns and texture of the wall behind them and the concrete yard beneath their boots. Without looking, he could have described the way each one held his arms, which of them was smiling, who looked suspicious of the photographer, and who hadn't fastened his tie properly that morning. He knew exactly the feel of the mahogany frame in his hands, the smoothness of the edges, the slight ridge in the wood near one corner that his finger always found, like a necessary flaw. He remembered the slight scratch in the glass that was almost hidden by the shadow of the chair one of the officers sat in on the front row. If you turned the picture towards the light, the scratch became obvious. He couldn't remember how it had happened. Somehow, it had always been there.

He put the photograph in the box first, wrapping it up carefully in tissue paper, then several layers of newspaper. Several less important prints went in after it. Perhaps the photograph would have been better protected if it had been on top. But it felt right for it to be at the bottom, deep in the accumulated objects of his life. It would have to take pride of place in the sitting room of his new flat, though. It would give a sort of tacit approval to the place. Cooper already had in mind the exact spot where it would go.

Soon after he and Matt arrived at Welbeck Street, the flat became a whirlwind of activity. His sister-in-law Kate drove down with the girls to have a look, and the three of them insisted on hunting for cleaning equipment and wiping down all the surfaces in the kitchen and bathroom until they shone. Matt stood in the conservatory and looked at the tiny overgrown garden and the backs of the houses that overlooked it. Then he walked through to the sitting room and looked out of the front window at the street. A row of cars stood directly in front of the houses opposite, and melting snow dripped slowly from the roofs.

'Rather you than me, Ben,' he said, after a while.

Cooper knew what his brother meant. Although Welbeck Street was only a few miles from Bridge End, there was a world of difference. But he believed he could adapt to it. It was Matt who would have the most trouble adjusting to a different life, if it ever came to selling the farm.

He had discovered that his new landlady had a Jack Russell terrier called Jasper. He could hear it now, yapping in the backyard next door.

A little later, Mrs Shelley herself came in from next door to see how he was getting on. Lawrence Daley was with her, and he was wearing his bow tie. He went round and shook hands with everybody, including Josie and Amy, which made them giggle hysterically for more than half an hour afterwards. Mrs Shelley watched Kate cleaning the kitchen, nodding approvingly.

Then Cooper's sister Claire appeared briefly. She always complained of being too busy for anything. But she had managed to spare him a few minutes, to help him settle in, she said. She brought him a card and a bottle of white wine, then vanished again in a perfumed breeze, off back to her craft shop in Bold Lane. In the conservatory, the girls were cooing over the cat, who was enjoying the attention immensely. His purrs were vibrating the windows.

Cooper sat on a suitcase and watched the activity. He felt very strange. He was surrounded by his family, the people he had known for many years, some of them all his life. He had lived in the same house as Matt for twenty-nine years. But because they were all in an unfamiliar place, he felt as though he were an alien among them. In half an hour they would be gone; the tide would go out again and they would ebb away, leaving him high and dry, stranded like a bit of seaweed tossed on to the rocks to dry out in the sun. When they all went home, he would stay here on his own in this little house, where he didn't even know how to find the electricity meter.

Even Uncle John and Aunt Margaret had stood in the doorway and made remarks about the convenient location until they felt able to make an excuse and leave. They had all come out of curiosity, out of bafflement that a member of the family was cutting himself off in this way. For that's what he was doing, in their eyes. Coopers did not live on their own. The family was there to provide support – why should he want to cast it aside? He sensed that Claire and his aunt and uncle had suspected there was a woman involved, someone he was living with on the quiet, but they had seen no signs of one. He was sure there would be later surprise visits to check.

Mrs Shelley had discovered that Matt was a farmer, and had decided he was the Antichrist. But she didn't say anything until he was gone, and then she confided her views in Cooper.

'I can't abide people who ill-treat animals,' said Mrs Shelley. 'What respect have they got for people if they treat animals like that? It makes me sick.'

'Yes, you're right, Mrs Shelley.'

'Don't let Miranda out at the front, will you? The cars are too dangerous. They go batting down this road like idiots. They have their music turned up full blast and their windows open. Music! It's a wonder their brains don't fall out.'

'Yes, you're right.'

'I see your brother has two children, though,' said Mrs Shelley. 'That's nice.'

'Matt says they're getting to be a difficult age.'

'Oh, I know. But they're beautiful when they're babies, aren't they? All that time I spent telling Lawrence he ought to become a father . . .'

'Auntie, I think Ben might prefer to be left to settle in now,' said Lawrence.

Mrs Shelley gave a little giggle. 'Lawrence says I talk too much. You *will* look after Miranda, won't you? Only I can't have her in my own house, you see.'

'Because of the dog, I suppose.'

Mrs Shelley glared at him. 'What's wrong with my dog?'

'Oh, nothing.'

'Jasper's a perfect guard dog – he protects his home and his little family. He lets me know if anyone's around.'

'I'm sure he does,' said Cooper, thinking of the bad-tempered yapping he'd heard from the yard earlier. 'Do you keep him outside or inside mostly?'

'It depends whether it's safe,' said Mrs Shelley. 'He barks when he's in the yard.'

'Oh, Jasper barks indoors as well these days, bless him. But I'm a little deaf anyway. I turn the sound up on the TV, and it doesn't bother me.'

Cooper was glad of the thick walls. He had heard neither the TV, nor the dog barking indoors.

'Not that I have the TV on all that often, you understand,' said Mrs Shelley. 'There's far too much news on it. I can't stand news – it's always full of people being cruel to other people, and to animals as well. I turn it off straight away when the news comes on, and I talk to Jasper instead, so he doesn't feel neglected.'

'Come on, Auntie,' said Lawrence. 'We said we'd only be a few minutes, didn't we?'

'All right. Bye for now, then,' she said. 'Duty calls.'

Then even Mrs Shelley was gone, back to her house next door. The dog, which had been yapping in her backyard, went back into the house, and everything was quiet again.

Cooper opened the kitchen window to let in some fresh air to disperse the smell of the disinfectant splashed around by Kate and the girls. A tinge of aromatic wood smoke drifted in. One of his new neighbours was having a garden bonfire. It smelled like apple branches they were burning. From the window of his flat, Cooper couldn't see any trees. They must be in the gardens between Welbeck Street and the shops on Meadow Road which were hidden from his view, except in the conservatory. He wondered if Mrs Shelley would let him knock a small window out of the back wall of the bedroom, so that he could see the apple blossom in the spring. Probably not. Maybe he would get used to seeing only tarmac and slate roofs.

He still had the telephone message in the pocket of his coat. Probably she had given up expecting to hear back from him by now. He wondered what she was doing with herself while she was in Edendale, when the people she wanted to talk to were refusing even to see her. Maybe Frank Baine had been showing her the sights.

Now seemed to be the best time. He rang the number of the hotel.

'Can I speak to Miss Alison Morrissey, please? She's a guest there.'

'One moment, please.'

There were still a couple of boxes of small items to unpack for the flat. One was a wooden figure of a cat, not unlike Miranda, black and overweight. Cooper had been given it many years ago, but couldn't remember now who the gift was from. It had stood in his bedroom at Bridge End Farm for over a decade.

While he waited, he placed the wooden cat on the window ledge overlooking the street. Carefully, he adjusted the cat's position so that it was looking into the room, directly towards the armchair where he would sit during the evening. He thought that he might find its fat little smile comforting.

'Hello?' Morrissey sounded cautious when she came to the phone. 'Who is that?'

'Ben Cooper. You left a message.'

'Oh, right. I didn't think you would call.'

'I almost didn't.'

'I wondered if you would be willing to meet with me. I don't feel I've managed to explain myself properly to anybody. But you at least seem interested. I hoped you might listen.'

'It would be entirely unofficial,' said Cooper.

'That's OK by me.'

'Tomorrow? I'm off duty then.'

'Great. Can you meet me in the lobby of the Cavendish Hotel? About eleven thirty?'

'Fine.'

For a few minutes, Cooper stroked the wooden back of the cat as he stared down into the street. He felt the need to familiarize himself with the minute details of his surroundings – the colours of the front doors on the houses opposite, the patterns on the curtains in their windows, the makes and models of the cars parked on the hard standings near the road. He noted which gardens had flowers growing in them and which were abandoned and weedy. He counted the wheelie bins standing at the entrance to a ginnel, and he noticed the Jack Russell terrier peering into the street from behind an iron gate. He wondered how long it would take before the place began to look like home.

'So this is it, then? The new bolt hole?'

Cooper almost dropped the lamp. She was the last person he expected to see. One of his new neighbours maybe, or another family member, coming to see how he was getting on. But Diane Fry? She hovered in the doorway like a bailiff, running a critical eye over his possessions in case she had to value them for a county court summons.

'I was just passing,' she said. 'And I saw your car outside. I figured this must be the place. It's not exactly huge, is it?'

'It'll do for me.'

Cooper put the lamp down carefully on the table, suddenly conscious of the second-best crockery and the pile of his clothes on the chairs in the sitting room. Fry always made him feel like this, as if he wasn't coming up to expectations.

The books he had bought from Eden Valley

Books were on top of the pile, only because they were the most recent. Of course, Diane Fry spotted them. She didn't miss much.

'*The History of Peak District Aircraft Wrecks*,' she read. 'I wonder why you've developed a sudden interest in this subject, Ben?'

Cooper didn't feel the need to reply. But that didn't stop her.

'The war was a long time ago, Ben,' she said. 'In fact, I can't understand why people call it *the* war. There have been plenty of others since then.'

'Not wars that affected so many people,' said Cooper. 'Not wars that changed the whole country.'

'If you say so. But it's not really old men you're interested in, is it?'

'Sorry?'

'Well, correct me if I'm wrong, but there's a bit of added interest in this for you, isn't there? A bit of excitement on the side? A Canadian by the name of Alison Morrissey?'

'What are you talking about?'

Fry smiled. 'Ben, make sure you keep your head. Keep your focus on what's important. Just because you're living on your own, you shouldn't be tempted to seek out the first person who pays you a bit of attention. It doesn't work.'

'It has nothing to do with you.'

'It has, if it affects the way you do your job, Ben. And at the moment, I've got doubts about that. You're letting yourself be distracted too easily. You're spending too much time on someone else's pet project. That's not what you're paid for. We can't afford to have you swanning off interviewing old soldiers to satisfy that Canadian woman's obsession. Do you understand what I'm saying?'

'I'll do it in my own time,' he said.

'Make sure that you do, Ben. Because I'll be keeping an eye on what you're up to.'

'Right.'

Cooper found himself breathing a bit too hard. He couldn't believe that Diane Fry had chosen to walk into his new flat on the day he moved in and try to humiliate him. He had to either throw her out or find something to help him to calm down.

'Would you like a coffee while you're here?' he said.

'There *is* a kitchen, is there?'

'Of sorts.'

'Thanks, then.'

Cooper went to make the coffee. First he had to find the box that the kettle was in, then unpack the shopping for the instant coffee and the milk, which he knew he should have put into the fridge straight away. His ears were straining for sounds of Diane Fry moving around in his new sitting room, but he heard nothing. Perhaps she had seen all she needed to see from the doorway and was reluctant to sit on the chairs, even if she could do so without touching his clothes. He realized he hadn't thought to get any sugar, and he turned to ask her if she took it in her coffee. But he didn't bother.

There was no doubt in his mind that she took it unsweetened.

But when he got back to the sitting room, he found Fry unpacking a box of pictures. She was arranging them on the walls, lining them up neatly on some tacks left by the previous tenants. She had found a cloth, too, and was wiping the glass covering a Richard Martin print of a squeeze stile with Win Hill in the background.

'Have you got a hammer?' she said.

'Er, yes. Somewhere.'

'I think this one needs to go on the wall over there.'

'You're probably right.'

Cooper found the hammer for her and perched on the edge of one of the armchairs with his coffee while he watched her fix the picture in exactly the right spot. She did the job as she did everything, with the correct procedure and no unnecessary fuss. And the finished job was perfect, precisely aligned and level. He had to admit that it was the ideal spot for the print. If he had been left to do it himself, it would probably have taken him several attempts until he hit on the right arrangement.

'Don't forget your coffee, Diane,' he said.

'Yes, in a minute.'

She was absorbed now, poking through the box for more pictures, peeling away layers of newspaper to see what she could find. She rejected some rather ordinary fox-hunting prints, then found a bigger picture at the bottom of the box, well wrapped in tissue paper to protect it from damage.

Cooper knew which picture it was. He wanted to tell her to cover it up and put it back in the box; he wanted to say that he didn't want her handling it. But he held his breath and said nothing, waiting to see her reaction. He expected a comment, at least. Anyone else would have said something – muttered some meaningless platitude, some embarrassed words of sympathy while avoiding his eye.

But Fry said nothing at all. Her expression didn't change. She took the picture by the frame and wiped it carefully with the cloth, rubbing at the glass to get the smears from the surface. And again she knew exactly where it had to go. This was one instance where Cooper had his own idea of the right place, but Fry didn't need telling. She hung it over the fireplace and positioned it dead centre, making minute adjustments to its angle until she was satisfied it was perfect. She stood back and examined it, then took the cloth again and wiped off her own faint fingermarks. He was astonished to see that she did it gently, almost tenderly. He had never seen her do anything in that way before.

The picture was the one of his father in his police uniform, lined up proudly with his colleagues – the last photograph taken of him before he was killed in the street. The way Fry caressed it with the cloth meant more to Cooper than any amount of words she could have used. Her instinctive reverence made his throat spasm uncomfortably. He wished she would stop now, and drink her damn coffee. He thrust the mug at her, forcing her to put down the cloth and stop what she was doing. He couldn't think of a thing to say for a few moments, until he managed to get his vocal cords working again.

'Where exactly were you passing on your way to?' he said, finally.

The tone of his voice made Fry look at him quizzically.

'I'm not always working, you know. I have my own private life.'

'Right.'

There was a small noise from the direction of the kitchen, a sort of tentative chirrup. Cooper turned and saw a broad, black face and a yellow eye that peered at Fry, hoping for attention.

'What on earth is that?' she said.

'That's Randy,' said Cooper. 'He's sort of part of the property.'

Fry stared at Cooper, then back at the cat, which had decided not to come any closer, after all.

'It's so typical,' said Fry. 'Only you, Ben, would take on a flat that came complete with its own stray.'

After that, they both seemed to run out of things to say. Fry looked at the window. Cooper could see that she was thinking of where she had to go next. She had put in an appearance, done her duty, and now she was ready to move on to more important business. She began to move towards

344

the door, then stopped and pulled something from her pocket. It was a small object wrapped in blue paper.

'I don't like you all that much, as you know,' she said. 'But I brought you this.'

'Thank you.'

Cooper took it and weighed it in his hand. It was solid, and heavy for its size. He began to tug at the tape sealing the parcel.

'No need to open it now,' said Fry. She swung her scarf round her neck. 'I can see you've still got things to do.'

'I suppose so.'

'See you on Monday, then.'

Cooper watched her slither down Welbeck Street. Presumably, she had been obliged to leave her car at the bottom of the street because of the number of vehicles parked outside the houses. Fry didn't look back, and she had soon disappeared. He had noticed when she was in the flat that she was wearing new shoes. He wondered whether she had bought some that had a bit of grip in the soles.

He went back to the sitting room and opened the little parcel. She had bought him a clock.

Cooper considered the advantages of living alone. He looked forward to being able to listen to the omnibus edition of *The Archers* on Sunday morning, without competition from videos or pop music or daytime children's TV. And, because he was on his own, it would hardly seem necessary to get dressed or have a shave on his days off. As long as he didn't have to go out of the house, no one would see him. He could slop around in his dressing gown or a pair of jogging bottoms for as long as he liked. He could sit at the kitchen table and drink coffee and eat toast and read the Sunday papers all morning, if he really wanted. If he had thought to put an order in to have any papers delivered, that is. At the moment, all he would be able to do while drinking his coffee and eating his toast was stare at the cat. Maybe he would have to unpack the box of books he had brought.

Finally, he realized why his thoughts were running on so fast. He was babbling to himself to cover the silence in the house. He had never known a silent house in his life. He had a foreboding of how depressing, how desperate, even how frightening it would be to come home every night to a dark and empty house. Every evening, the post would still be lying on the doormat where it had fallen in the morning; a single unwashed coffee mug would be in the sink where he had left it after breakfast because he had been in a rush to get to work again; the house would have that feel of having gone along in its own world without him all day, that his presence in it was unnecessary, maybe even unwelcome. That wasn't what you could call a home.

The first taste of loneliness was sour and un-expected, a burst of metallic bitterness on the back of his tongue. He remembered once breaking a tooth playing rugby at school, when he had got a boot in the face attempting a foolhardy tackle. The sudden gush of blood in his mouth had given him a moment of cold panic and made him feel nauseous. He had felt the taste of his own life trickling between his teeth and mingling with his saliva. Loneliness was like that taste. Just like the bitterness of the blood on his tongue.

The sound of every little movement made by the cat was reassuring. The touch of its claws on the tiles in the conservatory, the rustling as it changed position in its basket, even the faint snore when it was sleeping. These were now the sounds he listened for. Without them, the house would have been dead and hostile. Like a narrow crack of light entering his brain, he thought he had an inkling for the first time of why Diane Fry spent so much time at work.

The cat had moved up on him silently and sat watching him from the arm of a chair. When Cooper stroked its fur, he felt the sharp sting of static electricity, and the animal flinched away from his hand. The air was very dry. There would be another frost tonight.

21

Every morning when Diane Fry opened the door of her car she had to vacuum bits of polystyrene carton and fragments of greasy paper off the floor. She also had to spray air freshener inside until it was so thick she had to open the windows to prevent herself from suffocating. Sunday morning was no exception. The traces of Gavin Murfin lingered all weekend. She was sure Murfin used food as a means of avoiding talking to her when they were in the car. Ben Cooper at least had some conversation. He didn't have to buy a singing lobster to do his talking for him.

This Sunday morning, Fry finished cleaning out her car to find that her mobile was ringing and ringing. It was DI Hitchens.

'Diane, you'd better get into the office right away,' he said. 'Before the shit hits the fan.'

The Cavendish wasn't exactly the newest hotel in Edendale. There was the Holiday Inn on the roundabout at the end of the relief road, and the Travelodge in Eyre Street. And now there was the recent conversion of the old Conservative Club, with its portraits of Margaret Thatcher and John Major still hanging on the wall in the bar as historical souvenirs, like the heads of stags that had been shot and stuffed. But the Cavendish was the hotel that had 'character', according to the tourist brochures. It was the one where a waiter would bring you a copy of *The Times* as you relaxed in a leather armchair in the residents' lounge; it was the one where the Rotary Club held its charity dinners at £80 a head. In front of the hotel, there were iron railings painted green and topped with spikes. In most towns such ironwork had disappeared long ago, ripped up during the Second World War to make weapons. Somehow they had escaped this fate in Edendale.

Ben Cooper found Alison Morrissey waiting for him on the steps of the Cavendish. The morning was cold, but not unpleasant. It felt as though there could be rain at any time, which would at least wash away the snow still lying in the gutters and on the hillsides rising out of the town.

'Thanks for coming,' she said. 'I wasn't sure you would. I didn't think they would let you.'

'I'm off duty today. I can do what I like.'

'You can probably guess what I'm going to say.'

'Yes. But the reason I came is that I don't want there to be any misunderstanding.'

'Misunderstanding? I've had to accept that the

Derbyshire police weren't going to offer any assistance. I hadn't realized you would actively try to interfere and obstruct me.'

'That isn't the case,' said Cooper.

'No? You visited the Lukasz family before I could get to them. And then you went to see Mr Rowland. Don't try to tell me it's a coincidence. You're trying to thwart me. Your chiefs don't want me to talk to these people. They'd like me to get so frustrated that I give up and go back home. They've sent you to hinder me, to make sure that happens.'

Cooper felt himself shuffling his feet with embarrassment and tried to pretend that he was stamping them against the cold.

'I've had no instructions to do anything like that,' he said.

'No?' Alison hesitated. 'But you're the man to do it, aren't you? You talk the same language as these people. Every time you get there before I do, you make me seem so much more of an alien. They hear my accent and they shut up, like I'm a foreign spy. You'd think it was still wartime as far as they're concerned. Careless talk costs lives. They're still carrying the motto with them. Don't they know we were on their side?'

'It isn't like that,' said Cooper. 'They're naturally reticent people. You have to work a bit harder to get them to talk to you.'

'Yeah? It seems to me they're still living in the war. Suspicious isn't the word.'

Cooper shook his head. 'I'm sorry,' he said. 'But you're the one obsessed with the war. It's been over a very long time. Long before you and I were born.'

'You're wrong,' said Alison. 'It isn't over for me. It won't be over until I find out what happened to my grandfather.'

They looked at each other for a moment. Where they stood, on the corner near the Cavendish Hotel, there was an icy wind blowing round the stone walls. He saw Morrissey shiver. But then her mood changed suddenly, and she smiled.

'Well, you have to let me buy you a drink, at least. No argument,' she said. 'Where can we go – is there somewhere near?'

They went into the Wheatsheaf, where, to Cooper's surprise, Alison Morrissey asked for a pint of cider. Cooper realized that he didn't have to drive home any more when he was in town, and he ordered a pint of Derbyshire Drop. It was one of the strong local beers, its label a tribute to the original name for the unique semi-precious mineral Blue John, which attracted so many tourists to the Peak District.

'I've asked for the Sunday lunch menu, too,' said Morrissey. 'I hope you don't mind.'

'I can't let you pay for me,' he said.

'You're not going to be stuffy, are you? Didn't you say you were off duty today?'

'Even so, I have to be careful.'

'I see. You sound like a man treading a line.

351

Well, I can relate to that. It's exactly what I'm doing myself.'

Morrissey chose a vegetable bake, while Cooper settled for a lasagne. He felt ridiculously nervous. When the food was served, he couldn't quite think what order he should do things – where to put his napkin, what part of his meal to load on to his fork first, when to order coffee.

'What did you mean about "treading a line"?' said Cooper.

Morrissey raised an eyebrow. 'The line between two worlds, the line between the right and the wrong thing to do, the line between the past and present. Choose which you prefer. I'm treading them all.'

'And the line between rationality and obsession, perhaps?'

She looked at him, nursing her cider. Her cheeks were already turning pink from the alcohol and the warmth of the pub. Then, gradually, she began to talk. Cooper could feel her relaxing as the words trickled out.

'Yes, you're right – it *has* become an obsession,' she said. 'It became an obsession after I saw the report on the crash of Lancaster SU-V, and the list of names of the dead. From that moment, those men were no longer the crew of an RAF bomber – they were people. They had lives, they had wives and children. It was the fact that Dick Abbott had also been father of a young child that was the real trigger. Abbott was barely more than a boy himself. It set off something inside me, some urge, an instinct that has been driving me on to find out what exactly happened.'

'An instinct? Not curiosity?'

'Maybe. I don't understand what else to call it. But I had to know what happened. I had to know the truth, and in a way it was on behalf of that other fatherless child, as much as for myself. I wondered about Zygmunt Lukasz, too, and the family he might have. I can't explain why those British and Polish children mean anything to me at all. I know, in my logical moments, that the pictures of those children that I've been carrying in my head are nothing like the reality. I know they'll be well into middle age by now. But I found I was starting to live in some kind of parallel universe, where everyone was still as they were in 1945. So I made no attempt to explain it to anyone, not even to my mother. I was aware of the fact that I couldn't justify it, too afraid of the reasonable arguments that could be put to me, which I couldn't counter, but which would only make my determination stronger. Some people already call me obsessed, like you; I didn't want to give them an opportunity to call me mad.'

'I'll take the word back if it makes you feel better.'

'It doesn't matter. It helps if you understand how determined I am.'

'It's so far in the past, though . . .'

'Yes, I know. It was such an alien time. It makes

you appreciate peace. Do you know, it took me a long time to understand that an aircraft falling out of the sky was an everyday occurrence in wartime Britain.'

'And more than fifty aircraft have been wrecked in the Dark Peak area alone since the start of the Second World War.'

Morrissey looked at him in surprise. 'How did you know that?'

'I found a book,' said Cooper.

'Where?'

'In a second-hand bookshop we have here in town. Eden Valley Books.'

'That's interesting. I'd like to see it some time. Yes, I could hardly believe the figures when Frank Baine told me. I mean, on the map, the Peak District looks so small. It's no more than a few dozen miles across, locked in between the big cities. And the hills aren't even all that high. I mean, these summits are three thousand feet at the highest. We're not exactly talking the Rockies here, are we? Why was this area the graveyard for so many aircraft and airmen?'

'Some were damaged by enemy action, some suffered mechanical failure, or iced up and broke apart in mid-air. Other crashes were the result of pilot error or faulty navigation. If they found themselves over high ground in poor weather conditions, they were in trouble.'

'You really have done your research. Don't let it become an obsession.'

A group of men in their thirties came into the pub, let loose by their wives for Sunday lunchtime. They were talking noisily, joking about someone who had lost money through his ignorance when buying a second-hand car. They wore sweatshirts, and denim jeans with the waistbands rolling over from the pressure of their stomachs, and they made a fuss of choosing the specialist guest beers as if they were ordering cases of vintage wine.

'Then I had another problem,' said Morrissey. 'I had to consider whether to contact the relatives of the other airmen. Would they want to know the information I had? I had to try to put myself in their position. I was worried that I would be opening up old wounds. Just because those wounds are fifty-seven years old doesn't necessarily make them any less painful. I know that.'

Cooper tried to keep his eyes on hers, to encourage her to carry on talking. Often, that was all people needed, an air of attentiveness. But gazing into her eyes began to make him feel too disorientated after a while, and he had to look away.

'At first, it seemed an impossible task that I'd set myself,' she said. 'My imagination failed at the hurdle of putting myself in other people's shoes.'

'If you've never had that sort of experience yourself . . .'

'No. It wasn't that. It was because these were people who blamed my grandfather for their relatives' deaths. In the end, I decided that there was only one approach to take. I had to assume that the relatives, like me, would be happy to know what had really happened.'

She was talking constantly, barely pausing to eat, hardly waiting for him to nod or shake his head in response. It was as if she didn't want him to get a word in, as if she were afraid he might try to change the subject before she had finished explaining herself. Cooper began to feel he was unduly honoured by the fact that she had chosen him to explain it to. He wondered if anybody else had been given this privilege. Frank Baine, probably.

'You see, to me it felt as though I'd been reading a book but had been forced to put it down before the final chapter, and had never been able to finish it. It was a sense of frustration that drove me, I think. I knew finishing the last page would be a bitter-sweet experience. But it was an experience I had to go through with. Do you understand, Ben?'

The fact that she had called him Ben so naturally seemed to mark an important moment in their meeting. Cooper had interviewed enough people to know that unburdening herself of her thoughts had made Morrissey feel closer to him and had put him in the role of a friend. He had no problem with that.

'I think I understand.'

'Good. Did you know that last Monday was the anniversary of the crash?'

'Yes, I realized that.'

'I don't know why, but it seemed important I should come over here now.'

'Do you happen to have the medal with you?' asked Cooper.

'Yes. And the package it came in, too.' Morrissey placed the medal on the table. 'My grandfather kept it on him all the time when he was flying. It was a kind of lucky charm.'

Cooper used a dessert spoon to tip the medal towards the light from the pub window, so that he could see the shine from its metal surface.

Morrissey watched him with a smile. 'If you're looking for fingerprints, I have to tell you that the first thing my mother did was give it a good clean. She said it was dirty. Tarnished. She used metal polish on it.'

'Great.' Cooper could smell the polish. But there were pitted areas of corrosion on the metal, and damp stains on the faded ribbon. There were darker stains, too – small specks that could have been blood. The medal had arrived in an ancient leather pouch, which had crumbled and split until it was practically useless. On the inside were the remains of decayed stitching, where a label might once have been attached. The pouch had been wrapped in brown paper folded over several times and sealed with parcel tape, and the Canadian address was written in capital letters with a black felt-tipped pen.

'And the address is correct?'

'Yes.'

'I wonder how the sender knew your mother's address.'

'Brilliant,' said Morrissey.

Cooper looked up from the package. 'Sorry?'

'Don't you think that's what we've been wondering for months, ever since the medal arrived?'

'Of course.'

'It has to be someone who either had access to my grandfather's service records, or who was close enough to him for my grandfather to have given them his home address. Perhaps he wrote it down for them, so that they could stay in touch after the war was over.'

'You mean one of the members of his crew?'

'And since it was mailed from Edendale . . .'

'You concluded that it came from the surviving crew member, Zygmunt Lukasz.'

'Who else? When Frank Baine told us Lukasz still lived in Edendale, it seemed a pretty logical conclusion. Who else could my grandfather have known in this area?'

Cooper passed back the medal and the package. 'Families of the other crew members would have received their possessions from the RAF after the crash. Any one of them might have had your grandfather's home address among their belongings.'

'None of them lives anywhere near here.'

'You're certain, then, that Zygmunt Lukasz is involved in some way?'

'Either that,' said Morrissey, 'or my grandfather is still alive and living in Edendale.'

The atmosphere in the CID room was icy. Gavin Murfin was already there, and he looked green, as if he had finally eaten too many chicken tikka masalas. He saw Diane Fry come in and looked away.

'What's up with Gavin?' she asked Hitchens. 'Why does he look so sick?'

'He's been chasing down missing persons to match the Snowman, hasn't he? And he finally got around to circulating the description nationally.'

'Yes?'

'He did it properly, too. Sent details to all forces. *All* forces.'

Murfin definitely looked to be in a state of shock. His hair was standing on end, as if he had pushed greasy fingers through it in his agitation.

'One of the forces had a match?' said Fry.

'Yes, and they're on their way right now.'

'That's good.'

'Do you think so, Diane?'

'If somebody can spare the manpower to give us some back-up, that's great, surely? Well done, Gavin.' Fry looked at their faces, and saw how uneasy Hitchens was. 'It's not the RUC, is it? Don't tell me it's the Ulster troubles after all this time?'

'Oh, no,' said Hitchens. 'It's nothing so straightforward as a terrorist execution.'

'Who, then? Who've we stirred up? A neighbouring force?'

'No. A national force.'

'National?' Fry frowned. 'Railway police, you mean, sir? No? Not the National Crime Squad? Special Branch?'

'The military wing,' said Hitchens. 'Ministry of Defence Police. We've got two officers from the MDP arriving here today. They think they might know our Snowman. They think he might be one of theirs.'

'One of theirs? A missing serviceman?'

'The name of their missing person is Nick Easton. And when I say he's one of theirs, I mean one of theirs. He was an RAF special investigator. They'll be here in about an hour's time, so they're not messing about on this one. You'll be working with a Sergeant Jane Caudwell.'

Ben Cooper and Alison Morrissey split the bill between them and left the pub. For a few minutes, they walked in silence, until they found themselves on the river bank. In this one short stretch of river there were hundreds of birds on the water, calling and diving, splashing and arguing, cocking their heads at a few people on the paths. An old couple were discussing the difference between coots and moorhens. Two children argued over the last bit of bread, and tried to throw it to the furthest duck. Dogs became hysterical at the flapping of wings.

Near the weir, the water became shallower, and you could lean over and stare at the bottom, looking for fish. Rafts of dead willow leaves floated on the surface, swirling gently in aimless circles, clinging together in a dark scum as they touched the banks. Then, suddenly, a couple of feet away, the water roared over the weir. The meltwater was pouring off the hills, raising the level of the river. The water bounced so hard off the rocky bottom that it rose up again in white spurts inside the cascade. Then it foamed away towards the bridge, splashing over an old tree trunk that had lodged on the edge.

'It wasn't only my grandfather who was a hero,' said Morrissey. 'Klemens Wach had an admirable service record, too. When he arrived in Nottinghamshire, he was already one of the heroes of Poland, the ones who aren't forgotten, even now.'

'What do you mean?'

'Wach was transferred to Leadenhall from 305 Squadron, the famous Polish unit.'

'Was he?' said Cooper.

'Sure. It's in the file. They're a legendary squadron in Poland, apparently.'

'Right.'

They passed two bikers, a couple in their thirties, who sat on a bench sipping tea from paper cups, their helmets on the wooden slats next to them and their boots outstretched as they watched the ducks foraging for food. They sat without speaking, lifting their heads only to stare with amazement at a white-haired man in a black over-coat who attempted to hand them a religious pamphlet.

'How long are you staying in the area?' said Cooper.

'As long as necessary.'

'Have you no job to go back to in Toronto?'

'I'm a high-school teacher. But I took a sabbatical,' she said, with a small smile.

'Lucky you. And no family?'

'Only my mother and a brother a few years older than me. They support what I'm doing all the way. My mother and I, we're very alike. We think the same way on this. We have to know how the final chapter ends. We just have to, Ben.'

'So your grandmother was left alone in 1945 with a small baby she must have had to bring up on her own.'

'Not for long. She found another man. In fact, my mother's maiden name was Rees. She took the name of her stepfather, Kenneth Rees.'

'Your grandmother re-married?'

'How could she? Her husband hadn't ever been declared dead. She didn't actually consider him to be dead. But she needed a man to support her, to help her raise my mother. That's the way it was back then. And Kenneth Rees was a good man. He never questioned it, my mother says. I remember him very well, though he died fifteen years ago.'

Irritatingly, Cooper found himself longing for

a way he could ask Alison for a photograph of Kenneth Rees. He had an urge to compare one to the photos of Danny McTeague.

'Where was Rees from?'

'Newcastle upon Tyne. He was a structural engineer who came to Canada to build bridges.'

'Would he have been about the same age as your real grandfather?'

'About.'

'I suppose your grandmother had known him for a while? Or did she meet him after your grandfather went missing?'

Cooper found he was walking on his own. Alison Morrissey was no longer alongside him. He turned and saw that she had stopped a few feet behind him. Her lips were apart, and her breath came in angry spurts. She had shoved her hands into the pockets of her coat again in the way that he had last seen outside Walter Rowland's house. Her posture was angry, but defensive. Stubborn, yet awfully vulnerable.

'You think Kenneth Rees was my real grandfather using a different name,' she said. 'Why should he have married my grandmother – they were already married. He couldn't let anybody know who he was, because he was a deserter. He would have been sent to prison.'

'I didn't mean that.'

'Kenneth Rees was a Geordie engineer. He had red hair. He was only five foot eight. His accent was impossible to understand.'

363

'You say he's dead now?'

'Yes, but I can have his details faxed to you, if you want. A photograph, too.'

Cooper desperately wanted to say it wouldn't be necessary, but he knew he needed to see the evidence himself, for his own peace of mind. Alison simply nodded, understanding his lack of response. 'I'll phone my mother and get her to do it later today,' she said. 'So you'll have them first thing Monday morning. Is that soon enough for you?'

'Of course.'

'Do you have e-mail?'

'A fax will be fine.'

Morrissey looked across the road at the hotel. She seemed disappointed, but she had proved herself to be resilient so far, and he knew it would pass. He certainly hoped it would pass.

'Thanks for the lunch,' she said.

'You paid for it yourself,' said Cooper. 'I didn't do anything.'

'So you didn't.'

Cooper watched Morrissey pass the iron railings and go back into the hotel. He knew there was something wrong about what she had told him. And it wasn't just his wild suspicion about the Geordie, Kenneth Rees. Alison Morrissey's story wasn't the whole truth.

22

Diane Fry was waiting for Ben Cooper outside his flat in Welbeck Street, her arms folded as she leaned on her car parked at the kerb. Mrs Shelley's curtain next door was twitching anxiously.

'Diane? Another visit?'

'Where have you been?' she said.

'It's my day off.'

'You haven't been answering my calls again,' she said. 'I need you.'

Cooper saw a blond head in the passenger seat of Fry's car.

'But you've got Gavin,' he said.

'Yes, I know I've got bloody Gavin. But I need *you*.' She hustled Cooper towards the car. 'Gavin, get in the back,' she said.

Murfin stumbled out, and a shower of plastic wrappers fell around his feet on to the snow. Cooper could have booked him for a litter offence. 'Hi, Ben. Charged any window cleaners recently?'

'Shut up,' said Fry. 'And get in the back.'

Cooper hesitated at the passenger door. 'There's some sort of sticky mess on the seat,' he said.

'You two,' said Fry, losing patience. 'You two are *both* going to be a sticky mess on the floor in a minute. Now, will you –'

'I know. Get in the car. What's so important? Have we got another body or something?'

For a trained response driver, Diane Fry wasn't coping well in the snow today. She accelerated too hard and braked too suddenly. Now and then, Ben Cooper could feel the wheels start to slide a little and braced himself for a collision with the kerb or a car coming in the opposite direction. But she always seemed to correct the steering just in time. At the top of the High Street, she turned left at the lights into Clappergate, away from the pedestrianized shopping area. They passed the front of the railway station and the spire of All Saints parish church, where someone had built a snowman in the churchyard. It had been made to look like the vicar, with a black T-shirt and a circle of white cardboard for a dog collar, and marbles to create glittering eyes.

'Where are we going?' said Cooper.

'Back to West Street first,' said Fry.

'We're going the wrong way.'

'I'm avoiding the hill.'

'Yes – if you drive like this on the straight, you'd never make it up the hill, would you?'

'There are three things you need to know,' said

Fry, without smiling. 'One, we have an identification on the Snowman, who turns out to be an RAF investigator called Nick Easton.'

'Right.'

'Second, we've had a couple of goons from the Ministry of Defence Police at West Street this morning. It was the MDP who had been trying to trace Easton at the air museum.'

Cooper thought that was quite enough to take in at once. But it sounded as though there was even more. 'And what's the third thing I need to know?' he said.

'The third thing you need to know,' said Fry, 'is that, if you don't like my driving, you can get out and walk.'

'Oh. Right.'

Fry turned up past the High Peak College campus. Though it was uphill here, it was a gentle, winding incline, unlike the precipitous approach to the West Street divisional headquarters.

'Your mate's still missing,' said Gavin Murfin from the back seat, as if trying to cheer Cooper up.

'What mate?'

'Eddie Kemp. I checked his record. He's got quite a bit of form, hasn't he?'

They reached the top of the hill and worked their way through the back roads towards West Street. At least Fry had learned to find her way around the town now. It was no longer foreign territory to her, as it had seemed to be for a long time after she had transferred from the West Midlands. Some officers at West Street had called her 'the Bitch from the Black Country' in the early days. Cooper hadn't heard that title for a while. He hoped Fry herself had never heard it.

Sergeant Jane Caudwell and PC Steve Nash had driven up from the Ministry of Defence Police headquarters in Essex. Diane Fry had taken an instant dislike to Caudwell. She couldn't explain what it was about her – whether it was the dimples in her cheeks when she smiled, or the muscles that bulged in her broad shoulders when she took off her coat. Her sidekick, Nash, Fry managed to forget within moments. He sat in the background, saying nothing, not even 'hello'. DCI Tailby had come in for the meeting as well as DI Hitchens.

'Nick Easton was an investigator with the RAF Police,' said Sergeant Caudwell. 'We're arranging for his wife to make a formal identification, but we don't think there's any doubt. He's very well known. They called him "Magic Nick" Easton, because of his speciality.'

A photograph was passed round showing an RAF policeman in a blue uniform. It was clear to Fry that he and the Snowman were one and the same person. The attached personal details included a description of his tattoo.

'A speciality?' said Tailby, who looked even more unhappy today. But he always looked unhappy when his Sundays were disturbed.

'He was a children's entertainer in his spare time,' said Caudwell. 'His party tricks were very popular with the kiddies, I'm told. The top brass loved him – lots of opportunities for good PR, establishing friendly relations with the local community and all that.'

Paul Hitchens appeared to be on the verge of making a joke, but he looked at Caudwell and Nash and changed his mind.

'What case had Easton been working on?' asked Tailby.

'I'm afraid I can't tell you that at the moment,' said Caudwell.

Tailby stiffened and drew himself up to a greater height. He was several inches taller than Caudwell and two levels higher in seniority, but it didn't seem to make much difference.

'I think we're going to have to know, don't you?' he said.

'I'm sorry, sir. Not for the time being.'

'That's ridiculous, Sergeant. We have to be able to share information.'

Caudwell shook her head. The two stared at each other for a moment. Fry noticed that Caudwell hardly seemed to blink. Maybe she'd had her eyes stitched open to make her more frightening.

'I'll have to have a word with your chief,' said Tailby. 'This needs sorting out at a higher level. We need access to information.'

'Well, we'll see,' said Caudwell. 'It may not be

something we want to share. But that's not my decision. In any case, we don't know what Easton was doing in your area. We last heard of him in Nottinghamshire.'

'At the aircraft museum at Leadenhall,' said Fry.

Caudwell looked at her for the first time. She smiled, and her dimples made white holes in her cheeks. In the background, Nash was smiling, too. But he had no dimples, only a brutal haircut and eyes that strayed a little too close together.

'Ah,' said Caudwell. 'I see you know a little already.'

'I presume it was your people who had been to Leadenhall before us.'

'Since Nick Easton failed to keep in contact, we've been trying to trace his movements.' Caudwell turned back to the senior officers. 'What progress have you made on the cause of death?' she said.

'A small, sharp knife or scalpel, something of that kind,' said Hitchens. 'And we don't know that he was actually killed in this area. We think he was already dead when he was left by the side of the road, and we don't yet know where his body had been brought from.'

'Forensics?'

'Apart from the fatal wound, there were no traces on the body that couldn't be accounted for at the scene. There were some dirt stains on his suit that contained engine oil, and that's our only hope of identifying the vehicle he was carried in. It seems likely that his body was wrapped in something that left no traces – a plastic sheet, something of that nature. We found a bag, but it had been emptied. The snowplough had obliterated any traces of tyre marks.'

'Presumably Easton had a car?' said Tailby.

'A black Ford Focus.' Caudwell gave the registration number.

'We'll have all the car parks and usual dumping spots checked. And we'll ask Nottinghamshire to do the same.'

'There is one other place we think he visited after Leadenhall,' said Fry. 'We have a possible witness here in Edendale who says a man answering Easton's description visited her house on Monday.'

Caudwell leaned forward with interest. 'Name?'

'Mrs Grace Lukasz.'

The MDP sergeant smiled so broadly that even the dimples disappeared into the creases under her eyes. 'You have no idea', she said, 'how much that helps.'

Caudwell produced a sheet of paper, which she handed to DCI Tailby. He glanced at it and passed it to Hitchens.

'You might like to check whether the other names on that list mean anything, too,' said Caudwell. 'Then perhaps we can have another meeting, and we'll talk about sharing information.'

Fry watched Caudwell and Nash leave to check themselves into a local hotel.

'Can I see the list, please, sir?' she said.

Hitchens gave it to her, and Fry looked through the names. The list felt like a direct challenge, and she had an overwhelming desire to find out as much information as she could about all the people on it before she met Caudwell again. She could see the MDP were a problem, without a doubt. Anyone who was allocated to work with them would be on difficult ground. It would be like throwing someone to the wolves.

Ben Cooper had been trying to persuade Fry that Alison Morrissey's story was connected to the Snowman enquiry, and yet when the evidence was presented to him, it came as a surprise. Subconsciously, perhaps, he had been convinced that the connections he was making were imaginary, that he had been making them up because he wanted a reason to continue the McTeague investigation. But Fry had no reason for making these things up.

'So what do you say to that, Ben?' she asked.

'It was after Easton's visit that Zygmunt Lukasz started his journal.'

'Journal? What's this?'

'According to his son, Zygmunt is writing his account of the crash of Sugar Uncle Victor,' said Cooper.

'Oh, that.'

'Diane, don't you think it's time we conceded the possibility that the two things are connected?' he said.

Fry stared at him for a moment. 'What are you saying, Ben? Do you think Alison Morrissey might have been involved in the death of Nick Easton?'

'That wasn't what I meant. She wasn't even in the country at the time. She arrived after Easton was found.'

'Are you sure? Have you confirmed the time of her flight from Canada? Have you checked she was on the passenger list?'

'No.'

'Perhaps it's about time you did, then.'

Cooper stayed silent.

'It shouldn't be a problem,' said Fry. 'As long as you don't feel any personal involvement, that is. And I'm sure you don't feel that, do you, Ben? It wouldn't be like you at all. Not a competent and dedicated detective like yourself.'

Cooper felt himself flush. It was a habit he hated in himself, a ridiculous thing for someone approaching thirty years of age. Diane Fry had the uncanny knack of doing it to him. But, of course, it was usually because she was right.

'The connection is there,' he said. 'The link is the Lukasz family. Sergeant Caudwell knew the name – and I bet it's on the list she gave us.'

'Yes, it is.'

'I think Nick Easton was looking for Andrew Lukasz, though, not Zygmunt.'

'Why?'

'I don't know,' said Cooper. 'But it seems more than a coincidence that Andrew disappeared the day before Easton arrived. And something upset Zygmunt. His family have been worried about him. They say he's stopped speaking English. Personally, I think he's being damned awkward. But then, he hasn't got long left to live, they say.'

'Is his son very close to him?'

'They're all close. Yes, very close.'

'Peter Lukasz – what does he do for a living?'

'He's a doctor, works in the A&E department at the hospital.'

Fry opened a folder full of postmortem photographs of Nick Easton. Cooper still thought of him as the Snowman, since Easton had arrived in Derbyshire with the snow.

'According to Mrs Van Doon, the fatal wound on Easton was caused by a small, very sharp instrument. It could have been a scalpel.'

'OK, I can see what you're thinking. But Peter Lukasz is supposed to have been on duty at the hospital. We can easily check if he was where he ought to have been at the time Easton was killed.'

'Do it, then. What sort of car does Lukasz drive?'

'A blue BMW, three or four years old.'

'Good in snow?'

'I doubt it.'

'But there's a close little community there, you said.'

'It doesn't mean they'd conspire together to murder somebody. That would take a serious shared motive.'

'Yes.' Fry thought about it for a while, looked at the lists in front of her, and thought again.

'Ben, where else have you been?' she said.

'What do you mean?'

'On this business of Alison Morrissey's. Who else have you been to see? There was Zygmunt Lukasz, and the old RAF rescue man, Rowland. Who else is there? Tell me.'

'Well, there's George Malkin.'

Fry's face was grim. She looked as though she wanted to grab the lapels of his coat and shake him.

'Tell me who George Malkin is, Ben.'

'He was a farmworker, but he's been retired for years. The place he lives in at Harrop was his father's farm in those days, but there's only the old farmhouse left now. He was a child at the time of the Lancaster crash, but he went up to the site with his brother that night. Malkin is a lonely old man – solitary, going a bit strange, but he remembers the crash all right.' Cooper paused, thinking of Zygmunt Lukasz and Walter Rowland. 'Well, Malkin is not so old, really. Only in his sixties. It just happens that he remembers the crash very well.'

Fry continued to stare at him. 'It just happens?' she said. 'It just happens?'

'Well, yes.'

'This would be George Malkin, of Hollow Shaw Farm, Harrop?'

'Yes. What's all this about?'

Fry waved the file at him. 'Ben, George Malkin is another one of the names on Nick Easton's list. You've been wandering backwards and forwards across their enquiry, without knowing what the hell you were doing.'

Cooper felt a little surge of excitement, as if all his instincts had been justified.

'What are we going to do?'

'Have you got anything on for the rest of today?'

'Not a thing.'

'And have you got a phone number for the Lukasz family?'

'Yes.'

'Try them. We'll go and see them and Gavin can find his own way home.'

Cooper rang. There was no reply. 'They're not in.'

'Malkin, then.'

He tried another number. George Malkin was in, but said he would be busy.

'We'd really like to come today, Mr Malkin,' said Cooper.

'If you must. But be warned – you'll take me as you find me.'

Cooper nodded at Fry. 'He'll see us.'

'Let's go, then,' she said. 'I'll let DI Hitchens know the situation, and we'll see how your friend Malkin comes into this.'

But Cooper still wasn't sure where they stood.

The arrival of the Ministry of Defence Police had confused him, and so did Diane Fry's sudden interest.

'Diane, do you think I'm right, then – that there might be some connection with the Lancaster crash?'

'If it was just you, Ben, I'd say it was definitely your imagination,' said Fry.

'But it isn't just me?'

'No. When the MDP phoned this morning, one of the first things they asked for was to be shown the site of the wreck of Lancaster SU-V.'

Ben Cooper had never had any contact with the Ministry of Defence Police before, except when he had met some members of their surveillance unit on a training course. But he did have an old acquaintance in the RAF Police. Carol Parry was a local woman. Soon she would be finishing her time in the RAF, and she had been talking about applying to Derbyshire Constabulary for a job. Derbyshire would welcome her with open arms – officers with experience would be vital to balance the number of new recruits who were filtering into the ranks.

While he waited for Diane Fry, Cooper gave Carol Parry a call.

'The MDP are an entirely different animal to us,' said Parry. 'They have a much wider remit, and they deal with civilians. All our customers are servicemen, and most of them end up with the provosts in the Military Correctional Training Centre at Colchester. If the Court Martial gives them more than eighteen months, they transfer to a Home Office prison. So we're not really concerned with punishing serious crimes.'

'Who is, these days?'

'Well, don't tell the MDP you've spoken to me. They won't like it.'

'Why not?'

'There's no love lost between the services. It's like we take the mickey out of the Royal Military Police, and the RMP call us "snowdrops". But the MDP, they don't like either of us. Their numbers are being hacked all the time, because we're finding other ways of doing the job. It's the way of the world.'

'But *we* work together with the RAF Police when it's needed. We co-operate.'

'Ah, but that's because we need you. The RAF Police have no powers of arrest. *You* have the constabulary powers. But so does Sergeant Caudwell. By the way, are Caudwell and her staff armed?'

'What? I have no idea.'

'Seventy-five per cent of MDP officers are permanently armed.'

'In Derbyshire we have to be specially trained before we're approved to carry firearms,' protested Cooper. 'We have to pass regular tests.'

'So do they,' said Parry. 'Every one of them is fully weapons trained. It makes you remember what they're really there for. Of course, the only time the general public is likely to notice them is when they're escorting nuclear convoys up the A1. It's a very British way – if you don't make a fuss about it, nobody notices.'

'That's been a help,' said Cooper. 'I suppose.'

'What's the weather like there, anyway, Ben?'

'Warming up a bit,' he said.

23

At least Diane Fry had the sense to let Cooper drive
them to Harrop in his Toyota. She had glanced at
the road map and seen the clustering of contour
lines that indicated the steep descent on the other
side of the Snake Pass and the even steeper climb
to Harrop. There were still patches of snow and
lurking corners of black ice that would be worsening now as it grew dark again.

On the way to Harrop, they passed an empty
patrol car parked in a lay-by near Irontongue Hill.
The car displayed the force's website address on the
side – www.derbyshire. police.uk. Members of the
public were able to visit the site and read the Chief
Constable's report and news of the Bobby of the
Year Award. Cooper's favourite was the recruitment section, which stated that candidates had
to be proficient in the use of 'everyday technical
equipment', like telephones and riot shields.

A few yards further up the road, two officers in
fluorescent jackets were walking up and down the

road opening the yellow grit bins placed on the verges by the council. They were still looking for Baby Chloe.

'I was thinking about Marie Tennent yesterday,' said Cooper.

'Oh, yes?' said Fry.

'I was trying to understand why she did it. Why she went up there, I mean, to leave the baby clothes.'

'And did you succeed in understanding, Ben?'

'No,' he said. 'It didn't seem enough of a reason to me.'

'Nor me,' said Fry.

'I wish there were more time to spend on her. I'd like to be able to understand.'

'Finding the baby is what's important, for now. We can leave that to others.'

Despite Fry's words, Cooper didn't think she sounded entirely convinced. She, too, wanted to know about Marie Tennent. But there were procedures to be followed, priorities to be observed. A need to understand why people behaved the way they did was not enough to justify their time.

They drove on in silence for a while, following the twists and turns of the Snake Pass.

'So how's the new place?' said Fry. 'Settled in OK?'

'Sure. It's very handy.'

'You won't have any trouble getting into work on time, anyway.'

'I never did,' said Cooper.

'A lot of people don't think it's a good idea to live on your own patch. The customers can get to know where your home address is. It's been on my mind out at Grosvenor Avenue, but you're really in the thick of it where you are. Right on the doorstep for any tanked-up hooligan who staggers out of a town-centre pub and fancies throwing a brick through a copper's window. I know you're everybody's favourite bobby, but even you must have a few enemies, Ben.'

'I don't mind that,' said Cooper. 'I'll put up with that risk. I prefer to feel part of the community.'

'Oh,' said Fry. 'Community.'

'It's not a dirty word.'

'It isn't something real, though, is it? It's a word that we use in the titles of reports. Community liaison. Working with the community. Understanding the ethnic community. It's a word, Ben. It's not something you actually live in, not these days. You're living in the past. You should have been born fifty years earlier. You'd have loved that, wouldn't you? The days when a bit of friendly advice or a clip round the ear would solve most things.'

'Friendly advice still doesn't go amiss now and then.'

The Toyota crested the hill above Glossop, and the view over Manchester opened up in front of them. From here, the road wound down over western-facing moors to where the dry-stone walls ended and it became a different kind of country.

'Ben, I'm concerned that your mind seems to be on other things.'

'Like what?'

'I don't know. I wondered whether it was something to do with moving out of the farm. I know it's a big wrench for you. I know it's not easy living on your own for the first time.'

Cooper looked at her in amazement. This sounded horribly like a caring Diane Fry. But it wasn't really him she cared about. It was a question of doing the job right. No doubt she had been told to take an interest in the personal welfare of the officers under her supervision. He was probably her first attempt, a bit of practice.

'Ben? You were miles away again. What were you thinking about?'

'Nothing,' he said.

'And that's the trouble,' she said. Her voice had changed suddenly.

'What is?' asked Cooper, surprised.

'You never want to share what you're thinking. I don't know what's going on in your head, Ben, but sometimes it's obviously nothing to do with your job. There's a part of your life that you won't let anybody into.'

It was difficult to know what to say to her. So Cooper just kept quiet, and drove on.

Diane Fry was appalled by Harrop. It was like an outpost of the Wild West, without the cowboys. For a start, there didn't seem to be any roads, only potholed tracks, some of them barely wide enough for the car. There were no street lamps and no facilities of any kind. Nothing. Not a pub or a shop or a school, no village post office. Not even a phone box, as far as she could see. Just a few clusters of houses made of blackened stone, sheltering behind high walls.

The back of Irontongue Hill loomed over the village like the carcase of a dead whale, the outcrops of gritstone like patches of barnacles encrusted on its sides. Around Harrop, there was still deep snow lying in the fields, getting deeper as the grazing land deteriorated into open stretches of heather and dead bracken. The space between the houses and the rocky hillside was crammed with sheds and outbuildings, barns and derelict hen huts. In some cases, the supply of stone must have run out, because their builders had improvised with breeze-block and corrugated iron.

It was so desolate up here. Uninhabited and uninhabitable. But at least Fry had been able to see Manchester from further up the hill – a rare indication that civilization wasn't all that far away, after all. Down in the city, there would be restaurants and theatres and anonymous crowds, and concrete and tarmac instead of the relentless cold wind snatching at her clothes in this isolated moorland landscape. She had never felt so exposed in her life.

'We have to turn right and go up the hill a bit,' said Cooper.

'Up the hill? Aren't we high enough yet?'

'Hollow Shaw is the top farm, on the brow of the hill there.'

'I see it.'

Amazingly, the road got even worse as they approached Malkin's home. At one point, a ragged sheep stood in the roadway, chewing at a branch of a tree growing in a gateway. The animal turned and looked at the car as the headlights hit it. The light reflected from its eyes as if they were mirrors. Reluctantly, the sheep trotted away, its hooves slipping on the compacted snow.

'Do you know, if you'd told me what it was like, this is the last place I would have wanted to come in the dark,' said Fry.

'I expect it looks a bit better in the daylight,' said Cooper.

'You mean it *does* get light here sometimes?'

When George Malkin answered the door, he had his sleeves rolled up to reveal strong forearms, the hair on them stained with what looked like streaks of blood. He had taken his boots off in the house, but was wearing thick socks, as well as a brown sweater full of holes and plastic over-trousers on top of his blue boiler suit. His clothes were wet and sticky.

Cooper could sense Fry staring at Malkin's stained forearms, ready to jump to some wild conclusion from the man's appearance. But he could smell that unique odour of blood and birth fluids, both fruity and metallic at the same time – the scent of new life.

'Have you got some early lambs?' he said.

'Aye, I'm helping out Rod Whittaker – he's the lad who owns the land here now. He's got fifty head of ewes indoors.'

'We've a few routine questions, sir,' said Fry, who had learned to ignore agricultural conversations that she didn't understand.

'Oh, aye?' said Malkin. 'You'll have to come to the lambing shed with me, then.'

'Where?'

'This way. I can't leave 'em for long.'

They followed Malkin round the side of the house, through a gate and past a large steel shed with sliding doors that had been left open on their runners. Inside, there was a big articulated DAF lorry, parked next to a powerful Renault tractor with a snowplough blade attachment on the front.

'I take it that's your friend's truck,' said Cooper.

'Aye, he keeps the wagon here.'

'And the tractor?'

'Rod has to get work where he can – when it snows like this, he can't run the big wagon, but the council pays him to clear the roads around here, so he doesn't lose out. He can't afford not to have any money coming in – he has a family to keep. Contract haulage is almost as dodgy as farming, but he'll make a go of it.'

Behind the shed, they walked across a farmyard towards another building.

'Rod grazes his flock on these fields here. That grass comes up in the spring like little green rockets. He can afford to lamb the ewes early – he gets a good start with them.'

'You've split up the farm and kept the farmhouse for yourself,' said Cooper. 'So where does Mr Whittaker live?'

'Up the far end of the village,' said Malkin. 'It was my dad who sold off the land, when he couldn't keep the farm going any more. You could get a good price for land then, and it was enough. Rod has the land and these buildings here. Of course, he has the contract haulage business as well. That's why he can't be here to see to the ewes all the time. But he can't afford to pay for hired help, and he knows I don't mind.'

'You'll have lambed a few in your time, I bet,' said Cooper.

'Aye, a fair few.'

They entered the shed. It was much warmer than outside, and it was half-full of steel pens containing black-faced ewes. Cooper breathed in the warm smells of animals and straw. But Fry looked at the sheep and drew away.

'This isn't a very suitable place. Can we go back to the house?' she said.

'This lot are in the middle of lambing – you can see that,' said Malkin.

Fry gazed blankly at the sheep. Cooper knew she

could see nothing more than some mutton chops and several nice Sunday roasts milling about in the shed.

'They look all right to me,' she said.

'They can't be left to their own devices. Ask me your questions here.'

'All right. Do you recognize this man?' said Fry, producing the photograph of Nick Easton.

'It's no use showing me that – I haven't got my glasses on.'

'Well, where are they?'

'Back at the house, where I need them.'

'For goodness' sake!'

'I don't plan my day around you lot turning up, you know.'

Fry took a deep breath. Cooper could see her face twist as she drew in all the smells of sheep droppings and straw and sour milk.

'We're enquiring about a man called Sergeant Nick Easton. Does the name mean anything to you?'

'Never heard of him.'

'He worked for the Royal Air Force.'

'Oh,' said Malkin. 'Is it to do with the complaint?'

'What complaint?'

'About the low flying. There were some jet fighters came over here so low they almost knocked the chimney tops off. They frightened the sheep to death. Rod put in a complaint about it. He says he might be able to get compensation.'

Fry stared at him. Then she looked at Cooper.

'I think you'd have to prove the aircraft caused some damage or injury to the sheep,' he said. 'Did any of the ewes lose their lambs?'

'It's nothing to do with that at all,' said Fry.

'He's in the RAF, though?' Malkin said. 'He looks like he's in uniform in that photo. I can make out the blue, and the cap.'

'Yes, but you might have seen him in civilian clothes,' said Fry.

Malkin shrugged. 'Like I said – without my glasses . . .'

'Has anybody been here from the RAF recently? Or phoned you, maybe?'

'Not that I know of,' said Malkin. 'But I don't always answer the phone.'

'Your name was on a list of people Sergeant Easton was planning to visit. Can you think of any reason why that should be?'

'No.'

'Does the name Lukasz mean anything to you?'

Malkin seemed to tense a little. Before he could answer, a ewe in a nearby pen went down on its knees and began bellowing. Malkin turned towards it.

'It's all right,' said Cooper. 'Carry on.' And Malkin nodded at him, accepting his help without question as he handed over a spare pair of overalls.

Fry watched in amazement as Cooper took off his waxed coat and pulled the overalls over his clothes. She almost missed Malkin's next sentence.

'Lukasz. It rings a bell, that name. Something to do with the RAF, is it?'

'You tell me,' said Fry.

Out of the corner of her eye, she was aware that Cooper had climbed into the pen with the noisy ewe. The bellowing continued. It was the full-throated roar of childbirth. Fry couldn't shut out the noise, but she was trying to ignore what Cooper was doing as he bent down at the rear end of the sheep. Whatever it was, it made the sheep's eyes roll and its scream become even louder.

'Ben, what the hell are you doing?'

'There's a foot turned back,' said Cooper. 'Have you got a bit of baler band, sir?'

'Aye, on the pen side,' said Malkin.

Fry watched Cooper take a length of what looked like bright blue string, dip it in soapy water and fold it into a loop.

Cooper bent down again. Fry still didn't know exactly what he was doing, but she was quite sure it wasn't a usual occupation for a detective conducting an interview.

'Ah, here we come,' said Cooper, his voice strained with exertion.

There was a squelching sound, the sudden splash of fluids emptying into the straw, and the ewe fell silent. But then there was another noise. It was only a faint coughing, like the sound of a tiny child with something caught in its throat. It was followed by a sneeze. And Fry suddenly found she was desperate to see what was happening in there.

Malkin turned back towards her. 'The only thing I can think of is that he might have been an old airman. Polish, maybe, with that name? You should try old Walter Rowland. He used to be in the RAF. But that's years and years ago.'

'Yes, yes,' said Fry impatiently.

'Here, don't you want to know this? I thought you had to ask some questions.'

She could hear Cooper rustling in the straw, muttering to the sheep, crooning like some demented goatherd.

'It's a ewe lamb,' he said.

'Aye, that's good,' said Malkin, without looking round. 'Single, is it?'

'I'll tell you in a minute.'

Fry couldn't see anything except for Ben Cooper's back in the blue overalls. She tried to edge towards the pen, but Malkin was in her way.

'Any road,' he said, 'I don't know what else I can tell you. What else do you want to know? I don't understand what all this business is about the RAF.'

'Oh, shush!' she said.

Now a distinct high-pitched squeak came from somewhere in the wet straw. Fry leaned over to get a glimpse of something dark and wet, which hadn't been there a few seconds before. It was a creature with tiny, thin legs splayed in the straw and a head that was too big for its body. She watched in amazement as it began to struggle to its feet, wobbling dangerously, with its ears folded on to its head as it tried to get its balance. Although its eyes could hardly focus, its mouth was puckered and it was trying to move forward towards its mother. It had been in the world for only thirty seconds.

'Good, strong lamb,' said Cooper. 'We'll just get her suckling.'

'Where?' said Fry.

'From her mother's teats, where else?'

'It's too small. It won't be able to reach,' she said. 'Will it?'

'Don't you believe it.'

Within a few moments, the lamb had reached up and found a teat and was butting strongly with its head at its mother's belly. The ewe curved its neck and sniffed and licked at the lamb, which wagged its tail like a puppy.

'Look at it,' said Fry.

'A new life coming into the world,' said Cooper. 'It's always a bit of a special moment.'

'I can never see it often enough,' said Malkin, and they exchanged a meaningful look that Fry couldn't interpret, but which excluded her from its meaning.

'Have we finished?' Cooper asked her, un-buttoning his overall.

'Er, yeah,' she said, though she barely felt able to drag herself away from the lambing pen.

'If Mr Malkin remembers anything, I'm sure he'll contact us.'

Fry took the hint and presented Malkin with her Derbyshire Constabulary business card. Malkin took it between his thumb and forefinger, so as not to stain it. The card was white and shiny and pristine, and it looked as out of place in the lambing shed as if it had been an alien artefact from Mars.

Diane Fry walked back to the car while Ben Cooper asked to wash his hands. Malkin tapped him on the shoulder before he left. 'You're not a bad lad,' he said. 'I reckon you live on your own, am I right?'

'How on earth can you tell?'

Malkin gave him a sly wink. 'Like they say, it takes one to spot one. Have you got a good-sized pocket inside that coat? I bet you have.'

'Yes.'

'Stick this in it then. It's very fresh – you'll just have to clean it.'

He pushed a parcel wrapped in newspaper into Cooper's hand. Cooper felt at it for long enough to be sure that it wasn't a couple of kilos of crack cocaine or an illegal weapon he was being handed.

'I don't think I can take it,' he said.

'Don't be daft, lad. There's no harm in it. But don't tell your sergeant, eh? She wouldn't understand.'

Malkin winked at him again. Cooper was aware of Diane Fry waiting for him outside, but he was also conscious of the need to preserve this man's goodwill if he was going to get at his memories.

'I can only take it if I pay you something for it, Mr Malkin,' he said.

'Well, if you must. Fifty pence will do.'

Cooper dug out a fifty-pence piece. Living was proving cheap, so far. And he even knew how to prepare and cook rabbit. He and Randy would have a good supper from it.

'That's all open and above board then,' said Malkin, and winked again.

When the two detectives had gone, George Malkin went straight back to the sheep. He had to spread iodine on the navels of the newest lambs to stop them getting infections through their cords. And at the far end of the shed, there was another job he had to do, which he had postponed when the police arrived. The woman sergeant wouldn't have liked it much, and he had been reluctant to let them see what was in his pocket, the thing that he had gone to fetch from the house when they arrived.

Malkin enjoyed looking after the ewes. He was glad to be of use, happy to be working at his old job again for a short while. He had lambed hundreds of sheep in his time, and there was no need for anyone to tell him what to do. He could work alone, with his own thoughts for company. His help during the day meant that Rod Whittaker could go off to work on his driving job and take over in the shed when he came home in the evening.

He felt sorry for Rod, struggling to make a go of it. Farming was in the lad's blood, but he had no money to go into it properly, and little hope of making enough profit from his sheep to earn a living. Trying to get into farming was no life for a man now. Rod would be a lorry driver for the rest of his days, forced into earning his living some other way. Every morning, when he set off for work, he looked tired and bleary-eyed from a night dozing uncomfortably in the lambing shed.

Shortly before the police had arrived, one lamb had been born dead. Across the aisle, another ewe had produced two and was rejecting the second, refusing to allow it to feed. The tiny lamb was bleating, but its mother repeatedly butted it away in favour of its larger, stronger sibling, which was sucking vigorously at the teats.

Neither the dead lamb nor the rejected one was unusual, and Malkin knew exactly what he had to do. The fleece had to be skinned from the dead lamb and tied round the body of the rejected one, to give it the right smell for the bereaved ewe to accept it as her own. It was the old way, but the best one. The sheep were stupid – they never knew that they'd been fooled.

24

Diane Fry sat rigid and silent in the passenger seat of the Toyota on the way back from Harrop. Ben Cooper wanted to tell her that she had some straw sticking to her hair, but he daren't say anything. They were almost in Edendale before he felt her start to relax a little. It seemed to be the street lamps that did it, and the appearance of houses and petrol stations, with more light from their security systems and forecourts.

'We could try the Lukaszes, Diane,' said Cooper. 'Or do you want to wait until morning?'

Fry shook herself. 'Let's do it now. It could be too late in the morning.'

'OK.'

When they drove down Woodland Crescent, they found the Lukasz bungalow in darkness, and the BMW missing from the drive. Cooper rang the bell anyway.

'No luck,' he said.

'Damn. It'll have to be the morning then. I

suppose we ought to have known that some people have better things to do on a Sunday evening.'

'Hold on, what time is it?' said Cooper. 'Five o'clock? I know where they'll be.'

'You do?'

'Their *oplatek* dinner was due to start an hour ago. They'll all be down at the Dom Kombatanta.'

The Polish community seemed to be fond of their events. While they waited, Ben Cooper read the notices inside the entrance to the club. There was an Easter dinner in April, followed by something called the Katyn Day of Remembrance, which was celebrated by a Mass and wreath laying. Then 3rd May was Polish Constitution Day, with another Mass and a parade of standards. Cooper wondered if Zygmunt would be on parade for that day, with other members of the ex-servicemen's organization, the *Stowarzyszenie Polskich Kombatantow w W Brytanii*.

They had found someone working in the kitchen and asked them to take a message to Peter Lukasz, being reluctant to interrupt the event they could hear taking place through some double doors in the main hall.

'That's Peter Lukasz. Not Zygmunt Lukasz.'

Then Cooper noticed the final event on the spring calendar – the annual general meeting of the SPK itself, to be held at Dom Kombatanta. A poor turnout seemed almost to be accepted. The time of the AGM was set for 4 p.m., but underneath it was stated: *If there is no quorum, the AGM will begin at 4.30 p.m. in any case.* It gave Cooper a picture of the SPK – former soldiers and airmen, bent old warriors proud of the medals pinned to the breast pockets of their suits, some of them wearing their paratroopers' berets and their white eagle badges. But there were so few of them that they could no longer guarantee a quorum for a meeting once a year, acknowledging that death and illness would have intervened during the past twelve months.

He had seen them before, or old men just like them, lining up at the cenotaph every Remembrance Day. But their numbers were dwindling each year, as if it were only the fading memories of their sacrifice that had sustained them until now. Some of those taking part in the parade last year had looked so fragile and translucent that they could have been an illusion, anyway. Perhaps they existed only because of the public's belief in them, like Tinkerbell or Santa Claus.

'Peter says why don't you go through,' said the woman from the kitchen.

Diane Fry was still reluctant. 'Oh, but . . .'

'He says you're quite welcome tonight.'

Fry walked into the hall. Cooper hesitated in the doorway before following her. It was a strange feeling that he experienced, as if he were about to step into a foreign country. No – not a foreign country, but some kind of parallel universe where it was still England, but the people in it weren't English.

On the surface, the surroundings were familiar. It was a plain hall with a wooden floor and a stage, with a small bar to one side. The pumps and optics behind the bar looked like thousands of others, but the lettering on the bottles didn't make any sense. In the middle of the room were tables covered in white tablecloths and laden with cutlery and floral centrepieces. It could have been the Edendale old folks' Christmas party. It could have been the tennis club dinner, or a gathering of the Caledonian Society for Burns Night. The people sitting at the tables looked and sounded like any group of Derbyshire folk enjoying themselves – except that these people were speaking a language Cooper didn't understand. Their voices were raised, yet he couldn't make out the meaning of a single word. There were a lot of children here, too. Their presence gave a different atmosphere.

Then there were the smells. Food was being served – but it wasn't microwaved beef and Yorkshire puddings, nor even boiled ham and baked potatoes. The smells were too spicy, a combination of rich meats and strong herbs. Even the alcohol in some of the glasses looked the wrong colour. Cooper wanted to turn round and walk out, then come back in again, to see if the confusion cleared. The inconsistencies were too disorientating, the noise and the smells too redolent of a strange land.

He could see Zygmunt Lukasz and several other old men at a table. He watched them drinking glasses of clear liquid. Poles, like Russians, drank vodka, didn't they? The old men were knocking it back in one go, with a sharp flick of the wrist to toss the vodka to the back of the throat. And then they put down their glasses and attacked their starters – something that was decorated with small pieces of potato and cucumber, but smelled of fish.

Out of curiosity, Cooper picked up a copy of the menu from the bar. The starter was *sledzie w smietanie*. A helpful translation informed him that it was herrings in cream. His stomach gave a small lurch. He was sure that wasn't what he had smelled being prepared earlier. Maybe it had been the *pierogi* or the *bigos* that were on the menu for later. It hardly mattered. It would still be a frozen meal for one that awaited him when he got back to Welbeck Street.

'We're probably one of the most traditional Polish communities left in this country,' said Peter Lukasz, watching him read the menu. 'How long that will last, I don't know. A lot of it is down to the old people, of course. Like my father and my aunt Krystyna. Will you have a drink?'

Fry shook her head. 'That's not what we're here for.'

But Cooper was starting to feel he deserved a little freedom.

'Is there beer?' he asked Lukasz.

'*Zagloba Okocim.*'

'I don't know what it is, but that'll be fine.'

The shelves behind the bar were full of vodka

bottles, row upon row of them. Some of them were alarming colours, like a row of urine samples from people with virulent kidney diseases. He studied the labels. They were flavoured vodkas. He saw lemon, orange, pineapple, peach, cherry, melon and pepper. There was a pale green one that appeared to have a blade of grass floating in the bottle.

Lukasz was holding a tiny shot glass with a thick bottom and an eagle engraved on its side. Cooper noticed he was sipping his drink, not tossing it back in one go as the old men had done.

'What are you drinking yourself?' he asked.

'*Krupnik*,' said Lukasz. 'Polish honey vodka. Do you know, you have to pay nearly twenty pounds a bottle for it here, even when you can find it at all. Back home, it would cost about fifty pence.'

Cooper nodded. He was more interested in the fact that Lukasz had said 'back home' than in the information about honey vodka.

'Back home in Poland?' he said.

'Of course.'

Lukasz took another sip of his *krupnik*. Cooper knew perfectly well that Peter Lukasz had been born in Edendale and had lived in the town all his life.

Lukasz led them through into a small lounge bar. Cooper sat where he could watch Zygmunt and the other old men in the main hall. Several of them wore blazers, with their medals displayed on their breast pockets. It occurred to Cooper that any one of them could have been an eighty-year-old Danny McTeague. He could have changed his identity; he could have been living a different life for fifty-seven years. But why would he send his medal to his daughter after all this time? Did he want someone to come and find him? Was he seeking some kind of closure, as Zygmunt Lukasz was?

The other old men seemed to look to Zygmunt whenever he spoke. Women fussed around him, and children stood nearby and smiled at him. His pale blue eyes responded to everything with the same expression – a kind of calm pride.

'We need to talk to you about a man called Easton, Mr Lukasz,' said Cooper.

'Oh?' The name didn't seem to mean anything to him, but it was difficult to tell. Some people were better at hiding their reactions than others. They could be in turmoil inside, while calm on the exterior. 'What did you want to ask me?'

'It's a pity you failed to identify him when you came to the mortuary on Friday.'

'Ah, this is your dead person.'

'Exactly.'

'And why do you think I should have been able to identify him? At that time, you had some idea that he might have been my son.'

Cooper was conscious of the fact that he was a stranger here, an outsider. He had the feeling that people were watching him out of the corners of their eyes. He and Fry were guests here at the moment, but it wouldn't take much to transform them into the common enemy.

'We believe Nick Easton was the man who visited you on 7th January,' said Fry. 'Last Monday.'

'Who exactly is this man?'

'Perhaps you'd like to tell me that, sir.'

'I've told you – I wasn't even at home at the time. I was on duty at the hospital. My wife told me somebody had been, and she reported it to the police when she heard the appeals on the news. That's all I know, I'm afraid. Grace was the only person who actually saw him. But you've interviewed her, so you know that.'

'Mrs Lukasz didn't tell us everything, though. She didn't tell us why Easton came. Did she tell *you*, sir?'

Lukasz stared into his honey-flavoured vodka, and said nothing.

'I suppose we should ask your wife again,' said Cooper.

Lukasz sighed. 'Grace gets easily upset.'

'Then perhaps you'd better tell us yourself.'

'Grace says he was asking for Mr Lukasz. She thought he meant my father, because he was the only one home. He became insistent, and Grace was frightened that he was going to force his way into the house. So she sent him away. Grace tends to feel rather vulnerable when there's just my father and herself at home. And you have to realize, my father is terminally ill – we can't have him being troubled by people asking him questions all the time. Not this Easton, not the Canadian woman – and not you. We're trying to keep my father at home as long as feasible, but I'm afraid he'll be going into the hospice soon. His pain needs constant management.'

'Was it Easton's visit that prompted your father to begin writing his account of the crash of Sugar Uncle Victor?' said Cooper.

Lukasz looked surprised. 'Why should you think that?'

'The timing. And the fact that Nick Easton was an RAF investigator.'

Lukasz put his glass down suddenly. The bottom of it hit the table so hard that it almost shattered, and a splash of honey-flavoured vodka flew over the rim.

'Royal Air Force?' he said.

'Yes, sir. Have you any idea why Easton should have been asking to see your father?'

'I have no idea. None at all.'

Lukasz's expression was hard to read. He was puzzled, certainly. But also, Cooper thought, he was relieved.

'Have you heard from your son yet?' asked Fry.

'No.'

'Have you any idea where he is?'

'No.'

'Can you tell us what Andrew was doing during his time here in Edendale?'

'He said he had business up here.'

404

'What sort of business?'

'He didn't tell us. To be honest, the conversation was more, er, family-orientated.'

'What do you mean?'

'He's got married since he's been living in London. We weren't invited to the wedding. We only met his future wife once, and Grace took against her immediately, I'm afraid.'

'There was some bad feeling?' asked Fry.

'Yes.'

'So had your son come to make peace?' asked Cooper.

'I just told you, he was here on business.'

'It's *oplatek* time,' said Cooper. 'Doesn't that mean forgiveness and reconciliation?'

Lukasz smiled. 'You pick things up quickly. But Andrew didn't stay for *oplatek*. He disappeared again as suddenly as he came. He walked out last Sunday and we haven't heard from him since.'

'Had there been an argument?'

'He'd been talking to my father. I don't know what about, but I know my father was angry. Grace heard him shouting in Polish. I wasn't there at the time, because I was at the hospital. And now my father won't tell me why he was arguing with Andrew.' Lukasz turned and looked through the bar at the small group of old men enjoying their *oplatek* dinner. 'You see, Detective Constable Cooper, it isn't only you he won't talk to.'

'Mr Lukasz,' said Fry. 'What sort of business is your son Andrew in?'

'He works for a medical supplies company.'

'We'll need you to come in and make a statement first thing in the morning, Mr Lukasz,' said Fry. 'Your wife, too. And I'm afraid we're going to have to arrange for a translator so that we can interview your father.'

'Is that really necessary?'

'It's beginning to look extremely necessary,' said Fry.

The noise level had risen in the main hall, as if in expectation of forthcoming excitement. Sure enough, preparations were being made on the little stage. Cooper was reminded again of the old folks' parties the police choir sometimes sang at. Usually, half their audience had fallen asleep by the time they got to the third song – food and a glass of sweet sherry saw to that. But this audience was only warming up. He wondered what form of entertainment was appropriate to the evening.

Lukasz followed his gaze. 'There's a Nativity play,' he said.

'A what?' said Cooper.

'A Nativity play. Surely . . .'

'I know what a Nativity play is. But it's the middle of January.'

'This is our *oplatek* dinner,' said Lukasz. 'It's the time for the community. Not like *Wigilia*, which is for the family. The Nativity play will be performed by the children from the Saturday School.'

'You mean Sunday School,' said Cooper, thinking he was getting the hang of it. Many of the Poles were good Catholics, and he had seen the Church of Our Lady with its little school next door.

'Saturday,' said Lukasz. 'On Saturday mornings, the children study Polish. This year, some of them will take their O-level. I took it myself. I got a Grade 2, and Dad was very proud. He said I spoke the language almost as well as they do back home. Now my youngest children, Richard and Alice, are learning at the Saturday School, too.'

'We'd better be going,' said Fry.

'You could stay for the Nativity play, if you want,' said Lukasz. 'You're very welcome.'

'No, thank you. Oh, one more thing – we need Andrew's address in London.'

'Of course.'

Cooper hesitated, finishing his beer. There was no detectable peach or melon or pepper flavour, no blade of grass lurking in the bottom of the glass. It was a bit disappointing really. Yet the aftertaste had an indefinable strangeness that he knew would stay with him for the rest of the night.

'Mr Lukasz,' he said, 'before Nick Easton's visit, had something else happened to upset your father?'

Lukasz nodded. 'You're right. My father has been outraged at the pillaging of the aircraft wrecks that has been going on for years. The final straw was when his cousin Klemens' cigarette case turned up. It was an old silver case that Klemens had brought with him to Britain from Poland, and it had his initials engraved on it. My father was very angry about that. He wanted to know where it had come from, and who had taken it from Klemens. He thinks that taking things from the wrecks is desecration, because they're war graves that are being robbed. All his old hatred welled up again over that cigarette case. It was directed against the people he calls vultures.'

'Vultures?'

'Yes, vultures. Carrion feeders. My father says these people are picking over the remains of the dead, like vultures.'

'Did your father see this cigarette case himself, or did someone tell him about it?' asked Cooper.

'Oh, he saw it, and held it in his own hand. He identified it beyond any doubt.'

'Who showed it to him, Mr Lukasz?'

'Well . . .'

'Let me guess. Was it your son Andrew, perhaps?' Cooper waited for the slight nod. 'Do you think that might have been what they argued about last Sunday?'

Lukasz drained the last of his honey-flavoured vodka. 'Yes, I'm afraid it was.'

Ben Cooper felt the cold air hit him when they got outside the Dom Kombatanta and he found himself back in Harrington Street near Walter Rowland's house.

'We need to find Andrew Lukasz,' said Cooper.

'Put him on the list then,' said Fry. 'Baby Chloe, Eddie Kemp, Andrew Lukasz. I wonder if they're all lurking in the same place somewhere. That would certainly need your famous bit of luck, wouldn't it, Ben?'

'It looks as though Nick Easton must have been asking questions of the wrong people.'

'The vultures maybe? The ones the old man was so angry about for pillaging the aircraft wrecks?'

'Maybe so,' said Cooper. 'The other person we need to talk to is Graham Kemp, Eddie's brother. It sounds as if he's the number one collector of aviation memorabilia. If anybody knows where items like Klemens Wach's cigarette case came from, he will.'

'Does he live in Edendale?'

'Yes, according to the guy at Leadenhall.'

They reached the Toyota and waited for the heater to clear the beginnings of another frost from the windscreen. The sky was completely clear and full of stars. The gritting lorries would be out on the roads again tonight.

'I wonder how close Graham Kemp is to his brother,' said Fry. 'I wonder if he might have been involved with Eddie in the double assault on Monday night.'

Cooper looked at her. 'That would be a link.'

Fry rubbed her hands. 'I think we have a couple of promising lines of enquiry to put to the meeting in the morning.'

'It does give us the initiative,' said Cooper. 'Sergeant Caudwell will be impressed.'

'All right, Ben. I admit that might be a factor.'

'On the other hand,' said Cooper, 'what if someone thought Nick Easton himself was one of those vultures?'

'What?'

'If he was asking the wrong sort of questions, he could have given the wrong impression to someone who cared enough to be angry at the pillaging of the wreck sites.'

'Like who?'

'Only someone with a personal interest. Someone who had lost a close relative in a crashed aircraft. Someone who thought it was a desecration, the robbing of a grave.'

'Someone like Zygmunt Lukasz, you mean?'

'Peter Lukasz was very calm on the outside,' said Cooper. 'And he attributed the hatred of the vultures to his father. But inside, I wonder if he shares the same feelings?'

Cooper put the Toyota in gear and drove down Harrington Street. They passed the Church of Our Lady of Czestochowa, the Polish Saturday School, and the lighted windows of the Dom Kombatanta.

He supposed it was inevitable the *oplatek* traditions would die out with the old people. In the Lukasz family, Zygmunt and his sister Krystyna were the only ones left who had been born in Poland. The others were more English in their ways, even Peter Lukasz – though when the old man was around he seemed to take on the same set of the shoulders, the same look about the eyes

410

that Cooper had noticed in the photograph of the young Zygmunt and Klemens. Determination, a fighting spirit. A capacity for hatred.

Cooper felt himself on unfamiliar territory. Yet these people weren't recent immigrants, like the asylum seekers from Iran and Albania. The Poles had lived in Derbyshire for nearly sixty years. He had lived right alongside them all his life, and yet he knew almost nothing about them.

As they drove back down into the town, he lifted his head and looked at the barrier of hills to the west of Edendale. They were bare and glittering in the starlight, ancient and unchanged since the geological upheavals that had left them there millions of years ago. But as he stared at the familiar hills, Cooper felt his perception of them shift and blur, until they were no longer merely hills. For the first time in his life, they had begun to look like the walls of a prison.

25

Alison Morrissey stood in the cobbled alleyway of Nick i' th' Tor outside Eden Valley Books. She banged on the door, ignoring the sign in the window, and kept banging until Lawrence Daley appeared in the gloom inside and drew back the bolts.

'The shop is closed,' he said. 'I never open on Sunday.'

'Not for anybody?' said Morrissey.

Lawrence peered at her carefully, wiping a finger over the lenses of his glasses.

'I don't sell books on a Sunday,' he said. 'I work six days a week selling books. Sunday is my day off from selling books.'

'My name is Alison Morrissey. I'm the grand-daughter of the pilot of the crashed Lancaster on Irontongue Hill.'

'I know who you are,' said Lawrence. 'I saw you on the television news. You were in the papers, too.'

'That's good,' said Morrissey. 'Can I come in?'

Lawrence still hesitated, as if a great deal depended on making the right decision. Then, reluctantly, he pulled open the door of the shop.

Morrissey stamped her feet free of snow as she stood in the narrow passage near the counter. There was no light in the shop except from the open door to the stairs, and Lawrence made no move to find the light switch.

'What is it you want?' he said.

Morrissey kept her hands in the pockets of her coat as she looked around the shop, raising her eyebrows at the shelves and piles of books that gradually became visible as her eyes adjusted.

'If you know who I am, perhaps you know why I've come,' she said.

'I don't know anything about aircraft wrecks,' said Lawrence. 'I sell books on them sometimes, but I don't think I've got any in at the moment. I sold my last copies a few days ago. You're wasting your time.'

'I don't think so.'

Morrissey took her hand out of her pocket. Carefully, she unwrapped the package she had shown to Ben Cooper. The medal caught the light from the stairs and glittered, so that Lawrence could be in no doubt what it was.

'This is the reason I'm here,' she said.

Lawrence took off his glasses and wiped his eyes, whether from tiredness or some sudden emotion, it was impossible to tell in the darkness. 'It's nothing to do with me,' he said.

'Would the police agree with you, I wonder?'

'There's nothing illegal here.'

'You wouldn't mind the police coming, then.'

'As it happens, I know one of the local detectives very well.'

'Detective Cooper, perhaps? He mentioned your shop to me. And he's very interested in this medal.'

Lawrence's shoulders seemed to slump a little. 'This is very unfair,' he said.

Morrissey thrust the medal at him like an amulet that would ward off evil. 'Do you think it's fair to *me*? Fair to my family? Fair to the memory of my grandfather?'

Finally, Lawrence gave in.

'You'd better come upstairs,' he said.

Before he led Alison Morrissey towards the stairs, Lawrence took a last look outside, into the dark alley. He wondered who else might be out there, waiting to disrupt his life.

Back at West Street, Diane Fry found the file on Marie Tennent still lying on Ben Cooper's desk. It was only four days since Marie had been found on Irontongue Hill, yet it might as well have been weeks. Fry knew there had been search parties in Dam Street, where Marie had lived. Posters and newspaper appeals were everywhere, calling for information on the whereabouts of Baby Chloe. But Fry had been so absorbed in other things that she had lost touch with what had been going on today.

In the Tennent file, there was a report from a sergeant in the uniformed section to say that they had gone over Marie's house again, and had cleared the snow from the back garden, but there was no indication of recent digging in the frozen ground. There was no sign of a baby. They had gradually been extending their search, and should by now have searched the millpond. The area of hillside where Marie had been found had also been painstakingly picked over.

And Fry saw that, as far as Marie herself was concerned, they were still waiting for a postmortem result before the inquest could be opened.

Then Fry saw the faxes on Ben Cooper's desk. They had come on a machine that used the old fax rolls, and the sheets were curling up into thick coils. It took only a glance to see that they had come from Canada and were connected with Alison Morrissey. There was a yellow message form stuck to the top sheet, too. 'Please phone Alison,' it said. Fry tried the phone number it gave, and a voice said: 'Good evening, the Cavendish Hotel.'

'Do you have a Miss Alison Morrissey staying there?' asked Fry.

'Yes, we do. Would you like me to see if she's in the hotel?'

'No, it doesn't matter.'

She put the phone down. It seemed to Fry that there was no doubt where Ben Cooper's attention was at the moment. He had been told by the Chief

415

Superintendent himself that there was no possibility of helping Alison Morrissey in her hopeless quest. But for Cooper, anything that was hopeless seemed to represent a challenge. Fry recalled the woman she had seen on TV, the same woman who had been chatting to Cooper at Underbank the other day. 'Phone Alison,' the message said. So there was another attraction for Cooper, too.

Fry placed the message carefully back on the roll of faxes. She would have to think seriously about what she was going to do about it.

Turning her attention back to the Tennent file, she saw that it had been kept up to date with the inclusion of copies of reports on the baby's remains. She scanned through the SOCO's report, then a statement from one of the officers who had attended the scene after the air cadets' discovery of the remains. It was a thorough and detailed account of the scene, written by a young female officer who had put a lot of effort in, even when it might seem there was no point. She had spent some time looking for evidence of recent visitors to the aircraft wreck, despite the fact that the remains were so old. Reading between the lines, it seemed to Fry that the officer had been affected by the sight of the bones and the new baby clothes and had sought for something else to concentrate on.

Curiously, one of her observations related to poppies. Not real poppies, but the red plastic or paper ones sold during the weeks before Remembrance

Day every year to raise money for ex-servicemen. During November, many people wore them pinned to their coats; entire wreaths of them were laid at war memorials up and down the country. And it seemed that remembrance poppies were left at the site of the Lancaster crash, too. Fry supposed the wreckage was itself a memorial, in a way. According to the report, someone had left a poppy there very recently, despite the fact that it was January and Remembrance Day was long since past.

It seemed unimportant. But Fry knew that such details, observed at the right time, could turn out to be surprisingly valuable later on. She marked the line about the poppies with a red pen and was finishing the report when her telephone rang.

She walked back to her own desk, carrying the Tennent file. The switchboard operator apologized, saying that she had been told that DS Fry was in the station and wondered if she could deal with a call that had just come in.

'Who is it?' said Fry.

'Sergeant Caudwell, from the Ministry of Defence Police.'

'OK, put her on.'

For a moment, Fry pictured Caudwell and Nash sharing a hotel with Alison Morrissey, but recalled that the MDP officers had been sent somewhere cheaper and more basic, probably the Travelodge.

'Ah, still on duty, I see,' said Caudwell when she got through to Fry. 'That's lucky.'

'What can I do for you?' said Fry.

'Well, I soon got bored in this hotel we've found, and there didn't seem to be anything else to do in Edendale, so I asked them to send up the local newspapers. I found some interesting reading.'

'They've covered the story of the unidentified body extensively,' said Fry. 'A lot of speculation as usual, I'm afraid.'

'Oh, yes. But not only that. There was the woman who froze to death.'

Fry looked down at the file still in her hand. 'Marie Tennent. But –'

'And a missing baby, and all that. Rather worrying for you, I imagine. And now there are the remains of a child, found at the site of an aircraft wreck. The papers don't say, but it seems to me you might be linking the two incidents.'

'Yes, we think it likely the dead baby was Marie Tennent's earlier child.'

'I see.' Caudwell paused for a moment. When she spoke again, her voice had a different tone. Fry could picture her smiling. 'DS Fry, I'm going to ask you a favour. I'd be very grateful if you could send me over a copy of your file on Marie Tennent.'

'Why would you want that?'

'Just following a line of thought,' said Caudwell airily. When Fry hesitated, she added: 'The aircraft wreck. You realize that's Ministry of Defence property? We have an interest. We're entitled to full consultation. Strictly speaking, we should have been informed before any action was taken at the site. But I'm sure we don't need to argue about that.'

'I'll send a copy over to your hotel as soon as I can,' said Fry.

'Thank you very much. An hour would be fine.'

Fry replaced the phone and read carefully through the Tennent file again. She frowned at the line she had marked about poppies, then shrugged her shoulders. At least it should keep Sergeant Caudwell quiet for a while.

It had only been a day since he had moved out of Bridge End Farm, yet Ben Cooper found it was the most difficult time of all. After he had dropped Diane Fry off at West Street, he had walked through the town to the Old School Nursing Home. He had promised that he would visit his mother nearly every day, and that was what he was trying to do, even if she didn't know that he had been.

At the end of the visit, it was hard to tear himself away. He had to remember that he had his own home to go back to now. But all he actually had was an unfamiliar door in Welbeck Street and a dark, empty flat. Only the presence of a fat, idle cat in the conservatory made the idea tolerable.

On his way back through town from the nursing home, Cooper found himself standing in Clappergate, on the pedestrianized area near the corner of High Street. This was a spot he normally tried to avoid. Usually, he walked further up the hill and came into Clappergate from Back Lane or through the shopping precinct. That way he didn't have to see the flowerbed where council gardeners planted daffodils to grow in the spring. It meant he didn't have to see the plaque on the wooden bench next to the flowerbed.

But today, he'd had other things on his mind, and the street looked different in the snow. The flowerbed was partly hidden by a layer of frozen snow into which passers-by had thrust empty bottles and McDonald's cartons, spontaneously creating a piece of modern art. That was how Cooper had found himself right by the bench, staring at the memorial plaque as if it had dropped out of the sky in front of him, like a fallen meteorite. He realized he must be only a few yards from the door of the Vine Inn and the place where the blood had settled and stained the stone setts.

The plaque looked shiny and clean today, but he had been told it was sometimes vandalized and sprayed by graffiti artists with red paint. The paint was as difficult to remove from the plaque as the blood had been to clean from the setts. The inscription on the plaque read: *In memory of Sergeant Joseph Cooper of the Derbyshire Constabulary, who died in the course of his duty near here*. It was followed by the date – that day in November, a little over two years ago, when Sergeant Cooper had been kicked to death by a group of youths who had objected to him attempting to make an arrest.

Cooper thought his father would actually have

been satisfied with this way of dying. He would not have wanted to be one of those old men who faded slowly away in retirement, deprived of any role in life. Cooper was certain that his father must have had a deep dread of retirement. He could not have tolerated the prospect of ceasing to have any importance, of disappearing and no one even noticing he had gone. This way, Sergeant Joe Cooper would be remembered for ever as he was when he died, because the plaque accorded him a place in posterity. His death had given him immortality.

Ben turned away from the plaque and faced back towards High Street. Four women were walking towards him on the pavement. They moved slowly and straddle-legged like cowboys, their hats pulled low over their eyes, their arms hanging by their thighs, weighted down by shopping bags bursting with booty. On the pavement in front of the women were long shadows thrown by the light spilling out of the windows of Marks & Spencer. They had been to the January sales at the stores on Clappergate that opened on a Sunday. Now they were heading to the bus station for their journey home to the Devonshire Estate or the stone terraces of Underbank.

He didn't want to be among these people. Not because they were strangers, but because they might actually recognize who he was and feel sorry for him when they saw him standing gazing at the plaque. He decided to cut through one of the lanes that ran up to Hollowgate and under the town hall clock tower into the market square. He could walk across the square and through the passages at Nick i' th' Tor to get to the traffic lights at Fargate.

The market square was almost deserted as Cooper crossed it. A scatter of pigeons wandered around the square, forlornly searching for any scraps still left from the previous day's market. A man in a yellow cagoule stood staring at the war memorial in the middle of the square, as if he had nowhere else to go. Perhaps he didn't. Edendale had its share of the homeless, and some of them would fail to survive this winter.

Cooper reached the entrance to Nimble John's Gate, where a little footbridge crossed the river before dividing left and right into Nick i' th' Tor and Rock Terrace. The setts had been re-laid near the bridge, but the passages were tilted at uneasy angles where they negotiated the steep slope across the river. The snow lay deep against the walls on either side, and no one had ever thought to provide street lighting for the passages, which were in deep darkness between the tall buildings. Below him, the River Eden was loud and roaring where it squeezed into a narrow channel between the banks. Crossing the bridge, the sound of the water was almost deafening.

He hesitated on the corner of Nick i' th' Tor, thinking he had seen a movement ahead. But it was only the melted snow turning to water and dripping from the guttering at the back of the old cinema. The drips were creating ripples on the puddles that already lay among the cobblestones. The only light in the passage was from the street lamps behind him in the market square, reflected in the puddles and on the grey pillows of dirty snow. Cooper had never before worried about walking through the streets of Edendale, though he knew many a woman would automatically run through a mental checklist before she went anywhere at night – was her handbag safe, was the street well lit, would it be safer to take a taxi, could she run properly in these shoes?

He turned at a sound. Down at the far end of the passage, he saw a familiar figure pass in front of the lights in the market square. It was a man wearing a long overcoat, like an army greatcoat. Eddie Kemp? As if hearing his name, the figure paused in the entrance of the alley and turned his head. For a moment, Cooper almost caught his eye. He saw a woollen cap outlined against the lights. He was so sure, he could almost catch the smell.

As the figure moved on, Cooper took a step forward, then stopped. He remembered the mistake he had made when he arrested Eddie Kemp the first time, in Hollowgate. It was wrong to assume that Kemp was on his own and would be an easy arrest. He took out his radio and reported in to Control to ask for support. Then he walked carefully down to the end of the alley and eased his way round the corner. There was no longer any sign of Kemp.

Cooper looked at the doorways on either side of the alley entrance. There weren't many shops here any more – Woolworth's and W. H. Smiths had moved into the shopping centre on Clappergate. Now, the businesses in the market square were mostly banks and building societies, estate agents and pubs. The butcher's shop, Ferris's, was starting to look like a relic, some kind of folk museum. He carefully checked the doorways of Barclays Bank and the Nationwide Building Society. Nothing. He jumped as the town hall clock began to strike seven. It sounded far too loud in the empty square, its clangs reverberating off the tall buildings. The pigeons took off and clattered together for a few seconds as they circled the square before landing again and resuming their search for food.

Cooper paused for a moment and waited for the clock to finish striking. He listened for footsteps, but he heard only the engine of a bus, which pulled into High Street and stopped. He saw the three women clambering on with their shopping bags.

Next to Barclays Bank was the Red Lion pub. The lights were on, but it had only just opened and he could see no customers inside. Nevertheless, he went in to have a look in the darker corners. Large video screens were showing MTV. The barmaid shook her head when he asked after a man in a greatcoat and a cap with fur ear-flaps.

So Kemp must have walked on into High Street.

From there, he could have gone in several directions – over the river into Eyre Street, down on to the relief road, or back along the river walk towards the network of passages. Beyond them was Buxton Road and then the Buttercross, which was Eddie Kemp's way home. On his own, Cooper had to make a choice. It would be quicker to return the way he had come, back up Nick i' th' Tor.

But after the lights of the square, the passage seemed even darker. The shops here didn't bother leaving their lights burning at night, as the big stores did. The Italian restaurant didn't open on Sundays in January, and it was in darkness. Halfway up he passed Larkin's, the baker's, which was always busy during the day. But now its windows were empty. The coffee shops and the gift shop looked faintly ridiculous in the snow. Icicles hanging from the guttering had started to thaw, and drips of icy water landed on his shoulders and splashed his neck when he walked too close to the buildings. By the morning, the water would be frozen again if the sky stayed clear.

Ahead of him, Cooper heard the noise of the river again. It sounded almost as if a dam had burst up the hill, as if thousands of gallons of water were roaring towards him down the passage. The cobbles and the walls on either side were wet enough to suggest that it had happened before, and that any second he might get swept away and washed up in the market square.

Further up, on the corner of Rock Terrace, he

could see Eden Valley Books, nestling into the tall buildings around it. Starlight glittered faintly on the roof, and a light was visible in a window on the second floor. Here was someone else who didn't bother closing curtains. But up there were only the pigeons and a view of the back of the town hall clock tower. Lawrence Daley must have a good vantage point over the roofs of Edendale. He must be able to look down into all the yards and closes, passages and alleys between here and the market square. He must be able to look down on the River Eden where it passed below the bridge.

As Cooper looked up at the lighted window, a shape passed across it, then a second. The first, he was sure, was Lawrence Daley himself. But the second figure was female. Cooper couldn't quite believe who he thought it was. Then she turned towards the window to look out, and he was certain.

Cooper heard a cough. Eddie Kemp? Did he really have a delicate respiratory system?

Then his radio came to life. 'Ben, we're in Eyre Street. Which way did he go?'

'Diane? I think he's in one of the alleys between you and the market square. Somewhere near the bookshop.'

'Which ways shall we cover?'

'He'll come out either on to Eyre Street or up Rock Terrace on to Buxton Road. I'm at the market square end of Nick i' th' Tor.'

'OK.'

426

Slowly, Cooper began to move forward again. It was steep here, and the setts were slippery if he walked too near the walls. He passed Larkin's and one of the coffee shops and was almost at the bridge. Even if there had been footsteps, he wouldn't have heard them now because of the noise of the river under the bridge.

Where a broken remnant of stone wall concealed a delivery door to one of the shops, there was a sudden movement, and a dark shape on the edge of his vision. Before Cooper could turn towards it, he felt himself pushed heavily, and he fell hard against the door. Along with the sudden jolt of pain from the impact, he heard a thud of something hitting the door alongside him. Then there were feet clattering on the setts as someone ran off down the alley.

Cooper tried to push himself away from the door to run after them, but found he was unable to move. There was a strange tightness in his right side, and he couldn't force his body away from the door. It was as if he had lost all the strength down his right side. There was no real pain, except from his shoulder where it had collided with the door. He tried to raise his right arm above his head. It wouldn't move all the way, but was held back by the tightness in his side, so that his arm hung ridiculously in mid-air. He felt like a man patting an invisible small boy on the head.

Feeling ridiculously embarrassed, he lowered his arm again. Then he concentrated on each

427

part of his body in turn, wondering if there was a serious, major pain somewhere that he had missed. Perhaps his brain had suppressed it, and the agony would hit him in a moment. Perhaps he was in a state of shock. He had heard of badly injured people who carried on moving for several minutes before their wounds overwhelmed them and they collapsed.

Cooper clearly remembered an impact. And he knew, too, that he had heard a faint crunching of flesh and bone. Now his body refused to allow him to move to pursue his assailant. Something was definitely wrong.

He bent his head to look down at his side. Blood was soaking through the lining of his coat. A thick drop of it trickled from the hem and landed in the snow, splashing on the frozen surface. The blood was very dark, so dark that it was almost purple.

As the adrenalin drained away from his limbs and icy water dripped on him from the guttering, Ben Cooper began to feel very cold.

26

Diane Fry had not seen Eddie Kemp before. But when the man coming up the alley dodged back into the shadows as soon as he saw the light of her torch and the uniform of the officer next to her, she had no doubt who he was.

She used her radio as she ran. 'Ben – he's headed back downhill towards Eyre Street. We've got him boxed in. Ben?' She got no reply, but assumed he was too busy closing in from the other direction. Cooper was never a man to use more words than necessary when communicating with other people.

Round the corner Fry ran headlong into the man she had been chasing. He had stopped suddenly on the bridge when he saw the other uniformed officer approaching from Eyre Street.

'Edward Kemp?'

The man stepped back and swung a punch at her. Fry deflected it easily. He was far too heavy and slow, and she had kept her *tae kwon do* skills sufficiently honed to make her responses good. Within a few seconds, she had his arm behind his back and his face against the stone wall.

'Edward Kemp or not, you're under arrest.'

The two uniforms got the cuffs on and took the man away. Fry looked round. Still no Ben Cooper.

'Damn it, Cooper, are you doing your shopping again, or what?'

Her voice had risen on the last few words and echoed in the alley. The only answer was the noise of the river running under the bridge and the dripping of water from the roofs. Up on the road, the door of the patrol car slammed.

He'd said he was at the market square end of Nick i' th' Tor. Somewhere over the bridge then, past the bookshop and round the corner.

'Ben?' she called.

'Here.'

His voice sounded strange. Fry began to run, slithering on the cobbles as she crossed the bridge. Then she saw him. He was standing against a garage door, with his back to her.

'Ben?'

'Hi, Diane.'

'What are you doing?'

'Nothing much.'

'I think we got Kemp.'

'Good.'

'You're sure it was him? I didn't get a good look at him. Have they never heard of street lights

430

at this end of town? Or did the gas supply just run out?'

'Yeah, it's pretty dark all right.'

She looked at him, starting to get irritated. 'Why are you leaning against that garage?'

'Well, the fact is, I don't think I'm able to move.'

Fry moved to touch him, then stopped.

'You *think*? Is this some kind of joke? Because if it is, I'm going to make you drive round with DC Murfin for a week, and you can pay for his onion bhajis yourself.'

'It's not a joke, Diane.'

'Jesus, you don't *sound* like somebody who's injured. Let's take a look.' She pulled out the torch from her pocket and shone it at his chest. 'Where's the problem?'

Cooper unbuttoned the front of his waxed coat with his left hand and let it fall open. 'Round about here somewhere. I felt this –'

'Don't touch it!'

'What?'

Gingerly, Fry used the head of the torch to pull open his coat. She drew it back far enough to show him the protruding handle.

'It looks like the handle of a bayonet.'

'Thank God it missed me.'

'It didn't miss you,' said Fry. 'You're bleeding. I'm calling an ambulance.'

'No, it missed me.'

Fry shone her torch on the blood trickling into the snow. It had pooled in the big inside pocket of

431

his coat and there was a greasy patch where it had soaked through.

'Believe me now, Ben? You're bleeding.'

'No, it's the rabbit,' said Cooper.

'What on earth are you talking about?' She looked at him as if he were delirious.

'There's a rabbit in my poacher's pocket. George Malkin gave it to me.'

'You *are* joking.'

'It's true.' Cooper laughed unsteadily with relief. 'The blade of the bayonet has gone right through the rabbit. The point pinned my coat to the door, but it passed through the entrails of the rabbit. Malkin said it was fresh. He was right.'

'You're sure you're not hurt?'

Cooper studied the rip where the bayonet had penetrated his waxed coat, gone through a few inches of skin and bone and embedded itself in the garage door. 'This coat cost a fortune,' he said.

'As long as the only hole he made was in your credit card, and not in your guts.'

'No, I'm fine.'

'Get the coat off, then, and we'll get the whole thing along to Forensics. God knows how we're going to explain the rabbit.'

'It would have been rude to refuse it, Diane. Besides, I paid him, so it wasn't a gift.'

'You haven't got a couple of pheasant down your trousers as well, have you?'

'No,' said Cooper. 'I'm just pleased to see you.'

*   *   *

432

As soon as Peter and Grace Lukasz got into bed that night, the argument began. It was about something trivial at first, a disagreement that Grace couldn't even remember when it was all over. It might have been about the colour of the new wallpaper, or whether they could afford a holiday in Portugal this summer.

It had begun to change in character when Peter had told her not to nag, that he had other things on his mind that were more important.

Grace had looked at him lying next to her. His face was turned towards her, but was in shadow because of the bedside lamp behind his head. She had turned off her own lamp already, and had taken off her reading glasses. Peter's face was too close to hers, too blurred by the shadows, for her to read his expression. His eyes were open, but she could sense that his face was closed. She touched his arm, and she could feel that his muscles were tense.

'What's the matter?' she said.

'Nothing.'

'There's something wrong.'

'Nothing at all. What do you mean?'

'Tell me, Peter.'

'Leave me alone – I'm tired.'

He rolled over on to his back, thumping his pillow with the back of his head as if to beat it into submission. Now Grace could make out his profile, outlined by a halo of light from the bedside lamp. His expression was set into a determined scowl. It was the expression that reminded her most of his father, Zygmunt, the one that made her think of the old man as a warrior still. The same determination was there in Peter's face. And the implacable hatred, too.

'The Canadian woman coming here has upset you, hasn't it?' said Grace.

'She's not important.'

'She didn't want to go away, did she?'

'I think I made it plain,' said Peter.

'It was strange, though, about the policeman. I thought that was strange, didn't you?'

Peter didn't reply. Watching him, Grace felt a sudden surge of irritation.

'Why don't you talk to me?' she said.

He sighed. 'Yes, it *was* strange. I thought it was strange she had already met him, strange that he knew what she'd come for. It was very strange. But it was *you* that invited him into our house in the first place.'

'Oh, it's my fault, is it?'

'No, I didn't mean that.'

'Is that what it is? You're sulking because you blame me.'

'Not at all.'

'But all I did was to ring the police because of the description they gave of the man who died.'

'I know. That's all you did.'

Now it was Grace's turn to shift on to her back. She stared at the bedroom ceiling, not really seeing it at all, just more shadows. She was silent, waiting for Peter to speak, wondering if he would bother, willing him to feel her hurt.

'You did it because of Andrew,' he said.

Grace was surprised to find tears suddenly leaking down her face and on to her pillow. She fumbled for a tissue in the pocket of her nightdress.

'I couldn't bear to think of him lying dead somewhere,' she said.

'Who? Andrew? Or some strange man you've never seen before in your life?'

'You don't understand.'

'Andrew has gone back to London. You have to accept that,' said Peter.

'How can I, until I hear from him? Why isn't he answering his phone? Why hasn't he been in touch to tell us where he is?'

'All right. But what did you think you were achieving by phoning the police and telling them you recognized the man they found on the Snake Pass? That was stupid. More than stupid. You brought the police here, as well as that bloody woman.'

'Don't swear at me.'

'Well, it *was* bloody stupid. That was the last thing we needed. What do you think it would have done to Dad if the policeman had insisted on seeing him? I can't believe you didn't think about that. But, no, you were only thinking of yourself. Somehow you had to feed your obsession. It's always been Andrew, Andrew, Andrew – it's turning your mind. Can't you see that?'

Grace held the tissue to her face. She tried to control a small, spasmodic sob that rose in her throat, not wanting to show Peter her weakness.

'I want to protect Zygmunt as much as you do,' she said.

'You have a funny way of showing it.'

'But it's true – I do.'

'I can't stand this, I really can't.' He turned over on to his other side, crushing his pillow and dragging the bedclothes almost away from her.

'Don't turn away from me, please,' said Grace.

Without even touching him, she knew his body was knotted with tension. Peter was frightened, of course. But he would never admit it. It was a difficult time for him, since he was so close to his father. She accepted that. The last thing she wanted to do was make it worse for them both. She wiped her eyes and put her hand on his shoulder. He felt cold and resisting. She tried to pull him back towards her so that she could see his face.

'Peter –'

Then he rolled on to his back again. 'Look, Grace, for God's sake forget about Andrew for now. He's not worth it. There are far more important things to worry about. Do you understand what I'm saying?'

'Yes, Peter. I understand.'

Suddenly, the tension went out of them both. Peter rolled on to his side. He sighed deeply, as if overwhelmed by tiredness, and within a minute or two he was asleep. Grace smiled in the darkness and patted his shoulder gently. Then she turned over and pressed her body against his, for the sake of the warmth.

After Ben Cooper had been examined at West Street that night, Diane Fry made him sit in the CID room and do nothing for a while. She even got somebody to make him a cup of tea, for the shock. Cooper knew there would be activity going on down in the town – the passageway where he had been attacked would be sealed off, witnesses would be sought with the usual futility. Later, he would have to make a full statement. It was something he wasn't looking forward to.

Cooper could see a pile of faxes waiting for him on his desk. Curious, he picked them up. They had come from Toronto, marked for his personal attention. There was a head-and-shoulders photograph of a man with wiry hair and a square jaw, and another of him standing next to a woman slightly taller than himself. The man was named as Kenneth Rees, Alison's mother's stepfather. Despite the poor quality of the reproduction on the fax machine, there was no doubt this man wasn't Danny McTeague. Fleetingly, Cooper considered the idea that there was no real proof it was Kenneth Rees either.

He put the faxes down to study in the morning. There had been something else about his conversation with Alison Morrissey earlier that day that had been nagging at him, and he needed to check it. It had been a small thing, but it had undermined his faith in the accuracy of her information.

Cooper found the file that the Local Intelligence Officer had put together for the Chief. According to the information on Klemens Wach, he had done his initial training with the RAF at Blackpool at the same time as his cousin Zygmunt, and they had both been posted to the Operational Training Unit at Lymm, in Cheshire. At Lymm, they had gone through a very British system of assembling air crews – hundreds of men had simply been put into a large room together and encouraged to mingle until they formed their own crews with the right combination of skills. It sounded a bit like the way football teams had been chosen at school – you always had to have a good goal-scorer and a goalkeeper, and a couple of big lads in defence. But inevitably, there would be somebody left till the end, the boy who nobody really wanted. Cooper wondered who had been left to the last among the airmen. Might it have been Zygmunt Lukasz or Klemens Wach? It must have been even more difficult when different nationalities were involved. There were fewer natural bonds to bring them together.

But the crew had been formed, and had been sent to their first operational posting – a Lancaster squadron at RAF Leadenhall, where they remained until that fatal crash in January 1945.

According to the LIO's note, the information

on the airmen's service history came from the official RAF records. So Klemens Wach had only one operational posting, which meant he could never have served with the famous 305 Squadron, as Alison Morrissey had claimed. Morrissey had got it wrong. Until then, Cooper had been assuming that her research had been meticulous, with the help of Frank Baine. But now he was having doubts. There was a weakness in her research. He wondered what other information she had might be inaccurate.

But of course there was more than one inaccuracy; there had been a major gap. Morrissey had not known the identity of the Malkin brothers, even though the information had been readily available. Walter Rowland, for one, would have been able to tell her. Thinking back to his conversation with the old man, Cooper recollected that he hadn't seemed to have any great objection to talking to Alison Morrissey. He wondered who had persuaded Rowland not to.

'Well, the bayonet isn't some old military memento, anyway,' said Diane Fry. 'So the chances are it didn't come from one of your old soldiers.'

Ben Cooper looked across the office at her. Fry was holding up a latex evidence bag for him to see. There were still streaks of skin, dried blood and organ tissue along the sides of the long blade of the bayonet. The sight made Cooper wince and clench his stomach, as she had surely known it would.

'Airmen,' said Cooper. 'They're old airmen. They wouldn't have had much use for bayonets.'

'Who knows what they might have collected? But this one's quite new, the sort they sell openly in some shops, along with air rifles and hunting knives. The handle is a good surface. We might get some prints from it, or even enough traces of sweat from his hands to get a DNA sample, if he ever handled it without gloves. It could mean we've got Eddie Kemp tied up this time.'

'I don't think so,' said Cooper.

Fry lowered the bag. 'What do you mean?'

'I don't think it was him.'

'Ben, we arrested Kemp at the scene.'

'He was in the vicinity. But I don't think it was him who attacked me.'

Fry put down the bag and sat back in her chair. 'I hope you're joking.'

'He was some distance away from me, I'm sure. I don't think it was Kemp who barged into me. The person who did that ran off in the other direction, not towards Eyre Street. Besides, I would have recognized the smell.'

'He was certainly ripe when we processed him. The custody sergeant recognized him before we got him through the door. He said to thank you for sending "Homer" back.'

'That's what I mean.'

Fry sighed. 'Prints or DNA will settle it one way or the other.'

'I expect so.'

'If it wasn't Kemp, who else would have known you were there? Could somebody have recognized you?'

'Well . . .'

'Yes, of course, how silly of me,' said Fry. 'Everybody knows you round here, don't they? I don't suppose you've ever considered doing undercover work, Ben?'

'I didn't see him. Not clearly.'

'If we don't get a match from the bayonet, we're back to square one with Kemp – even for the double assault. The CPS think the witness evidence is insufficient.'

'I know.'

'It would have been nice, Ben, to have been able to charge somebody.'

'Well, I'm sorry – I'm only telling you the truth.'

She sighed. 'I suppose it'll be in your statement.'

'Of course.'

Fry sat at her desk. The mountain of paper on it was rising and becoming unstable. Cooper could see that a couple of buff files in the middle were sliding free under the weight of those on top. It would be best to be out of the office when the avalanche started.

'Well, I'm glad you're not injured, anyway,' said Fry.

'Thanks.'

'Because there's a special job for you tomorrow morning.'

'Oh?'

'You're to meet Sergeant Caudwell. You'll be going on a trip together.'

'Frankly, I'd rather be attacked with a bayonet in a dark alley.'

'Tough. I hope your stomach's feeling strong in the morning, Ben.'

'Why?' said Cooper suspiciously.

Fry smiled at him, though her expression lacked the confidence she was trying to convey. 'I've just talked to Sergeant Caudwell again,' she said. 'We've thought of a way of keeping you safe and off the streets.'

In his flat above the bookshop in Nick i' th' Tor, Lawrence Daley had heard the sound of voices echoing in the alleyways outside. He assumed it was a group of drunks leaving one of the pubs around the market square, although it was a bit early in the evening for them to be causing trouble. Usually, that happened later on, when Edendale's two night clubs closed.

Lawrence went to one of the windows. But instead of looking out of the front of the building on to Nick i' th' Tor, he went to the back, where his bedroom overlooked a snow-covered yard and gates that led out on to a back alley. There was frost forming on the window, slowly covering the glass in delicate patterns. The sky was clear tonight, and a crescent moon threw some light on the shapes in the yard. Lawrence shuddered, picturing human figures moving among the shapes, hearing the scuffling of their feet in the snow and the sound of their muttered curses in the darkness. But the yard was as secure as he could make it. The gates were firmly closed, and there was broken glass set into the concrete along the top of the back wall. For now, the yard was too full of snow to open the gates. According to the weather forecast, it would be the end of the week before it thawed. He had been watching the forecasts every day. Several times a day.

Satisfied for now, Lawrence went back to the book that he had been reading in front of the TV. On the floor above, he heard the noise of scurrying feet on bare boards, the faint scratching of claws on the wooden joists that ran across his ceiling. He didn't think the feet were those of the mice that lived in the shop downstairs, which sometimes darted out from among the bookshelves and startled his customers. The feet that scratched above his head belonged to something bigger and less quick, something that dragged a tail behind it along the boards.

Lawrence supposed it was possible that squirrels had found their way under the eaves to live in his attic for the winter. But he thought it much more likely that rats had moved into his life. And now they were thriving.

27

Ben Cooper hung on to the back of a seat as his view of the ground tilted and wreckage rushed past below him. Directly underneath the helicopter, the scene looked like the aftermath of a hurricane that had passed through a scrap-metal yard. Fragments of aircraft fuselage glinted in the light reflected from the snow. There should be part of a tail fin still protruding from the peat and the snow somewhere up the slope to the west. But Cooper had lost sight of where the horizon ought to be, and he felt his stomach lurch as his sense of balance was disrupted.

During his five years in Derbyshire CID, he had never been called on to take to the air in a helicopter before, and he wasn't sure it was something he was cut out for. He was a feet-on-the-ground man, no question. Half an hour this Monday morning had convinced him of it.

The passengers braced themselves as the pilot pulled back on the controls and banked to avoid the sudden upward rush of bare, black gritstone that the maps called Irontongue. The rocks were jagged and unforgiving, full of crevices that held streaks of frozen snow. Even rock climbers stayed away from the face of Irontongue. Its surface was too treacherous for all but the most experienced and best equipped.

The helicopter flew over the site again, banked, turned and came back to allow its passengers a good view of the remnants of the crashed aircraft. In the sharp morning light, the shadow of the rotor blades swept across the hill and over the wreckage.

'No, that's not the one,' said Cooper. 'That was a US Air Force Superfortress. Thirteen men died in that one.'

He looked back down at the ground. Broken scraps of the aircraft seemed to have started digging themselves into the peat, like burrowing animals anxious to escape the wind and snow, but never quite making it to safety below ground.

'There were so many during the war,' he said. 'The Peak District is littered with them.'

In fact, there had been so many that aircraft wrecks had entered local folklore. Even today, there were tales of a ghostly plane that had been heard, and even seen, over parts of the Dark Peak. Witnesses had been convinced that the aircraft must surely have crashed into the hillside because it was flying so low. No wreckage could ever be found, but it didn't stop the stories.

There was also said to be a German bomber that lay somewhere on the remote northern moors after being shot down during a raid on Manchester. German-made cartridge cases had been picked up in the area, but no one had ever seen signs of wreckage there, either. Cooper wondered if that was one animal that had reached its burrow, ploughing through the peat at a hundred miles an hour as it fell from the sky. A few years ago, archaeologists digging in a peat bog in Cheshire had found the body of an Iron Age man, petrified and almost complete. Would the peat here have preserved the bodies of the Luftwaffe crew too, with their skin dry and leathery and their eyes hardened like bullets?

'Although I don't think this one crashed during the war. It was 1948 – that Superfortress down there was from an American photographic unit. The crew had recorded the atom bomb tests at Bikini Atoll and filmed the Russian positions in East Germany during the Berlin Airlift.'

'But Derbyshire finished them off.'

Cooper lifted an eyebrow at the grim pleasure in Sergeant Caudwell's voice. He stared out of the helicopter window, surprised at the extent of the debris strewn across the moorland. On the way to the site, Cooper had found himself filling in the time by telling Jane Caudwell the story of the crash of Sugar Uncle Victor and the disappearance of Pilot Officer Danny McTeague. Before he had finished, her eyes had closed.

'I'm surprised nobody clears the wrecks away,' said Caudwell. 'Aren't they offensive to the tidy minds of our bureaucrats?'

'Not here. In the Peak District they let them stay. They're memorials, after all. They're official war graves. I always think it's funny how that can be, though. I mean – the bodies aren't still down there, are they?'

'We hope not, dear.'

They levelled out again and flew northwards, passing over acres of white, peat-flecked ground, rolling oceans of it that swelled in waves towards the fringes of the Dark Peak. It was barely more than a minute before they located another scatter of wreckage.

'That's the one. Sugar Uncle Victor.'

Caudwell gave a chuckle. 'Sounds like a naughty relative, doesn't it?'

As the helicopter banked, she hardly used her hands to brace herself, preferring to let her weight roll and wallow in the seat, at times pushing against Cooper's side like a heavy piece of loose cargo. Her colleague PC Steve Nash had barely acknowledged his presence since they had climbed aboard, and he wasn't sure whether it was indifference or whether Nash was silently terrified of the flight and dealing with it in his own way. Cooper was determined not to take it personally, anyway.

Below them, the remains of the Lancaster bomber's wings lay in tatters on the moor. Little of the fuselage was left, but there was a ragged line of burnt-out engines and undercarriage parts, and a single wheel still standing upright. Smaller fragments were scattered for several hundred feet through a series of water channels and groughs. Around the wreckage, the wind had scraped the dark peat bare. Against the snow, it looked like a pool of dried blood in which the broken body of the aircraft lay.

'They must have taken some of the parts away after the crash,' said Caudwell.

'It depends who you mean by "they",' said Cooper. 'There was no official salvage team. But there have been unofficial ones since. Apparently, there are two kinds of visitors to these wrecks – the aviation archaeologists, who want to preserve the remains, and the others, who have their own interests.'

'The vultures?'

'Some people call them that.' Cooper thought he detected a note of irony. 'The more valuable parts of the Lancaster have been removed over the years. I suppose things like the radio equipment would have been the first to go, followed by anything that was movable, anything that could be sold as scrap or might be considered a souvenir or collector's item.'

'Local people?'

'At first. For a long time, they would have been the only ones who knew the location of these wrecks. The others have arrived more recently.'

Who was it that had said the Home Guard men

sent to watch over the wrecked plane had not been too keen on their task? Cooper couldn't blame them, not in the dead of winter on the Dark Peak moors. Staying alive was enough for a man to concentrate on if he found himself out here, particularly at night and as ill-equipped as they would have been in those days, with hob-nailed boots and heavy service greatcoats. He could picture the Home Guard sneaking off to some sheltered spot to huddle together around a camp fire made of salvaged spars from the aircraft they were supposed to be guarding. They would have stood no chance of preventing local people from liberating items of value. It had been wartime, after all. It was every man for himself when it came to survival. But Danny McTeague had taken it further than that.

Caudwell was looking straight ahead, over the shoulder of the pilot, unmoved by the snow-covered landscape passing below them. She seemed to be watching for bad weather coming from the north, or maybe for the next outcrop of high ground appearing in front of them, just as the rocks of Irontongue Hill had appeared in front of Pilot Officer Danny McTeague in the final seconds.

The low sun misted the valley and gleamed yellow on the icy water of a small drinking hole made by a farmer for his livestock. There were cattle huddled below a wall, nervous of stepping on to the concrete lip of the drinking hole because they could feel their hooves slipping on the frozen surface.

Cooper found himself gazing up at Sergeant Caudwell as the helicopter banked. She yawned and stretched, almost pushing him off his seat. Her dark hair was scraped up inside a fake fur hat like a Russian commissar's. He felt unreasonably uncomfortable with Caudwell. Though on the surface she maintained the normal courtesies, there was a restrained hostility about her. It wasn't the overt edginess he had grown used to from others, but something deeper that he felt he ought not to rouse.

'Have you seen what you wanted?' he asked.

'I want to get down there. I need to get a closer look at the Lancaster wreck.'

'There's nowhere to set down safely here,' said the pilot.

'We're going to have to walk up then, I suppose,' said Caudwell. 'Detective Constable Cooper, could you arrange for a scenes of crime officer to accompany us, please?'

Cooper stared at her. 'I don't know what you're hoping to find. We carried out a forensic examination on Friday, after the remains of the baby were found. But they were old bones.'

'Not as old as the crew of the Lancaster, eh?'

Every police officer knew that there was nothing worse than going over cold ground, sifting through old bones. And there weren't many bones much colder than these. Wouldn't it have been better to let those fliers rest in peace, rather than raking over their graves and stirring up their ghosts?

'I think it's crazy,' said Cooper.

Caudwell smiled at him again, and her cheeks dimpled. Every time the MDP sergeant smiled, Cooper felt as though he was about to be swallowed up and spat out by a giant rodent, an enormous hamster in a fur hat.

'No doubt you're right, dear,' said Caudwell. 'Sometimes it seems the whole world's gone crazy, doesn't it?'

More hillsides and more miles of snow passed below them as the helicopter made its turn to head back to base. At first, the shape created by the spread of the wreckage had made Cooper think of a crucifixion. But he knew he had it wrong. This had nothing to do with Christianity – there was no message of death and resurrection, the forgiveness of sins. It was something more pagan that he was thinking of. Not a resurrection, only a celebration of death.

A few weeks ago, Cooper had been reading about the Danish invaders who had occupied Derbyshire and neighbouring counties for a while. Their army had made a point of executing defeated Saxon kings in the most gruesome way. Their chests had been cut open and their ribcages spread on either side like wings, to expose their hearts. It was a symbolic act, a celebratory sacrifice to their Norse gods. The act was called a 'Blood Eagle'. It was uncomfortably like the process involved in a postmortem examination – the cutting open of the sternum, the spreading of the ribcage, the

451

removal of heart and lungs and other internal organs. Cooper had never been able to escape the notion that every autopsy was a ritual sacrifice, a ceremony dedicating the victim to the new god of science.

But the memory had made the shape of the wreckage clear to him. It wasn't shaped like a crucifixion at all – it was a blood eagle.

On the way up to the Snake Pass, Ben Cooper had to put on his sunglasses as they climbed higher and the snow-covered slopes on either side dazzled him with their reflected glare. In the valley, the snow hadn't lingered so long on the banks of dead bracken, though it still showed through the copses of bare trees, like the exposed lining of a threadbare overcoat. The plantations of conifers further up the valley were different. In the sunlight, the lines of spruces glowed orange against the blue sheen of the snow.

Then, on the higher slopes, there was no bracken, only coarse grass with frozen snow clinging to its stems. Looking southwards, into the sun, the moor looked like an ocean, all its waves and swells solidifying as they reached the shore.

Today, there was no mistaking the flight path for Manchester Airport. In the sky were the vapour trails of six or seven jet airliners, each one white and distinct. One of the greatest fears of the emergency services was that an airliner would one day fall out of the sky as it was passing over the high ground of the Dark Peak. There were enough wrecks lying on the remote moors already for everyone to be aware of the difficulties involved in a rescue plan.

They parked their vehicles in the lay-by nearest to Irontongue Hill. It wasn't the one where Nick Easton had been found, but further up, almost at the highest point of the Snake Pass. Cooper pulled his Toyota in behind the MDP's Ford and the Scientific Support van. He was pleased to see that the SOCO they had sent was Liz Petty. She was conscientious, but she was also fitter than some of the other scenes of crime staff and would have no problem with the hike across the moor to the crash site.

'What a beautiful day for a brisk walk,' said Sergeant Caudwell cheerfully. 'How long will it take us?'

'About three-quarters of an hour, if we keep up a steady pace.'

'No slacking then, eh?'

'Will you be all right?'

'Don't worry about me. I'm like a camel. I may not look pretty, but I can keep going for hours.'

In the cold, bright morning, the walk to the top of Irontongue Hill was exhilarating. The sky was blue and cloudless, and the moors looked unsullied, their tracts of untouched snow glittering temptingly. The only patterns on the landscape were those caused by the different textures of light falling on the northern slopes, by the shadows in a sudden dip, or the bright highlights of a rocky summit. Further south, in the limestone areas of the White Peak, the dry-stone walls carved up the landscape into containable sections, forcing the snow into some kind of order, with here and there a line of trees breaking through. But on the empty Dark Peak moorland, the snow had its own way. It had filled every cranny, sculpting the world to a shape of its own creation.

These cold, bright days were good. But Cooper knew how quickly the weather could change. If cloud descended on the tops, they could be in the middle of a snowstorm before they got halfway back across the moor.

They crunched over the frozen heather into an easterly wind that picked up small swirls of powdery snow and blew them around like miniature blizzards before dropping them again, as if fussily rearranging the landscape to get the best reflection from the sun. In the deeper areas, the snow had been formed into whipped cream shapes or had been left draped in mid-air over a gully, like the scalloped edges of a tablecloth. Below it, a stream ran under a thin skin of ice.

Cooper could see that somebody had been this way already, but not today. A fine dusting of snow had blown into their footprints. There was a distant cackle of black grouse, and a human voice somewhere far away, over the other side of the summit.

They stopped for a breather when they reached the trig point on Irontongue Hill, where a cairn marked the summit. The bare rock face dropped away from them on one side, back down to the Snake. Across a narrow valley was the next outcrop of rock, High Shelf, where the wreckage of the American Superfortress lay.

'What a job you've got,' said Caudwell. 'And you say you're short-staffed!'

Liz Petty had hardly said a word all the way. But now she put her case down and took in the view.

'Days like this make up for the poor wages,' she said. Cooper smiled at her.

'Don't. You'll have me in tears,' said Caudwell.

Beyond High Shelf was a distant view down into Glossop. The hills fell away from the edge of the Dark Peak to a hollow in which the town sat, surrounded by the remains of the textile mills that had once been its main industry. At least Glossop seemed to have grown out of its landscape, like one of those complex eco-systems that formed of their own accord in a pool of stagnant water, given time.

But then, out past Glossop, Cooper could see nothing but a grey wall where the world seemed to come to an end. It reminded him of a scene from a horror novel he had once read, in which a small American town had been cut off from the rest of the country by an alien fog where vast monsters lurked. But he knew that, beneath the grimy blanket he could see in the distance, there were no monsters, only the city of Manchester.

On a warm summer's day, the white tower blocks of the city centre could look like the battlements of a fairy-tale city or a shimmering mirage lying in the plain. But not today. This morning, the uncompromisingly clear winter light exposed every atom of the pollution that hung over the city, every swirl of smoke from a factory chimney, every wisp of exhaust from the traffic choking the streets. With no warm thermals to lift it clear of the city, the smog had gathered and thickened, and now it lay like a huge grey rat coiled on its nest. Cooper shuddered. It would be a salutary experience for many a city dweller to take a trip up to High Shelf on a day like this and get a bird's-eye view of their city. They would hardly dare to breathe again.

Liz Petty turned away from the view and looked up at him thoughtfully.

'It's hard to imagine how they could have crashed here,' she said. 'It's so ironic somehow.'

'At night, in low cloud, it would be a different place altogether,' said Cooper. 'It would have been a far more dangerous place.'

Cooper pictured Lancaster SU-V coming low across the valley from the south, the rumble of its engines muffled by the blanket of cloud, the crew peering hopelessly from the cockpit windows or from their Perspex gun turrets. He imagined the bomb aimer, Bill Mee, lying in his position in the nose turret, looking down and catching a glimpse of the ground rising towards them. Perhaps Mee would have tapped urgently on the feet of the pilot above him, gesturing upwards as he mouthed: 'Climb! Climb!' And McTeague would surely then have heaved back on the controls and Lancaster SU-V would have begun to gain height.

At the rear of the aircraft, young Dick Abbott wouldn't have known what was happening, until he had suddenly been thrown forward in his harness towards the Perspex bubble as the aircraft climbed. He would have found himself hanging helplessly, almost upside down, with his view tilted so that he could see the hillside winking through a patch of cloud. And he might have heard the frightened voices shouting in his headphones.

But by then it was already too late. The stark face of Irontongue Hill would have been directly in front of them. Maybe the crew had seen it coming towards them a second before the impact, a huge black shape hurtling out of the cloud where there should have been only sky. But it had been too late by then. Far too late.

28

DCI Tailby looked around the conference room. He frowned. Diane Fry had noticed that he was doing a lot of frowning these days. He had never been a barrel of laughs, but his last few weeks at E Division were proving to be a burden on him.

'We don't seem to see much of DC Cooper at these meetings,' said Tailby.

'Everybody is so busy,' said Hitchens. 'There are so many actions. So many interviews to do.'

'I know that. Is Cooper all right? He wasn't injured in the incident last night?'

'No, he's fine. He reported for duty as normal this morning, and he's gone out with Sergeant Caudwell. The MDP asked to visit the site of the aircraft wreck.'

'He's with Sergeant Caudwell? You've thrown him to the dogs then?'

'I wouldn't say that exactly, sir,' said Hitchens.

'When things get difficult, there's a temptation to look around for a sacrifice,' said Tailby.

Fry blinked. She had never heard their old DCI get so philosophical before. Perhaps he wanted to put on a display of wisdom in his final days before he handed over to Kessen, so that the contrast would be all the greater.

'I'm told Sergeant Caudwell asked for a scenes of crime officer as well. What is she hoping to find?'

'I've no idea,' said Hitchens.

Tailby frowned. 'I'm happy that we're co-operating. But there comes a point when co-operation has to be mutual.'

'Yes, sir.'

'All right,' said Tailby. 'Well, here we are – it's Monday morning, and we've had some major developments in this enquiry over the weekend. We have a confirmed identity for the victim: our so-called Snowman is Sergeant Nick Easton, an investigator with the Royal Air Force Police. And I gather we've managed to piece together some of his movements, with the help of the MDP officers who have been sent to Edendale.'

'DS Fry and her team came in yesterday to follow that line of enquiry urgently,' said Hitchens.

'Excellent. I'm sure all the overtime will be fully justified, Paul.'

'Yes, sir. I'll let DS Fry tell you what she managed to achieve for the money.'

Fry shuffled in her seat as the two DCIs stared at her, one smiling, one frowning. Tweedledee and Tweedledum. They would never agree on anything.

'For a start,' said Fry, 'we know Sergeant Easton visited the air museum at Leadenhall on Sunday 6th January, between twenty-four and thirty-six hours before he was killed. The MDP believe he was enquiring about a volunteer there, Graham Kemp, who is well known as an aviation memorabilia collector.'

'This is the brother of Edward Kemp, I gather,' said Tailby. 'A gentleman we now have in custody again.'

'Yes, sir. We have his brother's address, and we're hoping to pick him up this morning. Of course, we've already been interviewing a number of Edward Kemp's associates in connection with the double assault last Monday night. It's worth bearing in mind that this incident happened within an hour or two of Easton's death.'

'OK. And from the aircraft museum . . .'

'We know Nick Easton stayed at a hotel near Chesterfield that night, then he visited Edendale the following day, Monday. He called at the home of a family called Lukasz in Woodland Crescent and spoke briefly to Mrs Grace Lukasz. It's odd that Mr Andrew Lukasz disappeared a matter of hours before Easton arrived.'

'Andrew?'

'Grace Lukasz's son. He lives in London, but had been visiting his parents. You might recall that we got the father and mother in to try to identify our Snowman because their son had disappeared rather suddenly.'

'And he hasn't turned up since? He's not back home in London?'

'Apparently not. The Metropolitan Police called at his home early this morning and talked to his neighbours, and apparently there's been no sign of him for about ten days, which would tie in with his arrival in Edendale. His wife is American, and she's been away at a family funeral in Wisconsin, but we're trying to make contact with her. Even more interestingly, his employers say Andrew Lukasz was on leave – but that he should have been back at work today. He didn't turn up.'

'What was Sergeant Easton's interest in the Lukasz family?' said Tailby. 'Do we have any idea?'

'We don't really know. And nor does Peter Lukasz. But he says that Andrew had argued with his grandfather. There was some disagreement over a cigarette case that had belonged to Zygmunt Lukasz's cousin, Klemens Wach, who was killed in an aircraft wreck during the Second World War. Apparently, Zygmunt expressed outrage that this item might have been looted from the wreck.'

'In other words, a piece of aviation memorabilia?'

'It looks like it, sir,' said Fry.

'Go on.'

'We don't know where Easton went after he left the Lukasz home. According to the MDP, he was using a black Ford Focus, but we haven't been able to locate it. And he wasn't booked into accommodation in this area for that night, as far as we can tell. DC Murfin checked everywhere yesterday, which meant a lot of phone calls and visits. I have to say, sir, that we simply don't have the staff for an enquiry as complex as this.'

'Point taken, Fry,' said Tailby. 'Have we made any progress on the time line for the morning Easton's body was found?'

'We've narrowed it down to a window of about half an hour, when his body could have been left at the side of the A57. But we've been unable to find any sightings of four-wheel drive vehicles on the road after it was closed because of the snow. There are so few houses on that stretch of road. The Snake Inn was our best bet, but the staff have been interviewed and it seems they saw and heard nothing but the snowploughs.'

'What about Edward Kemp's vehicle? A four-wheel drive, isn't it?'

'An Isuzu Trooper, yes. The rolls of plastic found in the back did have traces of blood, but the blood matched that of one of the assault victims. We think the baseball bats or other weapons that were used in the assault were hidden in the plastic rolls afterwards. Unfortunately, the weapons are now missing. However, we do have some possible traces from the plastic, if we can get approval for samples to go to the lab . . .'

'Yes, of course. Do it.'

'Also, the bayonet that was used in the assault

on DC Cooper. We might get a DNA trace from the handle.'

'Obviously.'

'My main concern at the moment is that we've not yet been given details of the enquiry that Sergeant Easton was working on,' said Fry. 'We need that information urgently.'

'The Ministry of Defence Police have promised us a meeting tomorrow morning, when full details will be shared as far as possible,' said Tailby. 'But at this stage, it seems clear that there's a connection involving aviation memorabilia. The Leadenhall Aircraft Museum, this collector, Graham Kemp, and an item that is known to have been in the possession of Andrew Lukasz. That's a very positive line of enquiry you've developed, Fry.'

'The most interesting point is that Easton called at the Lukasz home shortly after Andrew disappeared,' said Fry. 'Obviously, we'll be interviewing both the Kemp brothers. But, if you asked me at this moment, I'd say the person I'd be most interested in talking to about the murder of Nick Easton was Andrew Lukasz.'

'And, in what has now become our traditional manner, the person we most want to speak to is missing,' said Tailby.

'Yes, sir.'

Tailby spoke stiffly to DCI Kessen, who nodded. He had said nothing during the meeting. Fry feared that he was going to be out of his depth once Tailby departed.

'You're right, Fry,' said Tailby. 'There's a lot of work involved in this Easton enquiry, not to mention the assault on a police officer. We'll have to try to pull in some more assistance. But, Paul, do make sure you use the expertise of the MDP officers while they're here, too.'

'May I remind you we also have a missing baby, sir?' said Hitchens.

'Don't I know it? The papers say hope is fading for Baby Chloe. Is that right? Are our hopes fading?'

'If somebody has her, they're not coming forward,' said Fry. 'We're interviewing Eddie Kemp again after this meeting, both about the assault on DC Cooper and about the baby, since he was Marie Tennent's last-known boyfriend. But we've already checked his house and talked to his wife. I don't think he's been involved with Marie for some time, and it seems unlikely he'll have any information about the baby.'

'Bad news, then.'

'The bones of the other baby we found don't make the situation look good. If we can get DNA from the remains, we can confirm whether it was an earlier child of Marie Tennent's. But the clothes found with the bones were almost certainly left by her – Marie's mother identified them. It seems Marie might have gone up to the wreck to leave the clothes as some sort of memorial to the dead child.'

Tailby looked at her, horrified. 'That's rather macabre, Fry.'

'It's speculation, of course,' said Fry. 'But why else should Marie Tennent have gone up to the aircraft wreck on Irontongue Hill that day?'

The wreckage of Sugar Uncle Victor began a hundred yards below the trig point, on the windward side of Irontongue. Between the larger sections, the ground was covered in molten fragments of metal, slivers of glass and strands of torn rubber. A few tufts of ragged wool clung to an undercarriage axle where sheep had rubbed their itchy backs against it, glad to find something hard and solid in the expanse of soft peat. There were shreds of tyre still left, hanging from the huge hub of a wheel.

Close to the main wreckage, there were poppies on wreaths or attached to small makeshift crosses. Some of the crosses were wooden, but others seemed to have been made out of bits of melted tubing from the aircraft itself, tied together with wire. Parts of the metal on the undercarriage and fuselage were still uncorroded, even after so long. On the other hand, the poppies had faded completely to white, their original blood-red bleached by the sun and rain.

'One survivor and five fatalities, not including the pilot,' said Cooper, his eyes following the tail of a small aircraft as it headed towards Glossop.

Jane Caudwell seemed hardly to have heard him. The snow had spattered her boots and the legs of her trousers where she had stamped her feet in the snow. She was dressed in black – a totally impractical colour on the snow-covered peat moors. Bright colours were what you should be wearing, especially if the weather turned bad and the mountain rescue teams turned out to try to locate you. They could spot bright clothes. But black amounted to camouflage.

Caudwell took off her right glove, exposing a pale, plump hand with a gold ring on the middle finger. She held the hand up for Cooper's inspection, splaying the fingers into something that looked like an obscene gesture, multiplied several times over.

'Yes, five,' she said. 'But are you quite sure Pilot Officer McTeague was aboard this aircraft?'

'*What?*'

Caudwell smiled. 'Just a thought. By the way, I don't think it's a good idea for *her* to be up here, whoever she is.'

'Who?'

'Up there.'

Cooper turned and saw Alison Morrissey standing among the rocks near the trig point. She had a camera in her hand, though at the moment she was making no effort to photograph the officers working on the wreck site. The hood of her cagoule was pulled up to protect her ears from the wind that whipped the snow off the surface of the Irontongue rocks. But Cooper thought he could see the expression in her eyes, a dark mingling of satisfaction and pain.

'I'd better go and speak to her,' he said.

'No,' said Caudwell. 'Let someone else do it.'

She gestured at PC Nash, who scowled as he lumbered up the slope, kicking his feet in the snow. Morrissey watched him approach her, as she might have observed the movements of a bit of interesting wildlife. When Nash was within a few yards of her, with his head down, struggling to keep his footing on a stretch of wet scree, she raised the camera and took his picture. Nash heard the click and looked up angrily. He charged the rest of the way, thrusting against the rocks with his arms.

Cooper took a couple of steps towards them but felt Caudwell's hand on his arm and stopped. Morrissey had stood her ground and was listening with amused attentiveness to what Nash was saying. She didn't seem to reply, and he began to wave his arms, indicating that she should move back down the hill. Still she didn't move.

Then Nash tried to snatch her camera. Morrissey resisted. Nash towered over her, but there was a stubbornness plain from her body language that told him she wasn't going to be bullied.

'No.' Cooper pulled away from Caudwell and began to run up the slope.

'For heaven's sake,' called Caudwell, 'what's the matter with you?'

Cooper kicked up the snow as he scrambled across the scree, using his hands against the rocks to push himself up. He looked up. Nash had hold of the camera, but the strap was still tight round

Morrissey's shoulder and, when he tugged, it almost pulled her off balance. She slipped and flung out her arms to keep her balance. One of her hands hit the shoulder of his fluorescent jacket with a loud slap. Nash grabbed her arm.

'Let her go!'

PC Nash turned and looked at him. He wasn't smiling, but Cooper could sense that he was enjoying himself. Cooper felt at a complete disadvantage. He was standing down the slope from Nash, who loomed over him. For a moment, Cooper thought he had engineered a situation that was impossible to get out of. Nash looked past his shoulder and let go of Morrissey's camera.

'Go back to the road, Alison,' said Cooper. 'Please.'

Finally, Morrissey turned and walked away from him, with one backward glance. Cooper and Nash then scrambled down the slope together.

Ben Cooper took a deep lungful of air as he tried to calm himself. It was totally different from the air in the Lukasz bungalow or at Walter Rowland's house, or even at George Malkin's. This was clean and pure, straight off the top of the hill. It had even seemed a shame to walk through the virgin snow this morning. A single set of tracks was one thing – they were like a statement, emphasizing the untouched purity all around. But when several pairs of feet had trampled backwards and forwards and pressed the snow into slush, stained with dirt from their boots, it made the rest of the landscape look tarnished and seedy.

'So, these poppies,' said Caudwell. 'Who leaves them here?'

'I don't know,' said Cooper. 'Perhaps members of ex-servicemen's organizations who think the crew should be remembered. Or perhaps the local air cadets do it.'

'You think they come up here on Remembrance Day every year?'

'It's possible.'

'So what about this one?'

Cooper walked over to where she was standing. There was a single poppy on a wooden cross, tucked under the edge of the undercarriage. It was gradually emerging from a patch of thawing snow, and it was bright red, like a splash of arterial blood from a fresh wound.

'I think your officer was right. This doesn't look as though it's been here for two months.'

'There's been too much rain,' said Cooper. 'The colour would have been washed out of it, same as the others.'

'What was the date of the crash again?'

'January 7th, 1945.'

'The seventh was a week ago,' said Caudwell. 'The day Nick Easton was killed.'

'So?'

Caudwell gave him an exasperated look. 'Men don't know this,' she said. 'But anniversaries are very important to some people. Anniversaries of births, anniversaries of deaths. The day you first met the person you fell in love with. You know, dates that you never forget.'

'Yes, I do know,' said Cooper, thinking of the yearly visit with Matt to his father's grave, which would be an annual ritual until they became too old or infirm to make it to the cemetery. 'Relatives of one of the crew, then?'

Caudwell swapped her gloves for a pair of latex ones from a packet in her coat. 'Somebody who felt they had to leave the cross on the right day, whatever the weather.'

Cooper turned and looked down across the expanse of snow-covered moor to a spot which even now stood out from the rest of the area. It looked bare and brown, churned up by the boots of the men who had stood round a frozen body and made poor jokes about ice axes and thermometers.

To Cooper's surprise, Sergeant Caudwell spoke exactly what was in his thoughts.

'Marie Tennent,' she said.

Cooper stared at her. 'How do you know about Marie?'

'A combination of local knowledge, elementary detective work and inter-agency co-operation. I've read the file. We need to take the poppy.'

Liz Petty came over and took photographs of the poppy in position on its cross. Then she carefully eased the cross out of the ground. Cooper could see there was an inscription on the wood, written in white, as if it had been done in correction fluid.

'We found Marie Tennent's body a few hundred yards from here,' he said. 'She'd been there for days, in the snow. She's a presumed suicide. I don't think we've even had the postmortem results yet.'

'Don't tell me – you're short-staffed in the pathology department?'

Caudwell was peering at the wooden cross that Liz had placed in an evidence bag. 'What does the inscription say?' asked Cooper.

'It says: "Sergeant Dick Abbott – 24th August 1926 to 7th January 1945."'

'Abbott? He was the rear gunner. Tail-end Charlie.'

'It says something else,' said Caudwell. 'I don't know what this bit means . . .'

Cooper waited, thinking of Dick Abbott. The newspaper reports had said the rear gunner's body was severely mutilated. According to Walter Rowland, the rescue team had spent hours on the moor picking up the pieces of human bodies. The only consolation in Sergeant Abbott's case was that he might never have known what happened to him. From his rear turret, he would not have seen Irontongue Hill at all. There might have been a second when he heard terrified voices on the intercom, then he would have felt the impact as Sugar Uncle Victor collided with the gritstone buttress and flipped over to shatter his turret on the rocks.

'Is it Latin? It might be the squadron motto or something,' said Cooper.

'Oh, no,' said Caudwell. 'I can read the words. I just don't know what they mean. It says: "Justice at last."'

The manager of the Wise Buys shop in Clappergate remembered Marie Tennent perfectly well.

'She was a good girl. Hard working. Brighter than most of the others,' she told Diane Fry. 'I was sorry to lose her when she went. But the best of the young ones never stay long.'

Fry looked round the shop. Judging from the window displays, the main attraction of the stock was its price. The racks were filled with warm coats and colourful sweaters, trouser suits and matching scarf and hat sets. Spring fashions hadn't arrived yet.

'Did Marie tell you why she was leaving the job?' she asked.

'No. She just said she wanted to do something different. They get fed up after a while, you see. Dealing with the public isn't always easy.'

'I know,' said Fry.

'Oh, I expect you do.'

'But Marie didn't have another job to go to, as far as we know.'

'No, I didn't think she did. Personally, I thought there was probably a man. I expected to hear she was getting married before long.'

'Did she mention a particular man?'

'Not as such. Some girls talk about their boy-friends all the time, but Marie wasn't that type. She was more private. But I always wondered . . .'

'Yes?'

'Well, was there a baby, do you know?'

'Did she hint at that?'

'Not really. But there are little signs, aren't there? She became more absorbed in herself, as if she had other things to think about than joining in with the usual chat. She started to look a bit different, too. Being pregnant suits some, but Marie looked ill. Not anything you could really put your finger on – she was paler, more tired sometimes. She held herself differently. I've seen it before.'

'But you never asked her?' said Fry.

'It's not my place. She obviously didn't want to tell me, so I didn't pry.'

Fry watched a woman poke through a rack of dresses, find nothing that interested her and walk out of the shop.

'Did Marie ever mention her family?'

'Oh, yes, her mother in Scotland. She talked about her quite a lot. And she had a younger brother, I think.'

'Anybody else? Anybody in this area?'

The manager hesitated. 'Funny you should say that. Marie always said she was from Scotland. I mean, she spoke with a Scottish accent and everything, and that's where her mum lived. But I always thought she had some connection with

473

Derbyshire. She talked sometimes as if she knew a bit about the history of this area.'

Fry turned to look at her. 'Anything in particular?'

'It's hard to remember. But I think it was something to do with the war.'

'Could it have been the RAF? A crashed Second World War bomber?'

The frown cleared from the manager's face. 'Yes, I believe you're right. It was a funny thing for a girl like Marie to be interested in. But she mentioned those aircraft wrecks often.'

There was a crack as a gunshot split the frigid air. Recognizing the sound without even having to think, Ben Cooper dived to his left, rolling into the snowdrift behind the undercarriage, scrambling to take advantage of its cover. He looked around for Caudwell, but saw that she hadn't moved. She was still standing in the open, staring back over her shoulder at something beyond the wreckage.

Then Cooper heard a cackling and a drumming of wings as a brace of red pheasant panicked and burst up from the moor a hundred yards away. He caught a glimpse of the sunlight shimmering off their red backs like streams of blood in the air as they beat away towards the reservoir. And Cooper saw PC Nash laughing as he shoved what looked like a Glock pistol back into a holster under his jacket. So Carol Parry had been right – the MDP considered it necessary to be armed.

The natural sounds of the moor became audible again – the constant muttering of the wind as it nosed through the drifting snow, the barking of a dog and the clang of a bucket so muffled and distant that the world seemed to have slipped behind a thick curtain.

Caudwell turned back and watched Cooper picking himself up and brushing snow off his shoulders. She met his eye with a sardonic smile.

'Nash!' she called. 'Behave yourself. You're frightening the wildlife.'

Cooper sat in the snow for a few moments with his hands on his knees and watched Caudwell and Nash. He had to control his temper. He couldn't lose it – that was exactly what they wanted him to do. Probably exactly what Diane Fry wanted him to do, too.

Looking at the ground where he had fallen, Cooper noticed a glint in the dark peat. Another piece of aluminium? He picked it up and brushed the black fibres from it, revealing a peculiar whiteness. He puzzled over the material it was made from. It seemed to be a broken section of a narrow shaft, surely too brittle to have been part of the airframe. He lifted it to his nose and sniffed it, seeking the familiar smell of scorched metal. But instead he got a scent that reminded him fleetingly of Sunday dinners – a joint of beef with mashed potatoes and carrots round the dining table with his parents on a damp November day. He shook his head to clear the intrusive memory. Perhaps what he held in his fingers was a fragment from the aircraft's radio apparatus. It was almost like Bakelite, its broken ends grainy and hollow. But it was white . . .

He flung the object to the ground as if it had suddenly grown hot and burned his fingers. It lay on the peat, gleaming unmistakably now. He stared at it in horror. It was bone. Of course, it was more than likely a bit of a dead sheep, part of the carcase of a casualty from the flock across the hill that had been picked clean and dropped here by some scavenger. It didn't look as though it had been out in the weather for very long. But Cooper couldn't help associating it with what he had just been thinking of; as he held it in his hand, it had seemed like part of one of the shattered bodies of the airmen who had died in Uncle Victor.

'Ben – are you all right?'

Liz Petty was standing over him looking concerned, puzzled by his silence.

'Yes. Fine.'

But the truth was that Cooper had felt himself shift through time for a moment. He had been picturing that young airman, Sergeant Dick Abbott, hurtling through the torn and splintered metal edges of the Lancaster's fuselage, his limbs ripping from his body as the impact hurled him into the darkness, where he would bleed to death in the snow.

Cooper had once seen a sheep that had been hit by a car on an unfenced moorland road above the Eden Valley. One of the animal's forelegs had been smashed so badly that bits of its femur lay sprinkled on the tarmac like pieces of a jigsaw. This was far worse than that. Men's bodies had been torn apart here, their bones had been shattered and their blood had soaked into the peat. People talked about men who had sacrificed their lives. But this was more than a sacrifice. He was standing on the site of a massacre.

Everyone had blamed Pilot Officer Danny McTeague for the crash of Lancaster SU-V, for the death of five men. Cooper wondered what Marie Tennent, or anyone else, might consider to be justice for such a crime.

Diane Fry found Eddie Kemp in a more amenable mood. He looked like a man who was confident there was insufficient evidence against him. It was the sort of confidence that came to a man who had been questioned many times before without being charged, or who had appeared in court and been acquitted. Also, Fry couldn't detect the smell any more. Maybe the custody suite staff had scrubbed him up specially.

'Of course, my Vicky knew all about the thing with Marie,' said Kemp. 'Vicky had kicked me out at the time, so she couldn't really complain about what I did, could she?'

'I suppose not.'

'We sorted it all out, anyway. I went back to Vicky, and that was that.'

'When was this?'

'Last July.'

'About six months ago, then. Was the parting amicable?'

Kemp hesitated. 'Marie was a bit upset, and she said some things she didn't mean. She told me I smelled. But it's a medical condition I have, so that wasn't fair, was it?'

'And you haven't seen Marie Tennent since then?'

'No. There was no reason to.'

'Wasn't the baby a reason?'

Now Kemp looked a little less comfortable. Fry watched him squirm. 'I didn't know anything about a baby,' he said.

'Are you sure?'

'Sure.'

'Marie never contacted you to tell you about it? I would have thought she would be expecting some maintenance. If you were living with her until six months ago, we take it you're the father.'

'Is there any proof?' said Kemp.

Fry stared at him. 'I'm sure you know that we haven't been able to find the baby.'

'No, well . . .'

'Did she tell you she'd had a baby previously?'

'No.'

In the absence of any evidence otherwise, Fry changed tack. 'Mr Kemp, why did you break your bail?'

'All I did was go to spend a bit of time with my

brother,' he said. 'Vicky was fed up with me for getting in trouble again. To be honest, that's why she kicked me out the first time. So I cleared out for a day or two to let things calm down. I was still in town, though – I was staying with our Graham.'

'All right. Now I need to ask you about an assault on a police officer last night.'

Kemp shook his head. 'As for that,' he said, 'you definitely have no proof.'

29

Ben Cooper could see Alison Morrissey waiting for him by his car. He could see her from a long way off, as soon as the track levelled out on the last quarter of a mile across the peat moor. Her yellow coat stood out against his red Toyota like a splash of mustard.

'Your friend doesn't deter easily, does she?' said Jane Caudwell. She nudged Cooper and dimpled at him. 'Do you want me to set Nash on her again?'

PC Nash sniggered behind them. Liz Petty had been very quiet since they had set off back from the crash site.

Cooper was embarrassed. He hoped his flush wasn't noticeable in the cold. All the way across the moor, he alternately wished Morrissey would go away, then hoped she wouldn't.

'Funny how she knows which is your car,' said Caudwell.

Cooper turned and glanced at Liz. She glowered at him. It wasn't any better for her – she had to walk with Nash. His stride was twice the length of hers, but he was holding back deliberately so that they were shoulder to shoulder on the narrow path.

When they reached the cars, he found Alison Morrissey pale and shivering with the cold. She had her hands tucked under her armpits and her chin shoved into the collar of her coat to minimize the amount of exposed skin. Strands of her hair had escaped from her hat and were hanging in her eyes.

'Are you mad? You'll freeze to death,' said Cooper. 'Where's your car?'

'I haven't got one. Frank dropped me off.'

He noticed that she mumbled her words because her lips were so numb. There was hardly any colour to her lips at all.

'That was stupid,' he said. 'When is he coming back for you?'

'I told him not to. I thought you would give me a lift back to Edendale, Ben.'

'I can't do that.'

'Think of it as part of your service to the public, right?'

Liz Petty got into her van and drove away first, without looking back. As Caudwell and Nash changed out of their walking boots, Caudwell said something over the bonnet of their car, and Nash sniggered again.

'You're determined to get me in trouble, aren't you?' said Cooper. 'You can see I'm on duty.'

'You're worried what your colleagues will say. But they don't really care, do they? Not those two.'

It wasn't Caudwell and Nash that Cooper was worried about. He knew they would take the first opportunity to tell Diane Fry – if Liz Petty didn't get there first.

'You're making it difficult for me to help you.'

'Oh, is that what you're trying to do?' said Morrissey.

She was so pale that she looked very vulnerable. But a thought sneaked into Cooper's mind. He wondered whether her shivering was a little over-done, for effect. Caudwell and Nash drove past them. Nash played a little tune on the horn of their car, and Caudwell waved from the passenger seat, smiling graciously, like the Queen. They disappeared down the A57 towards the Snake Inn.

'They can't see us now,' said Morrissey. Her pale lips parted slightly, so that he could see her perfect teeth and the tip of her tongue. He felt her breath on his face and realized he was standing much too close to her.

'Damn it, Alison,' he said. 'You'd better get in.'

'Thanks, Ben.'

He unlocked the Toyota to let her in and threw his boots and cagoule in the back. He slammed the tailgate a little too hard, and she looked at him reproachfully through the back window.

'Is there a heater in here?' she said, as he opened the driver's door. 'I've lost all the feeling in my legs.'

'Why did you come?' he said. 'Did you know that we'd be up here this morning?'

'Frank did.'

'How?'

'A lot of people know Frank. I think the pilot phoned him last night to get the exact location of the crash site.'

'Damnation.'

'When he told me this morning, I asked him to bring me,' said Morrissey. 'I wanted to know what you were doing.'

'I can't tell you that.'

Cooper wasn't sure what he was so angry about. He turned the heater up full and revved the engine before he pulled out into the road. He was determined he wasn't going to speak to Alison on the way back into Edendale. She was deliberately putting him in a difficult position. But he knew she wouldn't be able to last all the way into town without asking questions. They drove in an uneasy silence for a few moments. When Morrissey spoke, it wasn't the question he had expected.

'Don't you find your job frustrating?' she said. 'All this grubbing around for evidence. A lot of it must be futile. A waste of time and effort, I guess.'

Cooper was taken by surprise at how she had

thrust straight to what he had been thinking himself. It made it impossible for him to refuse to respond.

'Yes, it's very frustrating at times,' he said.

'So why do you carry on with it?'

'Why not?'

'That's no answer, Ben. You're a man who has to have a reason for doing things. You have to believe that it's the right thing to do. So why do you carry on?'

Cooper frowned. He had never been able to explain it to himself, but now the words started to come when someone else asked him.

'Sometimes, just occasionally, I feel that I've done something worthwhile,' he said.

'And is that enough? Just occasionally?'

'Oh, yes,' said Cooper.

They passed the Snake Inn, where the staff had neither heard nor seen any cars on the night that Nick Easton had been killed, only the snow-ploughs. They passed the lay-by where the plough crew had found Easton's body. But Cooper wasn't thinking about Easton, or even Marie Tennent. Alison Morrissey knew exactly when to keep quiet. It was a skill that would make her useful as a police interviewer.

'You see,' he said, 'when it happens, when I feel as though I've done something worthwhile, it's like the world suddenly settles into place and looks as it ought to do for once, the way it was created, before we messed it up and made it cruel and dirty. It's hard to explain. It's not that anything in particular happens to the world, of course, not so that you would notice. It's something that happens to me. But whatever it is, it feels ... real.'

Out of the corner of his eye, he could see her nodding. Still she said nothing. They were on the long descent into the Derwent Valley. Glittering ribbons of water stretched ahead and alongside them as they drove into the long arms of Ladybower Reservoir.

'It's a sensation that isn't like anything else I've ever known. I suppose it's like taking a powerful drug. It gives me a buzz, makes me feel alive. It's good, for a while.'

She nodded again, and he felt her watching him. He was glad that she said nothing. He needed another moment to finish the thought, to get the words out that were suddenly jostling among themselves somewhere in his subconscious, waiting to be let out.

'But it's like any other drug,' he said. 'It does something to your mind. It leaves you always craving more. It leaves you willing to do anything, anything at all, to get that feeling again.'

They were soon through Bamford and approaching Edendale. Morrissey had left him alone with his thoughts. He was starting to feel embarrassed again that she was able to get him to say such things, yet he was glad he had articulated it to himself. It had made a kind of sense of his own feelings that he had never been able to grasp before.

'I'll drop you at your hotel,' said Cooper. 'Please don't do anything like that again.'

'OK,' said Morrissey. 'I'm grateful for the lift.' She sounded meek now, no longer provocative. 'I wanted the chance to say I'm sorry for getting annoyed with you yesterday. You're right to be sceptical about what people tell you. So I apologize.'

'That's all right. I've seen the faxes anyway.'

'Good. There's just one thing I'd like you to do for me, Ben.'

'No,' he said.

'Please,' she said. 'You know these people won't talk to me. I want you to go and see Walter Rowland again.'

'Why should I do that?'

'There's something that my grandmother told my mother, and my mother passed on to me. It was one of the allegations that were thrown at my grandfather at the time. But even Frank Baine doesn't seem to know anything about it. So I want you to ask Walter Rowland.'

'About what?' said Cooper.

'I want you to ask him what he knows about the missing money.'

As Ben Cooper tried to warm himself up back at West Street, two images stayed with him. One was the powerful impression he'd had of the dead

486

and dying airman. The other was an image of the bright red poppy on its wooden cross, which remained imprinted on his memory as if it had been burned there by the electric brightness of the snow. Sergeant Dick Abbott, 24th August 1926 to 7th January 1945. Who would take the trouble to remember Dick Abbott?

During that afternoon, Cooper tracked down the old inquest reports for the five airmen in the county archives at Derby and had them faxed to him. Of course, the verdicts on Klemens Wach, Dick Abbott and the other airmen had all been recorded as accidental deaths. There was some technical evidence given by an RAF accident investigator, who had referred to the fact that the Lancaster was well off course and over high ground in low cloud – that fatal combination. But there was also the suggestion of human error. Either the navigator had given the pilot the wrong course, or the pilot had ignored his instructions. Nobody could know, except those who had been involved. The navigator had died in the crash, and the pilot himself had gone missing.

The RAF's own investigation had placed the blame for the loss of the aircraft on the pilot. The pilot was always in charge, no matter what his rank. But no one seemed to have troubled to ask what the flight engineer might have known about SU-V's last few minutes. He was best placed to have noticed whether the navigator had got his calculations wrong, or whether the pilot had been incapable. But the flight engineer had been Zygmunt Lukasz, and the navigator had been his cousin Klemens.

The archivist had also sent him a copy of a report from the Accidents Investigation Branch of the Air Ministry. It had been signed in black fountain pen by someone called C.I. (Accidents), and it gave the results of a detailed examination of the main parts of the aircraft. No structural cause had been discovered. The report also covered weather conditions, the pilot's history and the airframe's history. The documents were useless to him. They told him nothing about the human lives involved.

But someone had known the background of Sergeant Dick Abbott. Alison Morrissey had mentioned finding out that another member of the crew of Sugar Uncle Victor had a young child, as well as Danny McTeague. That had been Dick Abbott, hadn't it? So where had Morrissey got her information from?

Cooper dialled a number in Edendale.

'Sergeant Dick Abbott, the rear gunner,' said Frank Baine. 'He was from Glasgow. He worked in a steel foundry before he joined up in the RAF.'

'He was married, with a child?'

'That's right, he was. Only two members of the crew of SU-V were fathers – Abbott and McTeague. Abbott was very young himself – eighteen. Maybe he had to get married because of the baby, I don't know.'

'Did you manage to trace his family?'

'Abbott's? Well, I went through the squadron historical society. They tried to contact the wife for me, but it seems she re-married and emigrated. I never took it any further than that.'

'I see. I suppose you know about these people who collect bits of aircraft wrecks. I've heard them called vultures.'

'Yes, I know all about them. Some folk think it's desecration, that the wrecks are memorials to the men who died.'

'I imagine relatives must feel strongly about that.'

'Naturally.'

'Alison Morrissey, for a start?'

'Alison? I'm not sure about her,' said Baine.

'What do you mean?'

Baine sighed. 'She always seems to be holding something back. Do you know what I mean? She's told me the entire story, all about her mother and her grandfather, Danny McTeague. I've had the whole thing. Sometimes it seems she's telling me far more than I need to know, and that makes me wonder . . . Well, I have the impression she does it so that I won't ask her questions. She doesn't like questions, though God knows she asks enough herself.'

'Is she paying you?' asked Cooper.

For a moment, Baine hesitated. 'Well, expenses really. Why do you ask?'

'You seem to be doing a lot for her, to say that she's a complete stranger and you don't even trust her yourself. Dropping her off near Irontongue Hill this morning was a bit stupid. It caused me a few problems.'

'I'm sorry, but she's very persuasive when there's something she wants you to do.'

'I know. I've found that, too.'

Diane Fry had entered the office while Cooper was talking to Baine. He wasn't sure whether she had heard him mention Alison Morrissey. But there was something about the way she toyed with her scarf, stretching and twisting it tightly between her hands, which made him think she had.

She walked up to his desk and lifted the pile of faxes. She held them in the air and waited for him to finish the call.

'So what's with the faxes?' she said. 'Anything interesting?'

'Oh, nothing important.'

Before he could take them from her, she was reading the top sheet. 'Who is Kenneth Rees? Should I know the name?'

'No.'

'He's not very attractive, is he? Also, it seems that he lives in Canada.'

Cooper gritted his teeth. 'He's Alison's mother's stepfather.'

'Ben, are you telling me that you're having details of her family faxed to you at work?'

'It's to do with Pilot Officer Danny McTeague.'

'Is it? Are you sure?'

'I happened to suggest the possibility that he might have got back to Canada and taken on a new identity.'

'Ah. Even you are sceptical, eh?'

'It's not impossible to change your identity. Deserters did it often.'

'And I suppose you're thinking that this Rees character is really McTeague with a new identity, who re-married his wife after a decent interval of mourning for his old self. Where on earth did you get that idea from, Ben?'

'He's nothing like McTeague anyway,' said Cooper. 'Kenneth Rees was a mining engineer from Newcastle. He had red hair, and was only five foot eight inches tall. You see, I checked.'

'Don't tell me – you read the idea in a novel. I read a novel myself once.'

'I didn't think you read novels, Diane.'

'I was sick at the time. It didn't do anything to cure me.'

'Right. Anyway, it looks as though McTeague never went back to his wife and baby. But the thing that worries me is that he kept telling his crew about his family back in Canada, and how he couldn't wait to get back to them. He wouldn't have deserted them, no matter what. He would have got in touch with them somehow and let them know he was alive, at least.'

Fry put down the fax. Cooper was surprised that she was still listening to him. It was the first time she had allowed him to talk about McTeague for more than thirty seconds.

'So what then?' she said.

'I'm convinced now that he never made it back to Canada. Maybe he suffered amnesia in the crash and forgot who he was. I suppose he could have taken on a new identity here and settled down in England.'

'Ben, I think the authorities were quite keen on knowing who people were at that time. They were paranoid about German spies landing and all that.'

'Right at the end of the war? I'm not so sure. We'd have to ask somebody who was around at the time. But Hitler was beaten by then. The war had turned. It was Bomber Command and the American air force who were flattening German cities by then, not the other way round. The most the Germans could do to this part of the country was to fire off a few V2 rockets and hope they reached Sheffield. And here, in the Peak District . . . well, I suspect there might have been people in this area who didn't ask too many questions. Let's face it, they're still like that today. During the war, they were short of men, short of labour for the farms. A lot of the farmers had to rely on German and Italian prisoners of war for their workforce. It's possible an airman with a Canadian accent would have been accepted on a farm somewhere, without any questions asked. They were strange times.'

He could see Fry was starting to get restless now.

'It's all speculation,' she said. 'You could never find out one way or the other, unless McTeague were to turn up somewhere.'

'I suppose not.'

'And, Ben? Reading that novel didn't do anything for me. It just made me feel sicker.'

Fry continued to tug at her scarf while Cooper told her about the visit to the crash site. He was economical with the details, but knew he had to tell her about Alison Morrissey's appearance. No doubt she would hear from Caudwell anyway. But it was the poppy and the cross she was most interested in.

'What makes you think it might have been Marie Tennent who placed the cross?' she said.

'January 7th was the anniversary of the crash. We've had appeals out for anyone who was up on the moor that day and might have seen Marie. But even the local ranger stayed away from Irontongue because of the weather. You'd have needed a pretty good reason to make it right to the top of the hill. But one person did go, to leave the cross. And one person died on the way back down – Marie Tennent. I'm suggesting they might have been one and the same person.'

'OK. And she was remembering this dead airman . . .'

'Sergeant Dick Abbott, the rear gunner. Apart from McTeague, he was the only member of the crew who had a child at home. Also, he was Scottish. We need to ask Mrs Tennent whether they were related. I think Marie could have been like Alison Morrissey – a granddaughter of one of the crew. Except, in this case, she knew exactly what had happened to Dick Abbott.'

He expected Fry to mock him. He expected her to say that it was a question of priorities, that there could be no possibility of sparing any more resources on a likely suicide or death by misadventure. But she didn't say any of those things. He knew it was the missing baby that made the difference for them both.

Normally, a mother who abandoned a baby left it somewhere that it would quickly be found, though she might make great efforts to remain anonymous. But if Marie Tennent had hidden her baby, she had chosen somewhere it couldn't be found. The remains of the earlier child were too depressing a precedent. Although DNA tests on the bones were awaited for confirmation, the circumstantial evidence was all too clear that they had belonged to Marie's first child. Surely Baby Chloe, too, must already be dead, succumbed to a lack of care perhaps, because she had been born to a woman who had no idea what to do with her.

'I hope something is obvious to you, Ben,' said Fry.

'What's that?'

She stood up. 'You're going to have big problems

justifying how you can spend so much time on this business of Alison Morrissey's. Think about Sergeant Easton. Think about Marie Tennent and her baby, instead of your Canadian woman. Think about the people who really *need* you.'

Cooper flushed. Why did Fry always have to be right? And why did she always have to speak to him in a way that prevented him from admitting that she was right?

'Whatever I'm doing to help Alison Morrissey, I'm doing it in my own time,' he said.

Fry smacked a hand on the faxes from Canada. 'Really? With these on your desk? I'm seriously doubting whether I can trust you to be out on your own, Ben. If we weren't so short-staffed, I'd be considering asking to have you replaced with someone I *can* trust.'

Cooper stood and began putting on his coat. His hand was trembling, and he fumbled with the buttons. But he needed to get out of the office. He didn't want to get into an argument.

Fry watched him, her voice quietening. 'Ben, I'm saying this for your own good. Forget about Alison Morrissey. Tell her to get lost. Seeing her again won't do you any good at all.'

'It has nothing to do with you,' said Cooper.

Ben Cooper went out to his car and started the engine. He found his mind was going round in circles, and he needed to calm down before he began to drive. He would only put his foot down too hard on the accelerator and break the speed limit on the relief road.

He picked up one of the books on Peak District aircraft wrecks. There was a picture of those men in their flying suits that was as clear in his mind as if it had been an actual memory. He could have been there himself, standing with the group of smiling airmen – perhaps feeling grateful, like them, for the bit of sun that lit their tired faces, and breathing in the familiar smell of aviation fuel and rubber from the aircraft that were lined up behind them on the edge of the runway.

Cooper could almost feel the wind that must have been blowing across the exposed Yorkshire airfield. He knew there had been a wind, because it had lifted Sergeant Dick Abbott's fringe of dark hair from his forehead. He wanted to reach out and pat the sergeant's hair back into place, because of the way it made his face look so young and vulnerable.

But that reaction was partly due to the knowledge Cooper had of what would happen to Sergeant Abbott a few weeks after the photograph was taken. He could no longer look at the photograph of the Lancaster crew without also seeing a phantom image superimposed on it – an image of splintered bones and torn limbs, of charred bodies trapped in twisted metal. He was seeing the ghosts of dead men, overlaid on the page by historical hindsight.

*　　*　　*

Diane Fry had watched Cooper go, noting the stubborn set of his shoulders as he buttoned his coat and pulled on his cap before stamping out of the room. Probably she had been wasting her breath in speaking to him. He wasn't in a state to be talked sense to. But she had meant what she had said. It was absolutely for his own good.

Still Fry regretted that she couldn't say to him what she really wanted to say. She couldn't tell him that she thought he was being used by Alison Morrissey, that he was going to end up being hurt. He would never take that from *her*.

In any case, the words would have stuck in her throat. Fry could imagine the look of embarrassed disbelief on his face, the first mocking laugh at the idea that she could possibly care.

Fry looked at the Marie Tennent file sitting on Cooper's desk. Still waiting for postmortem results. She decided to ring Mrs Van Doon there and then. If no one nagged, they might have to wait for days to get a report.

'Just done it,' said the pathologist. 'Your timing is admirable.'

'Preliminary results?'

'Cause of death was hypothermia and exposure. No surprise there, surely?'

'Any contributory factors? Injuries?'

'Frostbite damage to the extremities – feet, hands, parts of the face. And this is the bit you probably don't want to hear . . .'

'Go on. I can take it.'

'There was bruising and a number of minor abrasions on parts of the body.'

'Where?'

'Chest and abdomen, including two cracked ribs and some liver lacerations. Bruising on upper and lower arms. And an extensive bruise on the temple, near the left ear.'

'Are these injuries consistent with a fall? Like the Snowman?'

'Oh, your other body? No, I'm afraid not. This is different. The bruises and abrasions on the arms look like defensive injuries to me. The blow to the head is quite severe, as are some of the injuries to the torso, hence the cracked ribs. I imagine that she must have been in some considerable pain from her injuries.'

'Not in any condition to hike up Irontongue Hill in the snow, then?'

'It wouldn't have done her much good at all,' said the pathologist. 'She was already in a weakened condition. As for her general state of health, you'll have to wait for the results of all the tests. But I can tell you she was well nourished, though she hadn't eaten a meal for several hours. No immediate evidence of disease. Parturition within the last two months. Probably not the first. No surprises there either, eh?'

'Not really.'

'I've seen the newspaper reports. Are you still looking for the baby?'

'Yes.'

'Tragic. Another failure of the medical profession, I suppose. I see all their mistakes here, you know.'

'We're not jumping to any conclusions,' said Fry cautiously.

'No, I'm sorry. It's been a long day. A long week.'

'Oh, tell me about it.'

'Is there anything else you want to know?'

'Yes, what about a time scale? When were the injuries caused? How long before her death?'

'Right. Judging by the progress of the bruising, I would estimate the injuries were inflicted at least thirty-six hours prior to death – long enough to have become pretty painful. In fact, there was some fresh internal bleeding, which I imagine was the result of putting too much stress on the liver and chest injuries. She would have been in quite some pain at that stage.'

'She would have sat down to recover,' said Fry. 'Maybe even passed out from the pain?'

'Possibly.' The pathologist paused. 'Of course, I'm estimating the time of death, too. This person didn't die quickly, you know. In fact, she would have taken a long time to die.'

Fry didn't want to think about that too closely. She had one more thing to ask Mrs Van Doon.

'Could the injuries have been self-inflicted?'

'No way.'

Next, Fry rang Mrs Lorna Tennent, who had

gone back to Falkirk. Mrs Tennent was surprised at the question.

'Yes, of course,' she said. 'Dick Abbott was my first husband's father. We used to come down to Derbyshire to leave a poppy regularly every year when Marie was younger, but we stopped when I got divorced. I had no idea Marie still felt she had to keep it up. No idea.'

Fry put down the phone. She wanted to tell Cooper the news immediately, but she didn't know where he had gone. Probably he was off seeing Alison Morrissey again, purely out of bloody-mindedness. He was going to have to wait, then. There was no way Fry was going to interfere with his social life. At the moment, Ben Cooper was thinking only of himself.

30

Tonight, the Gospel Hall was in use. Through a side window, Ben Cooper glimpsed members of the congregation sitting on wooden chairs on a quarry-tiled floor. The sound of an electric organ reached him, and then voices singing a hymn.

On his first visit to Walter Rowland, Cooper hadn't recognized the other church, the one on the corner of Harrington Street. Now he saw that it was Our Lady of Czestochowa, the church attended by the Lukasz family and other members of the Polish community. It was distinguished by the representation of the Black Madonna over the door. And there was the little school alongside it, too – the Saturday School where Richard and Alice Lukasz studied for their Polish O-levels. Halfway down the street from here was the Dom Kombatanta, the club of the SPK, the Polish ex-servicemen's organization.

Cooper knocked on Rowland's door, but found it off the latch. He pushed it open a few inches.

'Mr Rowland?'

A tired voice answered him. A voice drowning in pain, barely managing to stay above the surface of despair.

'Aye. Through here.'

Walter Rowland was in his front room, and at least he had some heating in his house. The old man would long since have been dead if he had lived in Hollow Shaw.

Rowland was sitting in a curious position. He had his hands resting on the table in front of him, palms upward, as if he were expecting coins to drop from the ceiling and it was important that he should catch them. Cooper was reminded of a yogi sitting in a lotus position, with his hands held on his knees. What was it a yogi expected to receive when he meditated like that? Some kind of inner peace? But inner peace surely wasn't what this old man was expecting. Rowland's hands weren't relaxed at all; his fingers were curled in towards the palms like claws, and their flesh was dry and shrivelled, so that the joints of the fingers stood out in bony ridges. Those hands spoke so clearly of calmly accepted suffering and pain that Cooper revised his religious image from the meditating yogi. All that was missing from these hands were the nails pinning them to the wood.

Rowland noticed Cooper looking at his hands. 'It's not so good today,' he said, apologetically. He looked pale, and his eyes had sunk further into their sockets. 'If you want a cup of tea, you'll have to put the kettle on yourself.'

'Have you got anybody to help you?' asked Cooper, as he walked through into the kitchen.

'How do you mean?'

'If you're ill and can't look after yourself, you surely have some kind of home help, don't you?'

Rowland said nothing. Cooper plugged in the electric kettle and found two mugs with pictures of the Houses of Parliament on them. He noticed that there was a dent a couple of inches wide in the back door, and the wood was crushed. He wondered if the old man had fallen while trying to do some job in the kitchen.

Cooper glanced through into the front room. Rowland was staring at his hands. His fingers were as brown and as knotted as the pine table they lay on.

'Have you tried Social Services? Or talked to your GP?' said Cooper.

The old man shook his head.

'They could send you a home help,' said Cooper. 'At your age, you must qualify. It would make things easier for you. I mean, how do you manage to cook yourself a meal?'

Rowland just smiled. 'You'll find some tea in the top cupboard,' he said.

While he was finding the tea, Cooper looked through the kitchen cupboards, trying to slide the doors open as quietly as he could. There were plenty of tins of all descriptions – steak puddings and hot dogs, new potatoes and mushy peas, peaches and pineapple chunks. He wondered if Rowland were capable of operating a tin opener. A small fridge stood in the corner, and he could hear its coolant gurgling in the pipes at the back. He found some milk in it and checked the use-by date on the plastic bottle, remembering the sour taste of the tea at George Malkin's house. That taste had stayed with him for days afterwards. But Rowland's milk was OK for a day or so yet. Could that mean somebody did a bit of shopping for the old man occasionally? That was something, at least. Cooper wondered how he could ask Rowland the question, and whether he would get an answer.

He carried the two mugs of tea back through from the kitchen.

'What are the neighbours like? Will they fetch some shopping for you?'

Rowland didn't answer. He looked at his mug on the table. Cooper knew he was being told as clearly as he could be that it was none of his business.

'Don't worry about me,' said Rowland. 'I've got a routine to my day. I've got the telly, there. And when there's no more sex and violence on, I know it's time to go to bed.'

Cooper sat down opposite him. The television muttered in the corner, and he didn't bother asking Rowland to switch it off.

'We were talking about the Lancaster crash the other day,' he said. 'Do you remember?'

'Of course I remember. Sugar Uncle Victor. There

504

aren't all that many things happen around here that I wouldn't remember.'

'You said then that Pilot Officer McTeague was different from airmen who were sometimes in shock after a crash.'

'Yes, I did.'

'I want to ask you again why McTeague was different.'

Rowland breathed slowly for a while. But Cooper could see he had less resistance today.

'I smelled him,' said Rowland.

'What?'

'When we realized there was at least one crew member missing, we looked in the wreckage as best we could. Some of it was on fire, and our sergeant shouted at us to stay away. But we couldn't have left someone in the burning plane, could we? I went to look in the cockpit. It had broken away from the fuselage, so the flames hadn't reached it. And when I stuck my head in there – well, I could smell the whisky. The fumes fair knocked me out.'

'Do you mean Pilot Officer McTeague was drunk?'

'By the stink of the cockpit, he must have been pissed as a snake. Other folks might have taken what he did for shock, like you say. But I've never doubted that he was drunk when he flew that plane into Irontongue Hill.'

'If he was, his crew would have known.'

'No doubt. But only Zygmunt Lukasz survived, didn't he? And he never said anything.'

'Not officially, anyway.'

'No.'

'Do you ever meet any of the Polish community in Edendale?'

'Community?' said Rowland, confused by the use of the word.

'They have their own church up the road,' said Cooper. 'And an ex-servicemen's club, where Zygmunt Lukasz is a member. They even have a school.'

'So they do,' said Rowland, faintly surprised. 'But I've never thought much about it really. They keep up their own way of life, do they, then? I'm not surprised – like I said, they have their own beliefs, and they stick to them.'

Rowland watched Cooper quizzically, until he began to fidget uneasily.

'I can't blame them for that,' said the old man. 'If I had to live in Poland for some reason, it wouldn't make me Polish, would it? No, I reckon I'd still be a Derbyshire lad until the end of my days.'

Rowland closed his eyes momentarily. A voice continued to mumble from the TV. It was a different voice now – a woman with a Scottish accent. Soothing and reassuring.

'Maybe I was wrong about McTeague,' said Rowland. 'But I can only remember what I saw and heard.'

'But you didn't see Pilot Officer McTeague, did you? You didn't hear him or smell him, either.'

'He'd already legged it by the time we got there.'

'Exactly.'

'I always thought they would find him sleeping it off,' said Rowland. 'I had half a mind to try to find him myself and knock the living daylights out of him. But I don't think anybody else even noticed. The fire got to the cockpit, and that was that. Nobody said a word.'

'Mr Rowland, why didn't you say anything about this at the time?'

'What makes you think I didn't?'

'Because it isn't mentioned in the inquest report. It isn't mentioned in the accident report, either.'

'Always believe everything you read in official reports, do you?'

'Well . . .'

'I can't imagine you do. You probably write enough of them yourself to know the drill. Some things you put in, some you leave out. Now, don't you?'

'I suppose so.'

'I told the officers about it, but they left it out of the reports. I was only a young RAF squaddie. I did what I was told. We didn't question things in those days.'

'There's one more thing I want to ask you about,' said Cooper. 'The money.'

'Ah,' said Rowland. 'The money.'

'There isn't any money mentioned in the accident reports.'

'No, there wouldn't be.'

'As far as I understand it, Lancaster SU-V was

507

on a routine flight from its base at Leadenhall to RAF Benson in Lancashire. The aircraft had recently been through major repairs, including the replacement of an engine. Its crew were taking it on a test flight before it returned to normal operations.'

'Yes,' said Rowland. 'But when they set off on that routine flight, they were also asked to take the weekly wages to RAF Benson and three other RAF stations in Lancashire. It was safer than sending airmen armed with pickaxe handles to collect it from local banks – and some of those bases were in places where the nearest bank was a long way off.'

'I see. But the money never arrived. Because on the way there, the Lancaster crashed on Irontongue Hill.'

'And some bugger disappeared with the loot,' said Rowland. For a few seconds, there was a faint spark in his eyes. 'It was funny really. The RAF were going daft about it, but they daren't say anything publicly. Well, they didn't want crowds of folk wandering about on the mountain looking for the money. It was second nature with them anyway, to keep information to themselves. It was second nature to us all at that time. We never said anything, though some of us looked for the money ourselves when their backs were turned, I expect. There'd be one or two hoping to come across a few pound notes blowing about the moor.'

'It was never found?'

'Never. A couple of officers came out to the site. They got angry with us, but of course the rescue teams were more bothered about the human casualties. Some of us had been up there for hours and hours in the freezing cold, trying to piece the injured blokes together and get them off the mountain. We were in no mood to be harangued by some RAF brass with their posh accents and their Clark Gable moustaches. There were angry words, by all accounts. Some said that blows were struck, but no charges were ever brought, civil or military.'

'What happened in the end?'

'Two members of the Home Guard were suspected.'

'What? Dad's Army?'

'They were given the job of guarding the wreckage overnight. They were the only people who had the chance of removing the money, so the theory went.'

'This wasn't in the crash report.'

'Of course not. It was nothing to do with the crash. Do you think the RAF went round telling everybody there had been thousands of pounds in cash on board the plane?'

'Who were the two Home Guard men?'

'I can tell you their names if you want, but remember that they were men who were already too old for active service. They're long dead. Of course, the police ought to have been looking for somebody who suddenly got rich about that time. That amount of money would be like finding King Solomon's Mine for some poor bloody farmworker. They could hardly have spent it without anybody noticing. Not in wartime – think of rationing, for a start. But it was the two Home Guard blokes who took the blame. Walker and Sykes, they were called. They were questioned for days, but they were never charged. Without the money, they couldn't prove anything.'

'Did you know these men?' asked Cooper.

'Oh, aye,' said Rowland. 'Walker and Sykes were with the West Edendale company. One of them was the water board man that used to look after Blackbrook Reservoir. But his mate, now, he made a living working in the kitchens at the Snake Inn, as I recall. He didn't look quite English, you know. Too dark of complexion. He was one of those who always came under suspicion during the war. If you didn't fit in before the war, then you turned into a Nazi spy once it started. Aye, you were either one of us, or you were one of the enemy. That would be why he joined the Home Guard, I reckon – to show the local folk which side he was on.'

'But then, when the money went missing . . . ?'

'He was the obvious one to blame. When they found out he was on guard, everyone was convinced it was him that took the money. Nobody thought too much about how he did it – they just knew it was *him*.'

Cooper frowned. 'But, Mr Rowland, if it wasn't

the Home Guard men who took the money, then who was it?'

'I don't know the answers to these questions,' said Rowland. 'Why are you asking me?'

Cooper knew he should stop now. But he was sure that Walter Rowland knew more. He felt he almost had the one fact that would be the key to everything.

'Somebody local? Can you tell me who?'

'I've no idea,' said Rowland. 'It doesn't matter.'

There was a fatalism in the old man's voice that hadn't been there before. Though he was trying to answer the questions, it was difficult for him to rouse the interest. He was several inches nearer to the brink of despair. Cooper knew there was something wrong, and it was more, even, than the pain in the old man's joints.

'Just a minute,' he said. 'Sit there and don't move.'

He went back into the kitchen and looked at the back door. The lock was missing completely – there was only a round hole where the barrel should have passed through, and there was bare wood that had been recently exposed. He eased open the door by its outer edge and found he was looking into a small lean-to extension built on to the back of the house. There was a workbench, surrounded by wood shavings on the floor. But there were no tools – the racks above the bench were empty. There were marks on the bench where a lathe might have been clamped, but there was no lathe. The door that led outside had been forced, and fresh splinters of wood stuck out of it at dangerous angles.

'You've had a break-in,' said Cooper. 'They've ransacked your workshop.'

'Yes,' said Rowland.

'Have you reported it?'

'To the police? There didn't seem much point.'

'Why not?'

'Your lot would do sod-all. There's other folk that get more done about things around here. So I told them.'

Cooper stared at the old man. 'Who are you talking about, Mr Rowland?'

'Local folk, that don't like burglars and drug dealers. Folk that are prepared to do something about it.'

'You mean vigilantes?'

Rowland said nothing, avoiding his eye, and Cooper knew he would get nothing more out of the old man. But he was thinking of two youths who had ended up in hospital, and of a piece of CCTV film that would identify Eddie Kemp.

'I'll get somebody to come out to take the details of the incident and get some fingerprints,' he said. 'If you can make a list of what's been taken, we'll get people to look out for your property.'

Rowland lowered his head. He hardly seemed interested. He was still looking at his mug of tea, his twisted hands held in front of him as he watched the steam rise and vanish. With a shock, Cooper realized that the old man was probably unable to pick up the mug. He remembered that Rowland hadn't actually asked for the tea, just told him to get one for himself.

Cooper flushed with embarrassment. Now he didn't know what to do. There was no way he could help Walter Rowland, no way that he could offer to lift the mug to his lips to help him drink. The old man would never accept that sort of help from a stranger. Not from anyone, maybe. The only option was to leave him to it, to save Rowland the humiliation of having to sit there while the tea went cold, and to pretend that he didn't want it.

Helplessly, Cooper looked out of the window at the net curtains in the porch of the house next door. If he went to knock on the neighbours' door when he left, Rowland would see him. On the other side was the Gospel Hall, where the singing had stopped now. Cooper recalled hearing the sound of cars starting, and doors slamming. He could even imagine he had heard the noise of a key turning firmly in the lock of the big oak door before the hall fell into silence. He didn't know where else to look for help. His training had never prepared him for this.

Of course, where large amounts of money were involved, anything could happen. It could bring out the worst in everybody, whether it was war-time or not. Sitting in his car in Underbank, Ben Cooper considered the people he had talked to.

Had any of them suddenly become rich in the past? Walter Rowland or George Malkin? It didn't seem likely. And if Danny McTeague himself had walked off with the money from Lancaster SU-V, there was no way of finding out. That left only one man alive who had been there at the time.

He looked at his watch. He might just be in time. The Lukaszes should be at West Street to make their statements right now.

Diane Fry watched Grace Lukasz rub the palms of her hands on the arms of her wheelchair, leaving noticeable sweat stains. On her own, the woman was nervous.

'Mrs Lukasz,' said Fry, 'where did your son Andrew get the cigarette case that upset your father-in-law so much?'

'I don't know. Andrew wouldn't tell us. In fact, he was very secretive about it. You know, I'm not sure now what he wanted when he came. I thought he wanted to be reconciled, but something went wrong, and I don't know why he argued with Zygmunt. Since he's lived in London, Andrew has become like a stranger to us.'

'Did you have any idea who Nick Easton was, the man who came to your home on Monday?'

'Not really,' said Mrs Lukasz.

'Not really? What does that mean?'

'It means I only suspected. Nobody had told me anything, but I can put two and two together when it comes to my family. I thought he must either be a policeman – or something worse.'

'Worse?' Fry looked at Murfin and almost smiled. 'Is there something worse?'

'Yes,' said Mrs Lukasz. 'I think there are people who would want to do Andrew harm.'

'Why?'

'I've been worried about Andrew for a long time. You know we didn't see him for nearly five years after he left to go to London?'

'There was some question of discord over his wedding.'

'Yes, but it was more than that. He was always evasive about the details of his life and what he did. Nobody else would have noticed, perhaps. Peter didn't notice it. But I'm Andrew's mother – I didn't need to work it out logically. I started to feel sure that he'd become involved in something dangerous. Peter said I was talking nonsense.' Grace Lukasz toyed with the spokes of her wheels, while her eyes followed Fry's pen as she made notes. 'Then Andrew turned up in Edendale a few days after New Year, and he was still evasive – evasive about why he had come. He said he had business in the area, and I believed him. But I was worried what sort of business it might be.'

'Do you think it was something to do with the cigarette case?' asked Fry.

'Yes. It was what he argued with Zygmunt about that Sunday. I've never heard either of them so angry. I was glad that Peter wasn't there. Andrew said something about loyalty, and that was when Zygmunt really got angry. I thought he was going to have a heart attack. He shouted in Polish, and it was after that Andrew walked out.'

'Do you know why your father-in-law was so angry?'

Grace Lukasz nodded. 'You have to understand, this is *oplatek* time, the time for forgiveness and reconciliation. It means a lot to Zygmunt. We all know it will be his last *oplatek*, and he needs to leave everything straight.'

'I see.'

'I don't think you do,' said Grace. She wiped her hands on a tissue and crumpled it into a tight ball. 'In spite of *oplatek*, I think Zygmunt found he couldn't forgive. I think he realized it wasn't in his heart to forgive Andrew – and that was what made him so angry. I was frightened what Andrew meant to do when he left. He's in trouble, isn't he? I just know he's mixed up with the wrong people.'

Ben Cooper found Peter Lukasz waiting for his wife to come out from making her statement. He looked grey and worried, but there was an air of resignation about him, too. He looked as if he knew what Grace would be saying in her statement, and there was nothing he could do about it.

'Mr Lukasz, could you answer a question for me?' said Cooper.

'What is it?'

'I wonder if you could tell me when the Dom Kombatanta was built?'

Lukasz's mouth fell open a little. It wasn't what he had expected. 'Well, the original building was put up a few years after the war, when a Polish community first began to develop in Edendale.'

'So where did the money come from to build it?'

'The money?'

'It must have cost quite a few thousand pounds. Where did it come from?'

'Donations,' said Lukasz. 'Donations from the Polish community. Everybody put in a share, I suppose.'

'Some more than others, perhaps.'

'I don't know what you mean.'

'I'm wondering whether there was a particular benefactor, someone who was able to put a large amount of money in. It could make all the difference.'

'You'd have to ask Stefan Janicki. He's the treasurer. He might still have the records.'

'I will.'

'What does it matter, anyway? There have been lots of Poles who have made a success in business. Why shouldn't they put money into something that benefits their community?'

'No reason at all, I expect.'

'My cousin Tadeusz Kulczyck has contributed quite a lot for the recent improvements,' said Lukasz. 'He paid for the new stage and the toilet block.'

'Is he here in Edendale?'

'He doesn't live locally, but he visits us when he can. Tadeusz is an architect,' said Lukasz. 'He designed the Dom Kombatanta in Ottawa.'

'As in Ottawa, Canada?'

'Of course.'

'Your cousin Tadeusz is Canadian?'

'And why not? There are plenty of Poles in Canada.'

Cooper thought he was telling the truth. There were probably Polish communities everywhere, with long and indestructible roots, like bindweed. He remembered the old men with their closed faces, still oozing loyalty and determination. Hitler had mocked these people, calling them Sikorski's Tourists. But Walter Rowland said he preferred to have them on his side. Cooper wondered how he could get the Poles on *his* side, too. But, of course, Hitler had taught him that lesson already – what they needed was a common enemy.

'I have one more thing to ask of you,' said Cooper. 'This is more in the way of a favour.'

'Really?'

'Did your father ever mention a man called Walter Rowland? He was a member of the RAF rescue team who attended the Lancaster crash.'

'I think I know who you mean.'

'As it happens, he lives near to your church.'

'Yes? And what's this favour?'

'I wondered if you would visit him,' said Cooper. 'I just . . . well, I wondered if you would visit him.'

Lukasz kept a puzzled silence. Cooper thought he must have put the request badly. In fact, he hadn't really explained anything about Walter Rowland at all.

'He has no family,' said Cooper. 'But his history has links to your father's. Why not think of him as part of your community?'

Finally, Fry held open the door for Mrs Lukasz to leave. She and her husband didn't look at each other as he fell in behind her and steered her wheelchair down the ramp and out of the police station.

The Old School Nursing Home looked to Ben Cooper like a little haven of calm and security tonight. Its paths and drives had all been swept clear of snow, and sand had been sprinkled to avoid anyone slipping on the block paving. Nobody had bothered to do that at West Street yet. Also, there were lights on everywhere, and when he went inside, the rooms were warm and welcoming.

Cooper sat in the waiting room, aware that the staff always liked to have a few minutes to make sure his mother was ready to see him. Or rather, that she was ready for him to see. It made him smile a little to think that they were trying to protect him from the ugly realities of her condition, when he had already spent over a year dealing with its consequences at Bridge End Farm.

One of the care supervisors saw Cooper waiting and came to speak to him. The name on her badge was Rachel, and Cooper had met her several times.

'Isabel has had a good day again today,' she said.

'Thank you. I think she's settled here.'

'Oh, yes, it's much better for her. She has complete care, and her medication is monitored constantly. There's no need to feel guilty.'

Cooper raised his eyebrows. 'What makes you think I do?'

'It's normal for family members to feel like that. It takes a while to be reassured that you've done the right thing. But you'll see that Isabel is quite content. She's starting to make some friends now.'

'I'd still like to keep coming every day, if that's all right.'

Rachel smiled. She wasn't very old, twenty-five or twenty-six. He couldn't understand what made a woman like this want to look after other people's elderly relatives.

'Of course, it's fine,' she said. 'Come as often as you like.'

Then Cooper saw a familiar figure walking along the corridor on the way out. For a moment, he couldn't identify who it was. It was one of those moments when he saw somebody he knew but his mind failed to name them, because he was seeing them out of context. Maybe this man was dressed differently, too, from when he had last seen him. Cooper's brain floundered for a moment. Then the front door opened and a draught of icy air blew into the waiting room. It was the chill that prompted his memory.

'That was George Malkin,' he said.

'Oh, do you know Mr Malkin?' said Rachel. 'His wife is one of our residents, too. She's been here for some time now.'

'Yes, it must have been a while.'

'Sorry?'

'I was just thinking. I've been to his house recently. It doesn't show many signs of a woman's touch, you might say.'

'Poor chap. Some men are completely lost when it comes to living on their own, aren't they?'

'So I believe,' said Cooper.

'Florence Malkin has dementia. She recognizes her husband sometimes. But, funnily enough, those are the worst days. Florence has a bit of an obsession. She's convinced that George is going to pay for her to get private treatment. She says he's got the money to do it, and he's going to send her away to get her cured. Some days it's a top doctor in Harley Street, other days a famous specialist in America. She asks him about it every time he comes, when she remembers. She asks him over and over again, and he doesn't know how to answer her. Well, however she thinks he's going to afford that, I don't know. It's obvious neither of them ever had more than two pennies to rub together.'

Rachel sighed. 'You can see he's absolutely devoted to her. I don't know how he's managing to pay for her care here without selling his house. But it won't be for much longer. Poor man.'

'Yes,' said Cooper. 'Poor man.'

31

Ben Cooper rang Diane Fry's mobile. He had never
known what she did with herself in the evenings
when she went off duty, except that she sometimes
drove into Sheffield. Fry had told him once that she
had been trying to trace her sister, but she hadn't
mentioned it to him for months. She was much too
secret and solitary a person for her own good.

'Ben? Funny you should call. I've got some
news.'

'Yes?'

'You were right about Marie Tennent. She was
Sergeant Abbott's granddaughter. Strange, isn't
it? Two granddaughters of the Lancaster's crew
appearing at the same time. One dead and one
very much alive.'

'It was the anniversary of the crash,' said Cooper.
'Anniversaries are important. They both felt they
had to remember it.'

'That doesn't explain why one of them was
dead.'

'No.'

'Ben, we've also had the preliminary results of the postmortem.'

'On Marie Tennent?'

'Yes.'

'It's bad news, isn't it, Diane?'

'I'm afraid so. She suffered from more than just frostbite. She'd been badly beaten. She had bruises to her face and the upper part of her body, consistent with being struck by a fist several times. It looks as though she had been in a violent struggle not long before she died.'

'Damn.' The news made Cooper feel sick. Despite all the work on the Snowman enquiry, and all the time that he had spent on Danny McTeague and the crash of Sugar Uncle Victor, it had been Marie Tennent he had woken thinking about each morning. She had been there at the back of his mind – a sad, cold bundle lying on the hillside, waiting for somebody to explain what had happened to her.

'We've been neglecting her, Diane,' said Cooper. 'We have to find out where she had been, who she'd been seeing.'

'We'll interview Eddie Kemp again tomorrow,' said Fry. 'But if he moved back in with his wife six months ago, the chances are there's been another boyfriend since then.'

'One who might not have been happy about the baby.'

'Exactly.'

'There's his brother, too,' said Cooper. 'Graham,

isn't it? The guy at the aircraft museum mentioned him.'

'Yes, you're right. Graham Kemp was one of the people interviewed over the double assault. We have no evidence against him, though the CCTV film could help get an ID. The meeting with the MDP has been scheduled for tomorrow.'

'Hopefully Sergeant Caudwell might explain why she was interested in Marie Tennent and Sugar Uncle Victor.'

He heard Fry make a noise between a dismissive grunt and a resigned sigh. 'We're promised they're going to share intelligence,' she said. 'It's madness to keep details of this enquiry from us. They're making us work in the dark.'

'It would help to have a little more information of your own before that, wouldn't it?' said Cooper.

Fry was silent for a moment. 'What do you mean, Ben?'

'If you could have some evidence against the vultures.'

'*Vultures?*'

'It's what Zygmunt Lukasz calls them – the people who take things from the aircraft wrecks. Where are you, Diane?'

'Still at West Street.'

'More overtime? I think we could get some evidence. I think between us we could do it.'

'What? Ben, are you asking for my help?'

'A different approach might work. I thought we could tackle George Malkin again.'

'On what pretext?'

'There's the money.'

'What money?'

'The wages for three RAF bases were being carried on Lancaster SU-V the night it crashed. The money went missing and was never found. I suspect that Malkin once had at least a share in the money from the crashed Lancaster. Maybe his father was involved with the two Home Guards who were suspected of taking it. They could have got the money away and hidden it at Hollow Shaw Farm, to share it out later. I don't know. But Malkin has no money now. And he seems to have sold all the souvenirs he ever had, except for an old watch. I wonder who he sold them to, Diane. And I wonder what happened to the money.'

'I hope you're not on some flight of fancy again,' said Fry. 'Pick me up at the front door.'

It was completely dark when they reached Harrop. As they entered George Malkin's house, Ben Cooper was aware of Fry taking off her coat, then changing her mind and putting it back on again as she shivered with cold. She pulled her collar closer and tightened her scarf.

'Well, I *am* popular these days,' said Malkin. 'It's a proper social whirl I live in.'

'We're sorry to bother you again, sir.'

'Aye, I'm sure.'

The sitting room looked no different from when

Cooper had been there a few days before. Malkin didn't bother to draw the curtains at night. There was no point, since there were no other houses to be seen, and no one ever passed on the track outside, except Malkin's friend, Rod Whittaker, who ran his contract haulage business from here and kept his sheep in the fields.

On one window ledge was a collection of empty jars. They were the type that would once have contained strawberry jam or marmalade, but they had been stripped of their labels and washed clean for some long-forgotten purpose. Now they were left to gather dust instead. The jar nearest to Cooper had several small, dead spiders desiccating on the glass bottom. Their tiny, fragile legs, no thicker than a hair, had folded into their bodies as they had curled up to accept death in their incomprehensible prison.

'How long have you been living on your own?' asked Cooper.

'It's nearly three years since Florence went into the home.'

'Long enough when you're on your own.'

'Aye, if you're not used to it. It's thirty-eight years since we were wed. When you find yourself alone, you start to get into funny little ways. You don't realize it after a while, unless somebody points it out.'

'Like living without any heating, perhaps?' suggested Cooper.

Malkin laughed. The sound was like someone

shovelling loose gravel. A trickle of spittle formed at the corner of his mouth.

'I don't need it,' he said. 'Not for myself. And I'm not about to start a blazing fire, just in case I get visitors the likes of you. I suppose you live in a town, do you?'

Cooper was about to say 'no', then remembered that he did, in fact, live in a town. He had lived in a town since Saturday. He was touched by Malkin's concern for his comfort, but strangely offended by the man's assumption that his visitor was some kind of soft townie.

'You don't get the weather the same, not in a town,' said Malkin. 'If you're a bit nesh, lad, you should put on an extra sweater when you go out. That's what our mam always used to tell us.'

Cooper had never thought of himself as 'nesh' – soft, too sensitive to the cold. It was the sort of term normally reserved for southerners in the ironic way that local people had of winding them up. But he wasn't a southerner – he was local himself. Being nesh was for townies.

But Cooper could see that his way of living was a couple of steps away from that of George Malkin these days; his comfort level was several notches up the central heating thermostat. He had a lower degree of tolerance to discomfort and deprivation. So perhaps he was nesh, after all, in the eyes of the George Malkins of the world. Perhaps he had lost the link with these people that he once thought he had. In the end, the bond between them wasn't genetic but a social link that could be broken if it was stretched too far.

'I dare say Florence would be ashamed of how I live now, if she knew,' said Malkin.

Cooper felt a surge of sympathy. He recognized a man cut off from the support that had kept him on a normal course. Alone, it was too easy to fall into a way of living that seemed abnormal to everyone else.

'Detective Constable Cooper had a long talk to Mr Walter Rowland yesterday,' said Fry. 'DC Cooper is very good at getting information out of people. They seem to trust him.'

Malkin looked from Fry to Cooper, and his stare lingered. Cooper fidgeted uneasily.

'You and your family have always been known for collecting aircraft souvenirs,' said Fry. 'Is that correct?'

'I suppose it might be. A lot of things came our way over the years. My dad was a terror for it, I don't mind admitting. Us lads learned it from him. I picked up my share of souvenirs here and there.'

'More than just a broken watch, then.'

'I'm not saying I kept them. I'm not a collector – I can't see the point. But some folk will pay cash for stuff like that, you know.'

'Yes, we know.'

Cooper wondered if the souvenirs had brought a steady trickle of cash in for Malkin over the years. It would hardly have been enough to pay for private medical care for Florence. Perhaps she had heard her husband talk about his sideline and got the wrong idea about the value of the items. Poor woman – her husband had not lived up to her expectations.

'But we're enquiring into something more than just a few souvenirs,' said Fry.

'There was the money,' said Cooper. 'The wages for RAF Benson.'

Malkin took off his cap for the first time. It was such a surprise that it seemed to indicate better than anything his emotional response. His hair was remarkably thick, though going grey.

'Poor old Walter Rowland,' he said. 'He must be in a bad way now. He wasn't well last time I saw him.'

'No, he isn't too good.'

'If Walter knew about the money, he's kept quiet about it for fifty-seven years. I wonder what made him say something now.'

'He didn't. Not exactly,' said Cooper.

'Oh?'

'So you admit that you took the money that was on board the Lancaster?' said Fry.

Malkin turned his attention back to her. 'You've got good timing, you folk. You know when to ask your questions, all right. It doesn't matter to me now, you see. Not at all. So you might as well know everything.'

'Go on, sir.'

'Yes, it was me and my brother Ted who took the money. We were only lads at the time. I was eight years old, so I didn't really know what I was doing. But I don't suppose there's much point in me saying that now.'

'I think it's unlikely there will be a prosecution after all this time,' said Fry. 'Not for something you did when you were eight years old.'

'Oh, well,' said Malkin. 'It doesn't matter.'

'There was a lot of money,' said Cooper. 'We'd like to know what you did with it. What did you spend it on?'

Malkin smiled then, a sheepish, embarrassed smile. 'You won't believe me.'

'Try us. We've heard all sorts of things that people waste their money on. Foreign holidays? Women? Did you gamble it away?'

'None of those things.'

'What, then?'

'I didn't spend it at all. I've still got it.'

Cooper stared at him. 'You're kidding.'

'I said you wouldn't believe me.'

'You found yourself suddenly in possession of a fortune, and you're telling me that you just put it in the bank and saved it up for a rainy day? You didn't spend any of it?'

'No, I didn't. But I didn't put it in the bank either.'

'You're not making any sense.'

'I'm going to have to show you,' said Malkin.

George Malkin led Cooper and Fry up to the top of his garden, through a gate and across a snow-covered paddock. They had to lean into the wind and lift their feet high out of the snow to make progress. But Malkin seemed almost unaware of it. He ploughed across the field like a carthorse, with his head down and his shoulders hunched forward inside his overcoat.

At the far side of the field was a stile built into the dry-stone wall. They crossed it carefully, and found themselves floundering waist-deep in a drift that had been blown up against the other side. When they had struggled out of it, they were panting with the effort. In front of them was another field, but this one sloped gently up to the rocky base of the hill, and the snow became less deep as they crossed the last few yards.

It was only when they were standing at the foot of the hill that they saw they had reached the entrance to an old mine. It was no more than a cleft in the rock face, about as wide as a man's shoulders – not wide enough, in fact, for George Malkin, who had to slide through it sideways. A fine layer of snow had blown a foot or two into the entrance, but beyond that the rock floor was only damp, so that it gleamed in the light of an old bicycle lamp that Malkin took from his pocket.

'We should have brought a Dragon light from the car,' said Fry. 'I can hardly see a thing.'

'We'll manage,' said Malkin. 'We'll not be doing much reading or anything.'

Like all caves or mines, even the smallest and

most insignificant, there were unidentifiable noises and echoes in its darkest corners, and angles of rock that made sudden black fists in the edges of the shadows. The smell was of wet sand, and the dampness was as heavy as a blanket, as if they had stepped below the level of the water table.

George Malkin used the wavery beam of the bicycle lamp to locate a deep crack in the wall. He lifted a foot-wide boulder clear and fumbled inside with one hand until he drew out a length of baling twine. The twine was bright blue, and it seemed to be the only flicker of colour in the gloom. At first, there seemed to be no weight on the end of it, but then a small rope appeared, knotted to the twine.

'Maybe you could help me pull,' said Malkin.

Cooper took hold of the rope and they pulled on it together, while Fry held the lamp over them. The light failed momentarily and left them completely in the dark until she shook it, rattling the battery inside the casing to restore the corroded connection. Cooper could hear a dragging sound deep inside the rock. He could feel the resistance on the rope of something heavy that snagged on every bump. They seemed to be pulling at about a forty-five degree angle.

'It's a leather bag of some kind,' said Fry, peering over the shoulders of the two men into the hole. 'No, two bags – there's another one tied behind it.'

'Aye, there were two,' said Malkin as the bags

appeared over the lip of rock. 'We managed one each, just about. Of course, in those days, I was only a little lad. I was small enough to slide right down into that hole. It levels out at the bottom, like a shelf. Ted sent me down there and passed the bags to me. I remember they blocked the way at first, and they were so heavy I didn't think I was ever going to be able to get out again. But Ted was there. I knew he would rescue me if I got stuck.'

Malkin grabbed a leather strap as Cooper took the weight on the rope. 'It was totally dark down there,' he said. 'I hated the dark, always have. I've been scared of it since I was tiny. Darkness and deep water – those are the things that frighten me. I always had nightmares of being trapped somewhere with water coming in. You'd think you would grow out of that when you're not a nipper any more. But it just got worse after Ted was killed. I reckon it was because I knew he wouldn't be there any more to rescue me.'

They set the bags on the floor. Fry crouched over them with the lamp, rattling it every now and then to keep its beam alive. 'We really should have brought some more light,' she said. 'This is ridiculous.'

'Let's have a quick look, then we'll take them to the house,' said Cooper.

'It won't take you long to see what it is,' said Malkin. He was standing above them, and his voice sounded unnaturally distant and echoey, as if he

533

were back in the hole that his brother had sent him into as a child.

Cooper's fingers were clumsy in his gloves, and the straps of the first bag had stiffened and cracked, so that he had difficulty pulling them through the buckles. Finally, the flap fell open, and he saw it was a sort of saddlebag like those carried by Wells Fargo riders in Westerns. Inside, it was packed with something solid and white. Cooper couldn't believe what he was looking at.

'Bring the light closer,' he said.

Fry crouched alongside him. He could hear her breathing in his ear, and he could see a cloud of her breath drifting through the beam of light from the lamp. He tugged at the contents of the bag, and a lump of the white mass broke away into his hand. It wasn't solid at all, but consisted of tightly packed bundles which had stuck together in the damp that had seeped into the leather bag.

Cooper tilted the bag more, and the heaps of paper slid out. They were like wedges of frozen snow slipping on to the ground and separating into dirty crystalline rectangles. They were unfamiliar, yet he knew what they were.

'Bank notes,' he said.

'They can't be,' said Fry.

'I think you'll find they are.'

'But they're white. Has the colour faded? Is it foreign currency?'

'No,' said Cooper. 'They're British sterling.'

Cooper looked up. He could barely see George

Malkin's face. His expression was impassive. For a big man, it was surprising how easily he had almost faded into the rock among the shadows outside the light of the lamp. 'Mr Malkin?'

'Aye, you're right,' he said. 'But I'm not surprised you've never seen them before. You're much too young, the pair of you.'

'I've heard of them, though,' said Cooper. 'These are £5 notes, aren't they? White fivers. They haven't been in circulation for nearly fifty years.'

'That's right. White fivers. They're part of the wages for RAF Benson.'

Together, they carried the bags back to the house. On the sitting-room table, the bank notes looked almost at home, as if they were back in their own time again. It was as if a part of George Malkin's life had been frozen in 1945 and had never changed since.

'We thought at first it was a German plane that had been shot down,' said Malkin. 'There had been stories just before that of a Junkers that had been downed near Manchester. So we didn't think it was wrong to take the bags.'

'But you must have heard later that the aircraft was British.'

'It was too late then. We knew we couldn't tell anybody about the money. Ted threatened me not to say a word. Not that I needed telling. I always thought Ted would know what to do with the money. I thought he had a plan. He never told me what it was, but then I was only his annoying little brother, and I didn't need to know. When he went off for his National Service, I thought we'd do something with the money after he came back. I thought he would tell me what the plan was then, because I'd be seventeen and grown up enough. But, of course, Ted never came back.'

'What happened to him?'

'Ted was called up when he was eighteen years old, and they sent him to Malaya. He was dead before he was nineteen – shot by a Chinese communist rebel when his troop train was ambushed.'

'Did your mother and father never know about these bags?' asked Cooper. He watched Malkin shake his head. 'How on earth did you keep them secret all that time?'

'I left them in the old mine workings, where we'd put them. Sometimes, as a lad, I would go up there with a torch, and I'd get the bags out and look at the money. I didn't know what to do with it, but I knew I'd do *something* with it one day. It made me feel different from the rest of the kids. I really believed I was a secret millionaire. That helped a lot when I had bad times. They were like friends waiting to help me out when I needed them. Even after Mum and Dad died, I didn't bring the bags into the house. They never knew about the money while they were alive, and it seemed wrong to produce it when they were dead. As long as their memories still hung around the house, I felt as though I'd be giving away my secret to them.

It's surprising how long it takes people to leave a place after they're dead.'

Cooper nodded. 'So you never moved them?'

'Once. One day I saw some potholers coming into the mine. They had ropes and helmets and lamps, all the proper tackle. There was nothing I could do while they were in there, but I was terrified they would find the bags – my bags; I pictured one of them shining his lamp into the crack, and that would be that, all those years of waiting wasted. I thought of starting a rock fall to block the mine entrance, so that they would all die in there. It seemed like the only option. Then at least *nobody* would have got the money.'

Malkin paused, momentarily shaken by a desperate memory. 'But eventually they came out with their ropes, and they went away. And the bags were still there, where I had put them. I dragged them out and brought them up to the house. But then I started worrying about Florence finding them, so I took them back.'

Cooper stared at the bundles of notes. Those in the middle looked as though they might be as clean and pristine as when they were first issued.

'I don't know much about currency,' he said. 'But I've a feeling . . .'

'Oh, I know,' said Malkin. 'They took those notes out of circulation in 1957. I should have spent them when I was twenty years old, when I could have made proper use of them and set myself up for life.' He began to toss the bundles back into the bags. 'I remember the day I read the news that white fivers wouldn't be legal tender any more. It was like all my dreams had been smashed. That money was my future, as I thought. It felt as though I'd just lost a fortune. It was like thinking you'd won the jackpot on the National Lottery, then finding you'd lost the ticket. They're not even a secret any more, are they?'

'But why *didn't* you spend it when you were twenty?' said Fry, staring at him in bafflement.

Malkin shrugged. 'It might sound daft,' he said. 'Maybe it *was* daft. But I'd never been abroad or anything back then. I was too young to have gone away in the war, too old to take foreign holidays for granted like the young folks do today. I honestly didn't know what to do with the money. I thought if I took it to a bank they'd know straight away it was stolen and I'd be arrested. I was frightened to do anything with it. It seemed better to keep it as my secret. It was safer to sit here at home and dream of what I might spend it on. There seemed to be no risks that way.'

'Does your wife not know about the money?' said Cooper, recalling Florence's constant questions about her private medical treatment.

'I'd met Florence about three years before, and we'd started saving to get married. It was daft, but I let her think I had some money saved up. Well, I had, in a way. Then I found out they were scrapping the white fivers. Without Ted, I didn't know what to do. It was a couple of days later that I got the chance to go out to the old mine and check the bags one last time. I had to make sure the money was what I thought. Yes, white fivers, all of it. I knew I couldn't take it all to the bank to change it – it would look too suspicious, and the police would be round here. I couldn't risk that, when I was planning to get wed. So there was no money, as I'd always let Florence think.'

Cooper picked up the bag. 'What happened to all the souvenirs that you had, Mr Malkin? Who did you sell them to?'

'The only man who deals in that sort of thing around here – the bookseller in Edendale, Lawrence Daley. If you want to have a look at some stuff, you have to ask to see his upstairs room.'

Fry exchanged a glance with Cooper. 'We'll do that,' she said.

Malkin looked at the bag in Cooper's hands. 'There's just one thing,' he said. 'It's too late now, but it's something I won't stop thinking about until the day I pop my clogs.'

'What's that?'

'I wonder if I could have spent some of that money on getting treatment for Florence. Do you think it would have helped? Do you think I could have used the money to save her life?'

'But, Mr Malkin,' said Cooper, 'your wife is in the Old School Nursing Home.'

'Not any more, poor old lass. They phoned me just before you arrived. She died about two hours ago.'

32

Ben Cooper spent a few minutes ringing around his contacts before they set off back from Harrop. Eventually, he managed to track down a member of the antiques dealers association who specialized in coins and bank notes.

Fry waited impatiently until he had finished, tapping her fingers on the dashboard.

'So? Did he say why they would have sent all the money in £5 notes?'

'Counterfeiting,' said Cooper.

'Oh?'

'Apparently, the Germans were into it in a big way. They thought they could destabilize the British economy and bring the country to its knees. They were producing half a million counterfeit notes a month at one stage of the war. The Bank of England stopped issuing denominations of over £5, so that it wasn't worthwhile making counterfeits. Of course, there were £1 and ten-shilling notes as well then. The white fivers were the first to go, though.'

'So George Malkin's haul is worthless.'

'Not exactly,' said Cooper. 'Not now. If he had put them on the market judiciously, he could have been coining it in handsomely for a few years now.'

'How do you mean?'

'I'm told they're collector's items, those notes. According to the expert, white fivers from 1944 in good condition would sell for about £60 each.'

'Jesus,' said Fry. 'George Malkin had two thousand of them stashed away.'

'Nice, eh?'

'And we've got to return them to the RAF. Not so nice.'

'Blasted collectors,' said Cooper. 'Why don't they live in the real world? They distort the value of everything.'

'It's like anything else,' said Fry. 'Things are worth whatever somebody will pay for them.'

'It's crazy.'

'It's called a free market economy, Ben. That's why a footballer is paid millions of quid for kicking a ball about once a week; and it's why you can't afford to buy somewhere decent to live. Let's face it, mate, what you have to offer just isn't marketable.'

'Thanks.'

'Don't thank me. Thank the ungrateful public.'

But Cooper wasn't thinking of his own position. He had learned never to expect thanks. He was thinking of Walter Rowland sitting at his dining-room table, unable to lift a mug of tea, unable to help himself, and too stubborn to ask for help from anyone else. He was thinking of Rowland starving in a house full of tinned food because he was too proud to tell anyone he couldn't use a tin opener, of an old man frightened to turn up the heating because he didn't know whether he could afford the electricity bill. That was how much society had valued what Walter had done for it. And George Malkin had sat and watched his wife die because it had never occurred to him that people would be willing to pay much, much more for a bagful of outdated and useless bank notes than for the treatment to save a woman's life.

'Where are we going next?' said Fry. 'Shall I guess?'

Lawrence Daley was alone in the bookshop as usual. He looked over his glasses in outrage at Cooper and Fry when he finally answered their banging.

'Had any customers today, Lawrence?' said Cooper.

'I'm doing my best. A customer here, a customer there, you know. I expect to reach double figures by the end of the year. What do you want?'

'There are lots of other things in life apart from books,' said Fry. 'Can we come in?'

'You can find everything you want to know in

542

books. Life, death, love, the specifications for a 1968 Ford Capri ignition system.'

'And aircraft wrecks?' said Cooper.

'Sorry?'

'You sell books on aircraft wrecks.'

'You know I do – you bought a couple yourself.'

'I've heard there's quite a demand for that sort of thing. And not only books. Other items. Souvenirs. Collectibles.'

Lawrence nodded. 'I believe you're right.'

'Fetch a good price, do they? There's more profit in aircraft souvenirs than in books that never move off the shelf, I guess. A bit of diversification?'

Lawrence fidgeted with a set of keys, watching Cooper's eyes.

'Will you show us the upstairs room, Lawrence?' said Cooper.

The bookseller took off his glasses and fiddled inside his waistcoat for his tiny screwdriver. His eyes looked weary without the glasses. There were blue patches underneath them, and the tired creases that come with age.

'It's not illegal, you know.'

'Then there's nothing to worry about, is there?' said Fry. 'Lead the way.'

Lawrence Daley led the way to the foot of the bare wooden stairs, past the sign that said '*Staff Only*'. The stairs were narrow and unlit, and the

boards creaked alarmingly underfoot. Their footsteps echoed in the stairwell, and once they had
turned a corner halfway up, they lost the benefit
of the light from the shop. They could see their way
only by a naked bulb somewhere high above them,
and its reflection in a series of tiny stone-mullioned
windows set into the back wall. The light picked
out thick strands of blackened cobwebs clinging to
the ceilings and the highest corners. The banister
rail felt slightly sticky under Cooper's fingers, but
he was afraid to let go of it, in case the stairs disappeared in front of him and he lost his footing.

He could see that the building had once been
a town house for some wealthy family, a tall,
rambling place that the bookshop occupied only
half of. The stairs they were climbing were so
narrow that they must once have been designed
only for the use of servants, who were expected to
be thin and undernourished. Probably they were
expected to be able to see in the dark, too, and
survive the winter without any heating.

Along the skirting boards and on the window
ledges, Cooper saw more black mouse droppings.
He wondered if Lawrence would be interested in
having a cat.

Lawrence stopped in front of them and jingled
his keys. Cooper could make out a dusty corridor
ahead. Unsurprisingly, it was piled high with books
stacked against the walls. There were two or three
doors further down, but they were inaccessible
because of the number of books in front of them.

To the right, though, there was one clear doorway near the head of the stairs, tucked under a sloping section of roof. They must be close to the eaves of the building.

Fry stood behind him, just below one of the mullioned windows. Cooper turned to exchange a look. He saw her face was lit by a strange mottled pattern from the light reflected off the dust on the window.

'No wonder people like Eddie Kemp are never out of work,' she said.

All the doors were narrow and low, as if they had been made for the use of midgets. The paint on them was old and peeling, but must once have been dark green, and they had brown Bakelite handles that had got chipped over the years. There was no carpet on the floor of the passage, and probably never had been. The floorboards had been painted black, and that was the limit of decoration. Cooper shivered. The passage was cold, as cold as George Malkin's farmhouse, but with a different feel to the coldness. Malkin's house had dripped with the chill of emptiness, but this place felt full of phantoms. He could imagine a crowd of pale, thin ghosts in ragged clothes who walked continuously backwards and forwards, day and night, bearing bowls of hot water and candles for their masters.

'Useful-looking attic,' said Fry. 'Have you ever thought of converting it into student bedsits?'

A gleam came into Lawrence's eye for a moment

at the prospect of income from student rents. But he looked at the stacks of books, and his face fell.

'I don't think it's practical.'

'Let's have a look at this room,' said Cooper. 'It's what we came for, after all.'

The upstairs room at Eden Valley Books was full of aviation memorabilia, much of it of Second World War vintage. One of the most eye-catching items was an RAF pilot's Irving jacket, which fitted Ben Cooper fine when he tried it on. There had been a few repairs to the leather, but the zips and the belt still worked, and the lining was very warm. He could have kept it on and worn it all day.

'Two hundred pounds,' said Lawrence. 'It's still got the MoD label and everything.'

'I'll not bother.'

A cockpit clock was dated 1940. The label said it was in working condition, though it currently showed the time as four twenty-eight. It was priced at £75. A leather flying helmet with attached oxygen mask seemed to be one of the prime exhibits at £450. Cooper could see that Lawrence put more thought into the prices for his collectibles than he did into pricing his books.

'It's all perfectly legitimate,' said Lawrence.

'That depends on the origin of the items, doesn't it? Where do they come from?' asked Fry.

'People bring them to me.'

'Do they provide any evidence of their origin? What you might call a provenance?'

'Hardly ever. But these people are collectors, or other dealers. The things they bring have been changing hands for years.'

'If you have reason to believe that any of them are stolen or dishonestly obtained –'

'I don't.'

Fry nodded. 'In that case, you're right. It's legitimate.'

'Do you get any medals?' asked Cooper.

'Sometimes.'

'I was thinking of one particular medal. A Canadian Distinguished Flying Cross.'

'I don't think I've ever had one of those here.'

'Have you ever been offered one?'

'Not as far as I'm aware. I get job lots sometimes. I don't always sort them out. There might be a boxful of medals around here now somewhere.'

'Are you saying that someone could have browsed through your stock and found a medal like that? A Canadian DFC?'

Lawrence shrugged. 'It's possible.'

Cooper reached the table at the far end of the room. 'And what's this?'

He had picked up a bag. It was a leather bag with flaps, like a large satchel or saddlebag. The label said: *Original RAF leather money bag, 1945.*

'And where did this come from, Lawrence? How much have you been paying George Malkin for his collection?'

'I'm in business,' said Lawrence. 'I pay Malkin what I pay other people.'

There was a tiny window at the back of the room, so high that Cooper could only just see out of it. He rubbed some dirt from the pane, and found he was looking down from the back of the shop into a small yard illuminated by a security light. The backs of tall buildings were clustered all around it. There must be access to the yard somehow, because there was a pair of wooden gates facing him, set into a stone wall protected by bits of broken glass cemented to the coping stones.

'What's in the yard?' asked Cooper.

Slowly, Lawrence selected another key and opened the door. It let a burst of bright light into the room and a cold wind. Cooper could see the top of an iron fire escape, which led down the outer wall of the building. Down there, it was like a junkyard. All sorts of objects lay around. There appeared to be engines, propellers, wheels, and a section of cockpit, but many of the items were unidentifiable. A lot of them were covered in a layer of snow that had frozen on their horizontal surfaces, giving them an enigmatic appearance, like objects in a puzzle, seen from an unfamiliar angle. The snow on the ground was covered in the clawed footprints of birds, which seemed to have wandered aimlessly backwards and forwards, frequently crossing their own path, perhaps looking for food. The aircraft cockpit was one of the larger objects. In the snow on its upper surface, there were bigger, neater footprints prowling among the bird tracks. So there was a cat around, after all.

'I can see the stock,' said Cooper. 'But where do the customers come from? How do you advertise?'

'Through the website mostly,' said Lawrence.

'A website. Of course. Everybody has a website these days.'

'Most of the business isn't done here, you see – this is small-scale stuff. What the website does is put people in touch with each other, all over the world. We just have to maintain the site.'

'Do you have no control over who uses it?'

'We don't check on anybody's *bona fides*. Even if they have an entire aircraft to sell, we don't ask any questions.'

'Who's "we"?' said Cooper.

Lawrence fiddled with the keys. He pulled the door shut, as if ashamed of the view. 'There's a terrible draught with the door open,' he said.

'Who else is involved?' said Cooper.

'I have a bit of help sometimes,' said Lawrence. 'A few people who are interested in the aviation archaeology business.'

'We'll need names.'

'I can't do that. Confidentiality –'

'Rubbish.'

'Who else has access to the yard, apart from you?' said Cooper.

'No one,' said Lawrence.

'What about your business partners?'

Lawrence seemed to think for a moment. He

turned to Fry, but her expression was hard and unsympathetic.

'We need names,' she said.

When he finally got back to the flat in Welbeck Street that night, Ben Cooper was in no mood to find that there were two cats in the conservatory instead of one. The cat flap had been treated as an invitation to take in guests. The new occupant was a mackerel tabby with blue eyes, and it was another balloon on legs. He wondered how it had managed to squeeze through the cat flap at all without getting stuck.

'Randy, who's your fat friend?' he said.

Randy brushed himself against Cooper's legs as if introducing the other cat. Cooper put out his hand to stroke the newcomer, and immediately saw the drooping belly and engorged teats.

'Oh no. I hope you belong to somebody. You're not having your kittens in here.'

But Cooper looked out of the window at the frozen snow still lying in the garden and the icicles hanging from the branches of the trees, and knew he was just as soft as Mrs Shelley.

'Well, as soon as they're born, you go,' he said firmly. Both cats gazed at him and purred. He could have sworn they were laughing.

One thing that had been missing in his life was a physical relationship, and animals provided it. But why were they so like humans about some things? Why did animals never learn that it was dangerous to give their trust so readily?

33

DCI Tailby turned his head to look at the white-board where DI Paul Hitchens was writing names with a big black marker pen, occasionally switching to a red pen to draw lines connecting the names. The board squeaked as he produced curves and little circles, then completed the pattern by decorating his chart with a series of red dots.

'Can you see what it is yet?' said Hitchens.

'You propose to detain all these people?' said Tailby.

DI Hitchens was firing on all cylinders, ready to take over the morning meeting, given half a chance.

'We've liaised with our friends in the Ministry of Defence Police,' he said. 'And together we've drawn up this list of persons believed to be involved in the activities Sergeant Easton was investigating. If we pull them all in now, we expect to be able to start piecing together what happened.'

'As I understand the situation, the RAF Police

have been observing a number of servicemen who are suspected of the illegal sale of aircraft parts. Easton was attempting to establish who their contacts were on the outside.'

'Yes, sir. And these names are people involved in a circle of aviation memorabilia collectors. They have a well-established network, both by word of mouth and on the internet. DS Fry has identified the location where the memorabilia trade is based and where the website is run from. From what we're told, it seems to be a lucrative trade in itself. The prices for some of the items are extraordinary – but that's collectors for you. They'll pay the earth for something they really want. Strictly speaking, many of the items of memorabilia are probably illegally obtained, but it might take a lot of work to gather the evidence.'

'It doesn't sound worthwhile,' said Tailby. 'The CPS would say a prosecution wasn't in the public interest.'

'Yes. And it's insignificant compared to the trade that Nick Easton was trying to uncover,' said Hitchens. 'We've looked at the website this morning, and it's difficult to tell where the legal business ends and the illegal begins. Not all the collectibles are Second World War vintage by any means. There are items for use in restoring more modern aircraft, and interspersed among them there are a number of contemporary and definitely illegal items being traded. Some of the messages on the bulletin boards are probably coded anyway.

And the addresses given are international.'

Tailby sighed. 'That's going to be out of our hands. But it's just run from a bookshop, isn't it? Here in Edendale.'

'That was what Easton was looking for, but we don't think he ever found it. We think he was killed before he reached the centre of the operation. We have no evidence to suggest he ever visited the bookshop.'

'What about the owner?'

'Lawrence Daley,' said Fry. 'We think he was drawn in because of the money involved in the aviation memorabilia trade. We conducted an initial interview with him last night. He genuinely doesn't seem to be aware of any other type of business going on via the website or the bulletin board other than the memorabilia. One of his partners runs the internet side, which seems to be a mystery to him.'

'A gullible victim pulled into something illegal out of greed?' said Tailby.

'Yes. But he finally confirmed these names for us, which DI Hitchens has listed. These are the men principally involved. It seems possible that they killed Easton when he got too close to them. But we have no evidence to support that idea.'

'It's disappointing that we haven't located Easton's car yet. That would be very helpful.'

'It will turn up somewhere eventually,' said Hitchens. 'With a bit of luck, we'll still be able to get some evidence from it.'

DCI Tailby looked around the room. 'It's all circumstantial. Do you think we have sufficient evidence to bring them in?'

'Yes, sir,' said Hitchens.

Tailby looked at the MDP officers. 'And you, Sergeant Caudwell?'

'We're in favour.'

'Very well. I suppose you'll need more resources, Paul?'

'Whatever we can get, sir.'

'We'll call in the task force again. They've drawn a blank on the missing baby, so at least we can give them a bit of action.'

As the meeting broke up, Fry saw Sergeant Caudwell approaching.

'You win,' she said, showing her dimples. 'But, if I could make a suggestion, you might want to question what some of your officers have been getting involved in recently.'

Ben Cooper picked up Alison Morrissey from outside the Cavendish Hotel and drove her as far as Bamford, to the big pub at the crossroads. He didn't want to be seen in Edendale, not today.

Morrissey had a blue folder tucked under her arm. Not another file, surely? There had been enough of those, and some of the information had been misleading and wrong.

'What have you got there?' said Cooper.

'It's something Peter Lukasz sent to me. He says his father wrote it.'

'Ah. His account of the crash of Sugar Uncle Victor.'

'So you knew.'

'I saw Zygmunt writing it. At least, that's what Peter told me it was. I'm sure it will be very interesting if you can get it translated. But I don't suppose it really matters now.'

'Perhaps not,' said Alison. 'But Peter Lukasz has read it, and he thought there was one thing in it I ought to know straight away. Everyone said my grandfather was to blame for the crash because he had ignored his navigator's instructions. But according to Peter Lukasz, Zygmunt's account is different. He says that Klemens Wach made a mistake. It was his fault that they were so far off course. But everybody trusted Klemens, including my grandfather.'

'Have you heard a rumour that Danny McTeague was drunk when he crashed into Irontongue Hill?'

Morrissey frowned. 'The old man, Walter Rowland, put that rumour about, according to Frank. It was something Rowland had heard Zygmunt Lukasz say, something to do with celebrating the night before. Danny McTeague had been celebrating the birth of his first child – my mother.'

'There was certainly no reference at the inquest to the possibility that your grandfather might have been drunk. That might have been discretion, though, the withholding of allegations that might cause distress to relatives. Perhaps it would have been a different matter if McTeague had ever been found.'

'Perhaps.'

Cooper wondered if Rowland had mentioned the rumour about McTeague to George Malkin's father. He gazed past Morrissey at the wall of the pub, where there was a print of Chatsworth House, not unlike the one that Marie Tennent had kept under her bed. It was a favourite view for tourists. It appeared on all the postcards and in every guide book.

'Alison, how did you come to meet Frank Baine?' he said.

'Via the internet.'

'Really?'

'I found a bulletin board for aviation archaeology enthusiasts, and I put up an appeal for anyone with knowledge of aircraft wrecks in the Peak District. Frank saw the message and e-mailed me. He was a godsend. He had so much knowledge, and he was willing to research the details that I needed. At that time, I barely knew where the Peak District was, though my mother had mentioned it often enough. I'm doing all this for her, you know, as much as for me.'

'Baine says he's a journalist.'

'Yes.'

'I phoned around a few editors this morning. None of them had even heard of him.'

'Perhaps he just writes a few articles for magazines here and there.'

'Perhaps. And is that a living?'

'I don't know.'

'I'm sorry, I haven't helped you,' said Cooper. 'We're no nearer knowing who sent your grand-father's medal. If it somehow ended up in Lawrence Daley's shop, he didn't know about it – and from there, it could have gone anywhere. So, unless Zygmunt Lukasz has anything to say about it in his journal, I don't know where else to look. And I can't see Zygmunt hanging on to something like that – he believes people who collect souv-enirs from the aircraft wrecks are vultures. Even his own grandson, Andrew. They argued about a cigarette case that had belonged to Klemens Wach.'

Morrissey listened to him carefully.

'Where did Andrew Lukasz get this cigarette case?'

'I expect he'd bought it from a collector in London. It must be a widespread hobby, I suppose.'

'Yes, worldwide. I found that on the bull-etin board. There were a lot of US citizens and Canadians.'

Cooper watched her drink her cider for a while. She looked up and met his eye, and smiled at him. Cooper smiled back.

'Did you find out about the money?' said Morrissey.

'Yes, George Malkin still had it. He's never done anything with it.'

'Malkin?'

'At Hollow Shaw Farm. He was only a boy at the time, of course.'

Cooper stopped talking abruptly. He realized that Morrissey had never heard Malkin's name until now. Of course, she had said at the Chief Superintendent's meeting that she'd been unable to trace the boys who had seen her grandfather walk away from the crash. He searched for something else to say, before she started asking him questions.

'Do you want dropping at the Cavendish Hotel?' he said.

'Yes, please. Ben, this George Malkin –'

'How do you like it there? I don't suppose Edendale's hotels are up to Toronto standards.'

'No, not really,' said Morrissey, with a small smile.

Cooper looked at his watch. Time was catching up on him. If he stayed any longer here, Diane Fry would be paging him, wondering where he was, ready to give him another warning.

'Don't you think Zygmunt Lukasz could tell us so much about the crash?' said Morrissey.

Cooper shrugged. 'I don't know. Perhaps he's already said all he's going to.'

He wanted to add that it was George Malkin who remembered the crash best, but he had already said enough.

'I really have no more time to help you now,' he said. 'There was a meeting this morning. I don't know exactly what's going on, but I think there's going to be some action. The chiefs will be wanting arrests for the death of the RAF policeman, and I think the Ministry of Defence Police have come up with all the information that we were waiting for.'

'You'll be busy, then,' said Morrissey.

'I expect to get called away at any moment.'

'I want to say thank you for what you've done.'

'I didn't do anything.'

'But you tried hard, Ben. That's more than anyone else did. You must have thought you were doing something that was worthwhile. That was what you said, wasn't it? That you needed the feeling you'd done something worthwhile. That drug. You said it was the only thing that could give you the buzz and make you feel really alive.'

Cooper looked at her, watched her push the lock of hair from her forehead, knowing he didn't want to say goodbye to her, wanting to do something to keep the connection between them.

'I didn't say it was the only thing,' he said.

Diane Fry sat in her car with Gavin Murfin and watched the front of the Cavendish Hotel. She felt no sense of surprise when Ben Cooper's Toyota pulled up with Alison Morrissey in the passenger seat.

'Ben's already talked to her, then,' said Murfin, puzzled.

'I don't imagine they were talking about what *we* want to discuss,' said Fry.

They had a perfectly clear view as Alison Morrissey leaned across the seats of the Toyota and kissed

Cooper on the lips. They saw her hand slip behind his head, and Cooper's arm leave the steering wheel. The kiss seemed to Fry to last for a long time.

'I think Ben's a bit taken with her, like,' said Murfin.

Fry couldn't have said what else happened for a moment or two. Her view was obscured by a kind of red veil that rippled in front of her eyes, blurring the shape of Cooper's Toyota and its occupants. She took some deep breaths, and the veil gradually fell away. She found she was gripping the ends of her scarf so tightly that she was in danger of strangling herself.

Murfin popped some chewing gum in his mouth and rustled the wrapper as if he were in the cinema watching a Hollywood film.

'He's never had much luck with women, hasn't Ben,' he said. 'Maybe I should give him some tips.'

Fry stared at him. 'It isn't a question of luck, Gavin. Some people have a deeply ingrained stupidity.'

'Ben's not stupid,' protested Murfin. Then he thought about it. 'A bit gullible, maybe. You can always tempt him with a lost cause.'

'It comes of being a lost cause himself.'

Fry watched the Toyota drive away and Morrissey go into the hotel. She signalled to the car on the opposite side of the road. 'OK, let's go.'

*   *   *

Alison Morrissey and Frank Baine were standing in the reception area when Diane Fry and Gavin Murfin entered the hotel. Morrissey looked at them in surprise, then seemed to recognize what they were, if not who they were.

Fry showed them her ID. Morrissey stood her ground, then turned to glare at Sergeant Caudwell and PC Nash, who came in close behind. But Frank Baine looked as though he would try to fade into the background of oak panelling and potted plants and disappear into the corridors of the hotel. It was PC Nash who moved the quickest. He evaded Baine's attempt to headbutt him and snapped his handcuffs on to one wrist so that he could control him by the pressure on his arm. Then it was Sergeant Caudwell who read him his rights.

34

A week after the snow had arrived, it was still piled on the verges of the A57. Late that afternoon, as Ben Cooper drove towards Harrop in the dusk, he could see the occasional side road that had still not been properly cleared. On the hillsides were farms or hamlets that the council snowploughs never reached. Farmers had to fight their way down to the road themselves with blades mounted on their tractors. And there would be more snow today – he could feel it in the air.

When he was well above the valley, Cooper's headlights caught a blue Vauxhall parked at the side of the road at an awkward angle. As he got nearer, he could see it had skidded into a snowdrift that had hidden a soft verge, now churned to mud. The driver was out of his car, staring at the nearside wheels.

Cooper braked carefully and put his hazard lights on as he drew up in front of the Vauxhall. If Diane Fry had been with him, she would have told him they weren't a rescue service. If she had recognized who the driver was, she would have said it was no time to be stopping to buy a book. But Cooper turned off the engine, pulled his waterproof from the back seat and climbed out, his feet splashing in the slush. He opened the boot and took out his snow shovel. Some people laughed, but it was essential equipment in the winter. It ought to be standard on every police vehicle.

It was only when Cooper got out of the Toyota that Lawrence Daley recognized him. Lawrence didn't seem glad to see him, and he wasn't dressed for the weather either. He was wearing the same blue jacket he had been wearing in the bookshop, pulled over a thin sweater and shirt. His denims were already wet and stiff below the knee and would take days to dry out. The bookseller was shivering with cold and misery.

'What's up then, Lawrence?'

'I braked a bit too hard,' he said. 'My wheels went off the road, and now they just spin round when I rev the engine. I can't get any grip.'

He had the resigned air of the motorist for whom a car was a complete mystery once it stopped working. Cooper looked at the mud that had been splattered for several feet over the snow and into the road, and studied the deep ruts the car's wheels had created for themselves.

'You've dug yourself in a bit,' he said. 'Let me get behind and give you a push. But take it easy on the accelerator. Try not to make the wheels spin any more.'

'I was going to wait for the RAC,' said Lawrence.

'Have you called them?'

'I don't have a mobile. I can't bear the thought of the radiation frying my brain cells.'

Cooper thought it was a bit late to be worrying about that. There was not much more harm that could come to Lawrence's brain cells than had already been caused by whisky and being surrounded by too many books. Or maybe it was living alone that had done it. He had let himself be embroiled in something that had been tempting for two reasons – the money, of course; but also the feeling that he had been accepted as part of a group, a kind of family.

'Do you realize the nearest phone box is about four miles back down the road? You'd have to walk almost to the Snake Inn.'

Lawrence shrugged hopelessly. 'I suppose I would have got round to flagging somebody down.'

'Not everybody stops these days, Lawrence. They've heard too many stories of muggings and car-jackings to feel safe about picking up hitch-hikers.'

Sometimes Cooper could understand Diane Fry's impatience with people like Lawrence Daley. Lawrence had made no attempt at all to flag the Toyota down when he heard it coming. If Cooper hadn't recognized him, he might well have gone past. Would Lawrence have waved down another vehicle later on? Or would it have been too much of an indignity for him? Quite possibly he would have remained standing out here and frozen to death first, and become another Marie Tennent.

'Where were you heading to, anyway?'

'Oh, just to Glossop. I have a friend there. A fellow bookseller. Since you've closed my shop . . .'

'That's OK. As long as you weren't thinking of leaving the area.'

'No. Are you interviewing Frank Baine today?'

'He's being interviewed this afternoon. And some of the others, too. Eddie and Graham Kemp.'

'The Kemps?'

'Yes.'

'Eddie Kemp never tells the truth about anything.'

'We'll see,' said Cooper. 'Get in the car, and we'll give it a try.'

He leaned his weight on the boot of the Vauxhall, bracing himself to get a good grip on the road surface. Lawrence started the car and let off the handbrake. At first, it seemed as though the wheels weren't going to get any purchase, but then the offside rear wheel found a bit of clear road surface, and a second later the Vauxhall lurched forward out of the mud. Cooper lost his footing and fell on to his knee behind the back bumper. Lawrence drove the car a few feet on to the road and stopped.

'Thanks!' he called.

Cooper got up. Beating the snow off his gloves, he began to walk past the Vauxhall towards his own car. He stopped at Lawrence's open window. 'Before you go any further, I suggest you clear your windscreen properly,' he said. 'And scrape the snow off your headlights. Otherwise, if you run into my colleagues from Traffic, they'll book you.'

'I'll do that,' said Lawrence.

Cooper nodded, brushed off some more snow, and got into the Toyota. As he drove off, he looked into his rearview mirror. He could see Lawrence Daley waving goodbye.

The Ministry of Defence Police had taken their turn at interviewing Frank Baine on suspicion that he was the main contact for the servicemen the RAF Police had been keeping under surveillance. Diane Fry could see that Baine was certainly a man with a lot of contacts, and very little evidence of income from journalism. According to Lawrence Daley, Baine had also been running the website and the internet bulletin board.

A case against him for the murder of Nick Easton was going to be more difficult to construct. They had found no weapon and a potential link between Baine and Eddie Kemp had failed. They had not been able to show that Eddie Kemp's car had been used to convey Easton's body to the Snake Pass. Besides, there was evidence that Eddie Kemp had been involved in the assault on the two youths near Underbank on Monday night – he was recognizable on the CCTV footage.

Fry shook her head in exasperation. The two

young drug dealers were refusing to talk to the police on principle. But enquiries around Underbank had established that residents were well aware of vigilante groups who had taken it into their own hands to deter the drug gangs from the Devonshire Estate from moving in. Even the old man, Walter Rowland, had told an officer that there were people far more likely to recover his stolen property than the police. Sadly, he was almost certainly right.

The Kemp brothers seemed to have built themselves quite a reputation around Underbank. They were unlucky that the old couple who had identified Eddie that night had not been told whose side he was on.

She looked at the bayonet that had been used to attack Ben Cooper. She was anxious for her own opportunity to question Frank Baine – and she was hopeful the forensic laboratory would give her a match from the bayonet to Baine's DNA. That would clear up the assault on a police officer, at least. Meanwhile, she had both the Kemp brothers. And Eddie Kemp had some questions to answer about the death of Marie Tennent.

It proved to be a long afternoon before Fry got Eddie Kemp on to the subject she most wanted to know about.

'The baby,' she said. 'Marie's baby.'

'It wasn't mine,' said Kemp. 'She told me the baby wasn't mine.'

'How did you feel about that, Mr Kemp?'

'Feel?'

'Were you angry with her?'

Though they had given him the required breaks from questioning, Kemp was starting to look tired. He was still trying to act relaxed, completely unconcerned, like a man with nothing to fear. But Fry thought she could see the weariness in his eyes, the first sign that he was being worn down.

'Were you angry, Mr Kemp?'

'It didn't matter to me.'

'No. Let's think about that. If I remember rightly, a pregnancy takes nine months. If that baby wasn't yours, it meant Marie had been seeing someone else while you were still living with her.'

'So?'

'So I think you might have been angry about that,' said Fry. 'I think you might have lost your temper.'

'Well, any bloke might have done, in that situation.'

'So you hit her, did you?'

Kemp grimaced with irritation. 'You seem to have me pegged as the violent type. I don't know why.'

'How many times did you hit her?' asked Fry patiently.

'Look, it was a bit of a blur, to be honest.'

'Once? Twice? More than twice?'

'I don't recall.'

'Where did you hit her? On the face, on the body, or where?'

'On the body, I suppose.'

'Did you hit her in the face, too?'

'If I did, it was an accident.'

'I see.'

'I didn't really hurt her,' said Kemp.

'Sorry?'

'I mean, if I hit her at all, I would just have slapped her a bit. She wouldn't have more than a few little bruises. But she asked for it. She was far too full of herself.'

Fry decided to change tack and come back to the assault later. His story would change in the details until eventually they would have the full account.

'Did Marie tell you who the father of the baby was?'

Kemp blinked a little, then leaned forward across the table.

'Oh, yeah. But she didn't need to – it wasn't hard to guess.'

'And who did she say it was?'

Now Kemp wanted to talk. He wanted to be sure that she understood. Like so many others, he was convinced that everybody would think he had done the right thing, if only he could explain it properly. Some of them talked for ever once they had started, baffled by their failure to communicate.

'Look, you have to understand something about Marie,' said Kemp. 'She thought she was cleverer than the rest of us, but she never had the education. She got obsessed with books. That house of hers was full of books before she'd finished.'

'Yes, I've seen them.'

'Well, she thought she was going to better herself by reading. As if reading those novels she had was going to improve anybody's education. What a load of crap! But she thought because she could talk about novels she was an intellectual. She was easily influenced like that, always wanting to please some bloke. So she was round at the bookshop all the time. She thought she was moving in better circles, just because he took an interest in her. But he was after one thing from her, like everybody else.'

'The bookshop?'

'Eden Valley Books, of course. The ponce with the bow tie, Lawrence Daley. It was my fault she met him. And he's no better than the rest of us, is he?'

'Marie told you that Lawrence Daley was the father of her child?' asked Fry.

'That's it. Daley. There's only two things he's interested in, when it comes down to it. And they're the same things as the rest of us – sex and money. All the rest of the stuff is just airs and graces. Books? Rubbish. Sex and money. Yes, I could tell you a thing or two about that bookseller.'

Two miles down the road, Cooper was still trying to thaw out his hands when he took the call on his mobile phone.

'Ben, where are you?'

'A57, near the Snake Inn. I'm on my way to Harrop to get a statement from George Malkin about the items he sold to Lawrence Daley.'

'Perhaps you'd better pull in.'

Cooper tucked the Toyota into the first gateway that he came to. The driver of a Transit van sounded his horn as he pulled out to go past him.

'What is it?' he said.

'We've just interviewed Eddie Kemp again.'

'Yeah. Get anything out of him?'

'The name of the baby's father.'

'It wasn't his?'

'He says not. He says the father is Lawrence Daley.'

Cooper was glad he was no longer driving. He turned around in his seat. Lawrence's blue Vauxhall should have passed him by now. There was no road to turn off the Snake Pass until the Harrop road, the other side of Irontongue Hill.

'I've not long seen him,' said Cooper. 'A couple of miles back, I helped to get his car back on to the road. He told me he was heading this way, but I think he might have turned round.'

'I'm on my way. If you see him again, just keep contact.'

Cooper manoeuvred the Toyota in the gateway with difficulty, forcing more traffic to swerve round him. Finally, he got back on the road heading east. He didn't have to go far to find Lawrence's Vauxhall. Only two miles back up the A57, it was parked in another lay-by, but on the opposite side of the road. This time, it had been taken off the carriageway deliberately and was parked neatly. There was no sign of Lawrence Daley.

Cooper got out and scanned the nearby landscape. There was nothing but blank snow everywhere. It was about the remotest spot on the A57, familiar only by the sight of Irontongue Hill to the east. He checked the doors of the Vauxhall and found it locked. Then he looked in through the windows. He dialled Fry's mobile.

'What is it, Ben?'

'Lawrence Daley's car is here at the roadside. There's a length of plastic tubing and a roll of insulation tape on the passenger seat of his car.'

'It's a pity you didn't notice that when you were giving him a helping hand.'

'Do you think he drove out here to kill himself?'

'It sounds a bit like it. Can you see him? He can't have got far.'

'He'll be getting further and further away. But I don't know in which direction.'

Cooper turned to look to the north and cursed again. The weather was changing rapidly. Fat, heavy clouds were bumping over the flanks of Bleaklow and Kinder Scout. On the further slopes he could see the snow already falling. He shivered as the first cold gusts of a northerly wind reached him and bit through his clothes.

He cast about along the edge of the road, damning the slush and the deep tyre marks of every vehicle that had stopped in the last couple of days. Then he found the beginning of some footprints. They were fresh ones, the snow newly broken on the edge of the moor.

'I can see which way he went,' said Cooper. 'I should have guessed – he's heading towards Irontongue. But he'll never make it across that snowfield. It's treacherous under there. Groughs, loose peat, frozen bogs – you can't tell what you're walking on.'

The sky was darkening. The wind started to bluster around him, alternately whistling and moaning like an animal. The first flakes of snow fell – big, soft flakes that settled on the slush and began to freeze. Within minutes, they would be piling up, covering all the surfaces. Soon, he would be able to see nothing on the moor.

'Damn, damn and damn.'

'What are you doing?' said Fry.

Cooper didn't answer. He was opening the tailgate of the Toyota and taking off his shoes, balancing on one foot as he replaced his shoes with walking boots. He pulled on his cagoule, zipped up the hood.

'Ben, answer me. What the hell are you doing?'

'I'll take the phone with me. I'll try to keep in touch, depending what reception is like out there.'

He checked his rucksack for a compass, dry clothes, a torch.

'Ben, stay right where you are. I'm only a couple

of minutes away. We have to call out the mountain rescue team.'

'They'll take hours and it's nearly dark already.'

'We can get them to put a helicopter up.'

'In a blizzard? Because if you take a look to the north, you'll see there's one on the way.'

'Ben, I can see you now. Stay with the car.'

'Diane, if we let him do this, we may never find Baby Chloe.'

Cooper shoved his phone into the front pocket of his rucksack. He pulled on a pair of gloves. Finally, he began to walk up the hillside, following Lawrence's footsteps. He had gone a hundred yards when he heard a car pull up on the road.

'Ben!'

Cooper kept walking. Fry called after him again. But now there was an entirely different tone to her voice. No longer was there any anger, only fear and a strange appeal that made her sound like somebody else entirely.

He turned and stared at her wordlessly. It was entirely the wrong moment to try to think of words to say to her that could mean anything. Trust Diane Fry always to be choosing the wrong moment. For a second or two he looked at her, the snow landing on her shoulders and on her face, melting into damp patches that glistened on her cheeks. A remnant of common sense urged him to walk back towards her, so that they could sit in the car together and wait. He stared at her for so long that he thought he would see her red scarf for ever.

Then he carried on walking on to the moor. Just once, Cooper looked back, and he could see Fry still watching him from the road in the dusk, with the snow falling thicker and thicker through the headlights of her car. Then his path led him over the top of a rise, and he couldn't see her any more.

Diane Fry made the necessary calls with a shaking hand. Once she had done that, all she could do was wait. Ben Cooper would know that she had more sense than to do anything else, that she had enough self-discipline not to go flying in the face of procedures and the clear priorities of self-preservation and directing assistance.

Of course, Cooper would never in his life appreciate that she felt the same instincts that he did, that her first impulse had been to run after him into the snow. Not everybody could give way to those impulses – otherwise, where would the world be? What sort of mess would they be in now?

And Cooper would never realize that waiting was the worst thing. He would never know how hard it was to sit alone in her car watching the sky darken and the snow fall heavier and heavier until it filled his tracks and obliterated signs of his presence.

Fry switched on her wipers to clear her windscreen and looked at Cooper's Toyota. He said it always got him through the snow. But now his car stood abandoned in the lay-by while he faced the snow alone. Knowing Cooper, he had probably forgotten even to lock it in his eagerness to be a hero.

Fry shivered despite the warm air from her car heater. For some reason, she remembered the file she had in a locked drawer in her desk at West Street. She knew, in that moment, that she would destroy the file without hesitation, if Ben Cooper came back alive.

The distant moors looked entirely artificial in the twilight, like mounds of polystyrene packaging, their white surfaces split by cracks. Beyond Ben Cooper's immediate surroundings, the landscape was almost featureless. There was no horizon, just a vague softening where the low cloud lay on the tops, dropping more snow silently on the moors. The only landmark ahead of him was the outcrop of rock on Irontongue Hill, the blackest thing against a dark background.

Cooper was able to follow Lawrence Daley's tracks easily. There were traces of other walkers passing here, but they were frozen into the snow, like footprints set in wet cement, and Lawrence's were the only fresh tracks. Cooper tried to follow a line that avoided the gullies, but now and then he sank up to his knees in a drift and had to drag himself out. The snow was too cold to make his clothes wet. Instead, it stuck to his trousers, boots and gloves in small, frozen lumps. The depth of the drifts sapped the strength from his legs, and his calf muscles were soon aching.

He knew he needed to find Lawrence Daley before it became fully dark. The moor was a dangerous place to be at night in this weather. Not only dangerous but lethal, for anyone inadequately equipped. The heavier the snow became, the more difficult it would be to see Lawrence, unless he could close the distance.

He was climbing steadily higher towards the top of Irontongue Hill, where the wreckage of Sugar Uncle Victor lay. In the gullies, snow already lay over a thin layer of ice that cracked and gave way under his weight. In the deeper areas of snow, his feet plunged in. But on the smoother areas he was aware only of the crackle and squeak as the snow compressed under his boots. No other route he chose would be a good one – there were too many steep-sided gullies and groughs to cross, too many sudden hollows hidden by waist-deep drifts, too many icy streams and channels full of drainage water to stumble into.

Finally, there was a splash of colour in the snow, barely visible in the dusk. Cooper turned and headed towards it. Fifty yards away, he could see it was Lawrence's blue jacket. He looked as though he had simply lain down to rest at the foot of a rock, among the first scattered fragments of aircraft wreckage. But from the distress on Lawrence's face, Cooper could see he was exhausted and in pain.

'I think I've broken my leg,' said Lawrence. 'And my chest hurts. Badly.'

'Lie still. We have to wait until they come to find us.'

'You shouldn't have come after me, Ben.'

Cooper felt Lawrence's cheek. He was very cold. 'What on earth made you come out dressed like that?' he said. 'You could have died of exposure.'

'Oh, yes,' said Lawrence. 'So I could.' And he coughed into the snow.

'I've just been told about Marie,' said Cooper. 'Her grandfather was Sergeant Dick Abbott.'

'Yes, I know. When Marie was a girl, her parents used to bring her down to Derbyshire every year to leave a poppy. Sometimes they made a holiday out of it, staying in Edendale for a few days. It's very quiet in the winter – there isn't much to do, except browse in bookshops. That's how I met her the first time.'

Lawrence's voice faded. Cooper looked at his face. The bookseller's eyelids were drooping, and Cooper knew he had to stop him falling asleep.

'But Eddie Kemp came along, didn't he?'

Lawrence didn't reply.

'Did you know you were the father of the baby, Lawrence?' asked Cooper. 'If Marie told Eddie Kemp, then she must have told *you*, surely. Kemp was jealous. He beat her up when she told him the baby was yours. The pathologist said she was weakened by her injuries and too exhausted to make it back down the hill. That was after she left the poppy. She kept up the ritual. But she must have lain down to rest and gone to sleep. It's a mistake to go to sleep, Lawrence. You can die of exposure out here.'

But Lawrence seemed to have something else he wanted to talk about. 'It was nothing to do with the baby. Kemp couldn't have cared less about the baby.'

'What? Why then?'

'He wanted to frighten her. I don't think he meant to hurt her so badly, but he always went too far. He meant to warn her what would happen if she told what she knew to the police. That was my fault, of course. I let her find out what the business was. It never occurred to me how she would feel about it.'

'Because she was Dick Abbott's granddaughter, of course. She must have felt about it the way Zygmunt Lukasz did. So when she found out, she threatened to give you away. Is that what happened, Lawrence? And Eddie Kemp had the job of frightening her off. Didn't you do anything about it? For heaven's sake – she was badly injured!'

Lawrence sounded resigned. 'You don't understand. It was all too complicated.'

'No, I don't understand. And I don't understand why Marie didn't report that he had attacked her.'

'Because he threatened worse than that,' said Lawrence.

'Worse?'

Again, Lawrence seemed to go off at a tangent. 'Did you know Andrew Lukasz came to the shop?' he said.

'Did he?'

'He had a cigarette case he'd bought. He rang me and said he wanted to know the names of people involved in the business. He threatened he was going to speak to that RAF policeman that night.'

'When was this, Lawrence?'

'Over a week ago. On the Sunday, the day before Marie –'

'And did you tell him anything?'

'No. He frightened me. I couldn't face him on my own, so I phoned Frank Baine, and he came to the shop with Kemp.' Lawrence coughed again. 'I sent for the reinforcements.'

'But Easton was still looking for Andrew Lukasz next day. So he didn't meet him on Sunday night.'

'No.'

Cooper wondered where Andrew Lukasz was now. But time was running out, and there was a more important question that was preying on his mind.

'Lawrence, where's the baby?'

This time, Lawrence didn't answer. Then Cooper noticed the approaching noise. It seemed to come from the east, creeping round the sides of Irontongue Hill and enveloping the outcrops of rock. It moved down the slopes towards him, but at the same time was everywhere in the sky, spreading across the low clouds. It was more than a sound – it was a deep droning that he felt as a vibration in the air, a reverberation bouncing off the hillside and filling the space all around him.

As the rumbling continued, Cooper looked up, expecting to see an aircraft. But nothing appeared in the sky. There was just the same blanket of iron-grey cloud rolling away towards the horizon, the same steady drift of snowflakes, thousands upon thousands of them parachuting towards him. The sound came from within the cloud; it was rumbling around inside it, spreading itself across the sky, so that it was impossible to pin down the direction it was coming from.

'Where's the baby, Lawrence? Where's Baby Chloe?'

There was still no reply. After a few minutes, the noise gradually began to recede. It didn't exactly move away; there was no direction he could have said it had headed in. It simply became more subdued, a little quieter and more muffled, until eventually the cloud had swallowed it completely.

Cooper had the ridiculous idea that the clouds might have been troubled by indigestion that had now grumbled its way out into the open, perhaps in a sulphurous outbreak of gas into the atmosphere somewhere over Glossop. But maybe the sound had been thunder, after all. Or maybe it had been an airliner somewhere in the overcast, flying blind towards Manchester Airport, its engines booming inside the banks of cloud. Or then, maybe he had imagined the whole thing.

'We need to find Chloe, Lawrence. We have to be sure she's safe.'

Cooper moved to bring his other leg under his body. It was icy cold and hardly felt part of him any more. Now there was only the sound of the wind scraping its way across the moors, and the faint settling of the snow as it drifted past his ears.

He felt discouraged at the prospect of trying to get a response from Lawrence. But he had to keep him from falling asleep. He found himself casting around desperately for something to say.

'I know you wanted to keep the bookshop going, Lawrence. Did anybody ever buy any of those books that I priced up? No, I don't suppose they did, though there must have been some bargains among them. And coming to the shop helped me to find the flat. I didn't think you were very keen on me taking it at first. By the way, I suppose it's too much to ask – but could you have a word with your aunt about the noise of the dog? It barks too much when it's out in the yard. It wakes me up in the mornings.'

Cooper blinked his eyes. The wind was making them water, and the unending whiteness was playing havoc with his colour perception.

'Diane Fry will get help to us soon,' he said. 'She's good at things like that, very efficient. That's why she made sergeant instead of me, I expect. Who wants to be a sergeant, anyway? Who wants a management job shoving paper and dealing with other people's problems?'

He blinked again. Instead of Lawrence's blue jacket, he was seeing red. Cooper had met colour-blind people who were unable to distinguish between blue and red. But he knew he wasn't colour blind – proper colour perception was one of the physical requirements for joining the police force. Candidates unable to distinguish principal colours and those who suffer from pronounced squints are unacceptable. It was in the recruitment literature. Anybody could read it on the website.

'You could do with someone like Diane to run the shop,' he said. 'Someone efficient, someone a bit ruthless who would throw out all those old books no one will ever buy that are cluttering the place up. You could turn the business round completely. We can rely on Diane. She'll have help here soon. Very soon.'

Red, white and blue. Cooper used the back of his glove to rub his eyes. The colours had to be imaginary. But he was seeing both red and blue in the snow. Red, white and blue. Very patriotic. He fumbled for his torch and switched it on. The blue was Lawrence's jacket, the white was the snow. And the red was the blood. As it trickled from Lawrence's body, it was diluting itself from dark arterial red and spreading for a few inches until it thickened and froze, staining the snow pink, like strawberry ice cream.

'Lawrence, where are you injured? Did you say it was your chest? Have you fallen on something?'

Carefully, with numb fingers, he tried to feel under Lawrence's body. He touched metal, a sharp splinter of torn steel.

Cooper stared at Lawrence's white face, remembering the Irving flying jacket in that upstairs room at the bookshop. An Irving suit was exactly what he needed now to stop the steady leaching away of Lawrence's body heat as the blood seeped from his wounds. Without their Irving suits, airmen would have died of exposure in a Lancaster bomber on a winter bombing run over Germany. Rear gunners like Sergeant Dick Abbott had suffered frostbite despite their heated suits. Zygmunt Lukasz had lost two fingers trying to staunch the blood pouring from his cousin's wounds as they lay in the snow waiting for rescue. Even now, Cooper could clearly picture the two Polish airmen in their RAF uniforms, lying no more than a few feet from where they were now. Red, white and blue.

In the far distance, he could see a single light. Its rectangular shape blinked through the swirling snow like a beacon as it floated in the blackness over the snowfield. He thought for a moment of the bright star in the east that the Wise Men had followed. But this light was in the north, and it was not a star. Cooper realized it was the uncurtained bedroom window of a retired farmworker, where a man might even now be counting his regrets.

A little way to the west, there was a dark shape in the snow. That was the stone wall of the dam and the cold expanse of Blackbrook Reservoir. Cooper pictured Pilot Officer Danny McTeague, staggering from the wreckage of his Lancaster bomber and about to set off across the moor to find help. In another few minutes, it would be completely dark, as it was when McTeague walked away from Sugar Uncle Victor. And then he wouldn't be able to see the reservoir – only the light.

'At least you helped George Malkin, Lawrence,' said Cooper. 'His souvenirs produced a bit of money for him, didn't they?'

Still Lawrence didn't answer. But Cooper stared at his face as if he had spoken. It was as if Lawrence had just said something perceptive that Cooper hadn't thought of before.

'Yes,' said Cooper. 'You did help George Malkin – didn't you, Lawrence?'

The wind was really getting up now. Cooper heard an answering moan from the rocks behind him and felt a spatter of frozen snow on the back of his neck where it was blowing off the top of the drifts. There was a pain in his ears, but it was nothing to what Marie Tennent must have felt as she lay out in the snow the night she died. Where his hand had been plunged into the snow, it looked red and raw. He rubbed it on a dry part of his trousers and thrust it back into his glove. But the glove had got snow on the inside, too, and it didn't help, so he took it off again.

'I know you weren't involved in Nick Easton's murder. And Marie's death wasn't your fault. But you have to tell us where the baby is, Lawrence.'

Was that the noise of a helicopter, that dull thudding in his ears? Or was it his own heart struggling to push the blood through his veins? If he could convince Lawrence that rescue was on its way, perhaps he would decide not to die. Perhaps he would rouse himself and they could share their body heat to survive together.

Cooper held his breath in his hands to prevent it from drifting away, afraid it might take his life with it. But Lawrence wasn't going to rouse himself. There was no warmth left in his body to share. Cooper lay over him, covering both their bodies with the cagoule, leaving only his head and his feet free. He needed to be able to hear the helicopter so that he could signal their position. He didn't know whether he was going to be able to do that in the dark, but somehow he would have to. All he had was his torch, and the moor was a big place. If anyone were thinking properly, they would have thermal imaging equipment on board to locate their body heat. If there was any body heat left by then.

That was definitely the sound of a helicopter.

'I think they're here, Lawrence,' he said.

Cooper put his hand to Lawrence's face to attract his attention. His fingers touched something hard and cold, an incongruous blemish on Lawrence's cheek. It was a single tear, slowly freezing to the skin.

35

Diane Fry pulled out of the divisional headquarters car park and fell in behind the lights of a patrol car on its way down West Street. Dawn was creeping over the roofs of Edendale. Beside her, Ben Cooper looked pale and exhausted. He should have been at home in bed, but had refused to stay away.

'We should have insisted on looking in all the rooms while we were there,' he said.

'How could we? We had no search warrant. We had no grounds for making an arrest. Not then.'

'There were more rooms above that floor he showed us. That's where he lives – in the attic rooms. They would be the old servants' bedrooms.'

'We'll soon find out.'

Fry could tell Cooper was uneasy. He fidgeted with his seat belt like a restless child. But at least her car would stay clean. She had left Gavin Murfin behind this morning.

'I should have known there was something wrong about Frank Baine,' said Cooper. 'There were so many gaps in what he told Alison Morrissey. He didn't mention George Malkin to her, and he didn't let her see the books about the aircraft wrecks. Walter Rowland might have been willing to talk to her, but Baine discouraged him.'

'Yes, I suppose so,' said Fry.

'And of course, Baine told Alison that Sergeant Dick Abbott's family had left the country. But Marie Tennent was right here in Edendale. They ought to have been able to meet. It would have meant a lot to both of them.'

'I expect so.'

'There could have been some kind of reconciliation,' said Cooper.

'Yes, Ben.'

Fry drove through the roundabout and up Hulley Road towards the traffic lights. She was following the patrol car because she wasn't sure how to get into Nick i' th' Tor to reach Eden Valley Books.

'I should have known he was manipulating Alison. She was determined enough that he couldn't have stopped her coming over. But Baine was with her all the time, making sure he knew what she was doing, pushing her in the direction he wanted her to go, keeping her away from the truth. Of course, he'd been to see everyone himself before Alison ever arrived here, and he'd alienated them all, scared them off talking to her. Baine only started getting worried when he realized I was talking to the wrong people.'

Fry glanced at him. 'When he realized you weren't going to do what you were told.'

But Cooper ignored her. 'He saw me at the Lukaszes', then at Walter Rowland's. And he knew that I'd been to the bookshop itself.'

'Several times,' said Fry. 'Little did he know that you were just buying books.'

'Books on aircraft wrecks. Lawrence would have told him that.' Cooper paused. 'It was Frank Baine who tried to put me out of action that night, wasn't it? Not Eddie Kemp.'

'Yes, we think so. We're still waiting for DNA results.'

The patrol car turned into a narrow entrance off Eyre Street, and Fry turned after it. They bumped over cobbles and had to slow to a crawl as they entered the network of passages between Eyre Street and the market square. They pulled up near the bridge over the river, where a police officer was stopping people from walking further up than Larkin's bakery.

'I'll have to explain it all to Alison later today,' said Cooper.

Fry switched off the engine and sat for a moment looking at the bookshop, listening to the roar of the River Eden under the bridge. She didn't know what to say to him.

Outside Eden Valley Books, two police motor-cyclists were unbuckling the straps of their crash helmets. When they were bareheaded, the officers hardly looked any different. They both had bald domes as smooth and white as their helmets.

Ben Cooper pushed open the front door and walked among the shelves of books. The shop seemed dead without Lawrence's presence. Cooper felt as though he was walking through a set for a TV costume drama. In the little kitchen area at the back, he found a window open. A few lumps of snow had dropped inside and scattered on the draining board. A small heap of it lay on the base of an upturned coffee mug.

While Fry took a call on her radio, Cooper went upstairs and walked slowly through the upper rooms. The shop was so quiet that he was reluctant to open each door that he came to, for fear of what he might find behind it. On the second floor, the biggest room was the one that he and Fry had seen, where the aviation memorabilia was displayed. A second room had been converted into a kind of study, where a couple of computers sat humming quietly to themselves. No wonder so many books had been piled on the landing and in the corridor – they must once have occupied these rooms.

Between a couple of stacks of books, Cooper found what he had expected – a door that was a step up from the floor, a door that opened to reveal not a room but another flight of stairs, narrow and uncarpeted. The top floor of the building was Lawrence's living quarters. There was an untidy sitting room, a bathroom and a large bedroom with a vast iron bedstead. Cooper was looking for signs of Marie Tennent's presence when he heard a noise over his head. The sound of rats in a house was distinctive. They made so much noise on bare floorboards that they sounded as though they were wearing hobnailed boots. And there was that faint, dragging scrape that went with the footsteps – a sound that conjured up a clear picture of a scaly tail slithering across the floor in the dust.

Diane Fry stood in the doorway of the bedroom watching him, not speaking. He saw her shudder when she heard the scurrying in the ceiling.

'We've just had a call from the hospital,' she said.

'Lawrence?'

'I'm afraid so.'

Cooper sat down suddenly on the bed, which sagged and gave a protesting squeak.

'You did your best, Ben,' said Fry. 'Nobody could have done any more.'

'I could have done it sooner. I found Lawrence's bookmark in one of Marie's books almost a week ago. I knew she'd been here. Marie read all sorts of books, not only Danielle Steel. They were there in her house, on her shelves. She spent money that she couldn't afford, just to buy more books. Lawrence Daley was her type really, not Eddie Kemp. She was following her mother's advice and doing better for herself. When Marie told her mother that the baby's father ran his own business, she didn't mean he was a window cleaner, for God's sake.'

'There's nothing more we could have done, Ben.'

'No, there is,' said Cooper. 'We could have found the baby.'

Fry had to stand aside as he brushed past her. He went down the first flight of narrow stairs and into the big room where Lawrence's aviation memorabilia was displayed. The Irving suit and the flying helmets and the personal possessions of long-dead airmen looked particularly ghoulish now that their owner was himself dead. Cooper was starting to feel stifled by the atmosphere. He pushed open the outside door and stood at the top of the fire escape, allowing the cold air to blow into the room and stir the cobwebs. Below him, the yard was still untouched, its unidentifiable shapes covered by yesterday's fresh snow.

The back alley was full of police vehicles with their engines rumbling. There was a ripping sound and a loud snap as a member of the task force levered the padlock off the yard gates with a crowbar. But then the team found they had difficulty pushing the gates open against the weight of the snow. The more they cursed and heaved, the more the snow built up and compacted, so that they might as well have been pushing against a brick wall.

'Shovels,' called a sergeant. 'We'll have to dig a space clear.'

Cooper went down the fire escape. The steps were treacherously slippery, and his hands left imprints in the snow frozen to the top of the rail. Under the snow was a layer of ice, so that he felt as though his knuckles were scraping against sandpaper.

He stopped at the bottom and looked around the yard. Last week's snow had lingered here because no sun ever reached the yard, at any time of day. The backs of buildings were all around it, and they were too high to allow any sun through at this time of year. There was a pink glow behind the buildings in the east as the sun rose, but it only made their outlines darker, their shadows longer, so that they almost seemed to meet here in this yard, like old men leaning towards each other to whisper their secrets. They might have been saying: 'Have you seen Baby Chloe?'

Black cast-iron drainpipes formed an intricate spider's web on the back walls of the buildings, and a large part of Edendale's starling population was clustered on the edges of the guttering, chattering at the sunrise over the rooftops.

Cooper followed the pawprints of the cat that had walked through the fresh snow in the yard. It had crossed the tracks of the birds, but hadn't paused – presumably the birds were long gone by the time it arrived. Starlings weren't very bright, but they knew enough to make themselves scarce when there was a cat around. The prints went almost the full width of the yard, then veered away towards one of the snow-covered mounds. Cooper scraped some snow off it. It was a wheel, and part of an undercarriage leg. He caught a whiff of an acidic smell. There was a yellow stain at the base of the wheel, and a spattering of small, melted holes in the surface of the snow, where the cat had marked its territory. Then the animal had walked towards the next object and had circled it for a while, before leaping to the top and from there on to the wall and away into the adjoining yard.

It was easy to see what the object was. The barrels of two rusted Vickers machine guns poked through the snow from a domed shape like a giant helmet. It was a gun turret. Cooper touched the end of one of the barrels, and found it moved slightly on its pivot, dislodging a few inches of snow that slid slowly from the Perspex hood. Through the hole he had made in the snow, he could see the gunner's seat and something dark thrown over it.

Behind him, members of the task force were backing a Land Rover through the gates and unloading shovels to clear the snow. The vehicle's exhaust fumes began to fill the yard, and the reek of them overlaid the cool, clean smell of the snow.

Cooper couldn't wait for the orderly progression of the search. He wanted to know what was inside the gun turret, what items had been left behind in the confines of the same kind of prison in which Sergeant Dick Abbott had died on board Sugar Uncle Victor. Maybe there was another Irving jacket like the one he had seen in the upstairs room; maybe there was a parachute harness, a flying helmet, or some other personal piece of equipment that he could hold in his hands, hoping it would tell him the story of the man who had lived and fought, and perhaps died, in this cramped space.

The area he had cleared wasn't quite wide enough for him to see inside properly. Cooper wiped his hand across the Perspex of the turret, so that another patch of snow broke away and landed on his boots, with a faint swish and a crunch. He had trouble for a moment because of the water that streaked and blurred on the Perspex. But soon it pooled and ran away down the curved surface, and began to drip quietly into the snow.

The sound of the dripping water seemed to absorb Cooper's concentration, so that the noise of the officers behind him and the revving Land Rover engine retreated from him and became no more than distant intrusions on the edge of his hearing. He had to drag his attention away from the dripping sound and back to the blurred window he had made in the Perspex.

It was only then that he saw the eyes.

Grace Lukasz took the wafer in her mouth and closed her eyes as she sipped the wine. The body of Christ lay on her tongue, His blood dampened her lips. Christ had given His life, a voluntary sacrifice. But Grace also knew the Old Testament story of the Scapegoat, which had been forced to take the sins of the tribe on itself and had been driven into the wilderness. Not all sacrificial victims were willing.

Andrew had always been hot-headed, stubborn, a chip off the old block, the old people said. He was more like Zygmunt than Peter. He had the same stubborn jaw, the same blue eyes, the same capacity for single-mindedness. But Andrew was different in one important matter – his desire was for money. She'd understood that, at least. She understood that it was Andrew that Zygmunt meant when he talked about vultures. Peter had been forced to choose between them – and he had chosen Zygmunt, choosing his origins rather than his future.

Grace would have to make herself feel glad. There was no other way of facing it. It was the time of forgiveness, for reconciliation. The sacrifice had been made, and now there would be peace in the family. This morning, Peter had looked content. Not happy, perhaps, but less haunted. She had always been the one accused of living in the past. But there was no one like these Polish families for that, no one like these old men clinging to their wartime memories, their gnarled hands grasping so tightly at remembrance of the time when they were needed so badly, a time when they had a role in life. A time when they had an enemy to fight.

Grace knew that Detective Constable Cooper was sitting at the back of the church. He hadn't come forward to the altar for Communion, but had stayed in his seat watching. He looked like a boy who could be helped by faith, if he could only let God into his life. He was about the same age as Andrew, too. She felt the beginnings of a tear fill the corner of her eye. She felt for a tissue in the pocket of her skirt. The young people these days knew nothing except their own concerns. They had not learned the value of perspective. They cared only for their own short-term personal interest. They did not know that a small sacrifice could be for the greater good.

She eased her wheelchair away from the end of the pew and turned it in the aisle. The squeak of the wheels on the strip of carpet in the aisle sounded too loud. Members of the congregation turned to watch her as she propelled herself to the side door and wheeled down the ramp into the churchyard.

Ben Cooper was conscious of the faces turned in his direction as people watched her leave. He waited until the attention of the congregation had settled back on to the priest, then he slipped out, closing the door behind him as quietly as he could. He was glad to be out of the church and back in the cold air. It had a purer, cleaner feel to it that was closer to his own idea of something sacred. He saw that Grace Lukasz hadn't gone far. Her wheelchair was on the path between the gravestones, close to where the giant figure of the Black Madonna and Child was built into the outside wall of the church.

Mrs Lukasz didn't look round, but had heard him approaching. 'Will you take me back to the bungalow? Peter was going to come for me, but he'll be a while yet.'

'Of course.'

Cooper had handled a wheelchair before. He helped Grace Lukasz to position herself next to the passenger door of his car and held the chair steady while she manoeuvred herself in. He could see that her legs were almost useless. She had to lift them in after her. When she was settled, he folded the wheelchair into the back of the Toyota.

'I suppose you're wondering,' she said. 'It was a car accident. Andrew was driving.'

'Before he went to London?'

'Yes. We'd been very close until then. But after the accident, he couldn't live with the guilt. He couldn't bear to look at me in the wheelchair, day after day. So it was me who drove him away, you see.'

Cooper couldn't think what to say to that. Guilt, like other emotions, was hardly ever logical.

'But you can't separate yourself from your family for ever,' said Grace. 'He came back, in the end.'

'Why did he come back?'

'Andrew was starting to feel isolated in London. Isolated from his family, isolated from the community he grew up in. After a year or two, he started to regret cutting himself off.'

'Did he tell you this?'

'Yes, when he arrived. Do you know, he remembered all the stories that Zygmunt used to tell about the RAF, about the Lancaster crash. And of course, about his cousin Klemens, who died.'

Cooper got into the driving seat and fastened his seat belt. 'We think Andrew had started to collect Second World War aircraft memorabilia,' he said.

'Yes, but I bet he was looking for things with a Polish connection. The links are very strong, you know. The way our children are raised, they can't break the links so easily.'

'That's how he came across the cigarette case, then. He bought it from the website that Frank Baine and Lawrence Daley ran. He was a customer of theirs.'

'That's how it started,' said Grace. 'But it became his means of reconciliation.'

Cooper put the car into gear and drove towards Woodland Crescent. 'I don't really understand.'

'I managed to get it out of Peter and Zygmunt in the end,' said Grace. 'I think they're both ashamed. Peter certainly is. Zygmunt – well, I don't know about Zygmunt.'

'But reconciliation . . . ?'

'The way Andrew was feeling, I think that when he heard Zygmunt didn't have long to live, he knew it was time to be reconciled. He made his own enquiries into where these souvenirs or memorabilia came from, and who was involved. That's how he made contact with Lawrence Daley, here in Edendale. Daley trusted him, and Andrew worked out that there was far more to the business than the memorabilia. He contacted the RAF Police and told them the story.'

'He was getting on to dangerous ground,' said Cooper. 'Didn't he realize that?'

'I suppose so. But he's single-minded, you know. Stubborn, like his father and his grandfather. He had his mind set on *oplatek*. It was the time for reconciliation. He had to come here and show his grandfather that he was doing something about the people Zygmunt called vultures. Andrew thought his grandfather would be proud of him.'

They turned the corner into Woodland Crescent. Cooper had slowed down, because he wanted to hear what Grace Lukasz had to say before she reached the bungalow.

'But it wasn't enough for Zygmunt,' she said. 'I think he mocked Andrew for simply passing the information to the police, which was what he intended. I think Zygmunt said he should have found out names. He asked Andrew where his courage was.'

Cooper pulled up to the kerb and put the hand-brake on. He sat for a moment, saying nothing. As he had hoped, Grace kept on talking. It was as if Communion had prompted her to thoughts of confession. But surely it was somebody else's sins she was talking about, somebody else's need for forgiveness.

'It was seeing the cigarette case that made Zygmunt so angry,' she said. 'They argued terribly.

I couldn't make it all out, but I'm sure that's what it was. Then Andrew walked out.'

'Did you know where he'd gone?'

Grace shook her head. 'All I know is that he went off to prove himself to his grandfather, to show that he was worthy of forgiveness. He decided not to wait to speak to the policeman. And that's all I know.'

'I see.'

She turned her head wearily to look at Cooper. 'Andrew got himself into trouble, didn't he?'

'Let's go inside.'

But still Grace didn't move. 'There was another thing that Zygmunt always talked about too much,' she said. 'Sacrifice.'

At Grace's direction, Cooper opened the side gate and pushed her wheelchair down the passage past the garage to the back of the bungalow. He could see Zygmunt Lukasz in the conservatory. The lighting was strange inside because of the covering of snow on the glass roof, which gave a blue cast to the sunlight. But it seemed to Cooper that the old man was praying.

Zygmunt was seated in front of a tall candle that burned strongly in the enclosed space. His white hair shone with an unlikely purity in the snow-filtered light, as if it had recently been washed with bleach. The rest of his family were visible behind him in the house. There was Peter, and Richard and Krystyna, and even the youngest child, Alice.

Cooper began to feel embarrassed, and he wanted to slip back round the corner before they saw him. But Grace Lukasz banged on the glass without hesitation, and her husband came to the door, staring at Cooper.

'I wasn't expecting you to be ready to come home so soon,' he said to Grace.

'I'd had enough. And Detective Constable Cooper wants to speak to you.'

'I'm sorry to bother you, sir.'

'You'd better come in.'

Krystyna was in the kitchen cutting carrots and parsnips with a small knife. There was a chicken soaking in cold water. In the sitting room, Peter Lukasz had automatically picked up the television remote and was fingering the buttons. 'What is it you want?' he said.

'I wonder if you've heard from your son yet?'

'No. But we will soon.'

Cooper shook his head. It was strange standing here in the Lukaszes' home again. Over a week ago, he had arrested Eddie Kemp in the Starlight Café. He had never even heard of the Lukasz family then, but Kemp had just been involved in killing their son. There had been blood on the streets that dawn, in the snow. Now there was blood on Irontongue Hill.

'Mr Lukasz,' he said, 'I need you to come to the mortuary again to make an identification.'

Each of the Lukasz family stopped what they were doing. Grace spun her wheelchair to face him,

602

Peter put down the television remote, Krystyna paused with her knife in mid-air. Cooper turned and looked into the conservatory. Zygmunt had fixed him with his pale blue, knowing eyes. The old man raised his head, tensing his jaw as if facing a challenge. The dog was beside his chair, with a thin, pink biscuit in its mouth that it had been dragging around the floor. The biscuit was dirty, but a design was visible on it – a picture of a nativity scene. Cooper recognized it as a version of the *oplatek* wafer.

'Forgiveness for the animals?' he asked.

Then Zygmunt Lukasz spoke in English for the first time in Ben Cooper's hearing.

'Of course,' he said. 'There were animals in the stable when Jesus was born.'

'So there were,' said Cooper. 'And animals are much easier to forgive.'

Ben Cooper had never yet been next door, to the house that Mrs Shelley lived in. He had only ever met her at number 8, in his own flat. Of course, number 6 looked identical from the outside, apart from the fact that there was only the one bell.

'She's a bit vague,' he said. 'She might not understand what we're telling her at first.'

'It's lucky she knows who you are, then,' said Diane Fry.

'I'm not sure about that. She might not associate me with the police. She thinks of me as the young man who looks after the cat.'

'Promotion at last, Ben.'

Cooper turned to look at her, irritated by the jibe. But he saw from her face that she regretted having said it.

'If it's all right with you, I want to go to the Cavendish Hotel and see Alison Morrissey after this,' he said.

Now Fry couldn't meet his eyes at all. 'She's gone,' she said. 'She caught a flight back to Toronto this morning.'

'What?'

'I'm sorry, Ben. We agreed it was for the best.'

'Who's *we*?'

'I talked to her yesterday, after we arrested Frank Baine. I watched you take her back to the hotel. And I think she's already said goodbye.'

Cooper felt his mouth hanging open and a surge of anger flooding through him. But before he could demand an explanation, the door of number 6 opened and Mrs Shelley stood looking at them, a puzzled frown on her face.

'Can I help you?'

They could hear the Jack Russell terrier barking from the back of the house. Even in the hallway, the noise was deafening. Cooper was glad of the thick stone walls that stopped sound travelling between the two houses. He was reminded of the walls in the row of cottages where Marie Tennent lived. They were just as thick as these walls – thick enough, he remembered thinking, that her neighbours would not have heard a baby crying.

Seeing Cooper speechless, Fry took the lead. 'Mrs Shelley, we need to speak to you about Lawrence Daley.'

'Lawrence?' Mrs Shelley said, as if repeating the name might bring some meaning to the sound of it. 'Lawrence?'

'Your nephew.'

'Has there been an accident? Has there been a fire at the shop? I always warned him that he was working in a death trap. All those books – it only needed some thoughtless person to drop a cigarette end or a match, and the whole lot would go up, I told him.'

'Nothing like that, Mrs Shelley. Could we come in for a moment? It would be better than standing on the doorstep.'

'Oh, yes. Would you like some tea?'

'It might be an idea to put the kettle on, but we'll do it.'

'Why on earth would you do that? I'm quite capable of putting the kettle on.'

'I think this might be a bit of a shock for you.'

Mrs Shelley stared at them, her mouth moving slightly as she tried to puzzle out what they were saying. In a moment, Cooper expected her to ask him about the cat.

'He can't be dead,' she said. 'That isn't possible. Not both of them.'

'Both of them?' said Fry. 'Both of who?'

'I'll make that tea,' said Cooper.

He was glad to find that the dog, Jasper, was outside the back door rather than in the kitchen. His yapping sounded peevish and demanding. Cooper was getting used to being in other people's kitchens – Marie Tennent's, full of nappies and bottles of sterilizing fluid; Walter Rowland's, sparse and utilitarian; Lawrence's little cubbyhole at the bookshop; even his own kitchen next door at number 8, which he had not yet got used to.

And it ought really to have been the kitchen at number 8 that Mrs Shelley's reminded him of – they were the same layout, with a similar view out on to the overgrown gardens. But of all the kitchens he had been in, it was Marie Tennent's he was reminded of. It didn't take him long to find out why.

Down at the end of the room, in the alcove that was occupied in his own flat by a new chest freezer, there was an incongruous piece of furniture. It didn't belong in a kitchen at all. But it went with the smells, which he now realized were what had put him in mind of Marie Tennent's house in the first place. The smells had transported him instantly to Dam Street, as if he had opened a door and stepped back into Marie's hallway on that day nearly a week ago. It was a trick of the memory, a sense of *déjà vu*. Except that here he had in front of him the one item that had been so obviously missing from any room in Marie Tennent's home.

'What am I going to do with her?' said Mrs Shelley plaintively, coming into the kitchen behind him. 'Jasper is so jealous of the attention she's getting – that's why he never stops barking. And if Lawrence is dead, he won't be coming back for her, will he?'

'No, Mrs Shelley. And I don't think her mother will be, either.'

Cooper stood looking down into the cot. The baby's eyes were open, but she lay with her hands curled into fists and her face flushed bright red. She was lying very still indeed. Then the pupils of her eyes moved, as if she were trying to see something a long way off, and her forehead creased in puzzlement.

Finally, she seemed to become aware of Cooper's face. And Baby Chloe smiled.

36

Typically, the Peak District weather had changed completely within forty-eight hours. Once the thaw had begun, it had accelerated so fast that the last traces of snow were almost gone by Thursday, apart from a few frozen streaks in the deep gullies on the moors. Water cascaded off the hills and the rivers were swollen, threatening to burst their banks.

Ben Cooper drove out of Edendale on dark, wet roads, remembering how different the Snake Pass had looked on the day he had gone up to the wreckage of Sugar Uncle Victor with Sergeant Caudwell. The snow had still been pristine then, and the reflection of the sun off the hillsides had been so bright it had hurt his eyes.

Now, in the yard behind Eden Valley Books, there would be water running off the gun turret and the engine casings in rivulets, dripping and crackling as the snow melted. The body of Andrew Lukasz had long since been removed, though not without difficulty. His limbs had been folded to get him into the turret, and rigor mortis had made the pathologist wonder whether his arms would have to be dislocated to get him out. But they had managed. And when they turned the body over, they had seen the blood that had soaked into the seat, and the injury to the back of Andrew's head.

Cooper felt sorry for Lawrence Daley. His partners had made sure he was implicated in the death of Andrew Lukasz. With no Lawrence to testify against them, it was going to be very difficult proving whether it had been deliberate or an accident when Andrew had ended up at the foot of the fire-escape stairs. It might be true that they had simply opened the door to show him the yard. There had been ice for days, and snow had fallen by then. So did Andrew just lose his footing? Or had it been the only way that Baine and his friends could prevent him from meeting Nick Easton next day?

When he had visited the bookshop with Diane Fry to look at the upstairs room, Cooper had even stood at the top of the fire escape himself and looked down into the yard. Andrew Lukasz's body had already been there, waiting for the snow to clear enough so that it could be removed. Yes, poor Lawrence. He had never really known what he was getting himself involved in.

Now, with all the interviews completed, the work was going on to build a case against Frank Baine and the Kemps, and the MDP were still pursuing their own enquiry. The one thing they were still looking for was Sergeant Easton's black Ford Focus.

Alison Morrissey was back in Canada, and Baby Chloe had been taken into care. The baby had come to no harm while she was under Mrs Shelley's protection, kept out of the way of Eddie Kemp's threats. And Marie Tennent had been wrongly judged from the start. The only thing she had cared about was keeping the baby safe. No, there had been two things she cared about. She had also remembered the dead. She had combined an annual act of remembrance to her grandfather, Sgt Dick Abbott, with a need to keep alive the memory of her own dead child.

But it seemed to Ben Cooper there was one person left whose fate everyone had forgotten about. This whole business hadn't started with Nick Easton or Marie Tennent, or any of them. It had started with Pilot Officer Danny McTeague.

On Irontongue Hill, water was scouring the moors in every direction, carving channels through the bare peat, sculpting it into castles and mounds, dragging small stones into heaps and gathering in dark pools in the hollows. Further down the hill, the streams had turned brown with peat, bursting with far more meltwater than they could cope with. They were no longer picturesque.

Yet George Malkin's house at Harrop still had snow on the roof. Normally, that was a sign of good insulation, which prevented the heat from rising. But in Malkin's case, Cooper knew there wasn't enough warmth in Hollow Shaw Farm to melt the snow.

Malkin had been right about the grass in the field near his house. Even now, as the snow began to wear thin, the grass looked a brighter green than any other grazing in Derbyshire. The black-faced ewes lifted their heads and watched Cooper as he parked the Toyota and walked up the path to the house. Some of the animals nodded their heads, as if to say they had known this would happen. If they hadn't been sheep, they might have looked wise. But their constantly rotating jaws and unblinking eyes were only derisive.

'How was the rabbit?' said Malkin, when Cooper entered the house.

'It was a life saver.'

'Ah, grand.'

In Malkin's sitting room, a small drift of snow lay on the window ledge where the blizzard had driven it through the twisted window frame. The snow showed no sign of thawing, even now. The crystals glittered against the stained wood. Cooper didn't want to be inside this house today.

'Mr Malkin, would you come outside with me for a minute?'

'If you like.'

They walked a few yards up the slope of the hill, to where Irontongue was just visible in the distance, with the hump of Blackbrook Reservoir in between, its dam wall emerging from the snow.

'The night before last, I was up there in the

dark,' said Cooper. 'I wouldn't normally go up on the mountain in the dark, but that night I did.'

'I heard about that,' said Malkin.

'Well, when you're up there at night like that, in the snow, you're desperate for any signs of life, you know. For a long time, there was only one thing I could see anywhere – a light. It was the light from your window. I knew it was yours. You don't bother drawing your curtains.'

'I didn't know you were up there,' said Malkin. 'What did you expect me to do?'

'Nothing,' said Cooper. 'But if I'd been lost and didn't know which way to go, I would certainly have headed for your house. It was the one light for miles. It was like a symbol of safety.'

'If you say so.'

'I remember thinking that I would never have set off towards the other side of the reservoir and down to the water board road, which you can't even see from up there. You wouldn't even know it existed. You'd have to be blind or stupid to set off in that direction.'

Malkin seemed to catch on to the drift of what Cooper was saying. 'Or drunk?' he said.

'Pilot Officer McTeague was not drunk,' said Cooper.

The air felt damp, and Cooper could see that the cloud was lowering rapidly. He pulled his collar up and shivered.

'I checked the Accident Investigator's report myself,' he said. 'The whisky on board Lancaster

612

SU-V was a gift for the station commander at RAF Benson. The Wing Commander at Leadenhall had a black market supply, and he wanted to share it with his old friend in Lancashire.'

'Is that right?'

'Mr Malkin, I don't think you can possibly have seen or heard Pilot Officer McTeague walking down the road singing "Show Me the Way to Go Home".'

'Well, I might have been mistaken,' said Malkin. 'The memory plays tricks after all this time.'

'I think there are things you remember all too well.'

Malkin stared across the moor for a moment or two. Banks of mist were beginning to move across in front of Irontongue Hill, and soon they wouldn't be able to see it at all from Hollow Shaw.

'Would you like to tell me about it?' said Cooper.

Malkin stood quite still and rigid. 'You have to understand something,' he said. 'Ted and I had heard our mother and father and some of their friends talking about counterfeit bank notes that were supposed to have been printed by the Germans to upset our economy.'

Cooper frowned. 'What has this got to do with anything?'

'Listen to me. When I first went up to the crash with Ted, we heard two of the airmen talking to each other. They were talking in a foreign language. So we knew they were German.'

'No, it would have been the two Poles you

heard,' said Cooper. 'It was Zygmunt Lukasz and Klemens Wach. They were speaking Polish.'

'I know that *now*,' said Malkin, already starting to get irritated. 'That's why we stayed away from the crew, you see. Not that we would have known what to do if we'd found anyone injured. We were going to find a phone and call the police, but then we saw the bags that had been thrown clear of the wreckage. Ted stopped to take a look inside. And we found the money.'

Malkin paused. He looked across the moor towards the side of Blackbrook Reservoir and opened a field gate in the dry-stone wall before he continued.

'Ted said there were millions of pounds. It took us days to count the notes, but there wasn't that much. We could barely carry the bags between us. I was only little, remember, and I soon got tired. We planned to hide them before we called the police. We reckoned everyone would think the bags had been thrown into the reservoir in the crash, because there were plenty of other bits of the aircraft lying all around the edge of the water.'

'I understand all that,' said Cooper. 'So what went wrong?'

Malkin still stared at the reservoir. 'We saw the light,' he said. 'Out on the ice.'

'A light?'

'It was way out in the darkness, and we knew it was in a place no human being could possibly be. It was as if the light was floating in mid-air. You get daft ideas at times like that, but the first thing we thought of was the spirits that are supposed to be on the moor. We thought of ghosts. Even Ted was a bit scared, I think.'

Malkin seemed almost to be reverting back to his childhood as he spoke. Cooper could picture him as the excited, terrified little boy, in awe of his older bother. It wasn't all that hard to imagine how the young George Malkin must have felt. There had been times in his own past when Cooper had become almost sick with excitement at some adventure that Matt had got him into.

'And then we heard a voice calling for help,' said Malkin. 'It was weak, and there was a funny echo to it. We stood and watched the light moving, and we knew it must be one of the crew from the crashed plane. But we didn't think he could be alive at first. We thought it was his ghost, just a light and a voice. He was calling for help in English, but we weren't fooled. We'd heard them speaking in their own language, so we knew they were German.'

Cooper closed his eyes. 'They were Polish,' he said.

But Malkin didn't hear him. He was far away, re-living a moment that was permanently etched in his memory. Fifty-seven years had done nothing to weaken his recollection. He was talking now as if it didn't matter whether Cooper were there or not.

'Then Ted said the airman must be near the edge of the reservoir. He said the dam wall was behind him, because we could hear the echo when he shouted. So we watched the light for a little while longer. I've never felt so cold in my life, but part of that was the fear. I knew if we waited much longer, I wouldn't be able to carry the bag any further. I started to look round for somewhere to hide it, but there was nowhere near. There was only snow. And then Ted said: "He's on the ice."'

'The reservoir was frozen over, wasn't it?' said Cooper.

'At that far side, it was. The airman was walking across the ice, following the dam wall.' Malkin paused. 'I was worrying about the money. The man on the ice was the one thing that seemed to stand between the money and us. He would know it was missing. I said we should put the bags back, but Ted told me not to be stupid. I said the airman would reach the water board road, that he would be able to walk to the phone box half a mile away. But Ted said: "He won't reach the road."'

Cooper opened his mouth to ask a question, but changed his mind. It would be a mistake to interrupt now. The story was approaching a conclusion. He could feel it in Malkin's increasing tension, see it in the lines around his mouth, a tightening rictus of fear. Cooper could tell he had memorized every word that had been spoken as the two brothers stood clutching the leather bags, listening to a voice calling for help.

'And then we both heard it – the cracking,' said Malkin. 'It was clear in the night air, and it sounded so loud. It was like the sound of two pieces of metal being tapped against each other, and a little crunch of something breaking. Then the light disappeared. One second it was there, then it was gone. There was no shout or cry from him, not even a splash of water. Maybe a reflection of the flames on a piece of ice as it tilted on the surface. But then the ice fell back, and he was gone.'

Cooper shuddered, imagining the shock of icy water closing over his head. McTeague would have been dressed in heavy flying boots and a parachute harness. Trapped under a layer of ice, he would have been dead within seconds.

Now Irontongue had disappeared in the mist, which was rapidly approaching across the moor, racing towards Hollow Shaw, turning the air heavy with the expectation of rain. Cooper could feel the dampness on the back of his neck.

'I didn't understand what had happened,' said Malkin. 'Not until later. When we went up and looked at the reservoir next morning, I saw it was only on the east side that the water was frozen enough to walk on. It had a covering of snow, so it wouldn't have felt any different to a piece of level ground to a man in the dark. It's bloody hard work walking across that moor at any time, let alone in snow and in the dark. There are cloughs everywhere to get across.'

'He must already have been exhausted by the time he got to the reservoir,' said Cooper.

'Aye. He would never have suspected. But on the other side, near the weir, the water was still moving and the ice was thin, not enough to carry a man's weight. By the morning, there was barely a crack on the surface where he had fallen in. You know, that bloke had been over Germany, got back home and walked away from a crashed plane. Then he put his life in the hands of two young boys. And we let him die.'

Cooper knew that his own imagination could not match what Malkin was going through. The man had been over the events of that night too many times.

'I always thought he would come back and haunt us out here, on the moor,' said Malkin. 'At nights, he does come back. But only in my nightmares.'

Cooper stared towards the reservoir, where it lay in a hollow between the snow-covered hills. He nodded, thinking not of Malkin nor even of Danny McTeague, but of Zygmunt Lukasz.

'No forgiving. No forgetting,' he said.

And suddenly, Malkin snapped. His face reddened and the veins stood out in his forehead, twisting his face into an unrecognizable expression.

'Do you think I *want* to remember this?' he said. 'Don't you think I've re-lived it often enough already since the night it happened? How many times do you think I've had the nightmare in that time? How many?'

'I don't know,' said Cooper.

'How many nights in fifty-seven years?' said Malkin. 'Work it out for yourself, clever lad.'

*   *   *

George Malkin turned and began to walk back towards the farm. Ben Cooper felt for his radio. Should he call in? But it was ridiculous – this was surely an accidental death, fifty-seven years old. The witness had been an eight-year-old boy. After all that had happened recently, everyone would think he had finally gone mad if he made a drama out of it. Then he saw that Malkin wasn't heading for the house, but towards the big shed where Rod Whittaker kept his lorry. Malkin slid back the doors and disappeared inside.

'Mr Malkin?' called Cooper. He began to feel foolish standing in the field. He started to run towards the shed as he heard a diesel engine rumble into life. Cooper peered inside. The DAF wasn't there, but the big Renault tractor was, along with all its implements lined up against the wall – a hay baler, a harrow, a snowplough blade. George Malkin was sitting high up in the cab of the tractor.

'Mr Malkin!' shouted Cooper. 'Do you help Rod Whittaker with his contracting business, too?'

'Nay, I don't have an HGV licence,' Malkin called back.

'You can drive this tractor, though.'

Cooper saw Malkin put the tractor into gear. He dodged round to the side and pulled himself up on to the step to clamber through the passenger door.

'You said Rod Whittaker is contracted by the council. His contract includes clearing the snow sometimes, I bet. It's much cheaper for the council to pay farmers and local contractors to do it, rather than buy expensive snowploughs of their own.'

'Aye,' said Malkin, as the tractor began to move.

'So you could take this tractor out with the snowplough attachment, when it's needed to clear the roads around here?'

'I suppose I could.'

The tractor bumped across the yard and headed for the open gate on to the moor. Cooper remembered his visit to the Snake Inn, where the staff had said that one of the snowplough crews had stopped to fill their flasks on the morning Nick Easton's body had been found. But only one crew. They said the crews that came over the Pass from the north weren't council workers – they were on contract, so it was in their own interests to get the job done quicker. And one of them had been a big tractor with a snowplough. Very early on the job, it was. It would have come over from somewhere near Glossop, they said. It could easily have come from Harrop.

'You could get as far as the Snake Inn, couldn't you?' said Cooper over the roar of the engine. 'Nobody would think twice about a snowplough on the road after it had been closed to traffic. The staff at the inn didn't. They never saw or heard any other vehicles – just the snowploughs coming down the Pass, and then, later on, another one coming up. The one that found Nick Easton's body. And I think one of those that came down left him there.'

Blackbrook Reservoir appeared ahead of them in the mist. Malkin swung the wheel and reversed through the wet peat towards a padlocked gate.

'Stop,' said Cooper.

'Don't worry. I'm stopping.'

Malkin kept the engine running while he climbed down and swung open the gate. Cooper stood clear of the tractor's wheels, noticing that the padlock on the gate had been cut.

'You helped Frank Baine get rid of the body,' said Cooper. 'Did Baine have some kind of hold over you?'

'No, that's not right,' said Malkin.

He backed the tractor towards the edge of the reservoir, where a concrete slipway ran down into the water. Then Malkin fiddled with something at the back of the vehicle, and Cooper saw he had hold of a thick chain with a massive hook on one end. He watched in amazement as Malkin waded into the freezing water and was soon up to his waist. He bent and attached the hook to something under the surface. When he returned to the tractor, Malkin was soaked and white with cold.

'Frank Baine came here a couple of weeks ago,' he said. 'He'd worked out that I had the money. I sold a lot of other stuff to Lawrence Daley, and Baine is no fool. He asked Daley where it came from, and put two and two together.' Malkin climbed back into the tractor cab. 'Baine said the white fivers were worth a lot. He said they were collectors' items, that people would pay good money for them, proper money. He offered to sell them for me – in exchange for a cut of the profits, of course. We worked out there was over a hundred thousand pounds' worth. That was enough to send Florence to America for treatment.'

'It must have seemed like a miracle,' said Cooper.

'Aye, after all that time, the miracle I'd been praying for. You wouldn't reckon me to be a man that prayed, would you? But that's what I'd been doing, and I thought Baine had brought my miracle.' Malkin shook his head. 'Then the RAF policeman came. Of course, it was all too late by then. And everything I did after that was pointless.'

He put the tractor into gear, and the chain tightened. Cooper stood on the edge of the reservoir and looked down. The surface was black and oily with the mud that had been churned up by all the meltwater running into it, full of dark brown peat. Anything could have been lurking down there.

But as the tractor began to edge forward, it was something metallic and shiny that began to emerge from the water. Bit by bit, recognizable objects became visible. A bumper, a number plate and a back window. Eventually, the car stood on the concrete slipway, water streaming out of it, mud sliding slowly down its windscreen.

'Get your fingerprint kit on that,' said Malkin.

'It's Nick Easton's Ford Focus.'

'Clever lad.'

This time, Ben Cooper called in. George Malkin waited while he did it. He wasn't looking at Cooper, but gazing at Hollow Shaw Farm, as if he might be seeing it for the last time. It was the house he had lived in all his life, the place that had held his secrets.

Cooper shook his head as he looked at the dripping car.

'So you thought Nick Easton had come to take the money from you?'

'Of course he had,' said Malkin. 'Just when I thought I had that fortune in my grasp again, he came to snatch it away. I couldn't let him do that.'

'So you killed him.'

'It was blind panic. I don't think I really knew what I was doing.' Malkin's voice became a little unsteady. 'Once he was dead, I didn't seem to be able to think straight at all. I don't have any idea what I did for the next few hours, until I realized it was the middle of the night, and by then the snow had started. Rod had already put the snowplough blade on the tractor in case he was needed for road clearing, so I got the body in the back and took it down the Snake.'

'And there were no cars on the road,' said Cooper.

'You had that right. Nobody bothered about seeing a snowplough. But do you know what? I emptied the bloke's pockets before I tipped him out, and it was only when I found his keys that it dawned on me he'd have a car. How's that for stupid? I found the car parked just past the farm. I didn't see it on the way out, or I might have thought of putting him into the reservoir with it. At the time, all I wanted was to get him as far away as possible. Like I say, I wasn't thinking straight.'

Cooper frowned. 'But how did Nick Easton know you had the money? Who told him?'

Then Malkin laughed his coarse, gravelly laugh. The noise sounded alien in the damp stillness of the moor.

'I did,' he said. 'I told him myself.'

'I don't understand.'

'Years ago, it was. I'd known the bank notes were worthless for a long time. But they were on my conscience and I couldn't rest easy thinking that Florence might find them one day. It seemed to me that, if I owned up to the money, I might get the airman off my conscience too – that he wouldn't appear in my nightmares any more. So I got the number for the RAF Police, and I rang them. I gave them my name and address and told them I knew where the money from the crashed Lancaster was.'

'They would have had no idea what you were talking about.'

'Of course not,' said Malkin. 'Everyone had forgotten about it, but for me.'

'So what did they do?'

'Not a thing. They thanked me for the information and said somebody might get in touch with me. But nobody ever did. Well, they had better things to do, I suppose. They didn't care about what had happened all those years ago, and why should they? I suppose they just put a note in a file somewhere about this old idiot at Harrop, and then they left me with my nightmares.'

'Until Andrew Lukasz told Sergeant Easton the story. And Easton must have dug out the old files before he came to Edendale.'

'Aye.'

For a few moments, Cooper watched the ripples that were still disturbing the surface of the water, breaking sluggishly on the concrete slipway.

'You could hide anything in that reservoir,' he said. 'And it might never come to the surface. Danny McTeague's body never did.'

Malkin's face contorted again. 'Oh yes,' he said.

Cooper misunderstood him at first. He thought Malkin was agreeing with him. But there was something about the tone of the man's voice, an abruptness that choked the words in his throat.

'Mr Malkin?'

'He came to the surface when the ice began to melt,' said Malkin. 'Four days later.'

'You saw him?'

'Not at first. The ice gradually began to get thinner – so thin that we could see through it when we stood at the top of the reservoir wall. On the third day, we saw him. He was floating on his back, staring up at us, with his face squashed up against the ice. It was like he was pulling faces at us, sticking out his tongue to say that he had got the better of us, after all.'

'So what did you do about the body? Didn't you tell your father?'

Malkin laughed. 'Not bloody likely. He'd have beaten us black and blue with his belt and locked us in the coal shed for telling lies. And then he would have told the police. We thought we'd be put in prison for murder. Because we believed we *had* murdered him, see. It was our fault he died.'

'But if the body had been left there, it would have been found eventually.'

'Nobody found it, because we sent it back down to the bottom. There was a little rowing boat that was kept by the reservoir. We took it and filled it with stones, and we took our dad's fishing net from his shed. He noticed it was gone one day, but he blamed some gypsies who'd been hanging around.'

Cooper was starting to feel wet and uncomfortable. He almost wished he could see Irontongue Hill. At least the black buttress of rock would have been something solid and familiar. Yet together, Irontongue and the Malkin boys had been the end of Danny McTeague.

'We tied the ends of the net to the airman's body,' said Malkin. 'We tied it to his flying suit, his parachute harness, wherever we could. Then we filled it with stones and we threw it over the side. We didn't think he was going to sink at first, then his face stopped staring at us, and the stones pulled him down to the bottom, and all that was left were some bubbles. I kept looking, in case he came back up. I kept looking for months, even when the summer came. I spent so much time sitting staring at this reservoir that my dad thought I was turning peculiar. But the dead airman never came back up.'

'We'll have to send divers into the reservoir to look for the remains,' said Cooper. 'We might have to drain it.'

'Not much point in that,' said Malkin. 'They drained the reservoir thirty-five years ago.'

'But . . .'

'It was old and leaking by then, so they emptied it to put a concrete lining on the bottom. It's been drained twice more since, for maintenance. You don't just let a reservoir alone for sixty years, you know – it'd be so full of holes it wouldn't hold a drop of water. And what would be the good of that?'

Cooper wondered whether he had been spun a complete yarn. But Malkin wasn't laughing. His face was almost grey, and he made no attempt to wipe away the moisture that was settling on his cheeks as the mist gathered around them.

'Mr Malkin, are you telling me the truth?' said Cooper. 'Or was that some childish fantasy you had at the time?'

'Every word I'm telling you is true. But time

627

passes, and things change. A body doesn't stay a body for ever, not in water, not with fish and things nibbling away at it. By the time they drained the reservoir, there would only have been a few bits of bone and some rags buried in the mud on the bottom. Have you ever seen a reservoir when it's emptied? The mud is three feet deep on the bottom. Disgusting the smell is, too.'

'Yes, I remember the year there was a drought and all the reservoirs started to dry up. You could smell them for miles.'

'It was worse than that. It was foul enough to knock your head off. They scooped the mud out and tipped it into lorries. Nobody bothered to sift through it to find any bodies – they wanted to get it away as quick as they could. It all got tipped into a landfill site, over where Bents Quarry used to be. Later they put some top soil over it, and levelled it off. It grassed over nicely in a year or two – it makes a decent bit of grazing now. In fact, it's the pasture Rod Whittaker uses for his sheep.'

Malkin pointed back across the moor towards Hollow Shaw Farm, where Cooper could make out a scatter of white shapes among the remaining patches of snow.

'That's where your missing pilot is,' said Malkin. 'He's helping to feed those ewes.'

Cooper gazed at the sheep. One of the animals lifted its head and stared back at him. Its jaws were rotating steadily, and it had a look of sullen insolence on its black face. Cooper felt an irrational surge of anger. It had been such a long way to come, only to end with a field full of sheep.

'There's something I've often wondered since then,' said Malkin. 'What do you think the folk of Manchester would have said, if they'd known what was in their drinking water?'

Finally, the first patrol car bounced up the potholed road from Harrop. It had its headlights on as it climbed into the mist. George Malkin put his coat on, and walked with Cooper towards the car.

'The Morrissey woman – did you trust her?' said Malkin.

'Of course. I know some of her facts were wrong,' said Cooper. 'Frank Baine gave her false information.'

'That's not what I meant at all. She's known since Tuesday night how her grandfather died. She came here to ask me about the medal, so I told her.'

Cooper stopped suddenly. 'The medal?'

'I picked it up on the moor the night of the crash. It was in a little leather pouch, but with all the excitement about the money and the man on the ice, I forgot about it until later. Then I found it even had the airman's name and address on a label stitched inside the pouch.'

'So *you* sent her the medal.'

'I sent it back because I'd bottled the whole thing up long enough. It was when I finally knew that Florence was dying, and I needed to get it off my chest, I suppose. But I didn't put my name on the letter – I just said I was one of those boys who saw Danny McTeague walking away from the crash.'

Cooper's face twisted, as a remembered taste came to his mouth. It was that bitter, metallic taste, like blood seeping from his saliva glands, a bitterness that jerked a spasm from his throat. Alison Morrissey had been to Hollow Shaw after he had let Malkin's name drop on Tuesday, and since then she had known everything. The following morning she had been on a flight back to Toronto. Had she been as single-minded as she had claimed? Had she been concerned only with her own obsession, even as she had kissed him outside the Cavendish Hotel? Alison Morrissey had failed to mention that she had been kissing him goodbye. But Diane Fry had been watching, and she had known. No doubt she thought she had been right about Morrissey all along.

'It was all for Florence, you know,' said Malkin. 'She was the one real treasure that I had in my life, not the money. I carried the guilt with me so long that I grew not to trust anybody, in case they found out my secret. But Florence was the one person I never felt like that about. I trusted her and loved her, and I did what I could for her.'

A PC opened the door of the patrol car and Malkin ducked his head obediently to get in. But he paused and turned back towards Cooper.

'It means a lot if there's somebody you can trust,' he said. 'Even if they make a mistake now and then, you know they're genuine about what they do. Somebody like that is rare. If you're a clever lad, you'll find somebody like that and hold on to them, if you can.'

Cooper stared at George Malkin wordlessly. Now it was really raining, and the sky was hidden somewhere behind grey clouds. Cooper was glad not to be able to see the sky. He was glad not to be able to see the scornful faces of the sheep. He was particularly glad not to be able to see the tongue-shaped buttress of black rock on the hill, with its reptilian curl and its ridges and crevices. Irontongue had destroyed too many lives. He couldn't have tolerated its eternal derision.

'By the way,' said Malkin, 'I suppose you'll be wanting the knife.'

He pulled a blade from his pocket and held it out to Cooper. It was very sharp and stained with blood.

'My God. Hold on, I need to get a bag for it.'

'Don't worry,' said Malkin. 'It's sheep blood. I used it for skinning dead lambs. It's a messy job, but it had to be done. I couldn't see the orphans being left without any mothers.'

After Malkin had been driven away, Ben Cooper stood and listened for a moment to the rain dripping through the mist on to the peat moor. The sound was somehow reassuring. It was a totally natural cadence, a reminder that the world all around him continued as normal, no matter what happened in his own life. The moisture still condensed in the chilly air as it always had, and the rain drops still smacked against the wet ground, just as they would if he ceased to exist in this moment, if he were to vanish into a little pool of slush like a melted snowman. The rain was one of nature's primeval forces, oblivious to all human obsessions. The world that Ben Cooper moved in hardly impinged on it.

In the end, the secret of getting through life was to achieve the right perspective. At moments like these, all his own concerns seemed trivial. Back in Edendale, there were difficulties to face, pain to be dealt with, hard things to explain and a lot of work to be done to achieve any kind of reconciliation and forgiveness. But for as long as he could stand here listening to the rain on the moor, those problems and anxieties were so small in the scale of things that they could easily be overcome; they could even be washed away in the rain. Out here, life was simple and painless.

Cooper nodded to himself. Then he pulled up his collar and turned away from Hollow Shaw Farm. And the sound of the rain on the peat moor slowly faded behind him as he walked back to the car.